The Devil's C

MICHAEL LLOYD

On 22nd May 1997, the Rebel Army of Kabila entered Matadi,
a port on the banks of the Congo River, in what was
then called Zaire.

This is the story of a ship that was there.

'It matters not how strait the gate,
How charged with punishments the scroll;
I am the master of my fate:
I am the captain of my soul.'

W.E. Henley
THE CONGO RIVER

MONUMENT
SERIES

Monument Series
A Division of Witherby Publishing Group Ltd
4 Dunlop Square, Livingston, Edinburgh, EH54 8SB, Scotland, UK
Tel No: +44(0)1506 463 227 - Fax No: +44(0)1506 468 999
Email: info@emailws.com - Web: www.witherbyseamanship.com

First published 2012

ISBN: 978-1-85609-556-3
eBook ISBN: 978-1-85609-559-4

© Witherby Publishing Group Ltd, 2012

British Library Cataloguing in Publication Data
A catalogue record for this book is available from the British Library.

Printed and bound in Great Britain by Bell & Bain Ltd, Glasgow

Published by

Witherby Publishing Group Ltd
4 Dunlop Square, Livingston,
Edinburgh, EH54 8SB,
Scotland, UK

Tel No: +44(0)1506 463 227
Fax No: +44(0)1506 468 999

Email: info@emailws.com
Web: www.witherbys.com

The Congo River leads into the heart of Africa, but ships, regardless of how small, can only proceed as far as the rapids known collectively as the Livingstone Falls, 100 miles from the sea. Just below these rapids is where the port of Matadi lies. At Matadi, the Congo's estuary begins in a narrow channel which is only half a mile to a mile wide. From Matadi, the river forms the border between Angola to the south and the Democratic Republic of the Congo to the north.

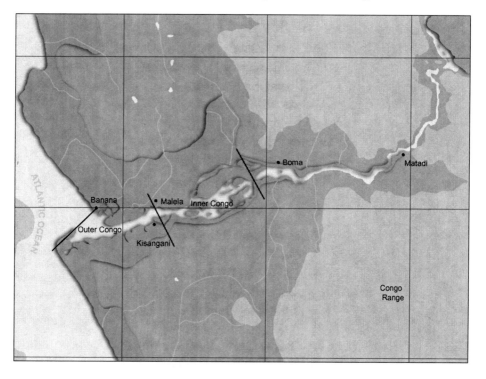

On the way back to the sea, there are two other ports: Boma and, where the river flows into the sea, Banana. The river eventually widens below Boma, but islands divide it into several arms. The river flows freely into the Atlantic Ocean, creating many shifting sandbanks. Due to the lack of navigational markings, along with the sandbanks and currents, ships only transit the river in daylight.

M.V. SEA QUEST

CREW LIST

Captain Harry Andrews

OFFICERS

Chief Officer (Mate) Julian 'Sandy' O'Donnell
2nd Officer (Navigator) Vijay Sinha
3rd Officer Graham Hennessey
Cadet Officer Jake Dale
Chief Engineer (Chief) Peter Anderson
2nd Engineer Godwin 'Chalky' Ayuba
3rd Engineer Davy Wilson

RATINGS

Bosun John McDonald
AB (Chief Coxn) Olav Bjerke
AB (2nd Coxn) Pat MacNab
AB Andy MacBride Medical Orderly (AMA)
OS Henry Duncan
OS James Stewart
Deck Boy Jim Bailey (promoted to OS)
Deck Boy George Huggins
Fitter Gwyn 'Taffy' Williams
Wiper Bert Morrison
Engine Trainee Mike Appleby
Cook Willie McBraith
Steward Ian Jarvis (Delilah)

Content

Saturday 17 May 1997

Chapter 1

Harry Andrews leant on the bridge wing, blew softly on his coffee and looked out over Africa. There were too many creases around his eyes from all the time spent peering through binoculars on ships' bridges. He was 47 years old and washed up; still slim, although his brown hair was tinged with grey.

Harry didn't like Africa, especially 100 miles up the Congo in the arsehole of the world, working for a lying shipowner on a wreck like this. That was being unkind, the ship wasn't really a wreck, just old and past its sell by date. He had been called by an agency to join the ship in the Persian Gulf where she was being converted from a Russian naval Arctic supply ship to a multi-purpose sea rescue and oil platform maintenance ship. It was a high sounding name for a ship which could be palmed off to the charterers as capable of doing anything they wanted, provided they didn't look too closely. The agent told him he was lucky to get the job.

It sounded good at first, British flag and, unusually, mostly British crew, which was at the charterer's insistence. They had not employed a Mate at this time, so Harry asked for his old Mate, Sandy, as part of the deal. So he and Sandy flew out to the ship together.

Nothing was as the agency said. The ship was over thirty years old when she was bought as a layup from a derelict Soviet cold war fleet. The conversion was botched; it was done as cheaply and quickly as possible to get the ship out on charter. The one good thing was that she was immensely strong; she had an ice class hull and was riveted. The antiquated Russian engines and instruments hadn't been replaced and constantly gave problems. Worse, the spares for the old Soviet engines were in short supply, not helped by all the repair manuals and signs being in Russian, a nightmare for the engineers. They had managed to keep things together throughout the contract but now it had come to a head. In fact everything had. The job in South Africa was done; the eighty oil field maintenance workers and their South African supervisors who had been on board for six weeks were off; the ship had been cleaned up and leave was due. Then head office said to bring the ship up to Luderitz in Namibia where they would be relieved. There were no reliefs. Instead, they were to do a short job and then bring the ship back home. The job was long and hard but worse was to come.

The office called once the job was finished and they were back alongside. As the charter was finished, they were changing flag from the Union Jack to some banana republic. The regulations and surveys were easier with no questions asked, but this meant the end of their employment. Another British crew on the beach. At least when they sailed they were pointing the right way, but after five months out, the port engine went down; it was just too old and there were no spares, so here they were.

Old ships have a particular atmosphere to them. They have lost their youth and have a comfortable lived in feel, similar to old clothes. Crews assume the homeliness these ships have and are usually more content than when on newer ships. Regrettably, a ship will become so old that it becomes desperate. When there are no spares, maintenance can't keep up with the deterioration, and the morale of the crew is affected by the general air of decay. Harry had the feeling that this ship was about to descend into this state. Worse, there was little he could do about it.

It was dawn, the only time of the day that was bearable in Matadi. Harry looked out at the mist. There was also blue smoke coming from the cooking fires rising above the town. It partially hid the tumble down poverty of the wrecked buildings, a reminder of the biggest war in the history of Africa. Even the port was half wrecked but this was more from neglect than war. A few working cranes still stood; the rest were either in the water or trying to join their friends like anxious pelicans peering down for fish. Harry looked at his watch: 0645. Any minute now he thought, and as if in answer, there was the sound of feet on the bridge stairway.

It was Sandy the Mate, or Chief Officer if you prefer, of this mighty vessel. The bridge door opened.

'Morning, Sir, and how is our happy Captain this morning?' Sandy asked as he moved over to the coffee percolator.

He was older than Harry, short, solidly built, with a red nose and broken veins due to being a hardened drinker, but his appearance was deceptive. Harry had seen him knock down two drunken sailors in a matter of seconds. He was also the best Mate this side of Suez, which was why Harry tolerated him. He was originally from Ireland. He had left many years ago and rumour was that he couldn't go back, but his voice still had a soft Irish lilt. He had a Glaswegian wife somewhere, although he never went back to her. His real name wasn't Sandy. On his discharge book it was Julian, but that was another life.

They first met many years ago in a little town in the Peruvian desert, when Harry was in charge of a Japanese owned ship carrying tonnes of mixed cargoes for the mine that supported the port. The ship was a typical Japanese build - cheap, bare minimum of equipment, poor accommodation, three cranes but a good engine, which was important in a Pacific winter. The crew was a real mixture: Indonesian engine with Filipino deck and catering ratings - a murderous combination, as they hated each other, especially as one bunch were Muslim and the other Christian. The officers were not much better, a mix of Romanians and Poles, a German Chief Engineer who had a picture of Hitler in his cabin, and was waiting for his resurrection to cleanse the world of anyone the Chief didn't like, and that was a long list. The British Mate had run for the hills on arrival, claiming sickness, meaning a new Mate had been required.

Harry was sitting on the veranda of the cantina in the dusty town square holding a bottle of cold beer with condensation dripping from it when a dusty jeep drew up and out fell an equally dusty figure.

'Bugger me,' said the figure when it managed to stand up unsteadily. 'Where is this?' Harry studied the apparition for a moment before replying.

'St Nicolas,' he said. 'In the middle of the Peruvian desert.'

'And don't I know it,' replied the figure. "I flew into Lima last night. A jeep turned up at the hotel when it was still dark before I could prepare for the journey. We've driven hundreds of miles through sand to get here. Christ, I could murder a beer.'

'Senjora,' called Harry. A stout sullen woman silently appeared. 'Dos cervezas, por favor.'

'Non,' interrupted the figure.

'Cinco,' he smiled at Harry. 'I said I could murder it, not tickle it.' He stuck his hand out towards Harry. 'I'm Julian, the new Mate of a ship that is parked somewhere around here.' Harry took the hand.

'Sit down.' He pointed towards the empty seat. 'I'm the Captain of that parked ship which is down that road.' He indicated to the road going down towards the sea with his bottle. 'You can't miss it, there's only one jetty and we're on it. Next, I'm not having a Mate called Julian. I'll call you Sandy, which you certainly are at the moment. The last Mate went sick; I suspect sick of the ship rather than ill. Are you an alcoholic?'

'Certainly not, it interferes with screwing.'

Just then the beers came. Sandy grabbed one and drank it quickly. 'Bugger me, that was good,' he said, picking up another bottle. He then sat back with a sigh, gave a loud satisfied burp and a lazy smile. 'Captain, you can call me what you like as long as there's a ship with beer on board and I get paid. How long are we here for?'

'About a week, then off to Chile for timber then back to Japan,' replied Harry.

Sandy looked thoughtful. 'Sounds like an interesting trip. So where's the brothel?' he asked.

'How do you know there is one?' asked Harry.

'Every town in Peru has one,' laughed Sandy.

'There is one brothel, two cantinas and a so-called restaurant which, once you've blown the flies off the food, isn't too bad,' replied Harry.

'So, I have a week to sort out the ship, screw the women, drink beer and sail away. Can't be bad,' said Sandy, reaching for another beer. 'Your health, your Honour.' He tipped the bottle in Harry's direction.

And that was how it began. He worked his magic on the ship and crew, drank and whored his way around the South American coast and showed that he could be the biggest pain in the arse; but he became a loyal and firm friend. Since then they had sailed together on many oceans.

'Sandy, you ask me that every morning and I never answer so why do you keep trying?'

'Ah, one day you will say happy.'

'Not while we're stuck here,' Harry replied. 'What are the plans for this morning?'

'It's Saturday, Captain. Clean ship ready for your inspection and then it's the weekend.'

The Captain's inspection is a tradition at sea. Once a week, the Captain and heads of department formally tour the ship. The crew have the morning to prepare for this. The alleyways, workplaces, messrooms and cabins are all inspected to ensure that the ship's accommodation, which could be overlooked in place of other work pressures, is always spick and span.

'Sandy, it's been one long weekend since we've been here. How long is it now?'

'We arrived three days ago,' replied Sandy.

'And the spares that were meant to be here weren't; they've been coming every day since,' said Harry.

'Do you think they will come today?'

'That's what the agent promised. I'll go up town later to see if they are likely to arrive.'

'What I can't understand,' said Sandy, 'is why we are stuck here? Why didn't we pull into Boma further down? Especially when there is a war going on and we're in the middle of it. The boys are getting a bit edgy. At least at Boma we would have been nearer the sea.' Harry was thinking the same thing. He was feeling edgy as well. The various reports they had received told of fighting getting closer each day.

'We may have been too deep to get alongside Boma. No one's been dredging the river or berths for some time. Up here the current is stronger and there's not much mud on the bottom. Boma only has an airstrip while the airport here is just over the bridge and, from what Burton in London said, port charges are negligible and that is probably the real reason.'

'From the state of the place they should pay us,' said Sandy.

They both looked over the wrecked state of the port. The insurrection had been going on for five years with no end in sight. It was just getting bigger with more armies and armed hordes roaming around looting, raping and murdering.

'You know,' said Sandy reflectively, 'the last time I saw this place the port was full; in fact it wasn't a bad place to visit.'

'When was that then?'

'Back in the seventies,' said Sandy.

'You still seem to be enjoying yourself. I suppose you're going up town tonight?' smiled Harry.

'Thought I might just have a stroll. Get some exercise.'

Harry laughed. 'You mean a stroll to Esmeralda's knocking shop. Plenty of exercise there. Between you all, you've nearly bought the place.' Sandy was about to reply when Harry put his hand up.

'What about the Cadet?'

'What about him?' asked Sandy looking puzzled.

'Sandy, he's only 17 years old and he's trying to keep up with you!'

'Hold on, Captain,' protested Sandy, 'Firstly he's nearly 18.'

'Nearly isn't 18,' interrupted Harry.

'Nearly 18,' repeated Sandy 'and he's got a girlfriend, not a whore.'

'Sandy, she's one of Esmeralda's girls!' said Harry.

'Actually, Captain, she's her daughter.'

'Well,' said Harry, looking crestfallen, 'what about his drinking?'

'Only time I've seen him pissed was at your birthday party in Cape Town and, if I remember correctly, you were buying the drinks,' replied Sandy. 'And from your stories when you were a Cadet, you…'

'All right, Sandy,' Harry interrupted. 'Point made but these are different times to when you and I roamed the seas as Cadets. Just keep an eye on him.'

'Well, 'the boy' is taking away the port daughter craft after breakfast,' said Sandy.

'Where are you sending him?' asked Harry.

'Up river as far as the rapids and then back. I want him to open her up, get rid of the cobwebs, test the radar and communications, the usual stuff.'

'Good,' said Harry. 'Talking of breakfast, looks like it's time.'

They looked out over the bridge towards the shore. The remaining dockworkers were streaming through the dock gates ready to start cargo work on the ship, which was alongside further down the jetty, but it was the small gathering of children and dogs by the stern of their ship that gave the game away.

'Funny isn't it,' said Sandy. 'Every bloody third world port is the same. Dogs, children and ships all gather together at feeding time.'

'Are you coming for breakfast?' asked Harry.

'I'm off to see the Bosun, Captain. I'll grab a bacon butty in the crew mess. See you for inspection at 1100.'

Sandy disappeared downstairs.

Harry stood on the bridge wing a for few more minutes. It was warming up quickly and soon it would almost be unbearable, the metal of the ship almost too hot to touch. He smiled, remembering how they used to demonstrate frying eggs on the ship's steel deck to passengers. He recalled the dreadful days in the tropics before air conditioning. Too many ships, too many seas, and now stuck in a river miles from the sea in the middle of a bloody war.

As he opened the bridge door and went down the stairway to his deck, the cold air conditioning enveloped him. At least that hadn't broken down – that would have led to mutiny.

Two more decks down and Harry entered the officers' mess. Only the engineer officers were present. As he moved to his seat, Delilah the steward appeared. His real name was Ian Jarvis, an ex-Royal Marines as the tattoo on his arm testified. Since then, he had decided he preferred 'Delilah.' He was a tall man in his thirties, with a craggy face and a permanent twinkle in his eye as if everything was a joke, which to him it probably was. He never spoke much about his life in the Royal Marines. Harry gathered there had been an altercation between him and an officer which resulted in the officer being hospitalised and Delilah looking for work. However, as long as he kept his dresses and wigs in his cabin for the occasional show in the crew bar and did his job, Harry couldn't care less. He was a bloody good steward.

'Coffee and toast, Captain?'

'Yes please, Delilah, and please ask the Cook if he has the provisions list ready.' Delilah disappeared back into the galley.

Harry sat beside the Chief Engineer, Peter Anderson. Peter was a small man who had a perpetual worried look about him, with good reason considering his problems. He was short, bald with thick glasses and came from a small village south of Birmingham. From the picture in Peter's cabin, Harry had noticed that his wife looked a rather large and intimidating lady. It was obvious that Peter was at times happy to get away from her. The trouble was that, once away, he worried about his family and wanted to get back. He had two teenage children with the usual problems. His main interest apart from engines was building model steam engines.

'Good morning, Peter,' said Harry. 'How's things?'

'Same as usual, Harry,' replied Peter. He was the only man on board allowed to call the Captain by his first name. This tradition in the Merchant Navy signifies the Chief Engineer's position and the fact that they got on well together.

'I've got problems with the main ballast pump now. It's in bits so we'll be busy today. Can my lads skip out on inspection? I really need them down below. I want to get this pump sorted out and back together by early afternoon. If I can do that I'll pipe them all down then. They need a break.'

'Sure, anything else we can do to help?' asked Harry.

Peter grimaced. 'Get me a new engine room. Is there any news of the spares?'

'I don't know yet,' said Harry. 'I'm going up to the agent's office after breakfast to find out what's happening. I'll let you know when I get back.'

Peter gave a cynical laugh. 'Bet I know the answer,' he said, pushing his chair back. He called across to the two engineer officers sitting at another table. 'Come on lads, the sooner we start the sooner we finish.' They groaned but stood up and followed the Chief out of the mess. Just then Delilah appeared with Harry's toast followed by the Cook.

Willie, the Cook, was from Aberdeen as were several of the crew. All ex-fishermen, they were the best of seamen, hardened by the winters of the North Sea and Arctic. He was of an indeterminate age, certainly older than his discharge book stated, but his home was the sea. He was a thin man with a thick mop of white hair topping a perpetually red face due to the heat of the galley. His startling blue eyes were always what people remembered. He had no family and when he went on leave he stayed in cheap doss houses or hotels until he could get another ship. He kept everyone filled up and for that Harry was very grateful. In Harry's eyes and probably quite a few others, he was the most important man on the ship.

'Morning, Captain,' Willie replied. 'Got the list. It's mostly fresh stuff, salad and the like. We've got plenty of meat and fish still from Luderitz, although I wouldn't mind some fresh fish if it's available. Don't want any river fish though, God knows what's inside them.'

'OK, Cook. I'm off to the agents, then I'll drop this off at the Chandlers. Is delivery on Monday OK with you, if we're still here?'

'Aye, that's fine, Sir.' Harry stood up and took the last piece of toast. 'I'll be off then, see you later. By the way, has the 2nd Mate been in this morning?'

'Been and gone,' said Delilah. 'I think he and the 3rd Mate were heading to the bridge this morning to get on with the paperwork.' Harry headed out through the door.

Meanwhile, Sandy went to the other side of the ship and entered the crew messroom. This was a standard arrangement, the messrooms on each side of the ship with the galley in the middle. The messroom was crowded with tobacco smoke hanging over the tables.

'Morning, Mr Mate,' called the Bosun, edging along the bench seat making room for Sandy. 'Peggy!' he shouted, and one of the spotty faced boy seamen appeared at the galley door. 'Bacon butty and a mug of tea for the Mate.'

'Coming up, Bosun,' said the boy as he disappeared back into the galley.

Boy seamen who carried out all the low jobs on board were traditionally called Peggy. In days gone by they were the old sailors who often had a wooden leg or another disability which meant they could no longer go up the mast or do hard seamanship work. 'So, how is the Old Man this lovely morning?' asked the Bosun with a wry smile.

The Bosun, John McDonald, was a rock of a man, always steady and calm. Another ex-fisherman, he hailed from Peterhead, was in his fifties and had been in deep sea for a long time. He was deeply tanned with scars on his hands from making and repairing nets during his fishing days.

'The usual,' said Sandy. 'He hates Africa, especially the West Coast.'

'You know what he needs?' said the Bosun. 'He needs to get pissed and laid. Get him off the ship tonight, Sandy. Don't like Captains on ships in port, it's not natural and they interfere in things.'

'It's an idea,' said Sandy. 'Still, we could have far worse. I wouldn't have stayed with him this long if he wasn't good at his job.'

'Hold on Sandy, I wasn't going for him. He's one of the best I've sailed with and I've sailed with the good, the bad and the complete wankers.'

'Haven't we all,' said Sandy. 'I think it's the business of changing the registry and hoisting that rag up. He knows it's the end of us when we get back. He's very much a sailors' captain, there aren't many of those left.'

'True,' said the Bosun. 'Anyway,' said Sandy, 'Apart from sending the boat away and cleaning the ship, anything else planned this morning?'

'There is a leak in the lower deck starboard heads. Nothing much. The engineers are up to their balls in work so I'll put one of the lads onto that. We're making a new canvas cover for the forecastle hatch, but that won't take long.'

'The paint locker needs squaring away,' said Sandy.

'Right, I'll get someone onto that as well.'

'Who are you sending away in the boat with the Cadet?'

'Thought I would send Pat, the Second Coxn and Henry.' Henry was an Ordinary Seaman.

'Pat's pretty good with the boat.'

'I know,' said the Bosun. 'When that squall hit us at the Cape, he did well. The wind rose to fifty knots with big rollers. He brought her through it like he was driving in a country lane. I want him to give the Cadet more training.'

'At least there'll be no problem with the waves up here.'

'More likely with the bloody crocs,' said the Bosun. 'Suppose we've got inspection this morning?'

'Of course,' said Sandy. 'Even if she was going to sink tomorrow she'd still have to be all tiddly fashion.'

'Right,' said the Bosun looking at the messroom clock, which showed nearly 0800. 'Let's get the boat away.' With that, he heaved himself up out of the bench and left the messroom.

Other members of the crew were also leaving, pushing past to get to their tasks. Good, thought Sandy, the ship's alive again. As he went out onto the deck and the heat met him, he knew it was going to be another scorcher. He looked down at the embarkation deck and saw the Cadet, Jake Dale, standing with his crew, waiting to board the boat which was now being lowered down to the deck. He was of average height, slightly built and deeply tanned with dark hair. His best attribute was that he was always cheerful. Cadets needed to be.

'Dale!' Sandy shouted. The Cadet looked up and saw Sandy. 'Take it easy when you get up to the rapids, slowly open her up on the way and make sure your fenders are inboard this time.' Last time he went out, the fenders were left trailing in the water. 'There is a strong current running this morning,' advised Sandy. 'Watch her when you hit the water.'

'I had noticed that, Sir,' he said. 'I'll have her ready to come ahead as we take to the water.'

When the boat came down to the deck level, the Cadet and crew boarded. These boats were known as daughter craft, designed for long distance search and rescue with a wheelhouse, radar, satnav, first aid equipment and able to go up to 35 knots. It was a very expensive piece of kit. The engines broke into a roar as she started, with diesel smoke billowing out of her exhausts. Sandy left them to it.

Chapter 2

Jake loved driving boats. His first experience of boats was when he joined the Sea Cadets aged 13. He knew then that he wanted to go to sea. Even at school he seemed a bit different, in trouble more than most, and usually leading others along the same path. Much to his parents' concern, instead of going to university, he decided he wanted to join the Merchant Navy. Then adding to their distress, instead of joining a regular shipping company, he went to one of the training companies which acted for owners of differing types of ships, hoping to do something out of the ordinary. He had certainly got that and was loving every moment of it. Now with nearly thirteen metres of heavy rescue launch under his command, he was in his element.

As the boat hit the water, he immediately released the hoist wire and angled the boat away from the ship's side. He increased power so that the strain was taken off the forward boat rope.

'Let go forward,' he shouted, signalling at the same time. Henry, an Ordinary Seaman, let the rope go, then he and Pat MacNab, the 2nd Coxn, joined Jake in the wheelhouse.

'Are the fenders in, Henry?' asked Jake. 'I don't want another bollocking.' Henry left to get them in. Jake eased the throttles forward and the boat surged ahead.

'Shall I switch the radar on?' asked Pat.

'Yes please,' said Jake. 'Make sure the scanner's clear.' The radar hummed as it warmed and then lit up.

'Where are we going today?' asked Henry, sitting down on a small bench seat.

'Just up to the rapids,' said Jake. 'We'll test the comms from there, then head back.'

The rapids were five miles up the river from the berth which meant the boat would have a good workout. The diesels roared as Jake opened the boat to full throttle. The boat bounced a little on the small wavelets of the river, causing them to hold on. Spray came over the wheelhouse and Jake switched the wipers on.

'One good thing up here,' shouted Jake above the engine noise, 'is there is no traffic coming down.' The rapids prevented any ships or boats, no matter what size, crossing from the upper parts of the Congo and vice versa. Matadi was the last place on the river before the rapids.

The radar was now fully ready and Pat switched the display on. Immediately a green coloured map of the river was displayed on the small screen.

'Take the wheel, Pat,' said Jake. 'I told the Mate I would test the radar.' Jake moved from the pilot seat over to the radar as Pat took control of the wheel. He put his head down onto the rubber screen cover.

'How's your heading?' Jake asked.

'032, 032, 032,' Pat repeated watching the gyro compass while giving the course.

'That's fine. She's all lined up.'

Harry sat at his desk, checking emails. The standard weather report was downloading but there was nothing from the company. The email service was expensive to use as it came down on the satellite, so company policy was to check in once a day in the morning.

He picked up the phone and called the bridge. The 2nd Mate, Vijay Sinha, answered. Originally he was from Bombay, but now lived in South Shields with his wife, a teacher at the local primary school and two children. Vijay was a shy man in his late twenties, but underneath his reserve he was a meticulous officer who could always be relied on.

'Vijay, can I borrow the 3rd Mate for a minute?' asked Harry. 'I want him to do the advances.'

'Certainly, Captain,' said Vijay in his precise English. 'I will send him down.' Harry put the phone down and went into his bedroom to change.

He checked his watch, 0830, plenty of time to get to the agent's and back in time for rounds. He heard the 3rd Mate knock at the office door.

'Come in,' shouted Harry. 'Just getting the cash.' He went to the safe, dialled in his code, opened it, reached in and pulled out a thick wad of dollars. He counted off four thousand and closed the safe, whirling the dial.

The 3rd Mate was a young lad of twenty two called Graham Hennessey. He had fair hair, with a tanned and freckled face. He had recently arrived on board, coming straight from the college after passing his Watchkeeping Officers Certificate. He referred to himself as a refugee from container ships and was still a little confused by the contrast to his previous seagoing life. Harry remembered when, on his second day on board, he was told to take one of the daughter craft away, only to have a shamefaced young man tell the Mate that he'd never had any boat work experience. It was quickly rectified with a week of intensive boat work, followed by weeks of further practical seamanship and ship handling. He was now fitting in well.

'Right, Graham. Here's four thousand dollars. That should be enough for those who want cash. No one is overdrawn but the limit is two fifty per man. If more is needed, I'll give that when I get back.'

'That's fine, Sir,' said Graham. 'I've got the advance book.'

'I'm off ashore now. Who has the duty today?'

'Me, Sir, until 1800, then the 2nd Mate takes over.'

'What, again?' asked Harry.

'He doesn't mind, Sir. He's saving up for his mortgage and doesn't want to go ashore.'

'OK,' said Harry. 'Off you go.'

He followed him out and locked his door, then went down the stairways to the main deck and out of the door onto the outside deck. The heat hit him like a flat iron as he walked to the gangway. The shore watchman was sitting there. He rose to his feet as Harry approached.

'Good morning, Captain Sir,' he said.

'Good morning,' replied Harry. 'All quiet?'

'Most certainly, Captain.' Harry smiled and went down the gangway. Poor bastard wouldn't be able to stop a couple of boy scouts, but at least he could feed his family, especially with the food parcels the Cook gave him to take home. Although they had to be alert to thieves coming on board, during the day there were plenty of crew around and at night the duty watch were fully alert. All the removable items were locked up anyway. He noticed that the children and dogs had gone so the crew had ensured they were fed.

He walked a short distance from the ship, then turning around, looked back. It was a typical rig support ship. The accommodation block was forward, aft of that various container offices were bolted on, then a large working deck with one heavy crane and a storing crane. The large starboard daughter craft referred to as Rescue 1 was in her davits taking up most of the side of the accommodation. Sandy had made good use of the time alongside, even though she was old. The hull gleamed with new black paint, with the five upper works decks also blindingly white in the sunlight. She looked a tough old ship, her three hundred foot long rugged hull ending in a blunt bow which was designed for pushing through ice rather than Congo River mud. There were various dents running down the hull, medals from battles with ice and ports over the years. An honest working ship. 'Strange how ships affect men,' thought Harry as he turned away and headed for town.

Rescue 2 had swept along up the calm waters of the river which were gradually becoming more disturbed as they neared the rapids. There were occasional white water crests showing where the rapids met the calm waters below in a swirling jumble of water.

Once Jake had completed the radar tests, he took the wheel as they approached the line of white water that crossed the river directly ahead of the boat. Behind this raging white water, black rock rose slightly following the river upstream. As he eased back on the throttles, the boat sat back down on the water breasting the current, rocking with the force of the turbulence. He picked up the VHF mike.

'Mother, Mother, Rescue 2,' he said. Sandy was aft on the work deck but had his portable walkie-talkie set with him. He heard the call clearly.

'Loud and clear, Rescue 2. How's the boat?'

'Running well,' said Jake. 'We are at the rapids now.'

'Right,' said Sandy. 'Start heading back. Have you got a dummy in the boat?'

'Yes, Sir,' said Jake.

'On the way back, throw it over and practice pickups.'

Jake turned the boat around and began to increase the speed. As they headed back down the river Henry called out, 'There's someone in the water! 2 points on the starboard bow!' Jake immediately slowed the boat and turned towards the direction Henry was pointing in. As they got closer, Jake could see it was more than one person but they were floating, not moving. He edged the boat towards them.

'Henry, get the boat hook and see if they are alive,' he called. Henry leant over the side with the hook. Then he knelt down on the deck and vomited.

'Shit!' said Jake. 'Pat, take the wheel.'

Jake went along the deck to where Henry was still kneeling and looked down. There were five bodies, spread out over the water close to the boat, two of them children all bobbing gently in the water. They were all missing limbs. From the look of them the limbs had been cleanly cut off. Jake gazed in horror; he'd never seen anything like this before. Stumbling back to the wheelhouse breathing heavily, he turned to Pat. 'There are five bodies, two of them are kids. They've all had their hands and legs chopped off!' He grabbed the mike.

'Mother! Mother!'

'This is Mother,' came Sandy's calm reply.

'We've found five bodies in the water. They've had their arms and legs chopped off!'

'All right. Calm down, Jake. Can I presume they are all dead?'

'Yes, Sir.'

'Then there is nothing you can do. Leave them and carry on with your exercise.'

'We can't just leave them, Sir!'

'Yes, you can. This has nothing to do with us. I suspect this is not unusual just now. Take a few deep breaths and get on with your man overboard drill, understand?'

There was a pause, then a quiet reply. 'Yes, Sir.'

As Harry passed through the dock gate, the guards came out of their hut; one port official and two Zaire soldiers, their uniforms a parody of officialdom. One soldier was quite drunk. Harry felt in his pocket and pulled out a couple of packets of cigarettes which he flipped at them. One of the soldiers caught them, waved his thanks and disappeared back into the hut.

Harry started up the hill towards the town. It was only a short walk but already he was sweating. There were no clouds in the sky, but that could change quickly. The odd person smiled at him as he passed, especially women. Harry smiled back. The women weren't flirting, they were just naturally happy, or at least seemed to be, which was strange considering the shit that most of them lived with. The many cripples sitting in doorways called softly, holding their hands out as he passed. Buildings that were once white with red tiles housing various offices were now deserted except for squatters. The roofs and walls were damaged, some had even completely collapsed, reminders of the insurrections visited on the town by various warring factions.

Dust kicked up from his shoes as he continued up the hill. As he passed some shanties and meagre shops clinging to the side of the road, some of the traders called out to him. Nearing the town, the road became busier and the buildings more substantial. People were walking about, bicycles clattered and there were a few cars – most were battered and ancient. Harry was a classic car buff and recognised some of the cars from his childhood, Citroens, Austins and Morris, but there were a few Japanese vehicles as well. Harry watched warily as some more soldiers ambled along, swinging their weapons. The agent didn't like him walking about even in daylight. The soldiers eyed him sullenly as he passed. Harry noticed there were a number of handcarts being loaded with household items and that some of the cars going past also had similar items loaded on their roofs.

A few hundred yards ahead was a three storey building where the shipping agency was housed. All ships when in port have a local agent to assist with all the formalities and arrange the cargo documentation. They were a go-between for the ship and port. The door was open this morning which meant that the air conditioning had broken down again or there was no electricity. Not an uncommon event.

When Harry entered the building, Louise the receptionist gave her usual cheery broad smile.

'Good morning, Captain. Go in. Mr Alvares is free.'

Mr Alvares was sitting at his desk wiping his face with a large red handkerchief. He was a fat, sweaty and perpetually harassed looking man, though what about in a pisspot office like this Harry couldn't imagine.

'Good morning, Mario,' Harry said, leaning forward to shake his hand. Mario was Goanese, one of the thousands of displaced persons of Africa who crossed the border during the Angolan wars to set up home here with his family.

'Captain,' he effused. 'I was going to come to the ship this morning but instead here you are. Louise!' he shouted. 'Water for the Captain!'

Louise appeared just as he finished shouting with a glass of water, gave Harry a wan smile and returned to her desk.

Harry sat down in a shabby chair facing Mario.

'So, any news about the spare parts?' The agent sighed and opened his arms wide.

'Captain, what do I say? There seem to be so many problems with transport. You know Kinshasa has been in the hands of the rebels for some time now and the place is a mess. The airport service is all over the place. Sometimes planes come. Other times they don't. The last I heard was that the spares were coming by road from Angola two days ago but there is no further news yet. There are terrible stories coming out of Kinshasa of murders, rape and looting. Kabila is allowing his army to do as they please. To be honest, Captain, the situation is not good. There is fighting about fifty kilometres away and there are rumours that Kabila is attacking towards Matadi.'

'Who is Kabila?'

'He has been fighting all his life, regardless of what for. For years he has been leading various groups of murderers masquarading as freedom fighters. Wherever he goes, massacres follow. There is no limit to the atrocities his men will commit. Now it looks as if he has beaten Mobutu so you can imagine what is coming here.'

'I noticed as I came up the hill that there were several cars and carts loaded with household goods.'

'People are leaving, Captain. They are scared.'

'Where are the government forces?' asked Harry.

'They are holding the rebels in the north. That's why most of the *Mechants* have left town, apart from those too drunk or drugged to move. Hopefully with the Angolans' help, we can kick the rebels back to the bush.'

'*Mechants*?' asked Harry.

'That is what we call them,' said Mario. 'It means vicious. We use it for anyone in uniform. Except your good selves of course,' he added hastily.

'Christ, Mario. Why did you bring your family to this place?' asked Harry in disgust.

'Where do we go, Captain?' Mario protested. 'We have been living in Angola for generations, then because we are Portuguese they kicked us out when independence came. Portugal doesn't want us because we are Indian. India doesn't want us because we have Angolan passports and are Goanese. This was the only place left. At least it has been safe enough to bring the girls up and provide a living.' Mario had three young daughters. Their picture stood on his desk along with one of his rather large wife.

'I'm sorry, Mario. You're right. I've seen it before. You've done well to keep it all going.'

He got up and reached across the desk to shake hands. 'I have to go to the Chandler then back to the ship, Mario. I suppose there will be no news until Monday now?'

'That's right, Captain. By the way, can you tell any of your crew who are interested that there will be mass at the cathedral at 11 o'clock tomorrow. They are most welcome. I imagine it will be quite full. People always look to the church when trouble is coming.'

'Surprisingly, Mario, you may see a few. I'll see you on Monday then?' asked Harry. 'I will be on board at eight thirty sharp.'

Just as Harry was going out of the door, he remembered. 'Sorry Mario. I completely forgot about the strawberry jam. I'll send one of the crew up with it.'

'No need, Captain. If someone brings it to Esmeralda's tonight, they can give it to her. She and my wife share everything.'

'Hopefully not you Mario.'

'No, Captain. I want to keep my balls a little longer.' Harry laughed and left the office saying goodbye to Louise, who was also laughing from the exchange.

With the current astern, Rescue 2 was speeding back to the ship.

'Rescue 2, Rescue 2, this is Mother. You're clear to come alongside.' It was the Bosun with the deck party. Jake swung the boat in a wide arc towards the side of the ship. He could see that the hoist wire was dangling above the water and that Jim, the other deck boy, was standing by with the boat rope.

'Get the fenders out, Pat,' he said. Then slowing down further, he brought the boat expertly under the hoist while the boat rope was thrown and made fast.

Pat quickly snapped the hooks in place and shouted, 'Hoist fast!' Jake gave the Bosun the signal to hoist and the boat immediately swung up out of the water. When it was level with the deck, the boat was swung against the ship's side.

'I see you remembered the fenders this time,' smiled the Bosun.

'I reckon if I hadn't, Sandy would have stopped my shore leave,' Jake replied, getting out of the boat.

'Leave her here,' said the Bosun. 'We'll put a hose of fresh water over her before hoisting her up.'

'Did you hear about the bodies we found?'

'Aye, lad, I did. Used to be a common sight around the China Sea, especially after a typhoon.'

'But not with the arms and legs chopped off.'

'No, that's true. But it's not uncommon in Africa, especially when they are at war. If you stay at sea, you'll see quite a few bodies in your travels, I promise you.'

'You all seem so complacent about it.'

'That's because we've seen it before and we'll see it again. There is nothing we can do about it. It's not our business. We're sailors. Same as Caesar: we arrive, we see and we piss off. Now I suggest you go and get ready for the Old Man's inspection.'

Harry went out into the street and across to the Chandler's office. Henri, the Chandler, wasn't in so Harry left his order with the clerk and headed back down the hill towards the ship. He was sweating profusely. There was no breeze, not even coming off the river. In the distance, walking up the hill amongst the sparse traffic, Harry could see the figure of Ernestino Perfidio, the Filipino Captain of the cargo ship which was the only other ship alongside. Ernestino wasn't bothered with the heat, as he was used to this in the Philippines. Even so his skin shone a little with perspiration.

'Good morning, Captain,' they greeted each other.

'We're sailing tomorrow,' said Ernestino.

'Bet you're pleased to be out of it,' Harry said.

'Certainly,' said Ernestino, 'but we are headed to Lagos.'

'Christ,' said Harry. 'That's almost as bad as here, except there isn't a war going on.'

'I know and they will rob us blind. We've hardly got enough supplies of whisky and cigarettes for the crew, never mind all those thieving port officials. Still, after that we go across to New Orleans. At least we'll be able to store the ship properly there.'

At that moment Harry looked up and saw a group of ragged soldiers wearing green berets approaching them.

'Watch out,' Harry muttered to Ernestino.

'Ey, Mondele!' one of the soldiers shouted. 'Tes papiers! Tes papiers toute de suite!' Mondele meant white man.

'It's alright,' said Ernestino. 'I met them yesterday. They just want beer money.' With that he dug his hand into his pocket and took out a handful of banknotes which he passed to the soldier with a smile. The soldiers grabbed the money and passed by without any acknowledgement.

'Filth,' said Harry.

'I used to think our soldiers and police in the Philippines were thieving bastards,' said Ernestino. 'But these make them look like saints.'

'How much did you give them?' said Harry. 'I'll pay you back later.'

'Nothing,' laughed Ernestino. 'I changed $50 this morning for two thousand banknotes! I work at an exchange rate of a handful to a dollar, that seems about right. I've been here many times and it never gets better, just worse. But then so do many other ports these days. When do you sail?'

'I don't know. When the spares arrive I suppose.'

'You should think about sailing soon. Look around. The locals are leaving because they know what is going to happen.'

'I assure you I will leave as soon as I can. Will you go ashore tonight?'

'Of course, it's last night.'

Harry walked through the dock gate where the guards didn't bother to leave their shack. The dust kicked up from Harry's boots as he trudged back to the gangway. On board he opened the main deck door and revelled in the ice of the air conditioning. He checked his watch: 0945. Time for a shower and change before inspection. As he climbed the ladder to his deck, the noise of music and chatter came from various parts of the ship accompanied by the clang of buckets. From one of the heads came the sound of scrubbing.

His door was open. On entering his office he saw Delilah winding up the cord of the vacuum cleaner. 'How was it ashore, Captain?' 'Hot and dusty. Some of the locals are starting to leave.'

'Don't blame them. There's trouble coming. It's strange but it's like when we were waiting for an attack. You knew it was coming but not when.'

Harry went into the bedroom, stripped off, and went into the bathroom where he turned the shower on full blast. Heaven. He leant against the bulkhead and let the water surge over him. Steam soon filled the room. He grabbed a towel, turned the water off and went into the bedroom drying himself. He noticed Delilah had put his epaulets onto a fresh uniform shirt. Once dressed, he went into the dayroom where coffee was ready. He drank quickly then looked at his watch. Coming up for 1030. There was no point in turning the TV on; the only available station was local and it was rubbish dancing or government propaganda. Some ships had satellite TV but not this one. Anyway, he wanted to see the 2nd Mate. He went out into the alleyway and up to the bridge deck.

Vijay and Graham were both wearing blue working shirts and were leaning over the chart table, which was piled with books and paper.

'How's the paperwork?' asked Harry. Paperwork was the Achilles' heel of all ships today. Computers were meant to help but all they did was increase it. Harry was lucky; Vijay was a good navigator and administrator and kept the ship on the straight and narrow. Too much so at times.

'These last few days alongside have been great, Captain,' said Vijay. 'We've caught up on weeks of work. Graham has been of considerable assistance.'

'Good to hear it,' said Harry.

'We are missing a number of notices to mariners,' said Vijay. Notices contained the weekly navigation changes to charts as well as other important changes regarding general merchant ship matters. 'I hoped they would be sent here but I suppose there's still no mail?'

'That's right,' said Harry. 'Anyway, we won't sink without them. I expect you've done the routing to Hull?' Hull was their final port of destination.

'All finished,' said Vijay pointing at a neat pile of charts to one side of the chart table.

'I need your signatures on all of these, Captain,' Vijay said, indicating another pile with yellow stickers sticking out. 'I've marked all the places. And you haven't signed the logbook for three days,' he finished.

'I know, I know,' Harry said.

Graham butted in. 'There are also some new risk assessment sheets that I've done for you to look over, Sir.'

'Right,' Harry said, holding his hands up in front of him. 'Dump everything wanting my attention on my desk and I'll sign, check, lick, kiss whatever you want, tomorrow morning. Vijay, I thought you could forge my signature.' Vijay looked shocked.

'I would never do that, Sir,' he protested.

'I know, I know,' said Harry. 'I was joking.' Vijay looked unsure. 'Graham, spread the word that there is mass at the cathedral at 11 o'clock tomorrow for anyone interested.'

'I'll put it on the notice board, Captain.'

'You can do that but no one ever looks at it. Just tell the heads of department and the Bosun. That'll do it. Anything else?' Harry asked.

'No, Sir,' said Vijay.

'Vijay, you're doing a fine job of the bridge.' As the Navigating Officer, this was Vijay's domain.

As Harry looked around, he saw everything was in its place. The brass sparkled, even the windows gleamed. It didn't matter that quite a few bits of equipment didn't work; no one knew what one strange item of Russian construction was even for.

'Thank you, Sir,' said Vijay, smiling with pleasure.

'Right, I'm off on rounds.'

Sandy came up from the crew deck and walked aft to the Cadet's cabin at the end of the officers' deck. The door was open and Jake was inside tidying his desk. It was a small cabin with a large porthole letting in the bright sunlight. It had a desk, bunk, wardrobe and a small shower and head.

'You ready, Jake?' asked Sandy.

'Yes, Sir.'

'How was the boat this morning?'

'Apart from the bodies, we did two runs at the dummy perfectly.'

'OK,' grunted Sandy. 'Mind you a river is simple. Wait until you do it in a North Sea gale in winter.'

Jake grimaced, 'that's what the Bosun always tells me.'

'Come on,' said Sandy. 'Let's not keep the Old Man waiting.'

Harry was sitting at his desk in his office when Sandy and Jake arrived.

'The agent still has no news, Sandy,' Harry said as Sandy walked in.

'That's no surprise,' remarked Sandy.

'Frankly, Captain, I think we're wasting our time here. Much better to get the hell out and go up to Lagos and see what we can get there.'

'We'll see what the office says on Monday. Meanwhile, that means we have a weekend in port.'

'A last weekend before the shit hits the fan. As long as we aren't here when it does start to fly.'

'How was the boat trip?' Harry asked looking at Jake.

Jake looked at Sandy. 'He found some bodies in the river,' Sandy explained. 'Their hands and legs had been chopped off.'

'There will be a few more of those soon,' said Harry. 'Are you going ashore tonight?'

'With the Chief Officer's permission,' Jake said carefully.

'Just be careful,' said Harry. 'How are the condoms holding out, Sandy?'

'Beer will run out before they do,' laughed Sandy.

'Right,' said Harry. 'Let's go.' He turned and took his cap from a coat peg by the door. It was a bit battered now; the oak leaves around the brim and the cap badge were a little tarnished. Just like me thought Harry.

'I've seen the bridge, so we'll start on the officers' deck,' Harry said leading the way. Harry got to the end of the alleyway and entered Jake's cabin.

'Did you leave something?' whispered Sandy. Jake nodded. As Jake was a Cadet, he was under training, and Harry was fierce in his inspections. Drawers and the wardrobe were opened, door mat was lifted, all in order. In the bathroom, the taps gleamed and the porcelain sparkled. Harry was not going to give up. Then he peered forward.

'Dale,' he called. Jake went into the bathroom and looked down to where Harry was pointing. 'The drain is dirty.'

'Yes, Sir,' said Jake.

'Get it cleaned after inspection and put it in the book.'

'Very good, Sir,' said Jake. On inspection, his job was to note all the defects Harry found, then give them to the department heads as reminders. Harry walked out of the cabin followed by Sandy, who turned to Jake with a broad grin and winked.

Going down the next stairway they reached the crew deck. This was much larger than the officers' deck and extended further aft. All the crew were accommodated here. This deck was where the galley and messrooms were, which was where Harry went first. The officers' messroom, as usual, was clean and already set for lunch. Just off the messroom was a small lounge area which had a small bar in the corner. The glasses and bottles reflected the light coming from the two portholes. On the bulkheads there were various pictures and crests presented by ports and ships. The carpet was plain blue as were the curtains. In one corner stood a TV with a DVD and video player underneath. Harry went over to the bar and opened the bar book. This was where all drinks purchased by the officers were recorded.

'Still very light,' Harry said to Sandy, who ran the bar.

'We are ashore most evenings,' said Sandy, 'though being the first Saturday in port for a long time, it might get a little heavy tonight.'

They turned and went into the galley where Willie was waiting for them. He was resplendent in his chef's hat, trousers and tunic. Again everything was gleaming. The covers of the galley drains were already lifted for inspection. The oven doors were open and the ventilation uptake grilles were out showing they had been cleaned.

'As always, Cook, nice and clean,' said Harry.

'Be even cleaner if people didn't keep tramping around in here,' grumbled the Cook. This was his perpetual complaint.

'You'd better speak with the Bosun about that,' said Harry.

'He's the worst bloody offender,' the Cook protested. 'Always looking for food. Don't know where he puts it.'

Harry turned to Sandy. 'Are we having a buffet lunch in the bar tomorrow?'

'Actually, I know we normally have a buffet on Sundays but I thought that as we are in this port on Sunday, it might be fun to have a barbecue. What do you think?'

'I don't mind,' said Harry. 'It depends on the Cook. How are the stores? Can they take a barbecue?'

'That's no problem, Captain. We've plenty of meat from Capetown. The only problem is fresh salad, but we're storing up again on Monday.'

'Right. Ship's barbecue tomorrow night. I presume you've already run this past the Bosun?'

'Yes, Captain,' said Sandy. 'The crew are all up for it.'

'Let's keep our fingers crossed that there's no rain. All you have to do is mention barbecue and down it comes. Thank you, Cook,' said Harry, leading the team into the crew messroom where the Bosun was waiting.

'Good morning, Bosun,' said Harry. 'The Cook is complaining about crew in the galley.'

'Morning, Captain. Old bugger's always complaining. It's his way of saying he's happy. I'll have words with the crew or he'll spit in my tea.'

'Everything working in here?' Harry asked, indicating to the refrigerators, microwave, hotplates and toasters on the counter.

'Just as before,' said the Bosun. 'One of the refrigerators isn't so good and the chairs need recovering.' It was a large messroom with three bench tables and bench seats that were fixed to the deck. One of the deck boys, Jim, was laying the tables for lunch.

'All looks clean in here,' said Harry, 'but if it weren't, I'm sure you'd fix it. Cockroaches under control?'

'Got 'em all tamed now, Sir. Be giving us a floor show next.'

They left the messroom and went into the crew recreation room. It was much bigger than the officers' lounge. Down one side ran a large bar and on one bulkhead there was a large TV with various players underneath. The room was decorated with various trophies either given or stolen. The room smelt of stale tobacco.

'Have either of you heard of secondary smoking?' asked Harry. The Bosun and Sandy looked at each other in feigned puzzlement.

'You used to smoke didn't you, Captain?' said Sandy.

'Yes and I stopped.'

'As lowly sailors, it's our only pleasure, Captain,' said the Bosun.

'I don't think Esmeralda would agree with that,' Harry declared. Jake chortled from behind.

The deck boys also kept the recreation room clean. 'How are the deck boys doing?' asked Harry.

'Totally useless and lazy,' said the Bosun 'but we'll keep them.'

Sandy interrupted. 'Jim Bailey is due for rating up to Ordinary Seaman.'

'When?' asked Harry.

'Looking at his book, a few days ago,' said Sandy.

'Are you both happy with him being rated up?' asked Harry

'Aye, he's alright,' conceded the Bosun.

'Right,' said Harry. 'We'll do it in the bar. He can put on a case of beer.'

'I'm sure he'll be pleased to do that,' said Sandy.

'Cadet, put down in the book that we need air fresheners for the ship, especially in the public rooms. Sandy, have words with the Cook. I saw his packet of tobacco on the table in the galley. If I catch him smoking in the galley I'll have his balls.'

'Right, Captain,' said Sandy.

They continued down the alleyway checking each crew cabin and the communal bathrooms as they went. At the end of the alleyway there was a door leading to the platform maintenance offices and personnel quarters, which were used by the repair and maintenance crews when they were on board. The ship could take up to eight supervisors and eighty workers who were accommodated on the next two decks down.

'Do you want to go through?' Sandy asked Harry.

'Just a quick look,' said Harry. Sandy opened the door and Harry went through into another alleyway with cabins, opening up at the end to a large office overlooking the main deck work areas. Standing here Harry could see the entire afterdeck. There were helicopter markings on the deck and two cranes, one on each side.

The next deck down was the main deck where all the storerooms, laundry, refrigeration chambers, air conditioning room, galley and messrooms for the repair crews were. Most of their accommodation was a deck further down, below the main deck. A ladder led to this from the office. Harry went down.

'I won't bother with the maintenance crew quarters. They were all squared away after Luderitz. We'll just check the laundry and freezers.'

Jake went ahead and pulled the heavy main freezer door open. This led to a small chamber from which three other doors led off. One was for meats, another for general frozen stores and the other was a cool room for fresh vegetables and salad items. All were clean, but as the Cook had said, they were running low on salad. They moved onto the ship's laundry where the washing and drying machines were running with a pile of bedding ready to be loaded.

'That about does it. Sandy, Bosun, good job. She's nice and clean,' said Harry.

'Thank you, Captain,' said the Bosun. 'Can I buy you a pint in the bar?' It was a tradition for the Bosun to invite the Captain to the crew bar after rounds on a Sunday, provided all had gone well. Harry looked at his watch; it was almost noon.

'Yes please,' said Harry. 'How's the beer holding up by the way?'

'We took on extra cases of Castle and Lion in Luderitz and six more kegs of draught for the bars so we have enough to last us to Hull,' Sandy replied.

'At least we won't go thirsty then.'

They went up to the crew deck and into the bar. Harry removed his cap as they entered. There were several crew already there, most with pints in their hands. A chorus of 'Morning, Captain,' greeted Harry to which he responded and then waited for Olav, the Chief Coxn who was acting as barman to pour his pint.

Harry took the glass then turned. 'Cheers all.' They responded in kind. 'Coxn,' Harry called, 'can you ring the bell please?' Olav rang the bell and the assembled crew looked towards the bar and Harry.

'Gentlemen, excuse me interrupting your drinks but we have a small announcement. Bailey,' he called. Jim Bailey moved forward. 'Congratulations, Bailey. On the Bosun and Chief Officer's recommendation, you are rated up to Ordinary Seaman.' A cheer went up from all the crew as Harry shook his hand.

'Doesn't mean you stop cleaning my cabin,' said the Bosun gruffly.

Harry moved away and found a corner. Jake was being handed a pint glass.

'What are the regulations on underage drinking in this banana republic whose tatty flag we now display?' he asked Sandy.

'Don't think they've got one,' replied Sandy.

'Doesn't matter then,' said Harry.

'It didn't matter under the Red Ensign either,' Sandy shrugged.

'Want a beer on Bailey?' He asked holding his hand out for Harry's glass. Harry handed it over without comment and Sandy went to the bar for refills.

Some of the crew, seeing Harry alone, came over.

'I know what you are going to ask,' said Harry before they could speak. 'No I don't know when we are going to sail, but hopefully on Monday some decisions will be made.'

'It's just that we are well over our time, Sir,' said James Stewart, who was an Ordinary Seaman.

'I know that,' said Harry. 'It's the same for all of us.'

'What do you think will happen when we get back, Sir?' asked Andy MacBride, the ship's medic. Harry looked at them.

'Lads, I really don't know but I think you can guess the same as me.'

'So we'll be out of a job?' asked Andy.

Harry sighed, 'That's my guess.'

'It's not so easy getting work at sea now for us ratings,' said James. 'Everyone wants cheap labour like Filipinos or Chinese.'

'It's the same for officers,' said Harry, 'and the older you are the harder it is.' Just then Sandy appeared with fresh pints.

'Here you are, Captain,' he said looking at those around them.

'One thing to remember,' said Harry. 'You've all been at sea long enough to know that anything can happen. Who knows, there might even be another contract for the ship.'

'Yes,' said Andy as they moved away. 'For the ship but not for us.'

'Bit despondent are they?' asked Sandy.

'Aye. They know that there's nothing for us when we get back,' said Harry.

'It's a shame. They're all good seamen. No one wants them anymore as they are deemed too expensive.'

'Until there's a war,' said Sandy. 'Then see how fast they need us. Talking of runs ashore,' said Sandy, changing the subject, 'the Chief and I were wondering if you would like to join us for dinner tonight?'

'Where are you going?' asked Harry.

'The Metropole.' The Metropole was the oldest hotel in Matadi; it had been in the town centre since the 30s.

'Why not?' said Harry. 'Yes, that would be good. What time?'

'Shall we meet in the bar at 1900?' suggested Sandy.

'OK,' said Harry. He downed his beer. 'I'm off for some light lunch. Are you coming?'

'I think I'll just have one more,' said Sandy.

Harry smiled. 'See you this evening then. Thanks Bosun.' He waved across to the Bosun who was engaged in a noisy game of darts, then left, heading for the officers' mess.

'Is he going ashore?' asked the Bosun.

Sandy nodded.

'Do him good.'

Chapter 3

It was dark by the time the three officers walked up the hill towards the hotel in the centre of the town square. Flares of paraffin lamps from various windows and doors, as well as the lack of light from the street lights, showed that once again there was no power; an occasional bright light and the thumping of a diesel or petrol engine from more substantial homes indicated there was a generator working.

As they approached the town square, there was more light coming from the lamps on stalls scattered around the square. The hotel was brightly lit. It was a substantial colonial style building facing across the square towards the river.

'In the bar or up to the restaurant?' asked Sandy. The bar was on the ground floor, but the restaurant was on the next catching the breeze and views.

'Let's go up and sit out on the veranda,' said Peter carrying on through the foyer and up the stairs with Harry and Sandy following. There were only a few tables occupied. Philippe and Sophie Smeyers, both Belgian nationals, were sitting out on the terrace with a dark haired woman whom none of them had seen before. Philippe was the manager of the hotel and Sophie was his wife. As they walked towards the table, Philippe stood up with a broad smile on his face.

'Good evening, gentlemen. How good it is to have you for dinner. Will you join us for a drink?'

Before Harry could answer, Sandy eased forward saying, 'Excellent idea.' Then he bent over Sophie and kissed her on both cheeks. 'The pearl of Matadi,' he said as Sophie laughed.

'More like just one on a string, knowing you Sandy,' she said. Peter also went over and kissed her, but Harry, who'd only been once before, stood awkwardly waiting.

Philippe quickly noticed and apologised. 'I'm so sorry, Captain. You haven't met my wife have you? This is Sophie.' As Sandy intimated, she was lovely. Harry guessed she was in her mid-thirties, fair haired and with wide blue eyes. But he was attracted to the other woman. She was dark haired, probably in her early forties, slight with a hint of Asian. She also had a stunning figure which was enhanced by her trousers and plain shirt. A faint hint of makeup enhanced her tan and her dark eyes which were staring at him. Harry realised that he was staring at her and hastily turned to Philippe.

'I'm sorry again,' Philippe said. 'My manners. Can I introduce Dr Carole Masters? Dr Masters is head of the Mission Hospital which is up in the hills.' The three men held their hands out in turn. Harry noticed her hand was warm and dry with a firm grip. Her greeting had a southern United States accent which Harry picked up on.

'Carolina?' asked Harry.

'South Carolina,' Carole corrected. 'I don't suppose you can name the city?'

'Savannah?' guessed Harry.

'That's in Georgia,' laughed Carole, 'but that's good enough. Charleston. You have obviously spent time in the south.'

'He was on a ship where the only movie was Gone with the Wind,' chipped in Sandy,

'Philippe! Are we getting some drinks around here?'

'Coming, Sandy,' said Philippe. 'I know you and Peter will have beer. What about you, Captain?'

'Same please,' said Harry pulling up a chair and sitting down.

'So when do you sail, Captain?' asked Philippe.

'Good question,' replied Harry. 'We have no idea. The spares have not arrived and no one seems to know where they are.'

'Can you sail without them?'

Harry indicated towards Peter. 'On one engine we can make around 7 knots,' said Peter. 'We could make our way up the coast towards Lagos but that engine is not too reliable either, so I wouldn't guarantee getting much further.'

'The problem is getting out on one engine,' Harry added. 'Just after the bridge is the Devil's Cauldron. It's a bad place for ships, as the current can run up to 8 knots and push the ship directly against the cliffs. The ship has to make a hard left turn to avoid the cliffs and to do this successfully requires maximum speed.'

'I know all about the Cauldron,' said Philippe, 'but not from a seaman's view. It seems quite wide there.'

'Two kilometres at the speed the ship has to go is nothing,' said Harry. 'From entering the Cauldron we can be on the rocks in minutes. Anyway, it's up to the pilot whether he is willing to take the ship through. If we use both of the harbour tugs we can possibly do it, although small craft don't like the place either because of the whirlpools. Also they have to get back out after we let them go.'

'But you came in,' said Carole.

'Yes we did, but it is much easier against the current and we took a long time. Anyway, when we came in, the current was only around 5 knots.'

Very quickly the waiters arrived with glasses, ice and cold bottles of Heineken.

'Cheers,' said Sandy, and raised his bottle. Everyone ignored the glasses and did the same. Harry was just putting his bottle back on the table when there was a rumbling of thunder from across the river. The room fell silent for a moment.

'I didn't know that rain was forecast,' said Harry. Philippe looked concerned.

'That wasn't thunder, Harry. It was guns.'

'That close?'

'They have been sounding on and off for a few days now,' said Carole. 'Sometimes they seem close, at other times they are distant and even silent for a while, but slowly they are coming closer. At that moment a string of lights came on along the bridge which crossed the river. This was followed instantly by the lights coming on in the town below them and in the hotel.

'Let's stop this talk of guns,' said Philippe. 'You are here to enjoy yourselves. Now please excuse me. I will get the generators knocked off. Better save fuel.' He stood up and disappeared back into the main restaurant.

'Have you been in Matadi long?' Harry asked Carole.

'About a year now,' she replied.

'That's long enough,' said Harry.

'Oh, I don't know, it grows on you.'

Harry grunted.

Sandy interrupted. 'Harry's has a thing about Africa, particularly the West Coast. He thinks it should be cordoned off from the rest of the world.' Carole looked intently at Harry.

'There's more to Africa than violence and poverty. The majority of the people want what everyone wants, which is to be able to bring their families up in peace. Cordoning it off isn't going to help them.'

Harry held his hands up in surrender. 'Hey Doctor, I'm just a sailor, looking in the window. If you're saying I don't know the problems, you're right, but I admire those of you who are here trying to help.' He smiled at Carole, who stared back, relaxed and smiled in return.

'You should see her clinic and what she has achieved,' said Sophie, 'especially her pygmies.'

'They're not 'my' pygmies,' protested Carole.

'Pygmies?' asked Harry. 'I didn't know there were pygmies around here.'

'They are what remains of a village group from the north, around Kinshasa, who were caught up in the fighting,' said Carole. 'They found their way down here and live around the mission.'

Just then Philippe returned looking distracted.

'Is everything all right?' asked Sophie.

'Yes, fine,' said Philippe. 'I've just come off the phone with Justine. He's getting concerned about the situation in the north and wants to take precautions. Let's order.' Two waiters appeared and they took the orders for dinner and fresh drinks.

When they had gone, Sophie continued. 'What precautions?'

'Justine has been talking with his company in Kinshasa. The rebels, if we can still call them that, are now well established and Justine is sure that Mobutu and his family have left or are about to leave the country. If that is the case, it is only a matter of time before Kabila is recognised as the new President and the government forces we rely on become rebel forces and Matadi a rebel town.'

'Do we know how the fighting is going?' asked Harry.

'Not really,' said Philippe. 'Each side makes claims that cannot be believed, but it hinges on the Angolans. Anyway, we are here to enjoy ourselves this evening and I intend to do just that.' There were murmurs of agreement around the table as the plates arrived and two bottles of champagne also appeared.

'Some kind of celebration?' asked Sandy.

'No,' said Philippe. 'Just the pleasure of your company. So please, let's stop talking about the war.'

Once dinner was finished and as the drinks continued, the party became more relaxed.

'There's a piano over there, Captain,' said Sandy, indicating with his glass.

Harry ignored the remark but Sophie chipped in. 'You play, Captain? It would be good to hear it again. A lady used to come and play but she left. Since then it has been silent.'

'I don't play,' said Harry, 'I just tinkle.'

'Then please tinkle,' laughed Sophie.

'Go on,' said Carole, 'I would like to hear.'

Harry stood up. 'You asked for it,' he said moving over to the piano where he sat down and opened the lid. It was surprisingly clean. He ran his fingers across the keys and then began to play. The music floated over the room out onto the terrace.

'That's beautiful,' said Sophie. 'It's Rodrigo's Concierto de Aranjuez but I've never heard it played on the piano before.'

The restaurant had quietened down as the diners stopped talking and listened to the haunting melody of the piano.

'It's so sad,' said Carole.

'He likes sad songs,' said Sandy. 'He says it's because they are slow. He can play them easier. Whenever he plays it is usually sad and romantic.' They listened until the music finished; the room then burst into applause. The next number was an old romantic Sinatra piece and a few couples began to dance. Peter got up and held out his hand to Sophie who took it with a smile and they joined the dancers.

'Is he married, Sandy?' asked Carole.

'No,' said Sandy carefully.

'Tell me about him?'

'Ah now, that's not for me to say is it?'

She put her hand on his. 'Yes, you're right. So what about you? Are you married?'

'Not really,' said Sandy and Carole laughed.

'Now why am I not surprised by your answer?'

'I am a great believer in what Nelson said,' said Sandy. 'When a sailor passes Gibraltar, he becomes a bachelor.'

'Did he really say that?'

'If he didn't he should have,' said Sandy. 'He certainly became one, randy bugger.'

She made a face at him and got up.

'I'm taking Harry his drink.' She walked across to the piano and leant against it. Harry looked up.

'Come and sit here,' he said, making room on the piano bench.

'You play well,' Carole said. 'Where did you learn?'

'My mother taught me. She was very good. I'm not.' He finished the piece and broke into another.

'Casablanca!' cried Carole delightedly. 'I've always wanted someone to play that to me.' They looked at each other.

'Of all the gin joints in all the towns in all the world,' Harry started, 'she walks into mine,' they finished together. Harry finished the number to the applause of the dancers.

'That's enough,' said Harry closing the piano. He picked up his drink.

'I wondered if you would like to visit the mission tomorrow?' asked Carole looking at him. Harry thought for a moment.

'Tell you what, we're having a barbecue on board tomorrow night. I'll visit the mission if you'll come to the barbecue.'

'I would love to,' said Carole. 'I'll pick you up at 11 o'clock tomorrow morning?'

'That will be fine.' Harry took her arm and they walked back to the table.

Sophie stood up and kissed Harry on the cheek.

'That was lovely, Harry, thank you so much. Everyone enjoyed it. You do more than tinkle!'

'I'm pleased you enjoyed it, Sophie. Philippe, we are having a barbecue tomorrow evening on board. We would be delighted if you and Sophie could attend.'

Peter looked up. 'Actually, we'd already asked them,' he said, 'and they are coming.'

'That's great,' said Harry. 'Provided the weather stays dry.'

'According to the forecast from Kinshasa, it should be good until Monday,' said Philippe.

Sandy got up.

'Peter and I thought that we would finish the evening with a nightcap at Esmeralda's. Are you joining us, Captain?'

Harry was about to decline, when Carole piped up, 'Oh good! I have to go there anyway. I would love the company.'

Sandy looked at Harry. 'I suppose I could come for a drink,' Harry said lamely. Sandy smiled.

They paid their bill, said goodbye and went out into the night.

'I'll just tell my driver where I'm going,' said Carole disappearing off towards a row of cars and trucks.

Carole reappeared and linked her arms with Sandy and Harry.

'What a lovely evening,' she said, 'and so unexpected.'

'Why are you going to Esmeralda's?' asked Harry.

'I look after the girls,' said Carole. 'Esmeralda is remarkably good. She insists on the girls having regular check ups, especially as AIDS is so prevalent in Africa. I hope your crew wear condoms, Captain.'

'We give them enough to wear three at once,' said Sandy 'and yes, they're not stupid.'

They walked down the hill. Halfway down they turned off the main road into a side road where coloured lights could be seen and music was coming from the end of the street. As they approached the metal gate to a compound, they could see a group of people around the solid metal gate and a large sign saying Esmeralda's. There was also a military jeep parked there. As they drew closer they could see the UN flag and signs painted on the doors.

'Bastards!' exclaimed Carole.

'I didn't know you had UN troops here,' said Harry.

'We don't,' said Carole. 'The Angolan border is only a short distance away. They come over from there.'

'Why here?'

'They come looking for young girls. The younger the better,' said Carole bitterly. 'Also they know that here they can do as they want, then go back over the border where they can't be touched.'

'But surely there are girls in Angola,' said Sandy.

'Yes, but the Angolan authorities watch them and they have to pay there. Here they think they are free to do as they please, especially now, with the present situation and hardly any government troops or police around. Often the girls are never seen again.'

'What happens to them?'

Carole shrugged. 'Who knows. Probably sold as sex slaves or worse.'

Peter walked around the jeep. 'Ugandan,' he said pointing to the small flag painted on the door of the jeep.

'They come from all over Africa,' said Carole. 'Most are good but there are enough bad ones to be wary of them.'

The guards at the gate welcomed them. They pushed the crowd of beggars and children apart, and opened the gate for them to enter the compound where the music and lights emanated from the veranda. As they approached the entrance, Esmeralda came to the door. She was a large woman with an olive complexion, with flowing black hair and heaving breasts that almost fell out of her low cut frilly blouse.

'Sandy!' she shouted and enveloped him with her arms. 'I hoped you would come tonight.' She turned and embraced Peter. 'Good to see you Peter. Your girlfriend is waiting for you.' Leaving Peter spluttering she grinned at Carole.

'So you bring them all to my establishment, yes? And who is this?' she said looking at Harry. 'Don't tell me, I think I know. This is the Captain that I hear so much about but who has been avoiding me. You prefer other bars to mine, yes?'

Harry laughed. 'No Esmeralda, but the last thing the crew want is their Captain watching over their shore leave as well.'

'Well tonight you will see plenty. Come, Captain. Welcome to Esmeralda's,' she said leading the way in through the swing doors.

The place was full. The mix of black, brown and white skins of the men and women contrasted with the bright colours of the dresses and the room's garish décor. A combination of cigarette smoke, the smell of cheap perfume and alcohol pervaded the huge room, which had a band who were struggling in the corner to make themselves heard over the noise.

The tables overflowed with glasses and bottles and it appeared that every man had a woman balanced on their knee or hanging on their shoulders. Even the main bar was lined with men and women. Harry noted that, as well as his crew, the crew from the Filipino ship were making the most of their last night ashore.

The Bosun was sitting at a table near the far wall with Jake the Cadet, Godwin the 2nd Engineer and Olav the Chief Coxn. All had women around them. Harry noticed that Jake was with a particularly attractive girl.

'Cadet looks happy,' Harry said to Sandy.

'That's his girlfriend,' replied Sandy. Two fat, sweaty and drunk men wearing soiled white uniforms and gold epaulets staggered from the crowd and grabbed Harry's hand. It was the Harbour Master and the Chief Customs Officer.

'Good to see you, Captain,' said the Harbour Master slapping Harry on the back. 'We hear you are having a barbecue tomorrow night?'

'Word travels fast,' said Harry dryly.

'Well, Captain. You'll want permission to open the bond and have your friends on board.'

'Of course,' said Harry 'and you are included amongst our friends.'

They both beamed. 'It will be a pleasure, Captain. We will make sure that everything goes smoothly.'

I bet you will thought Harry, including your perks.

'I look forward to seeing you both tomorrow evening then,' he said turning towards Carole before they could continue.

'Shall we sit down?' Sandy waved to them from where the waiters had cleared a space and placed a table. A host of Primus beer bottles were already on the table.

'I don't suppose they have rum?' asked Harry. One of the waiters disappeared into the throng at the bar.

'Have a beer in the meantime,' said Carole holding her bottle aloft. 'Cheers all!' The others raised their bottles in salute.

Esmeralda appeared by the table holding a bottle in her hand along with a jug of what appeared to be lime juice with ice.

'Sorry, Captain,' she said. 'No rum, but I have a bottle of cane from South Africa. Will that do?'

'One of my favourite drinks,' said Harry. Esmeralda beamed and set the bottle and jug down.

'Enjoy,' she said and disappeared back to the bar.

Carole said, 'Let me,' and poured a generous measure of cane into the glass which Harry topped up with lime. He raised the glass and took a steady drink.

'Now that's a drink,' he said with satisfaction.

'Let's dance,' said Carole and stood up, reaching for Harry's hand. They made their way onto the busy dance floor and joined the throng. The band was gamely pumping out music. Carole moved in close. 'There's not much room to move around,' she said. 'I don't mind,' replied Harry holding her more closely.

At that moment from across the room came the sound of shattering glass and breaking furniture. The band stopped and the noise in the room died away except for angry voices.

Harry, still holding Carole's hand, walked towards the crowd at the edge of the dance floor. He pushed through and saw Jake and the Bosun facing four United Nations soldiers. The tables had been pushed aside and there were broken bottles and glasses on the floor. One of the soldiers had his arm around Jake's girl, and the Lieutenant and two other soldiers had wicked looking knives in their hands. The Bosun was holding Jake back, who was struggling and shouting at the soldiers.

Harry turned to Jake, 'Stow it!' he ordered.

'He's got my girl!' shouted Jake still struggling.

'He's also got a big fucking knife,' Harry said. 'Now just shut up. Bosun! Hold on to him.'

Harry gauged the scene. On a nearby table were the weapons the soldiers had brought in with them rather than leaving them in the jeep. Behind the soldiers were a number of the crew. Harry saw Sandy slowly moving behind. Someone appeared alongside him, and Harry saw it was the Filipino Captain. His crew were also making a circle around the soldiers. Harry looked at the soldiers, who were drunk and mean.

'Gentlemen, we have a problem,' Harry started.

'Who are you?' one of the soldiers shouted turning to Harry pointing his knife at him.

Harry ignored him and spoke directly at the Lieutenant. 'The girl is not a whore, Lieutenant. She is a friend of ours.'

'She is coming with us,' the Lieutenant snarled.

'No, Lieutenant,' said Harry. 'She is not going anywhere with you tonight.' He looked over the Lieutenant's shoulder at Sandy, who nodded and brought up a shotgun with a short double barrel. The Lieutenant's hand started towards his holstered pistol.

'Don't do that,' ordered Harry. 'Not unless you want to feed the crocodiles in the river. Lieutenant, you are surrounded by seamen. This is our territory not yours. I want you to keep your hands away from your pistol, and very slowly look behind you.' The Lieutenant looked hesitant but did not take his hand from his pistol. 'Behind you a shotgun is being pointed directly at your back. You will be familiar with the effect of a shotgun at short range of course? So is that man. One wrong move on your part and he will blow your back apart and that of your men, provided we do not get to them first. You have chosen the wrong night and the wrong place. Do not make the wrong decision.' Harry spoke to Jake and the Bosun, 'Move away from these soldiers.' Realising that this would clear Sandy's firing arc they did so quickly.

A voice came from the crowd. It was Esmeralda. 'He has taken girls before. They have never come back.'

'It's up to you now, Lieutenant. If you let the girl go, I promise you and your men can walk out of here and go back over the border. If you don't, then none of you will leave here alive.' Several sailors off both ships had drawn their knives. 'You are here illegally. You will just disappear and no one will care.'

The whole room was quiet; everyone watched Harry and the Lieutenant. Even the girl had stopped struggling, her brown eyes wide with fright. The Lieutenant looked at Harry for a long moment and then slowly turned and saw Sandy standing with the shotgun. Sandy smiled at him. The Lieutenant surveyed the room and all the seamen standing around.

'How do I know you will let us go?'

'There is no reason not to,' said Harry. 'You have nothing we want. We just want to be left alone. Now why not be sensible and leave?'

The Lieutenant turned to his men and spoke in a low native dialect. They looked at Harry malevolently but edged towards the table with the weapons.

'Just a minute,' said Harry. He saw Delilah in the crowd.

'Delilah, do you know these weapons?' Delilah nodded. 'Unload them and take the ammunition.' He turned to the Lieutenant. 'Just to ensure you don't change your mind when you leave. You can keep your knives but not the pistol. Delilah expertly emptied the guns and removed the magazines.

'If you want the pistol and magazines back, your Commanding Officer can get them from my ship on Monday.' He saw the Lieutenant about to speak. 'There's no argument Lieutenant, just walk out now.'

The room was silent. For a moment the soldiers hesitated then the Lieutenant lowered his knife.

'We will go,' he said to Harry, 'but we will remember you.' He took his pistol out of the holster and threw it on to the floor. The soldier who had the girl pushed her towards Jake, who grabbed her and moved her behind him. The soldiers backed towards the door and then turned and left.

'Sandy, make sure they go away.' Sandy waved acknowledgement and went outside followed by Delilah.

The room relaxed into an explosion of noise. Jake and his girl came up to Harry. 'Thank you, Sir,' said Jake.

'I hope you learnt something tonight,' said Harry. 'We were lucky there were so many of us and so few of them. Remember never take on a man with a knife, especially when you haven't got a bigger one.'

'This is proving a most interesting evening, Harry,' said Carole, 'Do you often get into these situations?'

'Not if we can help it,' said Harry dryly. Sandy came up to them. 'They're on their way, Captain.'

'Where the hell did the shotgun come from?'

'Esmeralda gave it to me from behind the bar.'

'Was it loaded?'

'Don't know, there wasn't time to check.'

'If they had gone for their weapons, it could have been a blood bath.'

'Not really,' said Sandy. 'They were pussies. Anyway we were watching for that. Now when we encountered the French Foreign Legion in Marseilles, that was a real party.'

'Do tell,' said Carole.

'That was long ago when the earth was young,' said Harry. 'Now where are our drinks?'

With that he led them back to the table.

'I'm going to go and see some of the girls,' said Carole. 'Back soon.'

The room was settling back into the customary noises, added to by the band which had started playing again.

'Where's Peter?' asked Harry.

'I think he is in deep discussion with a young lady.'

'Be a different discussion than the one he has with his wife in suburbia,' laughed Harry. 'It won't be about engines either.' He sighed. 'We're getting too old for this,' he said pouring another glass of cane.

'Well at least we're not stuck on some container ship rattling along on a milk run,' said Sandy. 'Now that would be slow death.'

'You know, there are times when that seems quite appealing. At least we would keep out of trouble.'

Sandy laughed. 'Those companies just want nautical truck drivers.'

'Probably,' replied Harry. 'That was quick,' said Harry as Carole rejoined them.

'Esmeralda operates a clean house,' Carole said, 'and the girls are very careful. Why can't you men just masturbate? It would save a lot of trouble and money.' Harry and Sandy looked at each other, not knowing quite how to reply to that. Carole laughed, 'You're all the same; you can talk about sex, but we can't.' She saw they were still looking embarrassed. 'OK,' she laughed. 'I'll drop it. Anyway it helps to pay the rent. Come on, Captain. Let's resume our dance.'

All too soon, Carole looked at her watch.

'Sorry,' she said. 'I have to do a Cinderella. I like to get back to the mission in time to make rounds before bed and it's nearly midnight now.'

Harry stood up. 'I'll see you to your car,' he said and took her arm.

'I'm packing in, Sandy. We'll probably have a heavy night tomorrow. Are you coming?'

'I'll hang around a little longer, Captain,' said Sandy.

'Right, I'll see you tomorrow morning. Night, Sandy, and thanks for your help tonight.'

'That's what Mates are for,' laughed Sandy, 'getting Captains out of trouble.' Harry smiled.

Harry and Carole weaved their way through the crowd, saying goodnight to various crew members as they passed. Esmeralda was waiting by the door.

'Thank you for tonight, Captain. Monique was in trouble. I hope those bastards will stay away for a while now.'

'I hope so too, Esmeralda. Thanks for the weaponry.'

'Hah,' she said. 'There aren't many businesses around here without something to protect them. It shouldn't be but then...' She shrugged. 'This is Zaire. Goodnight.' She leant up and kissed Harry's cheek and then embraced Carole. Just then Esmeralda's daughter came running up.

'Thank you, Captain.' She smiled, leant forward and kissed Harry on the cheek.

They emerged into the cool night air leaving the noise and smoke behind them. Outside on the road was Carole's Land Rover with two armed guards sitting inside waiting.

'At night, I never go anywhere without guards,' Carole explained. 'Especially now, with a war on and armed groups roaming around.'

'Will you be all right?' Harry asked.

'With these two, yes,' said Carole. 'They're ex-military and have been with the mission for two years,' she said. 'Harry, thank you for an interesting evening. At least I can now say I've been out with a sailor. What time shall I pick you up in the morning?'

'How about eleven?' said Harry. 'That will give me time to finish the paperwork.'

'Eleven it is,' she said. 'Hopefully the weather will stay as it is. Night.' She kissed him on his cheek.

'This is my lucky night,' he said. 'Three women kissing me in a few minutes.'

'If you go back in they will do more than that,' Carole laughed. 'Or do you want a lift back to the ship?'

'No thanks,' said Harry. 'It's only a few minutes down the hill. A walk will help to clear my lungs of all the smoke.'

'OK,' she said. 'See you tomorrow.' She got into her truck and as it drove away he waved goodbye. Now that, thought Harry as he walked down the hill, is an interesting woman.

Sunday 18 May

Chapter 4

Harry sat at his desk, working his way slowly through the various books and documents requiring his signature. Normally he would be getting more annoyed at this as he progressed through what he considered to be pointless procedures, but today he was quite cheerful and scrawled his signature on the pages indicated by the 2nd Officer. The sunlight was streaming into his office through the porthole. He was already changed and his sunglasses were tucked into his shirt pocket. It was 1030. Just a few more signatures to go and everything would be up to date, until next week. As it was Sunday morning the ship was quiet. Most of the crew were still in their bunks except for the duty watch. Even the galley would be quiet; it would be salads for lunch.

The footsteps on the stairs had to be Sandy – this was confirmed by his beaming face appearing in the doorway. 'Good morning, your Honour,' he said. 'I'm going up the road with some of the crew to the cathedral.' Harry wasn't surprised. Sandy kept in touch with his roots.

'Didn't know they had a bar there,' said Harry. 'No, but the hotel bar is just round the corner so we can refresh ourselves there after the service.'

'Better take the priest with you, treat him for shock after your confession.'

'He's heard it all before,' said Sandy. 'Anyway, I hope you have a pleasant day with the Doctor. I presume we will see you at the barbecue tonight?'

'Wouldn't miss it. What time does it start?'

'About 1900.'

'At least we will have the weather for it.'

'See you later, Captain.' Sandy left the office and clattered down the stairs.

Harry had left the logbook until last and now started to go through it for the last week's entries.

On the gangway Jake waited for Carole. His white shirt was gleaming with the Cadet's black and gold patches and his uniform cap sat squarely on his head. The shore watchman was quietly dozing in the shade of the overhead decking. Further down the jetty, the Filipino ship had made the two port tugs fast and was letting go the last of her lines. The tugs slowly pulled her off the berth as she came ahead on her engines, working her way further out into the river ready for turning to point towards the bridge and the way out to the sea.

At that moment Carole's battered Land Rover came through the dock gate and headed for the bottom of the gangway. Jake kicked the watchman's chair and went down the gangway as the vehicle drew up.

'Good morning, Doctor,' he said as he opened her door.

'Carole,' she said. 'My name is Carole.' Jake blushed.

'Carole,' he said. She smiled and gave him a quick peck on the cheek.

'There, that was easy. Am I allowed to kiss you on duty? I hope he's ready.'

'He's waiting for you topside. I'll take you up.' Carole looked at the Filipino ship. 'Can we watch for a minute? I like watching ships sail.'

'Of course,' he said and walked her aft where they could get a better view.

The ship was turning now in the fast flowing current and being swept downriver sideways as the turn continued.

'Where is she going?' asked Carole.

'Lagos,' said Jake. Carole looked at him.

'Would you like to be sailing?' she asked. Jake blushed again.

'Not really,' he said.

'Yes,' said Carole knowingly. 'I can understand.' She smiled again. 'Come on, lead me to his cave.'

They entered the cool accommodation and went up to Harry's deck. Jake tapped lightly on Harry's office door but Harry was already standing. Carole peered over Jake's shoulder.

'Just about on time am I?' she smiled.

'Good to see you,' said Harry. 'Come on in. Jake. Can you ask Delilah for two coffees?' He turned to Carole, 'Coffee all right or you can have tea?'

'Coffee is fine,' she said.

'Delilah was waiting for us when we passed the galley,' said Jake. 'He's already getting coffee.'

'Thank you, Jake', said Carole. 'You look very smart this morning. I wish I was younger.' Jake blushed and retreated.

'Stop seducing our Cadet,' said Harry. 'Come through to the dayroom.' He pushed aside a curtain and Carole stepped in.

'How lovely!' she exclaimed. 'Brass portholes, wooden walls and a chintz three piece suite. Just like the movies.'

'Dying fast, I'm afraid,' said Harry. 'You only see this on old ships. The modern ones are all plastic and steel. By the way it's not walls, its bulkheads.' Carole wrinkled her nose at him and went over to the bookcase.

'Roman history. Yours?'

'Yes,' said Harry. 'I've been interested in the Romans since I was a kid.'

'And through there?' she said indicating another curtained doorway.

'That's the bedroom.'

'Where your hammock is?'

'We've moved on a bit since then,' said Harry dryly.

'Can I see?' Without waiting for a reply she walked over and pulled the curtain aside. 'A double bed!' she exclaimed. 'Obviously they cater for Captain's habits.' She looked in the bathroom. 'My God! You have a bath. That's more than I have.' She turned back into the dayroom. 'Who looks after this?' Just then Delilah entered the cabin with a tray of coffee.

'I do,' he said. 'A woman's work is never done. What it really needs are some flowers to set it off.'

'Delilah,' said Harry warningly.

'Delilah's right,' said Carole.

'If Delilah had his way, it would be like a tart's boudoir. That's all, Delilah. Thank you.' Delilah scowled at him and winked at Carole.

'Nice to see someone with taste in here at last,' he said and departed quickly.

'Delilah is an interesting man,' said Carole sitting down on the settee. 'If that is the correct word. What is the story there?'

'He joined one morning in Kuwait. When I signed him on, he announced his name was Delilah. From what I gather he was in the Royal Marines for a while. If you believe the stories he was a sergeant. Somewhere along the line he started wearing dresses which didn't go down well with his brigade. There was a problem with an officer, which ended with the officer in hospital and Delilah looking for a job. Sometimes I wonder if he isn't taking the piss out of us all. Anyway here he is. He's like many of the crew. They have pasts but no one cares, as long as they obey orders and do their job.'

'Like a floating Foreign Legion?' Carole suggested.

'Not a bad analogy,' said Harry.

'And you? Do you have a past?'

'A few here and there. Let's finish our coffee and head off.' He went into the bedroom.

'Don't forget a hat,' Carole called. 'You'll need it.' He came back in with a safari hat on.

'My God,' she said. 'The White Queen's gift to Africa. Are we going hunting?'

'Apart from my uniform cap, it's all I have except for a baseball cap and I'm not wearing that ashore.'

'Well you'll certainly impress the natives,' she said, 'and probably scare the animals.' She stood up. 'I'm ready. Do you have any cigarettes?'

'Do you smoke?' asked Harry.

'Not for me, for the pygmies.' Harry went to a cupboard and took two cartons.

'Is that enough?' he asked.

'Plenty,' said Carole. They went out of the cabin and through the office. Harry paused to lock the door, and they then went down to the gangway, where Jake was waiting. He turned to the sign on the gangway showing the status of the senior officers on board and changed the Captain's sign to ashore.

'Tell the Chief Officer that I will be back for the barbecue at 1900,' said Harry. He turned to Carole, 'Does your phone work?'

'Spasmodically, when there is power. I'll write the number down.' She scribbled the number on a pad, tore off the sheet and gave it to Jake.

'If there is an emergency, call me at Carole's. If you can't get through, contact the agent and tell him to get me at Carole's mission station.'

'Aye aye, Sir,' said Jake. 'Goodbye, Carole.'

Harry nodded and they went down the gangway to Carole's Land Rover. Carole got in and opened the door for Harry who looked down at the AK47 on his seat.

'We can't go anywhere without these appearing,' he said.

'Can you use one?' asked Carole. 'Just in case.'

'Yes,' said Harry with a sigh. 'We have them on board.'

Carole put her foot down hard and they took off in a cloud of dust. The guard on the gate waved Carole through with a smile as they set off up the hill through the town.

'Which way are we going?' asked Harry.

'We start off on the main Kinshasa road. After about 25 clicks we turn to the left and go up into the hills, to where we are based.'

Harry was enjoying the drive. As they left town, there were fewer people on the road. The countryside was sparse brush but as they drove deeper into the country, the vegetation grew more green. There were occasional huts alongside the road, and children came out as they approached to sell bottles of drink.

'Why do you have guns on board, Harry? I thought you were a peaceful merchant ship.'

'We are. It's the other bastards who aren't so peaceful.' He looked at her but she was waiting. 'The seas are becoming like the wild west. There have always been pirates but now, because civilisation is retreating, many of these newly free countries don't have the navy or inclination to police their waters. The result is that ships are fair game off many coasts and even in oceans for that matter. Our ship operates in coastal waters, and we are slow and small with a low freeboard.'

'What's that?' said Carole.

'That means the deck is very close to the water so we are easy to board if pirates get close enough.'

'In other words, you are a tempting target?'

'You have it in a nutshell. Now, we can either sit back and wait for assistance, which I guarantee won't be there, let ourselves be boarded, which means at best we will be robbed or taken hostage or at worst murdered, or we can look after ourselves.'

'Have you ever been attacked?'

'They tried. We opened fire over their heads which made them turn around and look for easier prey. Young Jake was disappointed – he really wanted to shoot one of them.'

'It sounds exciting.'

'No, it's not. It's a nuisance and we shouldn't have to live like this, but that is how things are these days. You appear to have just as exciting a life,' he said, indicating the AK47. 'Have you ever used this?'

She nodded. 'Yes. The mission's been attacked twice but each time we drove them off. They were Mai Mai.'

'What are Mai Mai?'

'Supposedly para-military who support Kabila but really they are murderous armed gangs, mostly young men and teenagers, but they also use child soldiers.' The Land Rover lurched into a pothole. 'Sorry,' said Carole. 'Not watching the road.'

They were still passing the odd hut and occasionally a small settlement. Sometimes Carole slowed down to pass people walking or domestic animals, such as cows or goats, being driven along the roadside. Some of the people were entire families with their goods balanced on their heads.

'Everyone seems to be heading towards town,' said Harry. 'They're refugees from the fighting,' replied Carole.

'And yet there are people getting out of the town.'

Carole sighed. 'What are they to do? There is no safety anywhere.'

'There aren't many cars,' said Harry.

'Most have been stolen by the so-called armies,' said Carole. 'Anyway no one drives to Kinshasa anymore – it's too dangerous and the villages along the way are too poor for anyone to have a car.'

'Carole, if you know of all these dangers and that the rebels are getting closer, why don't you get them out, at least into the town or further south.'

She was silent for a moment, then replied, 'The mission is supported by a very wealthy organisation in America. When I elected to stay, they made contact with Kabila.'

'What, your bunch have been talking to the rebels?'

She ignored his outburst. 'I had nothing to do with this, but they have been assured that Kengi, our village, the mission and the pygmies will not be harmed.'

'And you believe this?' exclaimed Harry.

'I have to. I presume Kabila has been paid well.'

'Never mind how much he's been paid. I don't believe the politicians in Britain never mind some murderous thug out here in the Congo. Carole this doesn't make sense.'

'Look,' she said. 'It's very nice of you to be concerned, but you're on your way soon while the pygmies are left here. I'm all they've got. Wherever I take them it will be the same. At least I have a promise of protection if I stay put, which is more than I have anywhere else. Now please, let's stop talking about the war and have one day of enjoyment. What do you say?'

Harry shrugged. 'I give in. Maybe you're right. I don't know the place. OK, a day of enjoyment coming up.'

She laughed and drove faster, 'I'm thirsty.'

She pulled up at a roadside stall, and instantly the car was surrounded by clamouring children while beggars crawled out of the shade with their hands held out.

'Let's get some cokes,' she said. 'Unless you want beer?'

'No, coke is fine. I'll get these,' offered Harry.

'Do you have any local money?'

'No,' said Harry 'just dollars.'

'For Christ's sake don't show those. The entire village will surround us. Everyone wants them. With the war, the local currency is almost useless. That's why Esmeralda is so happy to see your ship in.'

She spoke to one of the children and two cold coke bottles appeared. She thrust some paper money at the child, who grinned. On the other side another child offered gum. She waved the children aside and drove back onto the road. Harry passed her a bottle.

'What was the language you used?'

'It's called Lingala. Most people speak that around here, but you'd be surprised at how many can speak a little English and French.'

'How do you put up with the poverty and sickness, Carole?'

Carole looked at him. 'Are you trying to say that I am heartless?'

'Hell no, Carole. Don't get so prickly,' Harry protested. 'It's just that it's everywhere.'

'That's the point, Harry. It's everywhere, just like green grass in England. In the end you don't see it. Oh yes, you know it's there. Malaria is endemic; over half the population is sick from it. The orphans, the mutilated. They have had two manic insurrections in the past few years when the army went berserk, killing and chopping limbs off. That's why there are so many with limbs missing. But because there is so much, it becomes part of the landscape.' She looked at him again. 'I can't cure them all, Harry.' He put his hand on hers.

'I understand. I've seen my share around the world, believe me, but that has been due to poverty and natural disaster. Here it is just so casual and deliberate.' He was silent for a moment. 'I was in Indonesia when Sukarno ordered his troops to shoot the people. We were unloading aid at the time and the bags of rice were breaking and spilling on the jetty. The starving people broke through the fencing. There were over 200 dead on the jetty when they had finished, mostly women and children.' She squeezed his hand back.

'When I first arrived here, there was an old French doctor who was going home. I asked him the same questions and he told me, 'It's background.' That is how he dealt with it. Mind you it was not as bad then.'

The road was getting worse as they drove on.

'Not so many people around now,' commented Harry.

'Most have the sense to stay indoors at this time of day,' said Carole. 'Not too far now.' Saying that, she slowed down as they approached another village in the distance. 'Kengi,' said Carole. 'Our local village.'

There was a dirt road on the left which Carole turned into. Instantly the car bounced heavily. They immediately started to head up into the hills with lush green foliage on each side of the track.

'It's strange,' said Harry. 'I thought it would be like the scrub in Namibia or like the Amazon jungle, but it's more like forest in Europe.'

'In the hills it is very beautiful.'

'What about wild animals?' said Harry.

'Not many left,' said Carole. 'Game is still around, but most animals have been killed for meat.'

'Any gorillas?'

'Not in this State. The last sightings in Bas Congo were near Boma but that was a long time ago. There are still some hippos and crocodiles but they are mainly in the small marshlands and lakes off the river. Plenty of snakes though. We have a good stock of antidotes in the mission. Lots of people get bitten.'

'Just as long as I don't see any,' said Harry.

The Land Rover continued to lurch as they drove higher into the hills, where the air became cooler.

'It's really very pleasant up here apart from the holes in the road,' Harry commented. They came to a bend in the road and, on rounding it, a white building came into view surrounded by several other smaller buildings as well as a number of huts built like igloos.

'Home,' said Carole.

As they drew to a stop, people started to come out from the huts.

'They really are pygmies,' Harry exclaimed. 'Incredible. I never thought I would meet pygmies.'

Most of the pygmies held back. The women all seemed to be holding children either in their arms or by their hands. They wore only loin cloths, some of the men had spears in their hands.

'Can you speak their language?' asked Harry.

'Not a chance,' said Carole. 'But some can speak KiCongo, and one knows a little English. God knows where he learnt it, possibly trading with the villages.'

Carole moved into the group of pygmies leaving Harry alone. Two of the men studied him with open curiosity. One of them was obviously translating for Carole, and they were chattering to her in a language with clicking sounds. Carole was talking to some of the women while handing out sweets to the children. She turned and smiled at Harry and then pointed at him while talking to the crowd. They all turned and looked at Harry as she spoke.

'I am telling them that you have a very large canoe with many people who live on it. They have never seen a ship so canoe is the best I can do.'

The pygmies were smiling at Harry now, and one of the men came up to him and offered his hand. Harry took it and they smiled at each other.

'That is the Kombeti,' said Carole. 'He is a kind of headman. I think it's time to give them the cigarettes.'

Harry turned back to the Land Rover, took out the two cartons of cigarettes and gave them to the Kombeti who brightened considerably. He turned to the others shouting and waved them in the air. Carole rejoined Harry.

'They are from the Aka people. They are very unhappy living here in a village. Traditionally they are forest people. They do not have a village as such, just encampments where they move about as they wish. They eat the game they catch, particularly monkeys. They are also experts at finding honey. In many ways they seem like children when they are out of the forest, but they know more about the forest than anyone else in Africa. There we are the children.'

'They have pointed teeth,' Harry said pointing at one of the boys.

'When the boys are ready for circumcision, that is when the girls and boys have their front teeth pointed. Do you see that woman over there?' She pointed to an old woman sitting on the ground by one of the huts. 'She is the Nganga.'

'Witch doctor?'

'No, not really. They do practise witchcraft but she is more of a healer. People from the other villages, towns and cities will also go to her.'

'Rather than you?'

Carole laughed. 'Let's say we work in partnership. Come on, I'll show you the hospital.'

They walked towards the larger white building. It had a broad veranda where a pygmy girl was sitting on a chair. As soon as Carole came onto the veranda she ran to her and hugged her leg, hiding her face from Harry.

'She's adopted me,' explained Carole. 'It is a terrible story. When the Mai Mai came to her camp, they caught her family.' She stopped, thinking for a moment. 'I know it sounds hard to believe but,' she paused again, 'they ate her family in front of her.' Harry stared in shocked silence. 'Not the whole bodies you understand. Just the interesting parts.' Carole looked away from Harry for a moment. 'They would have eaten her as well but she ran away into the forest and found the other survivors. They travelled through the forests and came here. There is nowhere else for them to go. This is all that is left of her group.' She waved her hand at the huts. Harry didn't say anything. He was staring at the girl.

'Trying to understand?' Carole asked. Harry nodded. 'You can't. The pygmies in the Congo are regarded as no more than vermin, yet they are credited with mystic qualities. It is not uncommon for them to be eaten, as many believe they will get magic powers from their flesh. It is the same with their sexual organs; by wearing them you gain increased sexual power. In many areas pygmies are actively hunted.'

Harry put his hand out to the girl but she shrank away from him holding tighter to Carole's leg.

'She won't come,' said Carole. 'You can understand.' She put her hand in her pocket and took out some sweets, and the girl's face lit up. Giving her the sweets she called across to one of the women who came over and took the girls hand.

'This is her aunt,' Carole explained as her aunt took the girl's hand and led her away.

'I really don't know what to say,' said Harry. Carole took his arm.

'It's all part of Zaire life and this bloody war,' she said. 'Mobutu is the biggest thief in Africa and a despot but at least things got along to a fashion and people didn't go around killing each other, at least not as much. Come in and look around.'

They went inside into a small clinic.

'This is where we deal with minor injuries.'

'Are you very busy?'

'It depends. There are other hospitals around but the problem is getting drugs and medicines. I deal mainly with pregnancies and what they term 'women's problems'. Come on through.'

They went into the main hospital area where two female nurses in white dresses were working.

'This is Phoebe and Helen,' said Carole introducing them. They smiled at Harry and carried on with their work.

There were several beds but only two were occupied with pregnant women, both pygmies.

'Both of these ladies are expecting their first child. As you can see they are very small and can have severe difficulties for the first one. At the moment things are slow which is how I like it,' Carole said.

'Is this all your staff?' Harry asked.

'We have four guards as well. You saw two of them on Saturday night. They live here with their families. Phoebe is the wife of one and Helen is the daughter of another. It is not as if we are out in the wilds so that's quite sufficient. They also work as handymen. If we need any other help we just get it from the village.' Harry looked at the slowly turning fans. 'When the mains power goes out we have a generator out the back but we try not to use it too often to save on the fuel. Luckily up here on the hill it's not too hot.' They went back outside.

'What is that building?' Harry asked indicating another large hut with open sides.

'That used to be the school. It was full a month ago, but the two teachers were withdrawn and flown out because of the war.'

'But you stayed?'

'They wanted me to go but who would look after them?' she said pointing at the pygmies. She looked at her watch. 'Let's go and have a bite to eat.'

They went around the huts and came to a small bungalow with the standard veranda and thatched roof. The shutters on the windows were open and a cool breeze blew in. It was a pleasant room, with wooden floors, a scattering of native rugs and low easy chairs. In the corner there was a television and a large bookcase against the wall. A door set in the opposite wall obviously led to a bedroom. Harry went over and examined the books. Medical books took a large section of the case but there were also whole rows of assorted novels.

Carole went to the refrigerator, took out two bottles of beer, uncapped them and handed one to Harry. 'Cheers!' They were cold and welcome.

'So have you had any of the local food?' she asked.

'Only at the hotel.'

'Hah,' she exclaimed. 'That's not local.'

She went into a small kitchen.

'Get yourself another beer when you're ready. I'll have another as well. One good thing here is that there are no breath tests for drivers, in fact driving improves with the alcohol.' Harry opened two more beers and took one to Carole in the kitchen. 'I made it this morning, so all it needs is reheating. Could you take the glasses and plates to the veranda, and I'll bring the rest.'

As Harry sat down, Carole appeared with a bowl and bottle.

'This is called Saka-madesu; it's stewed manioc leaves and beans.' She spooned a generous helping onto Harry's plate. 'I thought as we were going to a barbecue tonight we would not want a large meal.'

'This is fine,' said Harry and tasted the stew. 'It's delicious,' he exclaimed.

'Good,' she said. 'Now try this.' She filled Harry's glass.

'What is it?' he asked.

'Congo wine.'

'Congo wine? Really?'

She laughed. 'It's called Lunguila. It's sugar cane wine.'

Harry gingerly sipped his drink.

'Bloody hell! It's strong for wine.'

'As you like rum and cane so you should like this.'

He took another mouthful from his glass, this time more deeply.

'It's good, but I don't think it will catch on in France.' She laughed and filled her glass.

'Here's to you, Harry.'

'And to you, Carole.' There was silence for a moment as Carole looked at Harry.

'So here we are,' Harry said. 'A doctor and a captain miles up the Congo river in the middle of a war surrounded by pygmies and drinking local wine. An interesting way to spend an afternoon.'

She smiled, 'Can I ask you something, Harry?'

'Sure,' he said a little warily. She took a deep breath.

'I know you are not married but is there someone else?' Hastily she carried on. 'Please understand, I don't care but I like to know a little about the men I'm with.'

Harry thought for a moment. 'Sandy's been talking.'

'Only because I asked and he wouldn't say much.'

'I was married,' he said slowly, 'but that was a few years ago now.' She nodded.

'And you?' he asked.

'Same,' she said. 'That's why I am here. We were both doctors in Charleston. We had a good life but after trying for a family for a few years, we discovered that I can't have children. I was all for adoption but he wanted his own children. It didn't take long before he was screwing around, I didn't mind the screwing so much as finding out it was with my sister. It was too much, so we divorced and he married her. They have two children. I couldn't stay in Charleston after that so I joined this medical mission. I did a few years in Brazil, then they sent me here.'

She looked at him, 'I presume you also went through the mill?'

'Not like yours. I was involved in what they call 'an incident'. My ship was badly damaged in a storm so I tried to put into a port. There's a tradition of the sea called Port of Refuge. If a ship is damaged, ports are meant to assist by allowing them entry to effect repairs to continue the voyage or to take crew off if they are in danger. In this case, the port refused entry.' Carole looked puzzled. 'It's to do with pollution. These days bloody seagulls are more important than seafarers. Anyway, they decided that my ship would pollute their port. As the ship was in danger of sinking, I went into the port anyway. I got the crew off, but it did leak oil. I was arrested and thrown into prison.' He laughed bitterly. 'Quite common these days. The outcome was that I was fined, did six months in prison, my wife ran off with the lawyer defending me, and no shipowner will touch me unless they are desperate.'

'Christ, Harry. I thought I was hard done by.'

He shrugged. 'Water under the bridge. Let's drink to a good barbecue.' He finished his glass. 'Any more of those and I won't even get there!'

Carole stood up. 'Come on, let's get some fresh air. I want to show you the countryside. Leave the plates. One of the girls will tidy up.'

She went inside and through to the bedroom. When she came back she had a large bag slung over her shoulder. When they went to the Land Rover one of the guards came forward. 'No, Samuel,' she said. 'We're going up the hill.' He smiled and stepped back.

They got in and drove back onto the track then turned up the hill. The track here was now no more than ruts in the dirt, and the trees and bushes brushed the vehicle.

'It's about two kilometres to the top,' she said 'but it clears soon.' Slowly the trees and bush died away breaking through to a savannah like plain of grass dotted with boulders.

'A few years ago you would see all kinds of game here but now it is almost bare. However we still have a few antelope. Look! Over there!' Harry looked at where she was pointing. A group of antelope leapt through the air running away from the sound of the Land Rover.

'I think they survive because not many people come up here,' she said.

They came to a flat outcrop of rocks where Carole stopped.

'Don't get out yet,' Carole said as she blew the horn several times.

'What was that for?' he asked.

'Just to give any snakes a warning and to get them to move away. They are more frightened than we are and if you give them warning there is no danger. They can't hear, but the horn causes a vibration in the air which they can feel. Most bites occur by accident when someone steps on them.'

'That's good to know,' said Harry.

'It's all right now,' she said laughing as Harry gingerly stepped out of the Land Rover. 'They like to lie on the rocks in the sun.'

They walked up onto the rocks, and below them the view opened into a panorama.

'Over there is Matadi,' she said pointing to a haze of wood smoke. 'If you look to the right you can see the Congo river. In that direction is Kinshasa.' The view was stunning. 'It looks so peaceful and beautiful from up here,' said Carole.

'Probably the best way to see the place,' said Harry.

'You could say that about a lot of places,' replied Carole.

'Yes, you're right,' he conceded. They stood for a moment taking it in.

'Just think what it could be,' said Carole.

'Not for a long time yet,' Harry said sadly.

'Come on,' she said. 'We have a little further to go.'

They got back in the Land Rover and headed across the plain. Entering forest again, they started to go downhill.

'Where are we going now?' Harry asked.

'You'll see.'

They carried on until the track almost disappeared, and Carole then brought the Land Rover to a halt.

'We walk from here,' she said getting out and slinging her bag over her shoulder.

As they walked down through the trees, Harry heard the splash of water. The sound got louder and as they went further down they emerged from the trees in front of a waterfall dropping into a pool. She started unbuttoning her shirt.

'Beat you in?' she said as she removed her shirt.

'This is unfair,' said Harry. 'You never said anything about bringing a swimming costume.'

'Oh dear,' she laughed. 'You'll just have to make do won't you? I seem to have forgotten mine as well.'

Harry looked at her. She was only wearing her underwear. 'It's all right… I'm a doctor.'

She stripped off and ran to a rock jutting out over the water and did a perfect dive into the pool. She surfaced and turned towards Harry who was now naked and making his way gingerly into the water.

'I see it's true what they say about white boys!' Carole shouted.

'Quality not quantity,' Harry shouted back and dived in. He surfaced quickly. 'Bloody hell, it's cold!' he spluttered.

Carole swam back to the rocks and pulled herself out. She went to her pack and got out a bar of soap and shampoo. Harry watched her. She was beautiful and she knew it. She walked back into the water, pouring shampoo into her black hair and working it into a lather. She then ducked under the water and washed the lather out. She threw the shampoo back onto the rocks and swam over to Harry.

'So, Harry. How do you like my bathroom?'

'It's still bloody cold,' he said.

She reached down. 'Obviously,' she said laughing. He yelped and splashed back and lunged for her pushing her under the water. She put her arms around him and hugged him hard.

'I brought towels in the bag.'

They swam to the rocks where he helped her out. She took the two towels out of the bag and spread them down on the grass. Reaching into the bag again, she pulled out a bottle of wine, a corkscrew and two glasses.

'You be mother,' she said handing the bottle and corkscrew to Harry. 'A present from Philippe.'

Harry uncorked the bottle, poured out the wine and handed a glass to her.

'Well, I never thought I would be standing naked with a beautiful woman by a pool up a mountain in Africa drinking wine today. Not that I am complaining,' he added.

She took the glass from his hand and placed it down on the rocks, then went to him and put her hands on his shoulders.

'No strings, no commitments, just for fun, OK?'

'Exactly as I like it,' Harry replied and then kissed her.

They drove through the dock gates just after 1930. As usual there were no guards on the gate at night. As they passed the gate Harry could see brightly coloured lights coming from his ship and as they approached they could hear music.

'Bloody hell! I thought they were having a quiet barbecue,' exclaimed Harry.

'How lovely!' cried Carole. 'A party! Philippe's here already, that's his car.'

There were other vehicles including a truck, parked alongside the ship. Carole parked the Land Rover at the end of the line. She had changed into a coloured skirt, a white shirt and had tied back her hair. In the back her two guards sat holding their weapons. As Carole got out, she indicated towards them.

'Can they come up, Harry? It seems a shame to leave them here all evening.'

'Of course,' said Harry. 'Their weapons can be locked in the ship's office.'

He spotted Jake on the gangway. Jake was wearing a straw hat with a red shirt and was looking more like a pirate than an officer. He hastily put his drink down.

'Jake,' Harry called. 'Get these weapons locked away in the ship's office.'

'Right, Sir,' Jake replied.

'Is Jake permanently tied to the gangway?' asked Carole. 'No, but he is the ship's Cadet which means he gets all the jobs the other officers don't want. He doesn't do badly though.'

'Quite a crowd here tonight,' Harry said to Jake.

'It was the Mate's idea,' Jake explained. 'It just seemed to grow. The chap from the hotel turned up this afternoon with some food and drink. The Harbour Master and Customs Officers are also here.'

'And quite a few others I should think. Never mind, we haven't held a party for a while.'

They walked aft towards the ship's working deck where the barbecue was laid out. As they came out onto the deck, it was apparent that there were quite a few others. The coloured lights and flags were strung out above the crowd. Down one side was a large crowded bar presided over by Delilah and the Bosun. On one barbecue the Cook was basting a large pig on a spit and on the other there were three chickens looked after by Esmeralda.

Sandy appeared at Harry's side. 'Good evening, your Honour.' He took Carole's hand and raised it to his lips. 'Carole, it's lovely to see you.'

'Sandy, the entire town is here,' remarked Harry.

'The numbers seemed to grow. I think they just want to forget about the war for an evening if possible. The last party as it were. Look over there.' Sandy pointed towards the north. There was occasional lightening in the sky. Delilah told me that's artillery fire, and it's getting closer, Captain.'

'There's nothing we can do about it tonight, so let's have a good time.' Harry looked around. 'There are a lot of women here,' said Harry, and then he realised. 'Sandy, we've got all of Esmeralda's brothel on board!'

'And the band too!' laughed Carole.

'The band?' queried Harry. Then he noticed them setting up their instruments.

Esmeralda came up to him and gave him a distinctly wet and alcoholic kiss on his lips.

'Captain, what a lovely idea. Thank you so much. The girls have a night off on Sundays so it's lovely for them to have such a party to come to.' Harry looked across at Sandy who looked back in wide eyed innocence.

'Any more surprises, Sandy'?

'Only the children.'

'What children?'

'The ones we've been feeding. They were on the jetty watching, and as we had so much food I told Jake to let them come on board.' Harry looked around and saw a group of laughing children sitting holding large plates of food. 'The lads are keeping them filled with food and cola.'

The band had now started up and people were beginning to dance. Harry whispered in Sandy's ear. 'Just make sure the women are off before morning, Sandy. We are not going to look like a floating brothel.'

'Absolutely, Captain,' Sandy said.

'Carole, let me have the first dance.'

'Delighted, Sandy,' she said as Sandy whisked her away onto the deck.

Harry went to the bar. 'A large rum and pineapple,' he said to Delilah.

'Coming up, Captain.' Delilah's hand went under the table and pulled out a litre bottle of Appleton's Estate Reserve with CAPTAIN written on it in black letters. He poured out a generous measure and topped it off with pineapple. 'Good health, Sir,' and raised his glass of beer.

'Same to you,' replied Harry. 'Good health, Bosun.' The Bosun raised his glass.

'Looks like it will be a good evening, Sir. The hotel manager gave us a few cases of beer and wine,' he said pointing to some of the cases stacked by the bar beside two dustbins full of ice and drink.

'As if we needed more,' muttered Harry. Well, he might as well enjoy the party. He laughed as he thought, only a ship could arrange a party where the town brothel and band turn up.

Sandy and Carole finished their dance and joined him with Philippe and Sophie in tow.

'Good to see you both. Sophie, you look lovely,' he said kissing her cheeks.

'Thanks for the beer and wine, Philippe. That was kind of you.'

'I'd rather you had it than the rebels.'

Harry looked quizzically at Philippe. 'The news is not good,' he said. 'It seems definite that Mobutu has fled the country and the army is collapsing.'

'Apparently, the rebels are breaking through,' Carole said. 'Only the threat of the Angolan Army is stopping them.'

Sophie chipped in, 'I'm flying out in the morning.'

Philippe spoke up. 'Do you remember the phone call I had from our friend Justine? Well he is flying his family out tomorrow and taking Sophie with them.' He turned to Carole. 'There's room for you, Carole. It could be the last chance.'

She shook her head. 'I can't leave my patients or the pygmies. I am the only one they trust.' Harry looked at her.

'Are you sure, Carole? You can always come back in a few days if the situation stays calm.'

'I'm sure,' she said. 'I will miss you, Sophie. Just hurry back.'

'Right,' said Harry. 'That's enough gloom for the evening. Let's dance.' He took Carole's arm and lead her onto the dance area.

It was a slow number, giving him the chance to pull her close to him. 'What a lovely day, Harry,' she spoke into his shoulder. 'It's so nice seeing everyone enjoying themselves regardless of the problems.' Graham Hennessey, the 3rd Officer, danced by clutching one of Esmeralda's girls followed by Jake and his girlfriend. 'He's going to miss her,' said Carole.

'Sailor's story,' said Harry.

'What about you, Harry. Will you remember me?' Harry looked down at her.

'Yes, I will.'

'Until the next port,' she joked.

Just then there was loud shouting from the crowd. They turned to see a stunning woman join the party. She wore a long dress that glittered in the lights and hugged her figure.

'Oh no,' groaned Harry. Just then the drunken Harbour Master pounced on the new woman and dragged her onto the dance floor where he held her tightly.

'She's lovely,' said Carole. 'I've never seen her before. Who is she?'

'Delilah,' Harry groaned.

'What?' exclaimed Carole in astonishment.

'Delilah,' repeated Harry.

Sandy came up. 'I think the Harbour Master's in love,' he said.

'Does he know?' asked Harry.

'Does he care?' responded Sandy. They looked at each other and laughed.

The appearance of Delilah set the pattern for the evening. As the food and drinks were consumed, the band played to the most appreciative audience they had known for a long time.

'A great night,' said Harry to Sandy as they watched Carole dancing with Godwin the 2nd Engineer.

'She's quite something, isn't she?' said Sandy. Harry said nothing.

'She keeps looking at you,' Sandy continued.

'It could be you.'

'Hell no. Three of Esmeralda's girls would scratch her eyes out for that. I just noticed that you were watching her as well,' Sandy said.

'All right, Sandy. Yes she's attractive, vivacious and yes I like her. But that's all.'

'Of course,' said Sandy, 'I wasn't trying to suggest anything else.'

'Like hell you weren't,' laughed Harry.

The Cook staggered by held up by Delilah.

'Just getting a little air, Captain. The heat of cooking got to him,' explained Delilah.

'Along with the bottle of whisky,' said Sandy.

At one in the morning, the party was still in full swing. Harry and Carole were standing at the rail looking across the river.

'I've had a wonderful evening, Harry. If this is shipboard life, sign me up.'

'Doesn't happen very often these days,' said Harry 'but yes I'll sign you up. Prefer you waking me up to Delilah.' She laughed and put her arms around him.

'Kiss me, Harry.' He did so, for a long time.

'When do you think you will sail?'

'I really don't know. We could be told to sail tomorrow. It's all up in the air.'

'You won't get any spare parts tomorrow; rain is coming. Sophie is only able to fly out because it's a private plane. There won't be any more after that.'

'Well then we will just have to stay,' he said grinning.

'If you do have to sail will you call me? I would like to see you before you go.'

'What about tomorrow? Why don't you come into the town and stay here. It may be safer.'

'I can't. I have to go round the villages, then I have an operation to attend in one of the other hospitals. I don't think I can get away, but I can come into town on Tuesday. We could have lunch, if you are still here. They have very nice rooms at the hotel,' she smiled.

'You have a date.'

'I really must make tracks. Will you say goodbye for me; I don't want to break things up. My two guards are already waiting in the Land Rover and Jake has given them back their weapons.'

'I'll walk you down to the car.'

'I'm not driving tonight,' she smiled. 'Too much wine I think.'

Harry opened the door on the passenger side. She turned to him. 'Thank you for a lovely day, Harry.'

'I should thank you,' he said. 'I'll call tomorrow.'

'Please.' She raised her face to his to give him a farewell kiss but he took her in his arms and hugged her.

'I look forward to lunch.'

'And the dessert!' she said getting in the car. 'Good night, Harry.' The car backed out of the parking place and headed to the dock gate, the backlights disappearing in the dark.

Monday 19 May

Chapter 5

It was pouring with rain. Harry stood inside the bridge looking through the windows at the yellow wet weather gear of the crew on the deck and jetty as they loaded the stores using a sling on the crane. The 2nd Mate was in charge of the operation. He stood under an awning with a checklist. Typical, Harry thought. Either barbecues or storing, it had to rain for one. Anyway it would do their sore heads good. Harry had left the party after saying goodbye to Carole, but as he went to sleep he could still faintly hear the music in his cabin.

He checked his watch, nearly 1000 hrs, almost time to call the office; it would be 0900 in the UK. He went down to his deck and met Peter coming up.

'Morning, Peter. How's the head?'

'Good morning, Harry. A little sore but it was a great night.'

'It was,' agreed Harry. 'Come into the office.' Before he sat down Peter spread an old newspaper on the couch. 'We'll wait for Sandy before we start. What is the situation in the engine room, Peter? Could we use the port engine if we had to?'

'Only if you want to permanently wreck it. We managed to shut it down before too much damage was done but we really need the spares, and even then it will take two days to repair it.'

Sandy appeared. As usual he showed no signs of the night before. He shook his oilskins outside and hung them on a hook.

'Good morning, gentlemen. It's really pissing down now. Makes us feel like sailors again.' He sat down beside Peter.

'It's warm and dry in the engine room,' said Peter, 'if you were able to find your way there that is.'

'I wouldn't want to embarrass you with my skills, Chief.'

'We were just discussing the situation before we call the office,' said Harry. 'We have one engine, no spares. We've been here nearly a week and the war is getting closer. I am certain that there will be no planes landing now. If that is the case, we must consider sailing.'

'Where to?' asked Sandy.

'Who knows, possibly Lagos. It's in the right direction and at least there's an international airport there to get the spares. Any problem with the starboard engine getting there, Peter?'

'No, provided it keeps going.'

'That would be useful,' said Harry. 'The only question is how we get out on one engine.'

'We came in on one' said Peter.

'Yes, but the current was low and remember how long it took us to get through the Cauldron and we were going in the right direction. Getting out will be far more difficult. The pilot will probably refuse to take her out. The ship will be more difficult to steer with the current astern; it's a matter of speed. We need it to steer the ship, particularly as we will be continually veering to port. If we have the current astern that reduces the speed of the water passing over the rudder. The more current there is astern, the harder it will be to steer. The Cauldron will be a real problem. The river narrows to less than one kilometre and the current can reach 7 knots, which is the same as the 7 knots that one engine gives us. We have to make a 90 degree turn while in the Cauldron and there are rocks on both sides.'

Sandy nodded. 'It's a bad place. But we can order the tugs to stay with us and use them to help us get through.'

'That's what I'm thinking as well,' said Harry. 'I intend to ask the pilot if he will take us through using them. If we put one tug on the bow and the other on the stern, the stern tug can be used as a brake while the one on the bow will help to pull us round. Combined with the bow thrust that should be enough. Anyway let's phone the office and see what's happening.'

Harry picked up the satellite phone and dialled in the London office number. When the operator answered, Harry asked to be put through to Mr Burton.

'Burton.'

'Good morning, David. This is Harry Andrews.'

'Hi, Harry. How are things in Matadi?'

'Not good. David, I have this on speaker phone as I have the Chief Engineer and Chief Officer here in the office. The situation is that we still have no spares nor any sign of them. It is pouring with rain and I am reliably informed that there will be no flights today.'

'Damn. I was told that the parts would be with you by the weekend.'

'So where are they now?' asked Harry.

'Well, they were in Lagos and should have arrived some days ago.'

'So much for planning. Anyway it's all going to fall apart here pretty soon. The war is getting nearer. Mobutu has apparently fled and the rebels are closing in on the port. We don't want to be here when that happens.'

'I understand,' said David.

'I'm not sure you do. The situation on board is that while we only have one engine I believe we can sail out as long as the river pilot will agree. The biggest problem will be getting through the Devil's Cauldron, but if we can hire two port tugs to assist then we can get through. Once we get clear we can be in Lagos in a few days, pick up the spares, do the repairs and be on our way to Hull.'

'That seems sensible,' said Burton. 'I will contact the owner and tell him about the situation. Then we will have to get the approval of the insurers for sailing through the Cauldron. What is it anyway?'

'A very nasty piece of river that you don't want to know about. The insurers will know.'

'OK,' said Burton, 'How much will the tugs cost?'

'I don't know, but the agent will.'

'Right. What about fuel?'

'No problem. We have enough to get us to Hull and beyond.'

'How is the money holding out? I can't get you any more there.'

'That's not a problem. US dollars go a long way here especially now it's all going to hell in a hand basket. We have enough for our immediate needs.'

'Good, anything else?' Harry noticed that Sandy was waving to him. 'Just a minute.' He looked inquiringly at Sandy.

'Crew,' said Sandy. Harry nodded.

'Did you hear that, David?'

'Yes, crew. Any problems?'

'Not with them, with you. We are all overdue for leave and when we return it's likely that we will all be redundant.'

'I wouldn't say that,' said Burton.

'I've said it for you then. You know the story and so do we, but in the meantime, I suggest an immediate bonus for the crew backdated to when their contracted time ran out.'

'I can't authorise that without speaking to the owner, Harry.'

'That's fine. You're going to speak to him about sailing so you can ask him then. Tell him I suggest 50 percent and relief in Lagos.'

'Christ, that's pushing it, Harry.'

'It's no more than we've been pushed around.'

Burton sighed, 'All right, Harry. I'll do what I can. I'll call you back shortly.'

'Thanks, David. I'll be waiting.' Harry put the phone down.

'That's it gents,' he said looking at Peter and Sandy. 'I'll let you know as soon as he calls back.' They both stood up. 'Sandy when you go down, ask the 2nd Mate to come up please.' He looked out of the porthole. 'Still raining. Stores should be finished by now.'

'I'll check,' said Sandy.

'And get the 3rd Mate to come up with the receipts.'

They left the office leaving Harry staring out of the port. He was still staring when there was a tap on the door. It was the 2nd Mate.

'Good morning, Vijay. Didn't pull you away from anything did I?'

'No, Sir.' Even if he had Vijay wouldn't have said. 'I want a passage time to Lagos,' he said.

Vijay's face lit up. 'Are we sailing, Sir?' he asked.

'I certainly hope so but don't say anything, all right? I don't want the galley radio broadcasting yet. Work on a speed of 10 knots from the Devil's Cauldron to the pilot station allowing for current, and then 7 knots from the pilot station to Lagos.'

Vijay departed for the bridge only to be replaced by a very wet Ship Chandler.

'Good morning, Captain.' His round black face was dripping with water but he still managed a broad smile.

'You're a bit wet, Henri,' said Harry. 'Take your raincoat off and sit down.' Harry went into his bathroom, collected a towel and took out a bottle of whisky from the drinks cabinet in his dayroom along with a couple of glasses. He went back into the office, tossed the towel to the Chandler and poured out two large whiskies.

'Your good health, Henri.'

'And yours, Captain. That's good whisky.'

'Help yourself,' said Harry gesturing to the bottle. 'How did it go?'

'Just a few items to be replaced. Your officer has the list. I'll send the truck back when I get to the office.'

'How long is this rain setting in?'

'All day, Captain, but tomorrow should be better. At least it gets the soldiers wet.' Henri laughed at his joke.

'How's that going?' Henri looked glum.

'It seems that Mobutu has definitely gone but it hasn't stopped the fighting. The gangs use any excuse to rob and kill. Captain, I am leaving Matadi for a while, so if there is anything else you want let me know today.'

'Where are you going?'

'Up into the hills for a while. I have a small house there. I want to get the family away from the town before these bastards come.'

'You think they will come now Kabila has won?'

'Yes, and he won't be able to stop them. He couldn't if he wanted to. Only the Angolans can do that now.' Just then Graham the 3rd Mate appeared, his wet weather gear crackling and dripping water.

'Good morning, Graham. I gather there are a few items to be changed.'

'Yes, Sir, not many and they are marked here.' He passed the checklist to Harry.

'Leave it with me. You'd better go and get dry. Tell the Bosun that Henri will send a truck soon with the replacement items.'

'Right, Captain.' Harry looked at the bill and went to the safe in his cabin. He dialled in the code, reached in and took out a wad of notes.

He came back to the office and counted out the cash with Henri.

'I'll pay you in full, Henri. That saves messing around when you send the other items.'

'That's good, Captain. Are you sailing soon?'

'I hope so.'

'It is wise,' said Henri. 'These Mai Mai bastards are out of control and what is left of Mobutu's army are not much better. They will come as well.'

'You think the Angolans will stand back?'

Henri shrugged. 'Would you rely on them? I must go, Captain. It has been a pleasure. Thank you for your business. If I can be of any help before I close tomorrow, please let me know.'

'Thanks, Henri. I hope it goes well for you.' Henri smiled.

'We have put up with Mobutu and his henchmen all these years, so we can survive Kabila and his gang.' They shook hands and Henri clattered down the stairs. Vijay was waiting outside.

'What's the steaming time?'

'Based on 81 miles to the pilot station at 10 knots and then 920 miles to Lagos at 7 knots, 5 days 19.3 hours.'

'Call it 6 days then allowing for berth to berth,' Harry said.

Vijay nodded in agreement. 'I think the currents will balance out as we'll have the Angolan current against us on the coast but we'll pick up the tail end of the Benguelas current as we come off the land.'

'Thanks, Vijay.'

'Shall I lay out the courses, Sir?'

'Not yet, but you can get the charts ready and get the satellite weather maps from tomorrow onwards.'

Harry was just about to put the bottle away when the phone rang. It was Sandy.

'Captain, we have a visitor. There is an army jeep at the bottom of the gangway; a UN Major wants to come on board.'

'It must be about that business in Esmeralda's on Saturday,' said Harry.

'You had better bring him up.' Harry straightened his uniform shirt and sat behind his desk. Sandy appeared at the door. Harry was pleased to see that he was in uniform as well.

'Major Patrick Kayemba, Sir.'

'Welcome on board, Major,' said Harry. The Major had the obligatory rows of medal ribbons and badges and was looking quite at ease.

'Please sit down. What can we do for you, Major, although I think I know why you're here?'

The Major smiled ruefully. 'Well, I was given a message that if I wanted our property back I had to come and get it. You understand that being UN we have to account for all our weapons and ammunition, and there seems to be some missing.'

'Not missing, Major, just being looked after. We will be most happy to return it. I do not know what you have heard but...'

The Major raised his hand. 'Excuse me, Sir, but let me tell you what I have heard. There are two stories, the one from my Lieutenant who tells me how your armed and drunken sailors assaulted them on the road and took their pistol and ammunition and the other story of how my soldiers abused their position, assaulted a young lady and that you dealt with the situation in a sensible manner allowing them to return to their unit. I think the second story is the true one.' Harry relaxed.

'I'm pleased that we don't have to argue our case with you, Major. Sandy, pour the Major a drink, What would you like, Patrick is it?'

'Yes, Sir.'

'Then I am Harry and behind you is Sandy, the Chief Officer.'

'Yes, he was the one with the shotgun, right?'

'That's right,' said Sandy. Patrick smiled.

'One thing though, Captain. There are no crocodiles in this part of the river. The water flows too fast for them, not that my idiot Lieutenant would know the difference.' Sandy was waiting. 'Can I have a beer please?'

'Sure,' said Sandy, 'and you, Captain?'

'I'll stick to scotch,' he said indicating the opened bottle on the table. Sandy went to the Captain's refrigerator, took out two beers, poured them into glasses and brought them back to the office.

'Your health,' said Harry and they raised their glasses. 'You are well informed,' said Harry.

'I am sure you realise, Captain, that in our armies in Africa, and I suspect elsewhere, certain officers have to be accepted who are unacceptable except for their connections.' He shrugged. 'This is part of our army life. As long as we know who they are, we can generally keep an eye on them. That is why they come over the border thinking I do not know what happens here.'

'No problem, Patrick. Our armed forces have been doing it for hundreds of years and from your accent, I would say you know that. Sandhurst?'

'Very good,' said Patrick. 'I remember it with great affection. And yes, there were fine men there and a few idiots as well.'

The Major looked around. 'You are very comfortable here, Captain. One thing I have always envied is that when the ships go to war they take their comforts with them.'

'Except that this is not a warship, Patrick. This is a merchant ship and our trade is peace.'

'Except when defending a lady's honour,' Patrick said and they all laughed.

'Captain, thank you for your understanding and hospitality. I must go now. You understand that our presence on this side of the border is not official.' Harry stood.

'It has been a pleasure meeting you, Major. Sandy, the pistol and the ammunition?'

'Bosun's already handed it over to the Major's driver.'

The Major hesitated, and then spoke. 'Captain, when are you sailing?'

'Soon I hope,' said Harry. 'Why?'

'Just that you should not stay too long. It's going to get complicated here.'

'Thank you, Major, but it is my intention to leave as soon as possible.'

'That is wise. Goodbye, Captain, and have a safe voyage.' With that, Sandy led the way out.

Harry thought for a while. It was obvious the Major was giving him a warning. At that moment the satellite phone rang.

'Sea Quest, Captain.'

'Good morning again, Harry. It's David. There is a bit of a problem.'

'Christ, what is it now?'

'Your spare parts are in Kinshasa.'

'Kinshasa? What the hell are they doing there?'

'It was the only airport they could get them to. We tried Boma but apparently for some reason it is closed.'

'That's down the river,' said Harry. 'Where we could have gone in the first place.'

'Yes well that's in the past. Anyway we are told that they are on their way to you now.'

'How?'

'By road.'

'But we've been told the road is closed and in case you didn't know it that means they have to come through the front lines between the armies. Just how are they going to do that?'

'All I know is what the freight agent has told us,' said Burton.

'This is stupid,' said Harry. 'We could have gone down to Boma, picked the spares up there and anchored while we did the repairs. So what are we supposed to do now?'

'They say they will be with you tomorrow at the latest.'

'So if they come tomorrow, that's two days to repair by which time this place could be up in flames.'

'You don't know that.'

'No. The same as I don't know if there's going to be bad weather when I sail but I still batten down the ship in case. If I get the spares on board I can still sail. Did you find out about the tugs?'

'Yes, but they are holding us to ransom and demanding extortionate costs.' 'This is bullshit, David.' Harry turned and saw that Sandy had reappeared at the door. He waved him to sit. 'Listen, David. You can tell the owner that under no circumstances am I sitting here with a bunch of lunatics creating mayhem around my ship. At the first sign of trouble I'm off. Do you understand?'

'Yes, Harry. I do.'

'Good. I'll check with the agent tomorrow morning and see what news there is of our spares. Apart from that, what about the crew arrangements?'

'The owner has agreed to a 20 percent bonus but you must all agree to stay on the ship to Hull.' Harry looked at Sandy, who shrugged. 'I can't speak for the crew, David. I'll put that to them and see what they say. Any further news on the ship?'

'Nothing, Harry. Between you and me I don't think there is a charter at the moment. She could well be up for sale, especially as we have changed flag.'

'That's what we guessed this end. OK, David, we will keep you advised of the situation here, but remember what I said. I don't want to get stuck here.'

'Thanks, Harry. I'm sorry I cannot do more.'

Harry finished the call and looked at Sandy. 'I meant it. I'm not staying. If the spares don't come tomorrow, we are sailing.'

'Good,' said Sandy. 'In the meantime I'll tell the lads that they have a bonus. That's something anyway.' He looked out of the port. 'As it's still raining, we'll run some exercises this afternoon. Fire, enclosed space rescue, something to keep them busy. We'll test all the alarms as well.'

'Well there's nothing else we can do today. I'll check with the agent this evening when I go ashore to phone Carole.'

Sandy smiled. 'Is she coming into town then?'

'No, she's too busy but we're having lunch tomorrow.'

'Looks like tomorrow could be our last night then. I'll tell the boys to make the most of it.'

Harry worked on his accounts for most of the afternoon and apart from Delilah with his tea no one visited his office. Just before 1730 the phone rang.

'Captain, are you joining us for a pint in the bar?' asked Sandy.

'Good idea' said Harry. 'I have to go ashore so I'll get changed and be down shortly.'

He threw his pen down and went into the bedroom. A few minutes later he arrived in the officer's bar. Most of the officers were there waiting for dinner and Sandy had his pint poured.

'You'll need your wet weather gear,' he said. 'It's still raining.'

'I don't know which is worse, the heat or the rain. Anyone else going ashore?'

'Not tonight,' said Sandy, 'Quiet night tonight after last night.'

'I'll be back soon. Just going to check with the agent on the spares and phone Carole.'

'Do you want dinner saved?' asked Peter.

What's on?'

'Chicken.'

'No thanks. I'll raid the fridge when I get back.' Harry drained his glass. 'I'd better get on my way or the agent will be locking up. See you soon.'

Harry walked up the hill to the agent's office. It wasn't dark yet but the clouds were black and water was streaming down the hill. The offices and houses already had their lights on – at least there was electricity at the moment. Harry opened the door and seeing that there was no one in the outer office knocked on the agent's office door and opened it to see Mario at his desk.

'Come in, Captain, and sit down. I was wondering if you would come up this evening. I was just about to close but thought I would wait a few minutes.'

'I'm pleased you did. Did you talk with London today?'

'Yes, Captain, and I told Mr Burton that we had not heard anything about the spares. Then I phoned the Kinshasa freight agents, and they told me that the spares are at the airport customs house. This means we will have to pay to get them, even though they are supposed to be import tax exempt. I have instructed our office to pay whatever they have to and get them onto a truck.'

'What about the road?'

Mario shrugged. 'I explained to London about the problem. They just look at the map and see that Kinshasa is only 300 kilometres. In your country that can be done in a few hours. With our roads, who knows. If the railway was working then that would help but unfortunately that's gone.'

'If they don't come tomorrow, I'm sailing,' said Harry, 'spares or no spares. Did London authorise the tugs?'

'Well, it seems the cost of having two tugs to go with the ship through the Cauldron was too much. Apart from that the Pilot says he is not willing to go through without both engines working. The current is running at around 5 to 6 knots, Captain, and that is very strong especially with the whirlpools.'

'Shit! What a mess,' groaned Harry. 'Why don't we double the pilotage money?'

'I can try tomorrow but that still leaves the question as to who pays for the tugs?'

'If the situation gets worse here in Matadi, London will pay, don't worry.'

'The only problem is getting the money but if the Kinshasa banks are open again, it can be done through them.'

'How is the situation here?' The agent looked at Harry. 'It's not good. I was going to talk to you about it. There is a rumour going round that the rebels have broken through. If they have and they get here, it could be very unpleasant especially for those who are seen as being Mobutu supporters.'

'But you weren't a supporter of Mobutu.' Mario waved his hand impatiently. 'Look at me, Captain. I am Goanese. That is enough of an excuse, as if they need one. I am leaving town with my family for a few days until the situation calms down. Which it will do eventually.'

'What about my spares?'

Mario shrugged. 'I will stay as long as I can, Captain, but I must get my family away before the soldiers arrive.'

'Bloody hell, it looks as if everyone is going. All right. Tomorrow morning, I want you, the Harbour Master and Pilot on board to discuss the situation. Can that be done?'

'Certainly, Captain. I am sorry about this, but I have to put my family first.'

'That's alright, Mario. I'd do exactly the same. I would like to phone Carole Masters - do you know her?'

'Yes. She's the doctor at the mission hospital out at Kengi?

'That's right.'

Mario reached for the phone. 'Let's hope the phones are working. You have the number?'

Carole came on the phone sounding breathless.

'Harry, are you there?'

'Hi, Carole. How are things?'

'I'm so glad you phoned, Harry. We're in trouble and need help.'

'What's the problem?'

'The rebels, or whoever they are, are in Kengi. They've set fire to some of the houses. We can see the flames from here. It looks as if Mobutu's army is fleeing. The whole area is full of armed gangs and we could be next.'

'What did I tell you about trusting politicians? What do you want?'

'Harry, I need some transport to get the people out. If I can get them into Matadi for the night I can sort things out tomorrow. I am so sorry to drag you into this. I did say no strings.'

'Hold on, Carole.' Harry looked at the agent. 'What transport have you got?'

Mario looked startled, 'None, Captain. There's not much private transport around here anymore.'

'Carole, how many people?'

'About forty.' He looked at the agent again.

'The Chandler.'

'The Chandler?'

'Yes, he's got two trucks.'

'But, Captain, I don't know.'

'Then let's find out. Carole, don't go away from this phone.'

'OK Harry.'

Harry grabbed the agent by his arm and headed out onto the street. 'Where will we find the Chandler?'

'He lives behind his office.'

'Right let's go. Lead the way.'

Mario ran across the street with Harry following. They went down the alley at the side of the office and came to the door of the house just behind the office building. Luckily lights were showing through the windows. Mario banged on the door and shouted for Henri. They waited for a moment, then from behind the door came Henri's voice asking who it was.

'Mario and the English Captain,' Mario shouted.

The door opened and Henri was standing there with an old revolver in his hand.

'Where are your trucks?' asked Harry without giving him the chance to speak. 'I need them. Dr Masters has to get her patients and people out of the mission fast. The Mai Mai are attacking Kengi.'

'Captain, please wait. Those trucks are the only ones I have, and without them my business is finished.'

'It could be finished anyway,' said Harry.

'No, you don't know that! What do you think you are going to do anyway?'

'We are going to the mission to get the people out.'

'That is crazy, Captain! It will be dark soon, it is raining, and if the Mai Mai are in Kengi now, they could be on the road before we get there. Anyway I have no drivers.'

'Henri, I need the trucks. I will pay you for their use and for any damage.'

'What if they are lost?'

'Then I will pay you for the trucks.'

'This is madness,' said Henri looking at Mario for support. 'Who is going to drive?'

'You and me,' replied Harry.

'Now I know you are mad. Me, drive out there at night to see the Mai Mai? You think that because some of them are children they will welcome us? They are wild animals, Captain, and trucks are like gold dust.'

'Henri, I don't have time to argue. If they are at Kengi, as it is some distance from the mission, they will be busy looting and raping there before getting on the road towards the mission. We have time to get there. I will ask the Doctor to start heading towards us. If they can meet us on the main road where the turn off is to the mission that will save time and avoid going into the bush.'

Henri hesitated. 'I'll pay $500 for the trucks for two hours, Henri.' Henri thought for a moment.

'If there are any problems, Captain, then we stop and turn back, agreed?'

'Right let's get the trucks. Henri, you and I will drive them to the ship.'

They went over to the warehouse yard where Henri unlocked the steel doors and swung them wide.

'Mario, Dr Masters is waiting on the phone. Go back and tell her that we are coming with two trucks but she must get her people down the hill to the main road and we will meet her there. Besides with all this rain, the trucks would not get up that track to the mission. Got that?' Mario nodded. 'When we drive back from the ship, be outside your office and tell me what she said.'

'I'll be there, Captain.'

Henri went into the office and came out with the keys. He swung up into one of the trucks and Harry got into the other. The engine turned over and started spluttering, then caught with a roar. Harry managed to get the engine into gear and slowly drove off out of the yard, down the hill to the ship followed by Henri. They swung in through the dock gates and parked by the ship.

Harry ran up the gangway and into the accommodation, heading up the stairway. On the next deck up he saw Andrew MacBride, the medical orderly.

'MacBride, get the Chief Officer, Chief Engineer, Cook and Bosun up to my cabin as quickly as possible. You come up as well.'

'What's up, Captain? Are we sailing?' Andrew asked. Without stopping, Harry spoke over his shoulder. 'You'll find out soon enough.'

Harry went into his cabin and quickly changed into his dark blue work shirt. He heard the officers and crew coming into his office and went out to explain.

'Just a minute, Harry. Have you thought this through?' said Peter expressing the anxiety of them all.

'What do you mean?'

'I mean you are charging off into the jungle right into the middle of a war to do what? Pick up a load of refugees who you do not know, all for some woman.'

'It's not just for some woman!' shouted Harry. 'She has asked for help. There are a bunch of human beings who will be killed if I do nothing. Well I am going to try to get them out.'

'Killing is a way of life here, you know that.'

'Then at least I may stop some. Look, Peter, I understand where you are coming from. I haven't time to argue so I am going regardless of what any of you say.'

Harry turned to Willie. 'Cook, we need the workers' galley to be ready and make sure that all the equipment is there for them.'

'What about food, Captain?'

'Take what you think they will need overnight from our stocks. If you want, we can restock tomorrow. Rice I should think.'

'We still have some manioc left over from the last lot.'

'Good, anything like that. Also get bedding organised. Dr Masters can have one of the supervisor's cabins, one with a bathroom.'

'Bosun, get what help the Cook needs.'

'Sure, Captain.'

'MacBride, make sure the hospital is ready, just in case.'

'That's not a problem, Captain. The hospital's always ready.'

'Right, gentlemen, anything I have forgotten?'

'What about tomorrow, Captain?' asked the Bosun.

'We'll deal with that when it comes. The main thing is to get them here and settled in for the night. I expect that they will then go ashore somewhere. Thank you, gentlemen. Sandy, please open up the armoury and get me one of the AKs and a couple of magazines.'

Sandy said nothing but left the office with the others. Harry went back into the cabin and took a wad of dollars from the safe and a few cartons of cigarettes from his cupboard. He sat down for a moment thinking of anything he had missed. The ship would swing smoothly into action; they had done this many times before. Forty was a small number compared to the hundred or so they were used to carrying.

He waited for Sandy, who eventually arrived with the weapon.

'OK, Sandy, it's all in your hands.' Then he noticed that Sandy had changed and was carrying a rifle as well as the AK.

'What do you think you're doing?'

'You really don't think I'm letting you go charging off like Rambo into the jungles of Africa on your own do you? Anyway, as I remember, you're not very good with the AK.'

'I don't have to be. Just point the bloody thing in the general direction and let loose. Sandy, I need you here.'

'No, you don't. The 2ⁿᵈ Mate can handle things. He's already briefed and Peter is here to back him up and keep a watchful eye on him.' Harry hesitated.

'Come on,' said Sandy. 'We're wasting time.' Harry gave an exasperated sigh and muttered thanks as he followed Sandy out.

Chapter 6

When they got to the gangway Harry saw several of the crew standing by the trucks.

'What's going on?'

'Just a few more lads to add support.'

'No Sandy! They are not involved in this.'

'Of course they are, Captain! The whole crew wanted to come, but these guys have military experience and anyway we don't have any more weapons.'

Sandy stomped down the gangway without waiting for a reply. Harry swore and followed.

Delilah met them. This wasn't Steward Delilah, this was Sergeant Jarvis, ex-Royal Marines; the transformation was astonishing.

'Evening, Sir' he said to Harry. 'I've checked all the weapons, the safeties are on and the men know where they are. I've taken the liberty of appointing myself as military adviser.'

'No problem,' said Harry.

'Captain, Godwin should drive the truck. He's got a heavy goods vehicle licence and has driven trucks in Nigeria.' Godwin had a round very black face which sat square on a large full body.

'You happy about this, Chalkie?'

'Not a problem,' Godwin smiled, his teeth gleaming in the darkness. 'If you can drive in Nigeria, Captain, you can drive anywhere,' commented Godwin.

'Who else have we got here?'

'The Fitter, Taffy Williams. He's ex-Royal Engineers and can handle a weapon with his eyes closed. Also, I suggest we take Andy MacBride. I know you told him to get the hospital ready but it's in perfect order, and the Bosun and Cook can deal with anything that needs doing. Andy's had weapons training and could be very useful if we get into trouble.' Harry saw that in addition to his weapon, MacBride had a first aid kit slung on his shoulder.

'Right, is that it?' asked Harry. 'Just one more,' said Sandy, and out of the shadows came Jake.

'No way,' said Harry.

'Captain, not only is he a bloody good shot, but he is young enough to get up that track fast. If they are not there, someone has to go and see what is happening. Look at the rest of us. We're not going anywhere fast. Anyway he remembered to bring the walkie-talkies.'

'Alright, alright,' Harry said wearily, 'but it's on your head. You tell his parents if it goes pear shaped. Right listen to me everyone. This is not an expedition. We're a bunch of merchant seamen going a few miles down a main road to pick up some people. We are not taking on armies or wanting any trouble. We just want to get back to the ship in one piece. I want no shooting unless on my direct order; the weapons are for protection only. We haven't done anything wrong yet and I want to keep it that way. You got that Delilah?'

'Yes, Sir.'

'I'll go in the first cab with the Chandler, with Delilah and Andy in the back. In the second truck, Sandy in front with Chalky, Taffy and Jake in the back. Four walkie-talkies between the cabs and the back.'

'Last thing,' Delilah shouted. 'Remember, if someone is pointing a weapon at you, it is your job to put them down regardless of who they are. Have you got that? No hesitation or they will shoot you. A kid pointing a weapon at you is just as dangerous as anyone else. Keep your safeties on till I tell you to release.'

'Let's go!' Harry grabbed Jake as he was getting in the truck.

'You keep your head down you understand,' he shook him. 'If you get shot, you'll wish you'd never seen the decks of my ship. Do you understand?' Jake nodded wide eyed, the rain running down his face.

'Good. Now get on board.'

The trucks set off out of the docks and up the hill. As they neared the agent's office they could see Mario standing in the road waving.

'She will be waiting for you, Captain,' he shouted.

'Thanks, Mario,' Harry shouted back and waved the truck on.

The dim lights of the trucks cut through the rain as they left the town and headed along the Kinshasa road. There was no traffic on the road, just a tunnel of the trucks' lights as they drove along. Even the shacks at the side of the road were in darkness. Henri drove slowly but steadily, hampered by the single noisy wiper that scraped the screen rather than wiped. It was difficult to see more than fifty metres ahead, and Henri was leaning forward peering through the screen. They passed through Palabala, which was in darkness apart from a few dim lights coming through shuttered windows.

'It is only 10 kilometres to Kuyi,' said Henri. 'I think we must be careful when we get there as it's not far from Kengi.'

'OK, Henri.' He pressed the broadcast button on the walkie-talkie and passed on the warning. Everyone acknowledged.

'Captain, Delilah.'

'Yes, Delilah.'

'Captain, if the road is blocked, don't try to drive through it. They could have RPGs. They're as common as the AKs.'

'What are their range?'

'Up to 1,000 metres but for complete accuracy 100 metres.'

'Nice,' said Harry.

'What I suggest is, if the road is blocked, stop and let us out. They will want the trucks so, once we are out, drive slowly towards them. We can walk beside you to the side and be ready.'

'OK, Delilah. Let's hope that the road is clear.'

The rain was easing off now and the visibility improving. Some figures appeared out of the darkness walking towards them on the side of the road.

'They are escaping from the fighting,' said Henri. He let them get closer then stopped. Harry told everyone to hold tight. Henri leant out of the truck and spoke to the refugees.

He turned to Harry. 'They say that they came through Kuyi and there was nothing, but there are small armed gangs on the road between Kuyi and Kengi. Not soldiers, Mai Mai filth, not that there is much difference.'

Henri started driving again. Occasionally shadowy figures appeared on the side of the road trudging wearily in the direction of Matadi. They came to Kuyi where there were more people clustered around the village houses. There was a fire burning at the side of the road and people were gathered around it. Henri stopped the trucks and spoke to them.

Returning to the truck he said, 'They are from Kengi. It is bad there. Killings, rape, many of their homes have been looted and burnt. They want to know if we are from the government sent to help.'

'I wish we could,' said Harry, 'but there is nothing we can do for so many. Poor bastards. We have to keep going, Henri.'

As they drove, they continued to pass refugees, many holding their hands out in the darkness and calling to them.

'Not far now,' said Henri, 'Look!' he pointed through the windscreen towards a glow on the skyline.

'Kengi,' said Henri, 'it's burning.' Henri suddenly braked.

'What's the matter?' said Harry with alarm.

'Listen!' Henri turned off the engine. Harry could then hear the gunfire. It was coming from ahead.

'Turn the lights off, Henri.' He told the other truck to do the same. Harry got out of the truck and went to the back 'Sandy, we have a problem.' Then he went to the back of the other truck. 'Everyone out.'

Delilah climbed down with the others. He listened for a moment. 'There's a heavy machine gun firing as well as light weapons, I would say about 500 metres ahead.' He went to the side of the road and bending down scooped handfuls of mud onto his face. 'Taffy, get this on,' he said. He turned to Harry. 'Taffy and I will go up the road to see what is happening. All of you stay here. Get off the road on each side of the trucks. Won't be long.'

They disappeared into the darkness.

Now that Harry and the others were out of the trucks they could hear the deeper sounds of battle and see the flashes in the sky above the fire glow from Kengi.

'You take one side of the road, Sandy, with Chalkie and Andy I'll take the other with Jake. Henri, you stay with the trucks. This is not your battle,' said Harry. Sandy nodded and took his party off to his side.

They waited in silence listening to the intermittent gunfire. After about 10 minutes Harry's walkie-talkie crackled.

'Captain?' It was Delilah. 'We are on our way back. It looks like there is a fire fight going on at the junction near your lass's mission. As I thought, there is a heavy machine gun mounted on a truck, and we counted six others with light weapons. I guess they have your lass and her people pinned down up the hill. Do they have any weapons?'

'Yes,' said Harry. 'They have guards and Dr Masters is armed as well.'

'That explains the fire from up the hill. Be with you soon.'

Harry waited and then Delilah and Taffy appeared out of the darkness. They all came out onto the road to see them.

'OK,' said Delilah. 'I see no real problem. They seem to be holding position and are quite relaxed. There is only the machine gunner and three others shooting. The rest are standing behind the truck. It's as if they are waiting for reinforcements.'

Harry spoke. 'Which means we have to act quickly.'

Delilah looked at Harry. 'With your permission, Captain?' Harry nodded. 'The good guys are up the hill and the bad ones are on the road but are only firing AKs. At that range they are useless except for keeping heads down and the occasional lucky kill. I don't know what other weapons they have but the machine gunner must be the first down. On the left side of the road there is a rise up the hill. I want one party in position there. Another party will slowly go up the road keeping to the side. Taffy and I will go back and close in. We are the killing team. Who is going up the hill on the left?'

'I will, and I'll take Jake with me. I can keep an eye on him there,' said Harry.

'Right,' said Sandy. 'That leaves me, Chalkie and Andy for the road.'

'Good,' said Delilah. 'Now remember, your job is to distract them from me and Taffy. Only aim at the centre of the truck area. I don't want you blowing us away,' he smiled.

'When we get in position we'll let you know, then I'll give the order when we want you to engage. Just fire in the general direction and keep your heads down.'

'How close should we get,' asked Harry.

'About 100 metres will be fine. As I say you are not killing anyone, we are. Everyone understand? Don't forget, as soon as you let off a few rounds, get down as they'll swing that machine gun round in your direction. Good, now all get dirt on your faces, except Chalkie. Chalkie, no smiling.' There was nervous laughter all around.

'Right,' said Harry. 'Let's go. Be careful everyone.'

'Just like the Falklands, hey Taffy?' joked Delilah.

'Better,' said Taffy. 'Not so fucking cold.' Delilah and Taffy disappeared again into the darkness coming off the road into the light vegetation on the side.

Sandy turned to Harry and gave him the rifle.

'Captain, your position is higher up than me and the rifle will be better from there. Anyway, with respect, you're not very good with the AK. You have the rifle and give me your AK. The safety is on and it's the lever here by the trigger guard. Magazine holds eight and there is one in the spout already so it's all ready to go.'

'If you're sure,' replied Harry. 'I feel better with the rifle.'

They exchanged weapons and both parties headed off to their respective positions.

'Are there any snakes?' asked Jake

'No,' lied Harry, 'they're asleep.'

The sound of firing was louder now.

'Let's turn off and head upwards' said Harry. 'Then we can see where they are and move in closer if we need to.' They moved cautiously up the slope at the side of the road.

'Have you done this kind of thing before?' asked Jake.

'Loads of times,' lied Harry.

They reached the top and looked down at the road. They could see the truck and quick flashes of the occasional weapon firing followed by loud discharges. Harry sighted along his rifle.

'We are still too far away. I want to try to take out that machine gunner before he turns his gun on us or Sandy. Come on.' They started to crawl towards the truck. Harry wished Jake had not mentioned snakes. He was more bothered about them than he was about the buggers on the road.

Sandy and his party walked slowly on each side of the road, brushing through the sparse vegetation. The ground was flat and wet from the rain and the night sky was illuminated by flashes from artillery that thundered in the distance. The crackling of small arms fire grew as they got closer. 'Are we sure there are no other rebels around,' asked Chalkie nervously. 'It's just that we could be cut off from the others.'

'If we are,' said Andy, 'I will give you both covering fire so that you can try to get back to the trucks.'

'What about you?'

'Listen, Chalkie. If it gets to that stage, just get into a truck and go like lightning and don't stop till you're back on the ship.' Andy felt very exposed.

'Would be good if we could find some cover,' whispered Andy.

'That's what I am looking for,' said Sandy. 'Look!' He pointed, there was a clump of small trees on one side. 'That's where we'll go.' He softly called to the others to join him. They crawled to the edge of the trees where they could see the truck on the road.

'This will do,' said Sandy. 'Remember,' said Andy, 'a short burst for three seconds and then flat on the ground. It will take the machine gunner longer than that to swing round.'

Sandy spoke very softly on the walkie-talkie. 'In position.' Harry clicked an acknowledgement. Still nothing from Delilah. They crawled a few more metres forward and then Harry stopped again.

'How far do you think we are now?' he asked Jake. 'About 50 metres Captain,' Jake whispered. Harry sighted along his rifle.

'Yes, this will do. In position,' he said into the mike. Clicks came back. They waited listening to the gunfire both from the road and from up the hill. The fire from the road was continuous while from the hill it was spasmodic. 'I guess that Carole and her guards are trying to save ammunition,' Harry whispered.

Delilah and Taffy were slowly and methodically working their way forward and to the side. They were bent low, trying to blend into what little cover there was. As they got closer, in between the fire, they could hear the Mai Mai talking and laughing loudly.

'Stupid idiots. No guards. They think it's a turkey shoot. Just like the Gulf War. We used to creep up on the Iraqis the same way; they were never ready,' whispered Delilah.

They continued to move slowly into position until they were 20 metres from the enemy. Delilah looked at Taffy and nodded. Taffy nodded back. Delilah keyed the walkie-talkie.

'In position,' he whispered.

'I think I can take out the machine gunner,' Harry replied.

'OK, Captain. We leave it to you to open the party,' whispered Delilah in reply.

'Sandy, as soon as you hear the rifle shot, open up.'

'Done,' said Sandy. 'We're ready.'

Harry sighted along the rifle. 'As soon as I fire, let a quick burst go then get your head down,' he said glancing quickly at Jake, who was lying beside him with his AK pointing down the slope at the road.

Harry took his time, took a deep breath, sighted again and gently squeezed the trigger. The explosion thrust the butt back into his shoulder but the gunner went flying back off the truck.

'You got him!' shouted Jake, firing at the truck.

Delilah and Taffy charged the truck firing at the Mai Mai who were gathered there. They were screaming as they pressed forward. One rebel raised his weapon towards them but before he could fire, a burst from Delilah blew his head into a nightmare of blood and bone. Another turned to run but was cut down by Taffy who was firing his weapon in short bursts. Two others were on the ground one still but the other screaming holding his stomach. Delilah gave him a quick burst as they ran over him and he was silent. One more tried to reach the machine gun but was cut down as he mounted the truck.

Sandy, Chalkie and Andy all lay prone on the ground and opened fire together, aiming at the flashes around the truck in the road. Then they ceased fire and pressed themselves down against the earth.

The noise was deafening as Sandy and Delilah opened fire together.

'Get down!' Harry pulled Jake to the ground.

'Great shot!' Jake shouted. He was wide eyed with excitement. Harry held him.

'Calm down, let Delilah handle it.'

'There's someone under the truck,' Jake said.

'I see him,' said Harry and picked up the walkie-talkie. 'Delilah, there's one under the truck.' There was a quick burst then silence.

'We've got him,' replied Delilah. 'Right everyone, all clear. Good shooting, Captain.'

'Thanks,' said Harry. He turned towards the hill and walked to the track. 'Carole!' he shouted up the hill. 'It's Harry!' There was no reply but no firing either. He remembered the name of one of the guards. 'Samuel, it's the English Captain. We are here to take you to Matadi.' Again there was silence, then he heard Carole's voice.

'Harry?'

'Yes. We've come to take you to Matadi.'

'Thank God!' She ran out of the dark and grabbed him, kissing him wildly on his lips. 'My Rambo!'

'That's the second time someone has said that tonight,' he said and kissed her back.

'So what's the situation? Is anyone hurt?'

'No,' she said. 'We kept them at bay, but that machine gun was bad. We were also running out of ammunition. I've got the Land Rover up the track with two pregnant women in it.'

'Fine. We'll leave the talk till later. Get your people down the hill and onto the trucks. We've got them from the Chandler and maybe another one now if it works. I'll go down the hill and wait for you. Jake, you stay with Carole and give her a hand.'

She gave him another hug. 'I won't forget this, Harry.'

'You'd better not!'

Meanwhile Sandy had joined Delilah at the Mai Mai truck. Delilah pushed over one of the bodies with his foot.

'They're just kids, same age as Jake but they're dangerous.' Taffy appeared from the back pushing two prisoners in front of him. They had their hands on their heads.

'Look what I found in the back of the truck,' he said. They were mere children and were terrified. Their eyes wide with fear in the torchlight. One had urine streaming down his legs.

'Good to give them a taste of what they do to others,' said Sandy.

'I have an idea,' said Delilah. He keyed the walkie-talkie. 'Henri, bring the truck up here.' Then called, 'Chalkie! Go back and bring the other truck up. You can put your lights on.'

From down the road the lights of Henri's truck showed as the truck drew closer. Delilah walked down to meet Henri. The truck stopped and Delilah opened the door.

'Get down, Henri. We have two prisoners. I want you to talk to them. Tell them we are 100 Afrikaner mercenaries and that we are going into Kengi in the morning to take them out. Tell them that the last men we caught we impaled on red hot sticks.'

Henri walked forward to where the prisoners were. When he spoke to them Delilah caught the word Afrikaner and saw them visibly shaking.

'Ask them how many men in Kengi.' They immediately began chattering.

'About 100,' Henri said.

'Tell them we will have 100 heads tomorrow. If we find them there, they will have their skin torn off while they are still alive.'

Henri spoke again and they fell on their knees pleading, tears rolling down their cheeks.

'Right,' said Delilah 'Let them go. Go!' he shouted at them indicating down the road towards Kengi. 'Tell them we are coming for their heads!' They hesitated for a moment not believing they were free, then they ran for their lives with Henri shouting after them.

'Good,' said Delilah calmly. 'That should stop anyone coming up this road for 24 hours at least.' He looked at those around him. 'They might be horrific at what they do but the one thing they really fear is Afrikaner mercenaries and with good reason. They can be very bad boys.'

Harry appeared out of the darkness. He slapped Delilah on his back.

'Well done, Delilah. Anybody hurt?' No one answered and he looked around at the bodies on the ground.

'What are we going to do with these?'

'Leave them here,' said Sandy.

Harry bent down to look at one of them. 'Some of them are so young.'

'They didn't have to be here, Captain,' said Delilah. 'They could have run away or gone towards Matadi. I know everyone back home goes on about the child soldiers, but they've never been on the receiving end like the people in Kengi. The older teenagers are just as dangerous as an adult. They would happily have shot Carole and all her pygmies.'

'I know, Delilah.' He turned to them all. 'Carole is bringing them down the hill now. She has the pregnant women in her Land Rover. Does that truck of theirs still work?'

Taffy got in and started it. 'Apart from the bullet holes, yes Captain.' He used the stock of the AK to smash the shattered windscreen.

'Right, that gives us three trucks. Taffy will you drive that one?' Taffy nodded. 'Let's get them turned around and start loading people once they arrive. Taffy, you take the lead. Delilah, do you want to man the machine gun?'

'Exactly what I was going to suggest.'

'I'll follow with Carole. Henri, you next with Sandy, then Chalkie bring up the rear with Andy and Jake. Henri, thank you for what you have done. I didn't think I could trust you. I'm sorry.'

'I am pleased to help, Captain. I was frightened.'

'So were we,' smiled Harry, then looking at Taffy and Delilah smoking, 'well, some of us were anyway.'

They turned the trucks around and waited. It was not long before Carole and her people slowly appeared, Carole keeping pace with them in the Land Rover.

'Load them up as fast as possible. We don't want to hang around. Jake you go in the last truck.'

They opened up the backs of the trucks and led the people to them but there was shouting.

'What's the matter,' asked Harry impatiently.

'They have never been in a truck,' explained Carole.

'Carole, there is no time to learn. If they don't get in we'll bloody throw them in.'

Sandy and Delilah appeared. 'For fuck's sake, get them into the truck!' shouted Delilah. 'That bloody noise can be heard miles away. If they don't believe those kids we sent back, reinforcements could be here in minutes!'

At that moment Jake picked up one of the children and climbed into the back of the truck. He and the child smiled out.

'Carole, tell the headman or whatever he is that if the child is not frightened, why is he?' She talked to her translator who talked to the Kombeti. 'Delilah, start to pass the children up.' One by one the children were put in the back of the trucks. 'Now tell them that we will take their children and leave them here.' Again Carole talked waving her hands towards the trucks. Harry went over to his truck and reaching down pulled out a carton of cigarettes. He took these back to the Kombeti. 'Tell him that there are many more where these came from but he has to get in the truck now.' The Kombeti looked at him, then smiled and waved his people forward.

As Harry watched them boarding he turned to Carole.

'You know, I think that old bastard just took me.'

Carole looked towards the glow of the flames from the village. 'I should go there. I am a doctor. I know people there.'

'If you go there, they will kill you, Carole. It is too late. You have to look after your people first.' Harry could see the tears running down her cheeks. 'Come on,' he said, 'there'll be time for that later.'

As the convoy left, people began to come down the road from Kengi. Many of them were wailing and calling for help as they trudged along, holding children up to them but there was nothing they could do for them. To add to the misery it had started to rain again. The drive back was uneventful and they made good time. Harry switched channels on the walkie-talkies to 16 to see if anyone was listening out on the ship.

'Sea Quest?' he called. Luckily, Graham the 3rd Mate had the good sense to be listening and answered. 'Go to 6,' said Harry, not wanting a general broadcast on the emergency channel.

'Graham, all successful.' He looked at Henri. 'When will we be at the ship, Henri?'

'In about 10 minutes.'

'ETA 10 minutes. We have about 40 persons.'

'We'll be waiting.'

He clicked the set off. They swung through the gates right on time and he could see the 2nd Mate and crew in their yellow wet weather gear waiting on the jetty. The trucks came to a halt and the crew ran forward to unhook the tailgates. The Bosun met Harry.

'All ready, Sir. The Cook even has a hot meal ready for them.'

'Thanks, Bosun.'

The refugees were climbing down from the trucks and were looking in awe at the ship. The Bosun looked at Harry.

'I think the best thing is to take them onto the afterdeck and use the door there to the workers' quarters. That will avoid them getting lost in the alleyways.'

'Good idea,' said Harry.

'Take them all through to the afterdeck,' shouted the Bosun.

Harry went round to Henri's truck.

'Henri, you're a good man. I shall be kind about Ship Chandlers in the future.' He put his hand in his pocket and pulled out a roll of dollars. '$500 as agreed.'

'Are you sure, Captain? It seems a lot for a short drive.'

'Henri, without you we could not have done this. Give my apologies to your wife for taking you away this evening.'

'When she sees the dollars she won't mind.' Henri waved and drove off into the night.

The guards and their families went up the gangway without hesitation but again there was a delay as the pygmies looked up the gangway.

'Carole,' said Harry wearily, 'not again.'

'Try to understand, Harry, it's not easy for them.'

'Nor for us getting soaked.' He called to the crew, 'Pick up the children and take them up first.' Some children clung to the parents and refused to come but others went quite willingly. Slowly they were persuaded on board. They were gathering on the afterdeck, some peering inside the door. It was brightly lit and the Cook came to the door.

'Cook, bring a plate of food.'

The Cook disappeared and came back with a plate. He gave this to the nearest pygmy who sniffed it then dug his hand in and ate a mouthful. He turned to the others nodding and they came forward with their hands out.

'No way. Carole, tell them that the food is inside.' She did so, and they cautiously entered. Eventually the afterdeck was clear. 'Thank God for that,' said Harry, who was now completely soaked as were all those without rain gear.

The 2nd Mate came up. 'Sir, you can leave this to us now. Why don't you go in.'

The Bosun who was with him added, 'Have a drink; it looks as if you deserve it.'

'Great idea. I bloody well need one,' said Chalkie leading the way.

'I'm going up to the cabin to get changed and have a shower,' said Harry. 'Any problems call me.'

Delilah was waiting for Harry to leave and he beckoned Sandy to one side. 'Taffy and me would like to show you something.' They took Sandy back down the gangway to the captured truck. Sandy peered in and Delilah produced a small torch.

'What's that lot?' asked Sandy.

'That,' said Delilah, 'is enough to start a small war. In the long case is a brand new RPG, the case over there hand grenades, cases of ammo for the machine gun and the AKs and look.' He opened another case and showed Sandy. Sandy whistled.

'Bloody hell. What's that?'

'It's a Stinger, that's what it is.'

'Just as well they didn't use these.'

'They could have fired it at us but it's an anti-aircraft missile. Point it at the target, fire, it acquires the target and then homes in.'

'What the hell are a bunch of loonies doing with this on their truck?'

'I think they were bringing them from somewhere and then heard about the activity up the hill so stopped to have some fun.'

Delilah was looking at the cases. 'Sandy,' he said pointing. 'The cases have UN markings.' Sandy looked at Delilah.

'The UN is supplying the rebels? That's bullshit,' said Sandy.

'Not the UN, but rogue UN soldiers selling the weapons. It happens more than you would think,' replied Delilah. 'I suspect someone like our friend the Lieutenant might be involved.'

'So now what?' asked Sandy.

'Well,' said Delilah. 'I have a feeling that we are in very uncertain territory. No one knows what can happen and when I walk down a dark alley, I like to have a big stick.'

'So what are you saying?'

'I think we ought to bring these on board.'

'The Old Man would not allow it. No way.'

'Only if he knows.'

'Delilah…' Sandy started.

Delilah interrupted. 'Just hear me out. The Old Man has to refuse these coming on board, that's his job, but if we don't tell him we don't put him in that position. We can always chuck them over the side if they are not needed. Hell Sandy, the chances are that we would never need them, but what if?'

'Where will you stow them?'

'All sorted. The Bosun and his lads will be down once they are finished with these people and he will spirit them away.'

'Just make sure no word gets out, otherwise the Old Man will hang me from the yardarm.'

'Sandy, I guarantee it.'

Sandy looked again at the cases and turning went back up the gangway. Then he stopped and turned around. 'What about that thing?' he said pointing at the machine gun.

'Shame to leave it,' said Delilah. Sandy said nothing and went into the accommodation block.

Harry had had his shower and was now in clean clothes. He left his cabin and went down to the shore workers' accommodation. It was chaos. Children were running around, people were eating, talking and smoking, babies were crying and in the middle of it all was Carole.

'Harry, this is fantastic. I never thought that you would arrange all this.'

'Where were you intending to go then?'

'I hadn't worked that out. Getting away was the only thing on my mind. Your crew have been wonderful. The Cook has even given them sheets on the beds. They've never slept on beds before, never mind sheets.'

The food was going down well and in the workers' galley two of the guards' wives and some of the pygmy women were cooking and washing the metal plates.

'What about your pregnant women?'

'Come with me.'

They went out of the workers' mess and up the stairway to the hospital. The pregnant women were already in the hospital beds. The two nurses were also there together with Andy.

'Just checking, Captain,' Andy said 'They seem to have it all under control. Is there anything you want, Carole? Drugs? Medicine?'

'I brought what I want from the mission,' said Carole. 'But thanks anyway.'

'How close are they?' asked Harry.

Carole shrugged. 'When there are complications like they have, no one knows, but hopefully they will be off before anything happens if that is what you are worrying about.'

'I must admit, I really did not want to have a maternity ward,' said Harry. 'Have you seen your cabin?'

'Not yet.'

'Your bags have been taken there already. Come on I'll show you. They have everything in hand here.'

'The nurses will stay with them in the hospital. There are some empty beds, so they will sleep here.'

'No problem,' said Harry. They walked back to the door separating the ship's accommodation from the workers' cabins. Harry went through and opened a door putting the light on.

'This is lovely,' Carole said. There was a small dayroom with a couch, desk, telephone, refrigerator and a chair. There was also a bedroom and off that a bathroom. Her bags sat in the middle of the dayroom. 'Harry, your ship is amazing, it has everything.' Harry grunted. 'I want a long hot shower,' she said.

'Tell you what,' said Harry. 'I'll give you half an hour to get sorted, then I'll come to take you for a nightcap in the bar. He looked at his watch. 'Do you know it's only coming up to 2100. It feels as if we have been up all night.' He gave her a quick peck on the cheek. 'See you soon.'

Harry met Graham, the 3rd Mate, as he walked along the alleyway.

'Who's the duty officer tonight, Graham?'

'The Chief Officer's put us on sea watches now we have people on board, Sir, so we can keep an eye on them throughout the night. That means I'm holding the fort until midnight.'

'You all did a good job tonight.'

'Sorry I missed the fun ashore though, Sir.'

The ship seemed deserted, but Harry didn't have to guess where they all were from the noise that was coming from the crew bar. He went into the officers' mess and poured a coffee from the percolator. He knew he had a problem tomorrow. Just what was he supposed to do with these people? The idea had seemed good on paper. Now they had charged off, killed a bunch of so called militia, and brought a load of pygmies back to the ship. Just how do you explain that to the office ashore? In fact, he wasn't even going to try.

He finished his coffee and went down below to Carole's cabin, tapping on the door. She answered, wearing a pair of blue jeans and a jumper. She saw Harry look at her.

'It's the air conditioning, Harry. I'm not used to it,' she said explaining her sweater.

'You'd certainly notice it if it wasn't working,' he said. 'Can you hear the thumping?' She nodded. 'Well that's the generators. They give off heat under our feet. Imagine what the main engines do. The officers' bar is deserted so I imagine they are all in the crew bar. They walked towards the bar door, the noise of talking, laughter and music getting louder as they approached. Harry opened the door, and as they stepped in there was a loud cheer from the crew. Drinks were thrust into their hands and many glasses were clinked against them in celebration. The adrenaline and excitement of the evening's events were high.

'Just a minute.' Harry waved to Delilah behind the bar who was wearing a purple wig but no dress. 'Can you ring the bell, Delilah?'

'Cost a round,' he replied with a smile.

'Go on then.' Delilah rang the bell loudly until the noise died down. He turned the music off.

Harry held his hand up. 'Men we were very lucky, and that we owe to Delilah.' Another loud cheer swelled. Harry held his hand up again. 'But hopefully it's all over now and we can get back to the normal running of our ship and getting back home. Next round is on me.'

Another cheer went up, the music went back on and the noise level resumed its previous high.

Carole grabbed Harry's arm and pulled his face down. 'Harry, I'm bushed, and the drink and smoke are getting to me. I will quietly disappear.'

'I'll see you home,' said Harry.

'You don't have to leave,' she protested. 'No, it gives me an excuse,' replied Harry.

They said goodnight to those nearby and quietly slid out of the door. They walked down and came to her cabin. She hesitated.

'Harry…' she started. He put his finger on her lips.

'Don't say any more. I understand. We are all tired. Get a good night's sleep, I'll see you in the morning.' She smiled gratefully.

'Thank you, Harry. You and your crew have been wonderful.' She kissed him goodnight.

'Goodnight.'

Harry walked towards his cabin and found Peter waiting for him. 'I hope you don't think I was interfering this evening, Harry.'

'Of course not, Peter. It's your job to question what you think is wrong.'

'It's just that I am very worried at what will happen.'

'What do you mean?'

'Harry, these rebels are not totally stupid. They'll know what has happened. The town saw the trucks coming back and you even brought one of the rebel trucks with you. Everyone will know that it was us that rescued them and they will be after our blood. If we hadn't been in danger before, then we really are now.'

'I have no intention of being here when they arrive.'

'That may be easier said than done. What are you going to do with them all?'

'I'll decide that in the morning. Goodnight Peter.'

Tuesday 20 May

Chapter 7

The rain had stopped and the skies were blue again. The river was brown with the mud which had been washed down and was beginning to run harder with the rain swelling the current. Harry looked out and saw some of the crew putting an extra line out forward, just in case. The ship was moving on her berth with the swollen river.

He looked at his watch, nearly eight o'clock, time to go and have a look at the new 'passengers.' As he went down, he saw the Bosun standing with MacNab, the 2nd Coxn, and another seaman outside the Mate's cabin. They looked embarrassed as they saw the Captain. Wisely he walked on towards the workers' accommodation area. He went down the stairs to where they were having their breakfast. There was a strange unpleasant smell. He went into the galley where some of the women were.

'Good morning, ladies. What's that smell?' No one answered him. They continued to fill buckets with hot water. He came out of there and went along the alleyway where the bunkrooms were. The stench was overpowering. He opened a door and there on the deck was a pile of excrement and puddles of urine. The next cabin was the same. In the next cabin he found Carole with one of the ladies on their knees cleaning.

'What the hell is going on, Carole?' She stood up, her hair in disarray.

'Harry, be patient. They are used to the forest where they perform their ablutions as they please.'

'Shit as they please?' he almost shouted. 'They are shitting on the decks of my ship! Is every cabin like this?' Carole nodded miserably.

'Then why are you cleaning this up? Get them in here and make them clean their own mess up!'

'Harry, understand. This is women's work.'

'Women's work! I'll teach them women's work!' Now he was shouting.

'Harry! Please try to understand. This is very hard for them.'

'And for my ship!'

'Look! Leave this with us. We'll get it clean.'

'With what? Hot water? The whole place needs disinfecting. Look there are a row of heads right here!'

'Heads?' asked Carole.

'Yes heads, that's what we call them. Lavatories, toilets whatever you want, but get them to use them.'

'How do I do that?'

'Show them for Christ's sake.'

'Show them?'

'Yes. Sit on one. Wipe your bottom or whatever, but get them to use them.'

'They have. They've been using them as wells.' Harry looked at her and shook his head.

'Carole, just get them trained, right now. I'm going to get the disinfectant organised.'

He came up the ladder and walked along to Sandy's cabin. Whatever was going on hadn't finished.

'Am I interrupting something?' he asked.

'Not at all,' said Sandy, 'almost finished.'

'Sandy as soon as you can, get some crew with rubber gloves and lots of disinfectant down to the workers' bunk area. It seems that they have never used heads before except for drinking water and have decided the decks are for crapping and pissing on. The place is covered in it.'

'Well, well,' said Sandy, 'and there was I wondering what to do.' He looked at the two seamen who were looking very unhappy, but the Bosun was starting to grin behind them.

'Right, Bosun. I think we have two volunteers have we not?' The two sailors nodded miserably. 'Good. I'll inspect in two hours. I want to be able to eat off the decks. They're all yours, Bosun.'

'Thank you, Sir,' he said to Sandy.

'Come on, my lovely lads. Let's see who is going to throw up first.' They headed off to get started.

'That'll teach them to be late. Bit of a mess is it then?' asked Sandy.

'You could say that.' Harry was beginning to calm down. 'With Carole in the middle, trying to clean up. I was a bit rough with her,' Harry said.

'She's a doctor, she can take it. Probably got quite a temper on her if the truth be known. You go on up. I'll keep an eye on it.'

'Thanks,' said Harry gratefully.

'I'm expecting the agent with the Harbour Master and Pilot this morning. Come on up when they get here and bring Peter with you.'

'Aye aye, Sir.'

Harry went into the messroom. 'Delilah,' he called.

'Yes, Sir.' Delilah's head popped out of the galley.

'Breakfast, Sir?'

'Just bring me an egg and bacon sandwich with a coffee, Delilah.'

'Coming right up, Captain.'

Harry was sitting at his desk engaged in creative accounting, trying to lose the cash he'd paid for the trucks. Delilah had delivered the sandwiches and coffee and he was beginning to feel at peace with the world again. His phone rang. It was Graham, the duty officer.

'The Chandler has turned up with a truckload of food, Sir. Shall we take it on board?'

'I didn't order any extra. Did the Cook?'

'He thought you had, Captain.'

'Ask the Chandler to come up.' Harry put the phone down. Henri arrived out of breath from the climb up from the jetty.

'Good morning, Captain. I am sorry, I should have told you. I thought about all the people you have on board and that you may not have the food they like, so I loaded the truck and brought it down.'

'Let me see the invoice,' said Harry.

'There is none, Captain. This is from me. If I leave it in the warehouse, the *Mechants* will take it when they get into town.'

'Henri, that's very kind of you. Mind you, I hope I won't have them on board much longer. One moment.' He rang down to the ship's office on the main deck. When Graham answered, Harry told him to carry on and load the stores.

'Where will you send them, Captain?'

'That's not my problem, Henri.'

Henri scratched his head. 'They are pygmies. At the moment, wherever they go if they are not protected, they will be attacked. Maybe in Boma, up north in the forest reserve, they may be safe, but not here, Captain.' Henri stood up. 'Captain, it has been a pleasure. I wish you good luck in whatever you do. Maybe we will meet again in better times, but I fear that will be a long time in coming. There are too many people who want the killing to continue.'

Henri smiled again and then left.

Sandy arrived in the workers' quarters to find all the women and girls cleaning and washing. They seemed happy enough. He carried on to the sleeping areas and found Carole. Whatever Harry had found had gone and it all smelt of fresh disinfectant.

'Good morning, Sandy,' called Carole cheerfully.

'Morning, Carole, all going well?'

She grinned. 'After a few small hiccups. You probably heard.'

'Just a little,' he smiled back. 'His bark's worse than his bite.'

'I hope so. He was certainly in a foul mood this morning.'

'That's his prerogative, Carole. It's his ship. Harry is very particular about everything being spotless and I think that he was a little disturbed by the mess. Anyway, between you and me, he's more worried about upsetting you.'

'Is he?' Carole brightened.

'Good. The bastard told me to sit on the toilet or head as you call it and show them how to do it.'

'Did you?' asked Sandy.

'Don't be so puerile,' Carole wrinkled her nose at him.

'Your sailors have done a great job.'

'I was going to ask. Where are they?'

'They took the children out onto the deck. They were becoming restless and bored. The last thing I wanted after this morning was for them to start roaming around the ship. God forbid, they may even have invaded the great man's quarters.'

'Well, you seem to have it all under control. Did you hear that the Chandler brought a load of food down for our guests?'

'Yes,' said Carole. 'That was very kind of Henri. Some of it is already in the kitchen.'

'Galley,' Sandy corrected. She gave him an exasperated look. 'By the way,' said Sandy, looking at his watch, 'it's smoko now.' Seeing her face, he added, 'Tea break. We have one in the morning from 1000 to 1030 and another in the afternoon from 1500 to 1530. Luncheon is 1200 to 1300 and dinner 1800 to 1900. You'll eat in the officers' mess which is on the other side of the galley to the crew's messroom but anytime you want, you can go in the mess where there's always coffee brewing and the fridge is usually full.'

'Sandy, did you know Delilah brought me tea and toast this morning? Then he filled my refrigerator, and when I came back from breakfast, he had cleaned the cabin and made my bed?'

'Did you check your underwear?'

'What do you mean?'

'Sorry it was a lame joke. On the cruise ships the stewards used to pinch the women passengers' knickers.'

'I really didn't expect all this.'

'Most people don't. They only see cruise ships and warships on the telly. It's the only way a ship can run. Mind you, a lot depends on the Captain. With Harry, it's like a Swiss watch.'

'And he depends on the Chief Officer?'

'Who depends on the crew. It's a family. Anyway, I'm going to check on my lads. See you for lunch.'

Sandy walked out onto the afterdeck and found the younger members of the crew with young and old pygmies, playing basketball with the ring rigged up on the after end of the deck above. Peter the Chief Engineer was watching with Carole.

'I thought they would be teaching them football,' said Sandy.

'They were, but they lost two balls in ten minutes so switched to basketball,' said Peter.

'That gives me an idea,' said Sandy. He saw Jake watching from the side near the gangway. 'Jake, as soon as smoko is over, sound Man Overboard. We need to launch the Fast Rescue Craft anyway to give it a run. Let's see if our timing is up to standard.'

Sandy went to the gangway phone. 'Just to tell you, Captain, we're having an MOB exercise after smoko. It's just to exercise the FRC crew so the bridge team won't have to close up.'

'Thanks, Sandy.'

'Jake, as soon as the boat's in the water tell them to do a search pattern to find the footballs.' He looked at Jake. 'Where should their datum for a search be?'

Jake thought for a moment and looked at his watch. 'The first ball went over about twenty minutes ago, the current is around 5 knots. If we launch in 10 minutes then they should base their search from a position 2.5 miles astern.'

'Right and what pattern would you advise?'

'The balls will run in a fairly straight line. I would do a lane search using the base lane as a direct line from the stern in the direction of the current.'

'How long should the first lane be?'

'The FRC will do 35 knots with the current and will be in position approximately 5 minutes after launching. Their first lane should be no more than 2 minutes allowing for error.'

'Good. You're in charge. Get the balls back.'

Harry was desultorily going through his papers when the ship's bells rang three times, then the tannoy crackled. 'For exercise. For exercise. For exercise. Man overboard. Man overboard. Fast Rescue Craft away.' Even from his office Harry could hear the running of feet and shouting. He looked at the clock. Let's see he thought. They are probably a little stale with all this time in port. He heard the FRC launch winch starting up which meant that the Bosun's party was ready. One minute gone. Then came the whine of the davit being swung out, followed by the engines being started. Now the whine again as the boat was lowered down to the water, and the roar of the engines as the boat was on its way. Harry noticed the time. 1 minute 50 seconds. Not bad.

The agent, together with the Harbour Master and Pilot, appeared at the gangway. Graham the 3rd Mate immediately took them up to the Captain's office.

'Good morning, gentlemen. Please come in and sit down.'

By the usual magic, Delilah appeared in his white jacket. 'Gentlemen, coffee, tea?' All three ordered coffee.

'Would you get the bottle of whisky and four glasses out, Delilah. I know the Harbour Master would like a whisky to go with his coffee,' said Harry smiling. The three gave a brief but worried smile back and then waited for Harry. This is not going to be easy thought Harry.

Mario spoke. 'Captain, the Pilot has little English so I will translate. What is it you want to do?'

'First thing, Mario, have the spares arrived?'

'There is no word of them.'

'Have you told London?'

'Yes.'

'And what did they say?'

'They would check and come back to me.'

'Right, gentlemen, on that basis I want to sail tomorrow morning. That will give us passage in daylight hours through to the pilot station at Banana.'

The agent spoke to the Pilot, who then spoke rapidly to the Harbour Master. It was now the Harbour Master's turn. 'As you know, Captain, you only have one engine at the moment. If the spares come today, will the repairs be finished by tomorrow morning?'

'That is impossible,' said Harry.

The Pilot became agitated and spoke again. Mario turned to the Captain. 'It is the Chaudron d'Enfer, in English the Cauldron of Hell although you say Devil's Cauldron. He says that you do not have the speed to go through this and will be swept onto the rocks.'

'I fully understand, Mario. Please tell him I will charter the two tugs to go through with us.'

The Harbour Master interrupted. 'The tugs come under my jurisdiction, Captain, and they are not happy about going through the Cauldron towing your ship. They are really only meant to assist with berthing and unberthing and they only have 500 horsepower each.'

'But they have been before?'

'Yes but never towing a ship.'

'All right, let's get to the problem,' said Harry looking at the Harbour Master. 'How much?' The Harbour Master looked at Mario and spoke in Bantu to him.

They talked for a moment then Mario said, 'They want twenty thousand US dollars, Captain.'

'Bloody hell, that's extortionate!' exploded Harry.

The Harbour Master shrugged. 'Understand, Captain, I would like to help but I have no authority. I am leaving soon. Those coming do not like Mobutu's officials.'

A clattering on the stairway outside indicated the arrival of Sandy and Peter. They entered the office and after brief introductions they squeezed around the small table as Delilah appeared with a whisky bottle and glasses.

'Gentlemen, all of you except the Pilot know Sandy the Chief Officer and Peter the Chief Engineer. I will just recap for them. The Pilot has agreed to take us on Wednesday morning. However, he will not go without the tugs to get us through the Cauldron. The tugs want $20,000.' Sandy whistled. 'The other problem is that the tugs are not really tow tugs and only have 500 horsepower.'

'Hell,' said Sandy. 'That's not much.'

'That's why everyone is uneasy.' Harry addressed the Harbour Master again. 'As you are leaving, can you give me a clearance certificate? At least then I can sail when I want.'

'That is not a problem, Captain. I will give it to Mario when we go back.'

'Pilot, if we get the tugs will you take the ship tomorrow morning?' The Pilot hesitated. 'With a very generous present,' Harry added.

The Pilot spoke to the agent. Mario asked, 'How generous?'

'An extra $500 in cash.' The Pilot nodded his agreement. 'So we are back to the tugs.' Harry looked at the Harbour Master. 'Something is better than nothing,' he said. The Harbour Master said nothing. 'What is the lowest price you can give me?'

Mario turned to the Harbour Master and spoke in Bantu for a moment and then turned back to Harry. 'Maybe $15,000 but that must be in cash and in advance.'

'I don't have anything like that in my safe. I can probably raise around $4,000. Do you have any cash?'

'Hah,' Mario said bitterly. 'No one in Matadi is stupid enough to have that kind of money sitting in offices, Captain.'

'So we call London. Gentlemen, thank you for coming. I won't keep you any longer. Pilot I will see you tomorrow. Harbour Master, when are you leaving?'

'Probably tomorrow morning, Captain. The Pilot will also be leaving, so tomorrow is the last opportunity of having him.'

'Tomorrow morning it is, I hope that all goes well for you.'

'We will survive, Captain. After a week of doing what they wish with the town, Kabila will rope them in. He needs the port, and he will soon realise that he needs us, his new loyal supporters.' He grinned widely. 'Captain, good luck also. It is not often we have one of the old ship's parties these days, I will remember the barbecue.' His eyes twinkled. 'And the beautiful blond lady.' With that they left.

'Delilah made a conquest,' murmured Sandy.

'Maybe the Harbour Master did as well,' replied Peter. They looked at each other.

'No,' said Harry, 'don't think about it. Now Mario, let's phone London.' He picked up the sat phone and dialled the number. After several rings David's assistant answered. 'Mr Burton please,' said Harry. 'This is Harry Andrews on the Sea Quest.'

There was silence at the other end for a moment, then David came on the phone.

'Harry, what's the situation?'

'The same, David. The spares are not here and I'm arranging to sail the ship tomorrow morning.'

'I am dealing with the situation now, Harry.'

'No you're not. You're prevaricating. The tugs want $15,000 and the Pilot wants his fee and an extra $500. I will have clearance this afternoon provided you have paid the harbour fees. I have set up the sailing for Wednesday morning at 0600 which will get us down to the pilot station by dusk.'

'Harry, listen to me please. We have been directly on to the new government in Kinshasa. They are sending the spares by military escort tomorrow and they will be with you in the afternoon. I swear that this has been guaranteed. As soon as they are loaded, if you are bothered by the situation you can pull off the berth and anchor while the engine is being repaired, but Kinshasa have said there is no more fighting and that all is peaceful.'

'Really?' said Harry. 'Strange that we can hear the gunfire from the ship. Tell that to the people they attacked last night in a large village on the main Kinshasa road, burning the village down after raping and killing them. That doesn't sound like peace.'

'Harry, we simply cannot get that amount of money to you in Matadi.'

'You mean you won't pay that amount.'

'Please, Harry.' David sounded desperate. 'The spares have come from Russia. They were very hard to find and God knows if there are any more. I will do a deal with you. If for any reason the spares do not arrive you can pull off and sail on Thursday morning. I will arrange a banker's draft for the cash to be delivered to any account in Kinshasa, first thing on Thursday morning.'

'All right, David, spares by tomorrow afternoon. If they come and if necessary I will pull off and try to anchor somewhere although the current is very strong. If I can, I will do the repairs and sail. If the spares do not arrive, I will sail Thursday morning and you will have to arrange for the money to be paid for the Pilot and the tugs. Mario will call you and tell you where. Is that agreed?'

'Yes, Harry, and thank you. I will wait for Mario's call tomorrow as to where to arrange the payment.' Harry put the phone down.

'Gentlemen, it looks as if we are spending another day here. Mario, thanks for hanging on.'

'We have a small, as you say, "breathing space",' said Mario. 'It seems as though there are hundreds of South African mercenaries in town who are waiting for reinforcements.' Mario's eyes twinkled. 'Henri told me.' Then he became serious. 'What about the passengers, Captain?'

'What passengers?'

'Captain, the whole town knows you have a pygmy tribe on board from the mission. What do you intend to do with them?'

'Can they travel north into the hills with you and the other townspeople?'

'If they were anyone else but pygmies they probably could but no, Captain. It would be dangerous for them. They would be handed over to the rebels or whatever they are calling themselves now.'

Mario held his hands up. 'Nothing to do with me, Captain. I am sorry, I thought I would ask.'

'That's alright, Mario. I will think about it and let you know tomorrow.'

Mario got up. 'Gentlemen, once again thank you. I have a lot to do.' He shook hands with each of them. 'I will be in my office all day tomorrow, Captain, then I leave.'

They sat in silence after Mario had gone then Harry spoke.

'Peter, how quickly can you get that bloody engine going again?' Peter looked unhappy.

'I wish I could help, Harry, but I already told you two days and that hasn't changed. What you must also realise is that once it is up and running the parts must be run in, and I will have to limit the engine to seventy five percent revs for the first day and then slowly bring her up to speed. I may also have to stop to make any adjustments.' Harry was looking hard at Peter.

'I suppose there's no use us throwing more crew at you?'

'None at all except to load the spares. It's engineer's work. So if the spares come on Wednesday afternoon and there is no trouble we stay alongside. If, or more likely when, these rebels enter the town, we leave the berth regardless of the time and try to anchor somewhere. At least they can't touch us out there. Our repairs will be completed on Thursday afternoon. We then start the engine and run it continuously until Saturday morning and, pilot or not, we sail.'

'Peter, regardless of the state of the engine, I may have to use full power in the Cauldron.' He held his hand up, 'There is no discussion.' Peter looked glum.

'As you say Captain but...' he shrugged.

'That leaves the passengers,' said Sandy. 'There was a river ferry here when we arrived. It was from Boma - I wonder where that is? We could put them on that if it is still running.'

'We haven't seen it since then,' commented Harry, 'and we can't rely on it suddenly appearing. They'll come with us and we'll drop them off at Boma as we pass, or go alongside briefly to let them off. There are no laws being broken as they are simply travelling within the country.'

'That seems a logical solution,' said Sandy. 'Shall I tell Carole or will you?' Just then the phone went. It was Andy MacBride, the medic.

'Captain, thought you ought to know that one of the pregnant women is in labour. It looks like it will be pretty soon. The Doctor is here.'

Harry got up. 'Looks like I will tell Carole. I'm off down to the hospital, one of the women is about to sprog.'

Sandy and Peter were left in the office, Sandy reached for the whisky and poured a shot for them both.

'Your health, Peter.'

'And yours, Sandy.'

'Ever thought about sailing on a normal ship, Peter?' Sandy asked.

'Used to at one time; I was with Blue Funnel. That was a great time. When that went bottoms up, I went onto tankers but that was a miserable existence. Anyway, redundant again, another company and redundant again, so ended up on anything interesting; one contract at a time. And you?'

'Similar. Cadet with Bank Line tramping around the South Pacific. It was like a dream come true. I was only sixteen and came back from the South Pacific almost an alcoholic. But I was a seaman, had to be with that outfit. Then same as you. Redundant in the seventies, went onto bulk carriers, bloody hard work, but in those days you got ashore. Then redundant again, so went out east with an agency. Did some very interesting work. That was where I met Harry.'

'And Harry?'

'When I met him first it was in a Peruvian desert. He was in Port Line, same as us, redundant; he went east as well. He did a fair amount of time with the Royal Navy.' Peter looked surprised.

'Really?'

'He was a senior officer in the reserve.'

'He never flew the Blue Ensign on the ship,' said Peter.

'No but he carries it with him, at least he used to. Just be thankful that we saw how good it was Peter. They are good memories. Sod it. All this talk of the past has made me quite depressed. I think I will have a last run tonight up to Esmeralda's, coming?'

'Why not? A last evening of debauchery before work. I should think that most of the lads will be there as well.'

Harry walked briskly down the alleyway and stairway arriving outside the hospital, where he met a small gathering of pygmies and some crew. He eased his way through and looked in at the hospital door. Andy, Carole and the nurses were in attendance around the bed helping a groaning woman. Harry stepped back. It was no place for him at present, and they all seemed to be doing perfectly well without him. Instead he went to the galley where the Cook, Willie, was presiding over his steaming pots.

'Good morning, Willie. Any problems?' Willie turned, wiping his hands on a cloth.

'Morning, Captain. Not really, better than when we have the usual crowd of shore labourers. These women just collect food from the stores and get on with it. They're keeping the workers' galley and mess as clean as a new pin. I've just had a look.'

'That's good. I had words about cleanliness earlier this morning so it worked.'

'So I heard. Gave the Bosun some real work for a change instead of hanging around my galley.'

'How about provisions?'

'The Chandler dropped off a whole truckload, Captain. I've enough food to feed them for weeks.'

'Good, they will be here a little longer than we first thought. The idea now is that they stay on board until we get down the river, then we will drop them off at Boma which is about halfway down. That should, at the latest, be on Saturday afternoon.'

'That's not a problem, Captain. Excuse me a moment.' He turned to stir a brown gooey mess in a large pot.

'What's that?' asked Harry.

'The kids like sweets, so I thought I would make some toffee.'

'Good idea,' said Harry. 'I'm sure they'll like it. Nice to see the kids are being looked after.'

He went back to the hospital again to check on the events. From the smiling faces it was obvious that all had gone well. He eased his way into the hospital, to where the mother with baby were. Carole looked up.

'Harry,' she was flushed and smiling. 'It's a girl and guess what. She wants to call her "Ship". Harry smiled at her pleasure. 'I will keep her here for another day, as it was a difficult birth. Peter, his boys and Delilah are making a cradle.' Just at that moment, Peter came into the hospital.

'I hope this will do,' he said. 'It's been knocked up in a hurry.'

He was followed in by Davy Wilson the 3rd Engineer and Bert Morrison the Fitter carrying the cradle. Not just a cradle, it was covered in pink satin and lace, and inside there was a small mattress and pillow. Carole and the others gathered and clapped in delight.

'Peter, it's wonderful,' said Carole and gave him a kiss on his cheek.

Delilah then came in. 'Nice isn't it?'

'Nice!' exclaimed Carole. 'It's better than I could have ever believed.'

'Don't look too closely,' said Peter. 'The welding's still hot.'

'Where did you get the pink satin from?' The engineers all looked at Delilah.

'My best dress,' Delilah said. 'Still it's for a good cause, and there is enough for one more,' he said looking at the woman in the other bed.

Harry left the hospital and went up to the officers' deck and tapped on the door to Sandy's cabin. Sandy was sitting at his desk looking at a checklist, his reading glasses perched on his nose. Harry walked in and sat down on a chair.

'Sandy, it would seem that the whole ship is occupied in looking after our passengers.'

'Rather nice don't you think, Sir?' replied Sandy.

'I really don't know. It's like I've handed over my ship to a package holiday company.'

'Come on,' Sandy stood up. 'Time for a pint before lunch. I must say this stay in port is very civilised.'

'If you can forget what's going on outside.'

In the bar, Harry looked at his team.

'I want to run something by you all before the others come in. If we cannot get the tugs and we have to sail through the Cauldron, how would you connect the mooring lines to our boats?' They all looked at the Captain.

'Are you serious,' asked Sandy.

'Completely,' replied Harry.

'Well, as they are single hook launches, there are no hooks aft so I suppose you could take a turn around the wheelhouse but that's very messy. What is the strength of that structure?' said Sandy shrugging his shoulders.

'How about you, Peter?

Peter looked thoughtful. 'Tell you what. Chalkie and I will have a look after lunch.'

'I'll come with you,' said Sandy.

'Don't be worried about messing the boat up; we're past that. What I am looking for is a strong hook or bar arrangement aft that is part of the hull that we can hook the eye on or if necessary shackle the eye onto.'

'Even welding?' asked Peter.

'Yes. Seeing that cradle and your remarks about the welding being hot got me thinking. If together you could come up with an arrangement by tomorrow morning, I will make a decision then.'

'Do you really think the boats can do this?'

'I don't know, but at least we would be ready.'

The 3rd Mate and Jake came in followed by the 3rd Engineer and Carole.

'A flower amongst the thorns,' said Sandy.

'Stop it, Sandy. I don't feel much like a flower. Can I have a small beer please?' She turned towards Harry. 'Can I speak to you for a minute?' They went off to a corner of the bar.

'Harry, I heard you decided that we can stay on board to Boma. I just want to thank you. I know what this occupation is costing you and the effect it has had on you and the crew.'

'Carole, that's enough. It is the least that I can do. What did you think? That I could just dump you in the town with these bastards about to enter? We are coping very well and all seems, at least for the moment, to be under control.'

'I am losing my guards and their families this afternoon. They want to take their chances up in the hills rather than go with the ship. I'm not surprised. They are local after all and their friends and relatives are here.'

'Is that going to cause you any problems?'

'No. Andy was great today and I'm sure that between us we can look after our remaining patient.'

'When are they going?'

'After lunch. I'll take them up to town in the Land Rover. With a squeeze and the men hanging on I can get them up to the outskirts of town where they want to go.'

'Why not use the truck we won? That can hold everyone without a problem.'

'Chalkie,' Harry called. 'Can you drive Carole and some of her people to where they want to go this afternoon?'

'Not a problem, Captain.'

'I can drive myself, Harry.'

'Better you have someone with you.'

In the late afternoon, Sandy and Peter came up to Harry's office. Peter had a schematic diagram of the hull section of the daughter craft.

'The problem, Harry, is the whole structure of the boat. It is designed for speed. The main strength is concentrated forward for sea impact and in the area of the engines. The hull is GRP so we cannot weld anything there. The stern strength is at the bottom to support the engines.' Peter looked at Harry.

'OK, Peter, I'm following you.'

'Right. So there is nothing to support towing directly astern of the engine bay. The best place would be the forward part of the engine bay. There is a steel support beam on the base at bilge level and there is strengthening of the hull, with transverse girders here and here,' he said indicating the hull. 'That means the only way we can do this to get a good connection is to drill and bolt a curved bar aft of the deckhouse, from one side of the hull to the other and support this with a welded piece going from the steel support beam up to the middle of the bar. That means the bar is supported on three sides. Going to make a mess of the boats though,' said Peter.

'At this stage that is a minor consideration, as long as it doesn't interfere with seaworthiness.'

'The weight of the extra steel might slow the boat down a little and increase the draft, but as the boats have good stability that should be the only effect,' replied Sandy.

'How long will it take?' Harry asked Peter.

'If Sandy's lads can clear the site, we can measure up and prepare the welded pieces before we start, and we can fit each boat in about two hours. Hopefully, just lifting the engine bay access will give enough space otherwise we might have to cut some of the deck. I'll try to avoid that.'

Harry sat thinking for a moment. 'Get everything ready. I'll make a decision tomorrow afternoon on fitting.'

Peter got up. 'I'd better go and see what we have to make these pieces from.'

'Thanks, Peter. Let's hope we don't need them.'

'Are you serious about this?' asked Sandy once Peter had left.

'Bloody right I am. I might not have any other choice. If we have to sail and the tugs are not there for any reason, the only way might be to use our boats. I really don't know. On the open seas we are in our element and know the options but here in a river?' He shrugged. 'So what is your opinion?'

'It's a hell of a risk. Get it wrong and the ship is wrecked and no one is going to get her off those rocks except as small pieces of scrap metal.'

'Do you think I don't know that?'

'Sorry, Captain. I'm just trying to look at the possibilities.'

Harry looked away. 'I want to take Rescue 2 down to the Cauldron tomorrow morning to have a look at the conditions there.'

'I'll come with you. Two heads are better than one.'

'All right, we'll go after breakfast.'

'Be careful tonight. God knows what is roaming around. It might be an idea for everyone to stick together.'

'We're both taking one of the automatics, just in case.'

'Are Chalkie and Carole back?'

'Yes, they got back just before we came up. We're all going to use the truck tonight. It'll will keep everyone together. One other thing, the Cadet asked for permission to have his girlfriend on board this evening. I see no harm in it, but I thought I would run it by you as he is OOW.'

'No problem, provided it doesn't interfere with his duties. And she's off by breakfast.'

Sandy smiled. 'I'll make sure of that.'

'Better he screws her than that raddled bunch of whores up the road.'

'Sir! You're talking of the women I love!' They laughed together.

'Well I had better get tarted up for a sailors' farewell,' said Sandy grinning.

Harry looked at the drawings for the boats again before squaring away his desk. He looked up. Carole was in his doorway, leaning against the side.

'Hello, sailor! Want a good time?'

'How much?'

'Depends on what you want,' she replied smiling.

'Can you do any tricks?' She pretended to think for a moment. 'Take my teeth out.'

'That's different, but I'll take my chances with them in.'

'As long as I don't get too excited, you're safe.'

He went towards her and taking her in his arms, gave her a long kiss.

'God, Harry,' she said. 'I want you.'

'Same here, but we are going to have dinner first.'

'That's your idea of foreplay is it?'

'No, but I'm bloody hungry. Let's head down to the bar.'

They went into the messroom. To Harry's surprise it had flowers on the tables. He looked at Carole.

'Well you wouldn't have them in your cabin. When I went ashore I saw children selling whole bunches of them cheaply so I bought some.'

Delilah appeared. 'They're in the crew messroom too,' he said. 'Makes the place look really nice.'

'What does the Bosun think?' asked Harry.

'He's just a caveman,' said Delilah and disappeared back into the galley.

They carried on through to the bar and again flowers were in abundance.

'What do you think?' said Carole.

'I really don't know,' said Harry. 'Maybe it's because it is so unusual.'

Delilah arrived wearing his white jacket and went behind the bar. 'Your usual rum and pineapple, Sir?' he said in the tones of a London barman.

'Yes please, Delilah, but ladies first. Carole?'

'A glass of red wine please, Delilah.' Delilah winked and bent down and pulled up a bottle of very good red.

'Saved some from the barbecue. The hotel bloke gave us some good wine and I wasn't going to waste it on a crowd of drunks.'

'They got their drinks just as Sandy and the Chief walked in.'

'Bloody hell,' said Harry. 'That smell is not the flowers. What on earth is it?'

'Whatever it is, it smells lovely,' said Delilah. Sandy looked disconcerted.

'It's called white musk,' said Peter. 'He got it in Cape Town. It has pheromones in it. Makes him irresistible to women.'

'What do you think, Carole?'

'I'm trembling already.'

'So am I,' said Delilah. Sandy turned and glowered at him. 'I think you are needed by the Cook.'

'Certainly, Sir,' said Delilah who retreated smiling to the galley.

The Bosun popped his head in the bar. 'Excuse me, gents,' he said 'but all ashore who's going ashore. Transport's waiting.'

'Have a good night,' Harry called as Sandy and Peter left the bar. 'You too,' said Sandy smiling.

Harry took the bottle of wine off the bar. 'I think we will,' he said as they went into dinner.

Wednesday 21 May

Chapter 8

Harry stood on the embarkation deck waiting for the daughter craft to be readied for boarding. He had a chart tucked under his arm. It was hot under a blue sky and gold plate sun. The river looked like a sheet of steel with floating hibiscus clumps and the odd patches of debris floating past. Olav the Chief Coxn was already in the boat with Henry Duncan and George Huggins, a deck boy.

Harry felt remarkably fresh which was surprising considering the night that had passed. He had woken up in the morning to find Carole gone. As if in answer to his thoughts, Carole along with Sandy appeared next to him; she was dressed in work trousers and a shirt which was too large.

'Good morning, Harry,' she said. 'Sandy told me you were going to have a look at the Cauldron. I have heard so much about it and would love to come along if that is allowed.'

'Fine', said Harry. 'We shouldn't be too long. It starts at the bridge.'

Olav signalled that he was ready for them to embark. They stepped aboard and entered the wheelhouse where Olav was at the wheel.

'Did you bring the leadline?' Harry asked Olav.

'It's in the locker behind you, Sir,' Olav replied.

He started the engines up with a roar, and then settled them down. When he was satisfied, he signalled to the launch crew who swung the boat out and lowered it into the water where Olav released it. He expertly gunned the engines and swung the boat away from the ship in a wide arc. Although they were in the wheelhouse, there still was noise coming from the engines.

'He looks like one of those pictures of a Viking,' shouted Carole pointing at Olav. Olav was tall with blond hair, a short pointed beard and there was a gold earring dangling from one ear.

'Probably has Viking blood,' replied Harry. 'Olav comes from a small Norwegian fishing village. By the time he was 14, he was at sea on fishing boats. Then into the Norwegian Coastguard, followed by deep sea ships, just roaming around as the mood took him. He's been on tankers, bulkers, search and rescue ships and ended up here. Good sailors, the Norwegians. Enjoy their drink as well.'

'At least I know I'm in good hands,' said Carole. 'How fast will this boat go?'

'With only us on board about 35 knots flat out in calm waters,' said Harry.

Olav shouted to hold on and slowly eased the throttles forward to full pitch. The boat's bow came up as she sprung forward. Harry went over to the radar and switched it on. Olav switched on the wipers as the spray was coming over the wheelhouse. They lurched with the boat as she occasionally bounced on the small waves of the river.

'Once we get to the bridge stop her,' Harry shouted to Olav. 'I want to check on a few distances and the current. Take her down from the centre of the bridge.' Olav nodded and changed course to the centre.

They were quickly under the bridge where Olav eased her back and put the engines in neutral.

'That's better,' said Sandy. 'We can talk now.' Harry was taking distances on the radar from the bridge to the cliffs ahead on the far side of the Cauldron. Sandy came and stood beside him. They watched in silence for a while.

'6 knots,' said Sandy. 'This is the narrowest part.'

'Yes but look how quickly it's dragging us towards the cliffs ahead.' Harry unrolled his chart and put it on the small chart table beside the radar.

'The distance from the bridge to the cliffs is about a mile.'

Olav spoke. 'I'll have to start the engines, Captain. She's starting to spin.'

'Go ahead, Olav.'

Olav expertly handled the wheel, being used to handling small craft in the Leads on the Norwegian coast. He gunned the engines and brought the boat back on course.

'It's the whirlpools,' said Sandy. 'Look at that.' The boat was pitching in the turbulence as Olav took the boat to starboard trying to bring her out of the force of the current.

'Vicious, aren't they?' said Harry. 'Not just one either, they are all over the bloody place. Olav, keep the power on. I want to go close in to the cliffs keeping about 30 metres off and take some soundings there. Can you manage that?'

'I will try, Captain.' The cliffs were already towering above them.

'They are huge,' Carole exclaimed. 'How high are they?'

'About 250 metres,' said Harry. The rocks at the bottom of the cliffs were now clearly in sight.

'30 metres off now, Captain,' said Olav.

'Right, Duncan, sound with the line.'

Duncan cast the line, which rapidly sank into the depths, shooting through his hands.

'No sounding, Sir,' he called. He took several more soundings but again with no result.

'Olav, head towards the exit channel.'

Olav again turned the boat, allowing for the current that was trying to drag them onto the rocks, and headed for the channel. They stopped and Duncan sounded, but again there was no result.

'It's certainly deep,' said Sandy. 'I bet there is nothing until the rocks at the bottom of the cliffs.'

Harry was satisfied. 'OK, Olav, take us back. I want you to go close in to the Matadi side as you go under the bridge and we will take a few more soundings there. If we have to go through with one engine, then if we keep tight to that side as we enter the Cauldron, we will have less distance to travel broadside to the current to get out.'

'That makes sense,' said Sandy.

They arrived back under the bridge and again Duncan took a sounding. This time he called out, 'By the mark seven, Sir.'

'That's not bad,' said Harry. 'We are closer in than I would come.'

'What does that mean?' asked Carole who had come back into the wheelhouse.

'The leadline is marked by fathoms, which are each 6 feet, so when Duncan said by the mark seven he was saying that the seventh fathom was marked on the line. So that means that the depth of water is forty two feet minus the distance from the deck of the boat to the water.'

'You sailors do complicate things,' said Carole.

'It's been complicated for a long time. The leadline is the oldest nautical instrument and has been in use for thousands of years.'

Duncan called again, 'Still by the mark seven, Sir.'

'Alright, Olav, let's go home.'

Olav pushed the throttles down and the boat sped over the water towards the ship's side where the crew were waiting to hoist them back on board. When the boat was hoisted, Harry took the chart back to the bridge. He opened it up on the chart table and stood looking at it for a few moments, then picked up the phone.

'Are you up, Vijay?' he asked when the 2nd Mate answered. 'Yes, Sir.'

'Good, come to the bridge for a few minutes.'

Vijay arrived on the bridge a few moments later and went over to the chart table with Harry.

'We went to have a look at the Cauldron this morning. The current is running quite strong, especially at the bridge. It's about 6 knots and there are some strong whirlpools in the centre area. What I am trying to do is plan for the worst just in case the spares don't arrive and I have to sail with one engine with no tugs to assist. Look here.' They both bent over the chart. 'If, instead of taking the usual route under the bridge, we keep to the port side as tight as we can to the bank, the current is not so strong. We then have the advantage of approaching the exit passage by using the boats on the bow, the thrusters and the wheel to port. We turn into the exit sooner than from the middle of the Cauldron, and as we turn in we will soon get the lee of the bank.'

'The current will still be heavy on the stern, Sir, and that will force the bow to port towards the bank.'

'That won't be a problem as the main body of the ship will still be pushed away from the bank into the centre of the exit channel. If there is a problem then we can use the boats to bring the bow to starboard, although I doubt if that would be needed.'

'How tight can we come to the bank?' asked Vijay.

'Less than half a cable and we maintain that from the berth right down to the exit channel.'

'That's tight, Sir. There's not much on the chart showing that close in.'

'There's not much on the chart, period,' said Harry. 'That's based on our own soundings. Anyway on that basis, Vijay, draw up the courses from the berth and make out a navigator's notebook with the courses and distances listed to about two miles out of the Cauldron, so I can have them for the passage.'

'Very good, Sir. Do you know an ETD yet?'

'No, Vijay. That's all in the lap of the gods – yours and mine!'

The bridge phone rang and Harry answered. It was Delilah. 'The sat phone was ringing when I was in your office, Sir. It's London.'

'I'll be right down,' said Harry.

Harry entered his office and Delilah passed him the telephone. He sat down in his chair and listened.

'Harry? David. Just to tell you that the spares left Kinshasa at dawn this morning and should be with you this afternoon. They have a military escort.'

'What exactly is that?' Harry asked.

'I really don't know. All I know is that we have paid for some soldiers to travel with the truck.'

'Well at least that's something.'

'How are things there?'

'At the berth it's quiet, but the sound of gunfire is regular now. I don't know about the town as I haven't been ashore yet, but I am going up to the agent's office shortly.'

'Well, Harry, what I recommend is that once the spares are on board you leave the berth and anchor while you get the repairs completed.'

'I fully intend to. Thanks for the call, David. I'll keep you posted.'

Just as he put the phone down, the ship's telephone rang.

'Captain, this is Sandy. I'm on the gangway. You'd better come and look at this.' Harry went quickly down the stairway and came out onto the main deck by the gangway. There were four military vehicles and a jeep near the bottom of the gangway.

'How long have they been here?' Harry asked.

'They just arrived. Vijay called me.' More crew were now coming to look. Andy had arrived as well.

'The first two are APCs, that's armed personnel carriers, then there is a supply truck and the last is a light scout tank of some kind.'

The doors of the APCs opened and troops poured out dressed in tiger suits and black berets.

'Whatever they are, they are well dressed.'

'I don't know what is going on but I'm damn certain that this is not the escort for the spares,' said Harry.

He turned to the crew. 'All those not on duty, inside.' When they hesitated, he shouted, 'Now!'

The soldiers formed a line facing the ship holding their weapons at the ready. Some of them had bandages on and they all looked weary.

'These are not ordinary troops,' said Harry. 'They're too well disciplined.' From the jeep emerged two officers who came towards the gangway. As they neared, Harry could see rank markings on their tigersuits. The senior one even had a swagger stick under his arm. He looked at the three officers standing there, and seeing Harry's four stripes he saluted and in perfect English asked, 'Captain?'

'Correct,' said Harry returning the salute. 'Captain Harry Andrews, Sea Quest.'

'Lieutenant Colonel Laurent Monswengwo Saolona. May I present my Lieutenant Arthur Odya? I wonder if I might have a word with you in private for a moment please.'

'Come this way.'

Harry led him inside the ship and they went up the stairways in silence to Harry's office. Harry sat down behind his desk.

'Please sit down, Colonel,' he said indicating the chair in front of his desk.

The Colonel sat and looking around said, 'Very comfortable, Captain.'

'Thank you,' said Harry, 'but I'm sure you didn't come to admire the furnishings.' The Colonel looked steadily at Harry.

'Are your crew all British, Captain?'

'Mostly, but we have a few others on board.' The Colonel nodded.

'Who else is on board the ship, Captain?' There was something about that question that indicated that he knew something but what Harry was not sure.

'Before I answer that question, Colonel, may I ask what this is about?'

'Have you heard of the Special Presidential Division, Captain?'

'No,' said Harry. 'You must excuse me, I really know little about Zaire. We are here for repairs and all I want to do is sail my ship as soon as possible, hopefully this afternoon in fact.' The Colonel smiled and held his hand up.

'Let me continue. The soldiers you see on the quayside are what remains of my brigade. I am now the commanding officer.' He continued looking at Harry. 'As you probably know, Kinshasa has fallen and the rebel army are heading this way. We were intending to carry on by road to Boma and meet up with the government forces there, but unfortunately the road is now completely blocked. This means that the only way to Boma is by your ship.' There was silence.

'First,' Harry replied, 'we have nothing to do with your civil war. We are a merchant ship trying to sail. Second, I have no authority to take you as passengers, and even if I did, that would involve my ship and crew in your conflict. Finally, Colonel, my ship cannot sail until we get the spare parts we are waiting for.'

The Colonel raised his finger. 'I will keep it simple. We are boarding this ship either peacefully or by force.'

Harry looked at the Colonel, who was sitting quite calmly.

'Colonel, if you come on board you cannot sail the ship. What are you going to do then, shoot us?'

The Colonel looked steadily at Harry. 'Captain, that would not bother me in the slightest considering what we have done in the last few weeks. Your nationality will not protect you. In this country no one cares any more. However, we need you. My men and I are very tired and angry. We have been fighting for weeks. We have seen our comrades slowly killed until we are the only ones left. Worse, we have lost many of our families. Now all we are asking is that you take us and our vehicles to Boma. Once there, we will be gone. Is that worth all the trouble if you say no? Do you really think that we will quietly wait for Kabila's rabble to arrive and kill us and what is left of our families? Captain, if necessary I will take each of these pygmies that you have on board, yes I know about them, and shoot them one by one until you agree. Then I will start on your men. Is that what you want?' Harry looked at him with hatred in his eyes.

'All my instincts say get off my ship, Colonel, but in reality I have no choice do I?' The Colonel shook his head. 'All right, Colonel,' he said. 'You have forced your way on board. But first listen to me. Once you are on the ship, you are under my command. Do you understand?'

'Provided that does not endanger us, that is accepted, Captain.'

'Now, your troops will be quartered in the shore workers' accommodation with the pymies. These people are our guests. There will be no unpleasantness and they will share in the accommodation, galley and cooking.'

'My people will not like that, Captain, and neither will their families. I want them off the ship.'

'That is not possible.'

'I could throw them off the ship, Captain. That would solve the problem.'

'Colonel, look at me. I promise you that if that occurs this ship will not move despite your threats. I mean that. If you are going to get out, you need our full cooperation.'

They looked at each other in silence for a moment.

'Captain, this is what I will agree with you. They can remain and I will ensure that my people cause no trouble but, as you think so much of them, your cooperation will be their protection. If at any time you do not cooperate, I will not hesitate to kill them. That cooperation includes getting this ship out. This is our private agreement. Please believe I am perfectly capable of doing this.'

'No wonder there are rebels roaming around with people like you in power.'

The Colonel held his hand up. 'Captain, I am not interested in your opinions. What do you want of us?'

'How many are there of you?'

'Twenty three soldiers including my Lieutenant and myself and around forty women and children.' Harry shook his head.

'This is getting worse by the minute. Do you have any other surprises?'

'No, Captain.'

'Now, accommodation. You and your Lieutenant can have supervisor cabins in the shore accommodation. They are basic but have a shower and toilet.'

'Captain, this is more than enough.'

'Good. You and your Lieutenant can eat in the officers' mess if you wish or with your troops. That's it for the time being. Is there anything else?'

'Some of my men have been wounded. Do you have any medical facilities on board?'

'Yes and we also have a doctor. Speak to the Chief Officer and he will have them taken to the ship's hospital for treatment.'

'Are there any arms on board?'

'Yes, we have a small armoury on the bridge. It is locked and secure. The Officer of the Watch has a key as well as my Chief Officer and myself.'

'Now we are here, you will not need those keys. Give them to me. Now, perhaps I can help you. Where are your spares?'

'They are coming from Kinshasa on a military truck with soldiers.'

'When did they leave?'

'Early this morning.'

'Then I will send a party out to meet this truck and make sure it gets here as soon as possible. What are your intentions then?'

'We will leave the berth and anchor until the repairs are completed.'

'How long?'

'Two days.'

'That is too long, Captain.'

'Colonel, we cannot sail before then. It is a problem of navigation. I will explain this when you get settled on board.' The Colonel got up.

'This could have been far more difficult for us all. Thank you for your sensible attitude, Captain.'

'I didn't have any choice.'

'We all have choices, Captain. Will you instruct your crew as to what is happening? I presume there will be no stupidity.'

'There will be no stupidity as you call it, Colonel. Please hold your people back until the Officer on the gangway indicates that we are ready for boarding.'

'That's no problem, Captain.' He put his cap on, saluted and left the office.

Harry called down to the gangway. 'Sandy they are all coming on board but not until we are ready. Leave the 2nd Mate to show them the shore workers' quarters. When they are on board come up here.' He picked the phone up and called the galley. The Cook answered. 'Cook, we are taking on another 60 or so people.'

'Bugger me,' said the Cook. 'It's getting like a fucking cruise ship.'

'Have we sufficient food on board?'

'For a short time yes, Captain.'

'That's fine. Please go down to the workers' galley and supply what is needed there. Don't worry about the crew. We can eat later if needs be. Is Delilah there?' Delilah came on the phone. 'Delilah, we are taking on some more passengers. I need two other cabins readied.'

'Not a problem, Captain.'

'OK, I'll leave it in your hands.'

Harry put the phone down and went down to Carole's cabin. He knocked and went in. Carole was in her bathrobe with a towel round her hair.

'Captain, I could have been naked,' she smiled.

'Carole, we have a problem,' Harry said. 'I'm going to need your help. There are a bunch of soldiers and their families that we have to accommodate. They will be with your group. I'm aware that the pygmies may be frightened when they see the soldiers. Now they are not coming on board until we are ready.' He held his hand up. 'Wait, I know what you are going to say, but believe me we have absolutely no choice. They are the Presidential Guard. The only good thing is that they seem to be very disciplined. The other thing is that some of them are wounded and need attention.'

'Do you know how serious?'

'No but they seem to be walking wounded. The Colonel probably shot the more serious.'

'If they are the Presidential Guard, then that's more than likely. They were Mobutu's SS. I'll get down to the hospital right now.'

'I am sending the Bosun and some of the crew down to your people's quarters to assist you and watch over the settling in of the new arrivals. Anything you want, ask them. I'm sorry I can't explain more right now but I will tell you later.' She instantly grabbed her clothes and started to dress.

Harry immediately went to the gangway where the troops and their families were assembling on the jetty. He turned to Sandy.

'They are coming on board as far as Boma.'

Sandy looked at Harry. 'I suppose we don't have much choice?'

'You've got it.'

Harry went down the gangway just as one of the RPCs drove off. The Colonel was standing there watching. The soldiers and their families were milling around on the jetty sorting through their baggage. It was a colourful scene that in peacetime would have resembled an everyday ferry trip down the river. The Colonel came up to Harry and said, 'They are on the way to get your spares, Captain.'

'Thank you, Colonel. Now I forgot about your men's weapons.'

'What do you suggest, Captain? They must be able to reach them if required.'

'We have a ship's office. I will hand that over to you as an armoury and give you the key. Will that be sufficient?'

'Yes, Captain, but I want to keep four guards around, two on the gangway and two on the bridge. Just in case. We will also keep our hand weapons.' The Colonel smiled faintly.

'Sandy,' Harry called. Sandy came down the gangway. 'They will place two guards on the gangway and two on the bridge,' Harry explained, 'and they are going to store their weapons in the ship's office. Get Chalkie and a few crew to go up with the truck to the Chandler's warehouse and see if there is any food we can have. According to the Chandler it's going to be looted anyway, and at least this way we will pay for it. Tell them to take a crow bar and a hacksaw.'

Delilah came to the top of the gangway.

'Doctor says that she's ready, the cabins are ready and the Cook is getting food organised.'

Graham the 3rd Mate appeared with Jake.

'Graham, as the soldiers board I want you to check that all their weapons except their hand guns are placed in the ship's office. Four will keep their automatics as they will be guarding us.'

'Jake, you go off with Chalkie and some of the crew to the Chandler's warehouse and stock up on food. Make sure it is food that we can use such as rice or manioc, anything grain. And if there are any salads and fruit that's a bonus. Make a list of what you take.'

'OK, Sir. Shall I take tinned food?'

'Anything like that Jake. I leave it up to you. Off you go, but be quick. I have a feeling we don't have much time.'

'Colonel, your people can board now.'

The quayside was now filling with a mix of soldiers and their families as they climbed out of the various vehicles. The families looked as tired and bedraggled as the soldiers, and several of the children were crying as the mothers clutched them in their arms.

Harry stood aside as they began to board. Just then a battered car came through the dock gates and approached the ship. As the Colonel turned to give orders to his men Harry called to him.

'Colonel, it's my agent.' Mario got out of the car and looked at the scene with an open mouth. 'It's alright Mario. We're just taking on some extra passengers.'

'That's the Presidential Guard,' commented Mario. 'I heard rumours in the town but didn't believe them.'

'Well it's all under control, at least sort of. What's the latest on the spares?'

'According to Kinshasa they should almost be here. The truck reported in about 40 kilometres away saying it was making good progress. Captain, there are already various gangs in the outskirts of the town. They are mostly deserters from Mobutu's army. I have to get my family out now. I hope you understand.'

'Of course I do, Mario. You have done everything you can.' Mario put his hand in his pocket and produced an envelope. 'This is your clearance, Captain. It is undated so you can fill in what you like.'

'What about the tugs and pilot?'

'Call for the pilot on Channel 16 VHF; he will be listening unless he has already left. If you get the spares then you will not need the tugs, Captain.'

'But if I don't?'

Mario shrugged. 'Then it is up to your owners to arrange the payments. Who knows what will happen here now.'

Harry nodded. 'All right, Mario. Thanks for everything you have done. Good luck and take care.'

From the end of the jetty came an explosion and everyone instinctively ducked. One of the warehouses was on fire with thick smoke pouring from it. The Colonel was shouting at his people who were redoubling their efforts to board the ship.

'I must go now,' said Mario, who was visibly agitated. 'I think it is starting, Captain. You must get off the berth as soon as you can. Good luck.'

'And to you, Mario. Take care.'

'We will, don't worry.' Mario shook hands, got into his car and drove out of the gates.

Harry turned to the Colonel. 'What was that?'

'I think it was a stray shell, Captain. Not aimed at us but it shows how close they are. We must sail soon.'

Harry went back on board and into organised chaos. Soldiers were queuing to stow their weapons, women and children were being directed aft by the crew and then through into the shore workers' quarters. In the middle of this Chalkie and their team were going down the gangway to join Jake to go to the Chandler's warehouse.

He pushed through the crowd and went into the shore workers' accommodation. There were no pygmies to be seen and he assumed that Carole had kept them in their sleeping areas. The Bosun and the two coxns were there directing the new arrivals to their quarters, and the Cook and the deck boys were in the galley showing the women the various implements. He took the wise course and left, heading back to the gangway, where Sandy was directing the last of the new arrivals on board.

'Can we load the vehicles?'

'I think so. They are all under 20 tonnes and that's within our limit.'

'All right, Sandy. As soon as you can please. We have plenty of room on deck so take what you can. The truck will also be coming back from the Chandler with more provisions hopefully, so they must come on board. When you're finished what you're doing, you and Peter come up to the office.'

Harry was waiting in his office when Sandy and Peter arrived.

'Peter, I don't know if Sandy has brought you up to speed but we have what could be called a situation on our hands.'

'So I heard. From my side all I want is my spares. Any news?'

'The Colonel sent of one of his APCs with troops to try and locate them. According to the agent they should be within spitting distance. Now, presuming they arrive soon, we will get them on board and get ready for sailing out to anchor. So we will test gear now, then we will be ready as soon as they arrive. Are you ready to start work as soon as we anchor?'

'Yes. Will you want the other engine on standby?'

'Yes. The best I can do is 15 minutes' notice. The current is strong and the holding ground is just rock which isn't much good. We'll put two anchors down, give as much scope as we can and hope that it holds. In the meantime, are the parts ready for the boats?'

'Yes, Harry. Just finished.'

'Right, you can start fitting them when you are ready. Do the starboard boat first.'

'I'll get the fitter on to it now.'

'Is the boat ready, Sandy?'

'All stripped out in the engine bay. I'll have one of coxns standing by to give a hand.'

'When we're anchored I'll call the Colonel up here with you both. I think we'll get Carole up as well as she represents most of the passengers on board. Last thing before you go, Sandy. Will you get someone to make out a passenger list. At least we will know who is on the ship and how many. I've got the clearance from the agent so there is nothing to stop us from sailing.'

'What about the pilot?'

'Even if he's still here, which I doubt, I won't bother him to go to anchor. I don't think he'll mind and there is no Harbour Master any more to object to moving ship without a pilot. Any other immediate points, problems, observations, whatever?'

'Just the safety issue, Captain,' said Sandy. 'Once we come off the berth, we will have to restrict where people go. What about a boat drill, just in case?'

'They will have to be assigned boat stations. Once we have a passenger list, we can make up some form of boat drill, but the pygmies can't read and will probably panic at the first sign of trouble. The only thing we can do is treat them on mass with Carole as their guide.'

'Agreed. Leave it with me. I'll work something out with her, and for the others we can make out some form of abandon ship boat station.'

'Good. Now the main objective is to get the engine repaired, get to Boma, get everyone off, sail out to sea and home. Let's work towards that. I will speak to all the off duty crew in the crew mess when we are anchored.'

Harry looked at them both. 'Do not underestimate this Colonel. He may seem polite on the surface, but let me tell you he is a murderous bastard underneath.'

Chapter 9

Jake and his team had loaded up the truck with what provisions they could find and headed back to the ship only to find themselves in a queue. Most of the vehicles were on board and the remaining two APCs were being stripped of equipment to lighten their load on the cranes. Sandy was on deck with the Colonel arranging the parking. The scout vehicle was on its own at the after end, the transports were in the forepart of the deck, leaving space in the centre for the APCs. Delilah had also come out to watch.

'I see you have placed the 90 mm gun aft with a good field of fire, Colonel.' The Colonel turned and looked at Delilah with interest.

'Do you know the AML?'

'It was in the Falklands, only on the other side. We captured a few though. Very handy weapon, armour piercing rounds and range about 2,000 metres?'

'Correct. Are you the steward?' The Colonel looked a little puzzled.

'Yes,' said Delilah. 'Previously I was in the Royal Marines.'

'Ah,' said the Colonel.

'Are you intending to put the APCs on each side of the ship?'

'Yes. Again, that will give their machine guns their own field of fire if required.'

'Are they amphibious?'

'Yes and so is the AML,' said the Colonel.

'Can I ask, what you are expecting, Colonel? I thought that you were leaving the ship at Boma, which is only a few hours down the river.'

'I am sure you understand that it is better to be prepared just in case.'

'Oh yes,' said Delilah. 'It's the 'in case' that bothers me.' At that moment a soldier from the remaining APC shouted up to the Colonel. He turned to Delilah.

'Would you inform your Captain that we have your spares and they will be here shortly.'

'Right,' said Delilah, 'but I think there is something you are not telling us Colonel.' Instead of replying the Colonel joined Sandy.

Delilah went inside the ship and up to Harry's office where Harry was sitting with Peter.

'Sir, the spares will be here shortly. The news came in over one of the APC's radios.'

Harry and Peter looked at each other smiling broadly. 'That's the best news of the week,' said Harry.

Peter got up. 'I'll get my lads organised. I expect you will be testing engines soon.'

'Yes please, Peter, if you could wind things up now. I want to get off as soon as possible.' Peter left leaving Delilah standing there.

Harry looked at him. 'Is there anything else, Delilah?'

'Captain, I think that the Colonel is not telling us everything.'

'What makes you think that?'

'This business of getting the vehicles on board. Think about it, they can have any vehicle in Boma when they arrive. Why load these?'

'What are you saying?'

'I am saying that Boma has fallen and they know it. That's why they didn't continue travelling on the road. Look at what they have got. They could go through any road block with the kit they have without any problems. The way the Colonel is placing the armed vehicles is to give the best field of fire as possible.'

Harry was thinking. 'All right, Delilah. You may be right but at the moment I just want to get the ship out to anchor. Say nothing about this to anyone else for the moment.'

'Right, Captain.'

Delilah left as the phone rang. It was Sandy on the gangway.

'The spares have arrived, Captain. The vehicles and provisions are all on board and the engine spares are being loaded now. We should be finished and secured down here in a few minutes.'

'Thanks, Sandy. Peter is away to wind up the engine, and as soon as that's ready we're off to anchor.'

'Right. The mooring lines are tight and the stern is clear.' Without putting the phone down Harry called the bridge where Vijay answered. 'The Mate has reported that loading is finishing, all the lines are tight and the stern is clear so you're clear for testing the engine.'

'All the navigational equipment and steering have already been tested, Captain.'

'Good. We'll sail as soon as we can.'

Harry called London. David was out of the office so Harry left a message that the spares had arrived and that he was going to anchor.

A rumbling noise from deep within the ship and an initial vibration told him that the starboard engine had started up. It was soon followed by a sharper tone engine which was the thruster unit. Sandy appeared.

'I'm sending the FRC away to stand by for the linesmen. I will land one of the OSs and the deck boy.'

'Good, Sandy. As soon as they are ashore you can take in the gangway. At least we haven't got the usual number of officials looking for their last handouts.' Sandy disappeared again.

Harry sat for a moment listening to the various noises from the ship as she was prepared for sailing. Above was the muffled thump from those moving around on the bridge, interspersed with phones ringing and alarms being tested. From the boat deck aft the winch was in action lowering the FRC ready for the linesmen. Below was the throb of the engine and changing of the revolutions as the bridge engine controls were tested. The ship vibrated faintly with the power of the engine. All ships regardless of size start to come alive as their sailing time approaches.

Harry looked up. Jake was standing in the doorway.

'Yes?' asked Harry. Jake was hesitant.

'I have a letter for you, Sir.' He stepped forward and handed Harry a mauve envelope. 'It's from Esmeralda,' Jake added.

Dear Captain,

Please forgive me for adding to your problems, especially as you have helped me already, but I have a very special favour to ask of you. I closed the bar this morning. The girls and I are leaving the town for a few days. I do not know how safe they will be but at worst it will be sex without being paid. This will not be too serious for them but I cannot think of my daughter in such circumstances.

As you are going to Boma with Carole, I beg you to please take Monique with you and allow her to accompany Carole ashore there. I leave her in your care, I know that you will do all you can.

I hope one day to meet you again to thank you for this.

In gratitude,

Esmeralda

Harry finished reading the letter and looked up.

'Did you know about this?' Jake looked at Harry pausing for a moment.

'I suggested that she ask you, Sir.'

'Where is she now?'

'In my cabin, Sir.'

'And where do you think she should be accommodated?'

'She can stay there, Sir. I don't mind.'

'I bloody well bet you don't.' He tossed the letter on the desk. 'There isn't a lot I can do about this now is there? Have you told the Chief Officer?'

'Not yet, Sir.'

'Then you had better do so. Make sure she goes on the passenger list. Take her to Carole where she can help out.'

'Thank you, Sir.'

'She will mess in the officers' mess with you. I will discuss her accommodation with the Chief Officer.'

'Thank you, Sir,' Jake repeated and hastily left.

The phone rang.

It was Vijay. 'Engine tested and in order, Captain. The Mate has reported the gangway is up and deck secured, ready for sea.'

'Very good, Vijay. Call stations.'

The familiar pipe came through the ship's loudspeakers. 'This is the bridge. Hands to stations fore and aft.' Harry arrived on the bridge. It was still light but he noticed clouds were rolling in.

'What's the forecast, Vijay?'

'Rain tomorrow, Sir.'

'Looks like it.' Sandy arrived and looked over the bridge. He was listening to the walkie-talkie.

'Hands at stations fore and aft, Sir. Bridge closed up,' he called.

'Thanks, Sandy. Come over here and I'll show you where we're anchoring.' Sandy bent over the chart and Harry indicated a spot just before the rapids on the far side of the river. 'I want to keep as much distance between the port and the ship. This is almost three miles up the river and better still it's out of sight from port.'

'There'll be poor holding ground,' said Sandy.

'I know, just rock, but I intend to do a standing moor, depending on the scope of cable and hopefully both the anchors will catch on the rock on the bottom. If they don't, we will have to keep the starboard engine running ahead to take the weight off.'

'That will slow the repairs down.'

'Do you think I don't know that!' exclaimed Harry. 'But if you have any better suggestions I'll be pleased to hear them.'

'I wasn't criticising, Captain,' said Sandy. 'Just running over the thoughts in my mind.'

Harry sighed. 'Sorry Sandy, that's your job I know. It's just that we are running out of options. At least going over to the side of the river we will be out of the main thrust of the current. With a steady current against us at least she won't be swinging. Anyway if we drag, there is nothing astern of us to bang into and we'll keep the engines on fifteen minutes' notice.' He touched Sandy on his shoulder. 'Come on. You take her off and I'll anchor her.'

Harry sat in the command chair as Sandy went to the wing of the bridge. Harry watched as Sandy ordered the forward spring and headlines let go and all the lines aft except the spring. After warning the after line party to keep the lines clear of the propellers, he ordered the engine half ahead to meet the current. Then the forward breast line was let go and the bow started to swing out as the current pressed between the berth and ship.

'Starboard 15,' Sandy ordered. Then he ordered the remaining spring line aft let go. Finally, the ship was free and the gap widened as she came off the berth.

'Take her over to the other side, then we'll head directly up towards the anchor position.' Sandy ordered the engine full ahead and gave the course. Harry saw that MacNab had the wheel hard over to starboard as she fought against the current and was just about to make a remark when Sandy came into the wheelhouse and ordered the thrusters to starboard to assist the steering.

The ship now started to come onto the required course and MacNab eased the wheel. At that moment another series of explosions were heard from the town close to the berth. Over the houses came a cloud of yellow dust.

'Just in time, I think,' said Harry. 'I'll take her now.'

'Do you want me to go forward?' asked Sandy.

'No, the 3rd Mate can handle it. Probably the first time he's done a standing moor. Set up the anchor position on the radar. God, it's good to get away and get some fresh air in the ship, even though it's not far. Give me course and distances to the anchor position. I'll run up 500 feet from that and drop the port anchor then drop back to the position, then head out to starboard and drop the starboard anchor. We'll bring her up with eight shackles on each anchor and hopefully 45 degrees between the anchors. Let the 3rd Mate know what we're doing and tell him when he lets the port anchor go to keep the chain slack. I'm not too bothered about absolute accuracy. There's nothing in the way.'

The ship continued to steam up the river against the current and worked her way to the far side where she straightened her course and headed for the anchor position. The port anchor was let go with a roar as the chain left the chain locker, then ceasing as the anchor found the bottom and the brake was put on. With the engine stopped, the ship fell back. The engine was started again and the ship moved into position for the starboard anchor to be dropped. With both anchors on the bottom, the chain was adjusted to even out the amount on each anchor.

'Hold on at that,' ordered Harry. Silence descended as they waited to see how the ship settled.

'Current's not too bad here,' said Sandy.

'Yes, she should hopefully hold.'

Graham reported that both cables were moderately tight and holding. Harry was watching the visual bearings from the centre gyro repeater and Sandy was watching the radar. They looked at each other and nodded.

'Good,' said Harry. 'Full anchor watches of course.' He rang the engine room. 'That's it, Peter,' he said. 'We're anchored. I'll ring finish with engines but I want them on 15 minutes' notice just in case. Rain is expected soon and that will increase the current tomorrow.' He listened for a moment then put the phone down.

'Peter is going to try to work in shifts all night. We'll have an update tomorrow morning. When you're finished, come on down. Jake can square away the bridge.' He looked at the clock. 'He's on watch anyway.'

Harry went down to his cabin and found Carole waiting for him.

'I'm sorry, Carole. I haven't had time to see you.'

'I know, Harry. Don't worry.'

'How are things below?'

'Surprisingly, well. These soldiers are very different to the others we've come across. They are disciplined. Bloody cold though. You get the feeling they're like coiled snakes all set to strike. Just like their Colonel. I've patched up those who needed it. Nothing too serious.'

'What about your other patient?'

'She's getting near her time. There may be complications but we will see.'

Sandy appeared. Seeing him, Carole said she would head off. 'No, Carole, stay. Come on in both of you.'

He went to the fridge and took out three beers. They nodded and he passed them out.

'The plan, if it can be called that, is that we remain here until the ship is repaired. Then hopefully if he's still here, we will get the pilot and sail down river to Boma on Saturday morning first light. We will get to Boma around noon, where we will go alongside and land all our passengers. Then, once that is done we will resume our passage to the pilot station at Banana, drop the pilot and head on to Hull.

'What if we don't get a pilot?' asked Sandy.

'Then we have to take ourselves down river.'

'Not so easy with the sandbanks, and the buoys missing or out of position.'

'I don't think we have much choice. The main problem will be after Boma and I hope that we can get a pilot at Boma. Will you be all right at Boma, Carole?'

'Yes. There is a mission, in fact several north of Boma. If I can get my people there then they should be safe, at least far safer than here.'

'Is everything else all right below?'

Carole shrugged. 'All peaceful at present.'

'Sandy, Monique is presently berthed in the Cadet's cabin.'

Sandy shrugged. 'If he was on a cruise ship he'd be screwing himself stupid anyway, so why not here?'

Carole laughed. 'Monique is certainly far happier with Jake than on her own. She is quite shy you know.'

'Strange considering her background,' said Harry. 'I have the impression that you both think we should leave things alone. Fine, provided there are no problems. We have far more important things to concern ourselves with. From now on the ship is under seagoing routine and that includes the crew beer issue and bar opening times. Anything else?' They both shook their heads. 'Good. Sandy, get the crew together in the messroom and I'll tell them what's going on.'

'Give me five minutes, Captain,' Sandy said as he left.

Carole went to Harry and putting her arms around his neck pressed herself against him. 'I know we didn't plan for this, but we do have another night together,' she said.

'You'd better believe it,' he said kissing her.

When Harry arrived in the messroom, most of the crew were there except for the engine room crowd. The buzz died down as Harry entered.

'I won't keep you long. I just wanted to tell you what's going on, although you probably know most of it. As you know we now have an assorted collection of passengers on board and amongst them are soldiers of the Presidential Guard and their families. We had no alternative but to take them on board; their Colonel made that very clear. We have the engine parts and the repairs should be finished by Friday, at which time we will depart down the river, stopping at Boma on the way to disembark our passengers and land the vehicles off the afterdeck. Then on to Hull.

'By agreement with the Colonel, the soldiers except four guards have voluntarily made their arms secure. You will have seen that we have been making some alterations to the boats. This was in case we had to go through the Cauldron with only one engine and no tugs. Luckily, we now have the engine spares so we don't have to worry about that. That's about it, gentlemen.'

The Bosun stood. 'Thank you, Sir. We'll make sure that peace is kept while they are here. The soldiers are not bad so far.' Some of the crew murmured in agreement.

'Thanks, Bosun. Let's hope it will be over soon and we can get on our way home.'

With that he left the messroom and headed for Carole's cabin. He tapped on the door and waited for her to open it. As soon as she appeared at the door he knew something was up.

'You can't trust those bastards, Harry.'

'Which bastards? I seem to have a few around me at the moment.'

'The Presidential Guard; they were Mobutu's special thugs.'

'I don't have much choice.'

'You know what they did don't you?'

'Nothing to do with me, Carole.'

'But they were Mobutu's men. They looted and murdered on his orders.'

'There are a few shipowners that can give them a run for their money.'

'This isn't funny, Harry.' Carole looked distressed.

'Look, Carole,' he said. 'We're seamen. We go round the world and end up in places where dictators rule, where there are riots, revolutions, piracy, murder and mayhem. We berth in ports where corruption, bribery and mismanagement are normal. We are threatened, imprisoned, abandoned by our shipowners and no one gives a damn about us. Even in your 'land of the free' we are often banned from going ashore or imprisoned. And when the contract ends, there are no medals, no thanks, no bonuses, no bands playing to welcome us back. We just go to wherever we call home and wait for the next ship. Don't expect me to get worked up over one more son of a bitch.'

He put his hands on her shoulders and looked into her eyes. 'Carole,' he said softly, 'we have enough problems. As someone once said to me, it pays the rent.'

She looked up at him and blinked the tears from her eyes. 'I'm sorry, Harry. You have enough to worry about without me adding to it.'

'True', said Harry,' but then it's nice having you around.' He put his arm around her shoulder. 'I know what you mean, and no I won't trust them as far as I can throw them, but let's get the ship down to Boma and get rid of them as soon as we can, and then we can sort ourselves out. Now I suggest we go down and see what the Cook's managed to rustle up for dinner, then go and screw ourselves silly.'

'Harry, you're such a romantic bastard!'

Thursday 22 May

Chapter 10

The morning brought a dull grey sky heavy with rain clouds. The river looked sullen and dark and the air was damp with heat. The ship moved easily to her anchors with the current causing a constant murmur of water as it washed past the hull. Harry had finished breakfast and was sitting at his desk trying to catch up with paperwork that had been left over the last few days.

His phone went.

'Bridge, Captain. There's a boat approaching.'

'Shit,' said Harry. 'I was hoping they would be busy with the town and leave us alone. He quickly went up the stairway to the bridge. When he arrived, it was already crowded with Sandy, Graham, the Colonel and the four soldiers of the bridge guard. Graham handed Harry a pair of binoculars.

'It's one of the tugs, Sir, and there are a lot of soldiers on board.

Harry turned to the Colonel. 'Have your men ready, but no shooting. Not yet anyway. I just want to keep them away, understood?

'Understood, Captain,' the Colonel replied. 'But I will alert my other men.' He called out to one of the soldiers who nodded and went down. He looked at Harry, 'Just in case.'

Harry nodded and turned back to watch the approaching tug. 'Get me the loud hailer.' Graham grabbed it from the bridge front and switching it on gave it a quick blow to test.

Harry went out onto the bridge wing. The tug was decrepit. A battered black hull with rust streaks down the white bridge front and black smoke billowing out of the funnel. He looked at the name 'Malamba' on the bow.

'Malamba. Malamba. What is your business?' There was no reply, but Harry could see that the bow and bridge was packed with soldiers. 'Malamba, keep away from my ship.'

Sandy was at his side. 'We can't let those soldiers on board, Captain. It will be mayhem.'

'I have no intention of doing that,' said Harry. 'Colonel,' he called, 'I want you to fire a few shots in the air and bring your men out on the wing so they can see we mean business. Harry had hardly finished before the blast of gunfire cracked out. The tug veered and Harry could see a struggle on the bridge of the tug.

'It would seem that the crew are not too anxious about coming alongside,' Sandy said.

Harry again called. 'Malamba, state your business, but stay away from my ship.'

The tug was now about 50 metres off the ship. Then Harry saw the blue berets.

'There are UN soldiers on board mixed up with Kabila's rabble,' said the Colonel, who was now also on the bridge wing. The Colonel spoke into the handset he was carrying. 'Just to show them we mean business,' he said to Harry and pointed down to the deck. Harry looked down and saw that all of the guard were lining the side with their weapons ready. Then there was a whining noise.

'What's that?' said Harry.

'It's the turret of the AML swinging round,' replied the Colonel.

'Christ!' said Harry. 'We're not starting a war!'

'Better to warn them, Captain.'

The tug was now 30 metres from the side and Harry could see those on the bridge clearly. He passed the binoculars to Sandy.

'Recognise anyone?' Sandy looked. 'What do you know, it's our chum the Lieutenant.'

Harry called across, 'What do you want, Lieutenant.'

'It is not Lieutenant. It is Major now,' the officer called back.

'Where is the other Major?' shouted Harry.

'He has been recalled. He was not doing his job properly. He lost too many weapons. I am now in charge.'

'Fuck,' said Sandy under his breath.

'Use the VHF,' shouted Harry. 'Channel 12.' He turned to Graham. 'Put it on the bridge speakers and start recording.' Graham went through to the bridge and after a moment called out to Harry that it was ready. Harry picked up the bridge wing microphone.

'Malamba, this is Sea Quest.' The voice of the Major filled the bridge.

'Captain, I am speaking on behalf of the UN forces. You have UN weapons on board your ship that were taken illegally and they must be returned.' Harry looked puzzled at Sandy.

'What does he mean?' Sandy shrugged.

'We have none of your weapons on board, Major,' said Harry. There was a pause then another voice came over the air. This had a distinctly different accent.

'This is General Mende of the New Free Democratic Government of President Kalimba. Captain, we are the advance force for the Free Democratic Government. Tomorrow, Matadi will be completely occupied by our Army. We have occupied the port and the airport and are now the legal authority for the port. Captain, you are ordered to bring your ship back alongside.'

'Sorry, General. I can't do that. The engine is under repair.'

'Then the tugs will assist you.'

'General, I have cleared your port and will sail as soon as the repair is completed.'

'No ship is allowed to sail, Captain. You have Mobutu war criminals on board. They are to be arrested for treason against the people. You also are holding citizens of the republic of the Congo and they must also be landed.'

'General, all the people on board are passengers who have asked for transportation to Boma.'

'Boma is under our control, Captain. We are now the legitimate government of the Congo. I am ordering you to return to Matadi. Once we have taken the criminals and passengers off, you will be allowed to proceed. I give you my word. We will provide a pilot and the tugs will assist.'

'One moment, General.' Harry switched off the microphone and turned to the others on the bridge. 'You all heard, Boma is under the rebels,' he said looking at the Colonel. 'But you knew that already didn't you?' The Colonel shrugged. 'It doesn't matter now, Captain.'

'It will if we hand you over,' said Sandy.

The Colonel looked at Sandy. 'I have 20 soldiers that say you cannot do that. Anyway what do you think will happen to all of you and the pygmies? They will kill them, and there is no guarantee that they will not kill you all as well unless I have killed you first. You have no protection, Captain. Your government is not going to do anything for a few seamen and anyway you are not under the British Flag any more. That gives them the perfect excuse to do nothing.' The loudspeaker crackled again.

'Well, Captain. Are you coming back to the port?'

Harry looked at the others. 'We need time.' He switched on the microphone. 'General, if you guarantee that no one will be harmed, I will bring my ship alongside but not today. We cannot heave our anchors until the repairs are completed. We have to put the engine back in order tonight and we will come alongside in the morning.' There was silence for a moment.

'I will put my soldiers on board then, Captain, to assist you with the criminals.'

'No, General. I cannot have that,' said Harry. 'We will come in the morning and then I will welcome the assistance of the tugs.'

Again there was silence.

'We will be waiting, Captain. Just in case you are thinking of trying to sail, the bridge across the river is now guarded with troops and tanks. If you try to go under you will be blown out of the water.'

'I understand, General.'

'That is good, Captain. This way is better for all of us. I have someone else who wishes to speak with you.'

'This is Major Wabudeya, Captain. I will also be waiting for our stolen weapons. I look forward to seeing you again.' With that the loudspeaker went dead. They watched the tug backing away and turning towards Matadi, black smoke pouring from its funnel.

'It keeps getting worse,' said Sandy.

'It certainly doesn't give us many alternatives does it?' said Harry. 'We'd better talk about this. Let's go down to my office.'

They entered the office and Harry sat at his desk.

'Sit,' he said. 'Now before we start, what is that Major on about with his UN weapons? Colonel, do you have any?'

'No, Captain. I am as surprised as you are.'

'Sandy?' Sandy was looking down refusing to look at Harry. 'Sandy?' Harry asked again. Sandy looked up.

'We may have some items on board, Captain.'

There was silence for a moment. 'I'm waiting,' said Harry.

'You know when we captured that truck?' Harry nodded. 'Well there was some equipment in the back.'

'What kind of equipment?'

'Boxes and such.'

'What was in the boxes?'

'Well, there were some weapons.'

'With UN markings?'

'Yes.'

'And?'

'We decided to load them.'

'Who is we?'

'Well I did.'

'So you on your own decided to bring UN weapons on board the ship. Is that right?'

'Yes,' said Sandy.

'And no one else knew about this?'

'Well there were a few others.'

'A few others. Let me guess, the Bosun, Delilah and all of the crew. Is that about right?'

'Well...'

'Don't fucking "well" me Chief Officer! It seems that I am now carrying stolen UN weapons on board my ship. Did you get that? MY SHIP!' Harry exploded. 'And every bastard on board knew about this except me, the Captain! Is that about right?'

Sandy looked miserable. 'It would seem that way, Captain.'

'Fucking right it would. You bunch of lunatics! What the hell do you think we are, a battleship?'

'Captain,' interjected the Colonel. 'We might need them.'

'You!' shouted Harry, turning towards him. 'I haven't even started with you. You force your way onto my ship with your gang of thugs and now I have the whole rebel army after our guts.' The Colonel sat calmly.

Harry pointed a finger at Sandy, 'Where are these weapons?'

'In the forecastle store.'

'Show me,' he said getting up. 'And get the Bosun and Delilah along. Colonel you come as well. I don't trust you alone.'

Harry got up and stormed out. The Colonel looked at Sandy. Sandy shook his head.

'Don't say anything. He's pissed off and rightly so. He'll calm down though. I've seen it before. You follow him and I'll go and get the others.'

The Colonel followed Harry out of the accommodation and across the short foredeck to the store. Harry undogged the weather door and, entering, turned the light on. The deck was covered with cases of differing sizes some stacked on each other.

'Bloody hell, it's an armoury!' Harry exclaimed. He looked at the Colonel. 'Can you see what we've got here?' The Colonel stepped forward and bent down to read the writing on the cases.

'Enough to fight a medium sized war, Captain,' he said. Then he exclaimed 'Look here!' The Colonel pointed at four long cases at the back. 'What are they?' asked Harry.

'Stingers,' said the Colonel. 'Heat seekers as well. Anti-aircraft but they can be used for ground targets as well, firing by sight. No wonder they want these back.' He looked at the other boxes. 'Grenades, grenade launchers, anti-tank ammunition. There's even a mortar as well and the ammunition for it.'

Behind them Sandy appeared with the Bosun and Delilah. Harry turned.

'You two were involved in this?' he asked. They both nodded. 'Did you realise what you were doing?'

'They were acting under my orders,' Sandy spoke up.

'Shut up,' said Harry. 'The fucking blind leading the bloody stupid. Right, what's done is done. We now have to find a way out of this mess. I want you all in the officers' mess. Bosun, give Peter and Chalkie my compliments, and get them up as well. Never mind what they are doing. Delilah, get the 2nd Mate. Perhaps you can all manage that without fucking up. Oh, and get Carole as well.'

Chapter 11

Harry looked at everyone. It was a complete mix of experience and emotions. Peter, in particular, looked worried. Somehow this disparate team had to be welded together to get the ship out, or people were going to die. They did not know of the threat that the Colonel held over them all.

'Let me run through it as I see the situation. Peter, bear with me. Things have been happening while you all have been slaving away below. We are now prohibited from sailing by the so-called "new government," which are the current bunch of thugs holding Matadi. They want the Colonel here and his men who are our bunch of thugs.' The Colonel shrugged. 'They also want the UN weapons that are on board and they want the pygmies off the ship. To enforce that, they have blocked our passage out by manning the bridge with their army. We are supposed to go alongside tomorrow morning. If we do, what will be the consequences? Carole, you first.'

'The men will all be killed and the women raped and then killed. The female children will be raped, then all children will be killed and the plumpest ones will be eaten.' There was stunned silence.

'Ask the Colonel. He has killed enough of them,' she added.

'Colonel?'

The Colonel sighed. 'Doctor, no matter what you think, I have not raped, killed or eaten pygmies. I was too busy killing rebels. Yes, Captain, they will kill them. They will also kill me, my men and their families, which of course I will not allow to happen. And you are not in too good a position yourself, especially from the UN Major.'

'Sandy?'

'It is obvious that the UN Major was selling weapons to the rebels. His Major got the blame for them going missing and now this guy either wants them back to get the money for them or to return them to the UN stores. He is unlikely to report this to the UN. Either way he doesn't want us talking.'

'Thanks for that. Frankly I would welcome the proper UN right now. I could hand you over and be on our way. Any other thoughts?'

'Can't go alongside for sure. What about if we stay here?' Sandy said.

Delilah chipped in. 'When I came up, there were soldiers on the river bank. There must be a track running along from Matadi. If they can get troops there then vehicles can probably go there as well. If I was them I would get artillery or tanks up there.'

Harry turned to the Colonel. 'What have they got?'

'Not much in the way of artillery. They prefer mobility, maybe some M116s 75 mm. But they do have tanks.'

'What kind?'

'Best they will have are T62s 115 mm, range 1,500 metres but I don't think they would bring their tanks up there. They will keep them on the bridge.'

'There is another problem,' said Harry. 'In the morning whatever naval forces they have at Boma will head for us. Do you know what they have there, Colonel?'

'Last reports I saw was a couple of Shanghai Class patrol boats with twin 57 mm guns and a couple of torpedo boats. There will also be some small craft with machine guns.'

'What the hell do you want with torpedo boats on the river, Colonel?'

He shrugged. 'When weapons are offered we take them. The Chinese have been good to us.'

'You can be sure they were good to themselves as well,' Harry replied. 'What's the state of these boats?'

'There are Chinese technicians in Boma just to keep them in business so I presume they are operational.'

'If all their boats are working, they will be the first navy in the world to achieve that,' said Harry. 'Either way, we can't stay here.'

'I can't believe that you are really thinking of sailing the ship through all of this.' It was Peter. He was now standing, looking angry. 'This is madness. We're a merchant ship for Christ's sake not a bloody warship.'

'There's no alternative, Peter.' said Harry.

'Of course there is. We go alongside. They won't kill us.'

'What about the civilians on board, Peter?' asked Carole.

Peter turned to her. 'Carole, I know you're concerned about the pygmies and I am sorry about them, but the Captain's only duty is to his crew. At the moment he is putting us all into danger. No Captain! What you're thinking of doing is stupid and dangerous.'

'What about help?' asked Carole.

'What do you mean?'

'I mean from your government or the US government; I am an American citizen.'

'Don't think the Irish government will send a gunboat,' said Sandy.

'Neither will Vanu Vatu,' said Harry. 'Don't forget we're no longer under the British Flag, not that they would do anything anyway. Your bunch may do something Carole, but certainly not by tomorrow. No, we are on our own. We can't go alongside and we can't stay here. We have to go. Peter, when will your repairs be finished?'

'They won't be if this nonsense is going ahead.'

'That's enough!' shouted the Colonel, glaring at Peter. 'You idiot, you don't understand. You come from your nice homes, with lawns and supermarkets, you get your thrills from movies and then go home to your nice comfortable beds. This is real. This is not some television quiz show. Should we open the box or shouldn't we? The box is already open. Hundreds of thousands of people have been massacred in the country. Here in this town they are dying, hacked down with machetes, their women raped in front of them. The madness will get worse tomorrow until they are satiated by the blood. And you, you lunatic, want to stay here? Let me tell you something, my friend. Even if the Captain did want to stay, he knows that I would kill you all one by one until he sailed. Starting with her.' He pointed at Carole. 'My men are armed again and it will stay that way from now on.'

The Colonel sat down, breathing heavily, his eyes wide and bloodshot, sweat dripping from his brow. Peter stared, his eyes wide with shock. The sheer menace of the Colonel filled the room.

'Calm down, everyone,' Harry said. 'As you hear, we have no alternative but to sail. Now, Peter, once again, when will the engine be repaired.

'Not until tomorrow morning at the earliest Captain.' Peter was still dazed.

'Right, then we go on one engine. Colonel what will those tanks be like on the bridge?'

'They have night sights but one good point in our favour is that they have poor depression capability.'

'Which means what?' said Sandy.

'It means they cannot depress their gun much below the horizontal.'

'Which means,' said Harry catching on, 'that while they can fire at us at full range, as we get nearer the bridge they cannot hit us, right?'

'That's right. However, they will have grenade launchers and machine guns and be able to drop grenades onto you as you pass under.'

'That won't sink the ship,' said Harry.

'Make a mess of my decks though,' said Sandy.

'We are not defenceless, Captain,' said the Colonel. 'We will have our weapons ready and we can use the UN grenade launchers.'

'Yes, but we are firing up and they are firing down and probably with a lot more than we have. The biggest danger will come after we have passed under and the tanks are ready.'

'But we can be ready with the anti-tank launchers.'

Harry looked around at them all.

'We go tonight,' he said. 'Sandy, this afternoon, get the crew and close down all the deadlights. Put up the weather shutters on the bridge, but leave the centre and side windows clear, I have to see something. All deck lighting must be off, lower all the boats down into the water and put them on boat ropes on the port side so they can't be seen from the shore. Once it gets dark the Cadet can take the FRC quietly around the ship and look for any chinks in our lighting. I want a complete blackout. Can you fix that Bosun?'

'Sure Captain.'

'What are deadlights, Captain? asked the Colonel.

'They are metal covers that protect the portholes and windows from heavy seas. Many ships have them on their lower decks but ships of this type, which are low down and may often be in heavy seas, have them for all front and side ports and windows.

'We'll get back down below,' said Peter. 'The sooner we get started the sooner the repairs will be finished. Come on Chalkie.'

'He's not a happy man,' said Sandy when they had gone.

'I don't blame him,' said Harry. 'He's got a wife and kids waiting in suburbia. There will be others as well, which is why I am going to give them the choice of leaving the ship.'

The Colonel looked startled. 'Are you joking, Captain?'

'No, I'm not. Those who do not want to go, I will land this evening on the other bank opposite Matadi and they can see if they can make their way up into the hills until this is over.'

'That's mad.'

'It might be, but at least I have to give them that choice. We are not at war, Colonel. Until that day, merchant seamen are civilians. They didn't sign up for this and it is not their quarrel or fault that we are in this situation. Don't worry. I don't think many will want to go so there will be enough to sail the ship but you must not stop those leaving who want to. Is that understood?' The Colonel stared at Harry for a moment and then nodded.

There was a tap at the door. Harry looked up and saw it was Jake's girlfriend, Monique, standing there.

'I am sorry,' she said. 'I have come for Carole.'

Carole got up instantly. 'What's wrong?'

'It's the woman in the hospital. I think she is having her baby.'

'Coming now,' said Carole. 'See you later boys,' and she dashed out.

'Makes the day complete,' said Sandy.

Harry spread the charts out on the table. 'Let's see if we can have a better day tomorrow.'

'Here we are,' he said tapping the table on the side of the chart. 'Off the chart. Ships are not supposed to go where we are just now. No point as there is nothing here for them. But this is what I am interested in,' he said, pointing to the berths at Matadi.

'You're not thinking of going alongside are you?' said Sandy

'No, but right here at the end of the jetty is where the tugs are parked.'

'So what? We can't use them.'

'Who says we can't?'

'What? You mean steal them? We don't even know if we could start them, never mind the crews being on board.'

'No Sandy, not take them, use them as decoys.'

'Decoys?'

'Just think a minute. Look at where they are berthed, if they were let go they would drift with the current right under the bridge. Now, how do you think those guards on the bridge will react at night with those tugs passing under?'

Sandy peered at the chart intently, 'Jesus, do you think that we can let them go?'

'Why not? We have the boats and we are seamen if nothing else. Colonel what do you think?'

The Colonel had been silent listening intently. He stood by Harry looking at the chart.

'When the tugs are let go I will be level with them on the far side of the river. We will go a little slower to allow them to attract all the attention and then we will pass under the bridge near the bank on the opposite side.'

The Colonel looked up. 'What time?' he asked.

'I want to pass under the bridge in the dark and be well clear before dawn.' He traced his finger along the river from the Cauldron. 'We know that any of those warships which are operational will be ready or on their way at dawn. There will also be local traffic on the river which we want to avoid. This means we must be somewhere else.' His finger stopped moving along the chart. 'Here.'

They all peered forward.

'That's the Angolan side of the river,' said Sandy.

'That's right,' replied Harry. 'If you look here, just at the turn of the river there is Point Tridente. Just beyond that there is a small creek. There is a chance we can get the ship in there. The river is 1 mile wide at that point. With chaos going on at the bridge, those warships will know that we have sailed and they will be searching for us as they come up the river. I believe that they will mostly concentrate on the Zaire side. From Boma that means they have 28 miles of river bank to search until they get to the bridge, that's if they don't spot us on the way. That's 28 miles against the current. They will want to get back by dusk so it doesn't give them much time. When they get to the bridge, their first instinct will be that they have missed us. That should send them back to Boma at full speed.'

There was silence around the table for a moment.

'Christ, Captain, there's a lot to go wrong,' said Sandy

'Then are we any worse off?' Again silence.

'What about helicopters?' It was the Colonel. They all turned and stared. 'There are helicopters at Boma airport. At least a couple will be there and operational.'

'Colonel, if you were sure that the warships were going to find us, a theoretically unarmed merchant ship, would you bother launching the helicopters?'

'Maybe not straight away, but if the ships don't find you then yes.'

'Would you search the Angolan river banks?'

'Only after searching the Zaire side.'

'Then all the more reason why we must be tucked away in that creek by dawn.'

'What about planes?' said Sandy. 'If there is an airport they must have those.'

The Colonel spoke. 'All the operational military planes were pulled back to defend Kinshasa, but that airport is only a small airstrip and there are no jets stationed there. The main problem is that the helicopters are also maintained by the Chinese and they are well armed.' They stood looking at the chart. 'It could work,' said the Colonel, 'but what about getting past Boma?'

'Let's deal with this bit first,' said Harry. 'We might not have to worry about the next bit.'

Sandy grimaced. 'I'll say this, Captain. It's always interesting sailing with you.'

'Vijay, get me the times of nautical twilight and sunrise tomorrow please. And also ask the 3rd Mate to come here.'

The Colonel moved away from the table. 'I'd better go and speak to my people,' he said. 'When are you going to tell your crew?'

'After they've had lunch.'

'I would like to be there.'

Harry nodded and the Colonel left. Sandy looked at Harry. 'That man is not just a bastard but he's crazy as well.' Harry shrugged. 'At least for the moment he's on our side.'

'It's like saying a snake is on your side,' said Sandy. 'Getting back to the problem in hand, navigating a river that you don't know in the dark with a strong current and only one engine is very risky.'

'We can do it,' said Harry.

'Can I mention one small problem?' asked Sandy.

'Go ahead.'

'You originally planned to get through the Cauldron in daylight on the side nearest Matadi. That was bad enough without tugs, but now you are going to go under the bridge on the other side, and from where I am standing, you will then have to angle the ship parallel to the bridge, right across the current and cross the Cauldron in the worst place to get out through the gap. Another small point, we will probably have the whole of the rebel army firing at us.'

Harry shrugged. 'We have the two daughter craft for tugs.' Sandy looked steadily at Harry.

'I can do it,' said Harry.

'There will be a lot of people hoping you can.'

Just then Vijay came back accompanied by Graham. 'Come and join us, Graham,' said Harry. 'You have probably heard a little of what is going on here.'

'Yes, Captain.'

'Nautical twilight just before 0400, Captain, and sunrise will be 0445,' said Vijay.

Harry bent over the chart again. 'It's going to rain soon. The current should be up to 6 knots at the berth tonight which will give the tugs about 10 minutes before they go under the berth. Agree Vijay?' Vijay nodded. 'So if we hit the tugs at 0230 that would give us an hour and a half to get under the bridge through the Cauldron and up to the creek at just about twilight, which we will need to see something of where we are going.' Harry looked at the two junior officers. 'The plan is for you two to be in the daughter craft which will act as tugs to help get us through the Cauldron. How do you feel about this?' he asked. 'You don't have to go if you don't want to. You're not paid enough for this and I won't order you to do it.'

They looked at each other. Vijay spoke. 'We will do our best, Captain.'

'Right, the rescue boat will be used to get to the berth and that will leave the two daughter craft for tugs.'

'I'm going,' said Sandy.

'Going where?'

'In the boat.'

'No you're bloody well not.'

'Yes I bloody well am.' He saw Harry's face darken. 'Captain, listen. I have worked with boats in the dark before in Ireland. I know what I am doing.'

'Sandy, this is a game for younger men.'

'It's also a game for wise heads. We don't know what we will find when we get there. Once we let those tugs go I can be back here on board before you go under the bridge. We will have 15 minutes to get back.' Harry looked hard at Sandy then he sighed. 'You take care of yourself. I need you back here.'

Sandy smiled. 'You don't think I will let you go alone do you?'

'Now, crews. I don't want to touch the engine department unless absolutely necessary. It is essential that I have both engines as soon as possible. So, in the two daughter craft will be Vijay with 2nd Coxn Pat MacNab and one of the OSs, take Henry Duncan. Graham, you will have the Chief Coxn, Olav and OS James Stewart. Sandy, you take Delilah and a couple of the Colonel's men. Bosun that leaves you with Jim Bailey and George Huggins for the forecastle party. Andy MacBride will be running the davits for launching and recovering. I'll make do with Jake on the bridge until we get under way. Everyone happy with that? Good, no dissent.'

Harry looked at his watch.

'Hell, I didn't realise the time. Let's get this cleared away and let people have lunch. After lunch, Bosun, assemble all the crew in the messroom.'

Sandy bent over the chart again. 'What I intend to do is head at an angle towards the berth,' he said, tracing a line from the ship towards the jetty, 'allowing for the current, and then when we near the top end of the berth, I'll cut the engine, come alongside and let the current take us down the jetty to where the tugs are.'

'What about guards?'

'If there are any, they won't be anywhere except near the tugs. There are no other ships alongside. Hopefully in this rain, the guards will be sheltering on the tugs as well.'

'But if they aren't?'

'Then we have to take care of them. Quietly. I should think the Colonel's lads are pretty handy with their knives.'

'What about the lines?'

'The only lines we will have to worry about will be the headlines. If they are a ragtag bunch, they will only put out the minimum head and stern lines. I am thinking one stern line and a max of two headlines. Don't need springs anyway with a constant head current. With the force of the current we won't be able to slip the headlines so we will have to cut through them. I'll take a saw for that. Far easier than anything else for cutting a tight rope.'

'What about if they are using wires?'

'I doubt it. Buggers are probably too lazy to handle wire, but just in case we'll take hacksaws. It will take longer, but Peter's got some heavy duty ones and if we use wire cutters to assist then it shouldn't be too much problem. If we have the rescue boat near the bows, we can be away even as the boats start drifting away.'

Harry stood looking at the chart. 'The rain will hide you from the bridge. How will you find us?'

'Don't worry,' replied Sandy. 'You've got the beer!'

Harry laughed. 'OK Sandy. You make me believe that this can work. Mind you, we haven't asked any of the crew yet whether they will go.'

'That's going to be interesting.'

Chapter 12

The messroom was crowded and noisy with a thick fug of cigarette smoke in the air. Most of the crew were sitting, except for Peter and his men who were standing in their oily work clothing opposite the door. At the back Harry noticed the Colonel's Lieutenant and some of his men. Carole had taken a seat at one of the tables with the officers. She looked tired. Harry went over to her.

'How did it go?'

'It was hard, but you now have another female passenger.'

'We'll talk later,' he said and stood back.

The room was quietening down now. Harry put his hand up to still the last of the talkers. 'Many of you probably know what is going on but I will put it all together for you. The rebels now control Matadi. God knows what mayhem is going on there but we are better out here. On board we have the Doctor and the pygmies from the mission. That is my doing. We also have the remnants of the Republican Guard and their families under their Colonel. That is their doing. They demanded to board and we had no choice. We also have a quantity of weapons on board stolen from the UN Ugandan Force who want them back. That is your doing as it seems that everyone knew about this but me. We have been given an ultimatum. We either go alongside tomorrow, then after handing over all these people to what I am assured will be their death and once the weapons have been removed, take whatever they decide is coming to us. Or, we can try to escape.' He held his hand up as he saw some of the crew raise their hands.

'Wait till I have finished then we can have questions. We cannot stay here. They will have guns or tanks up on the banks opposite us. They have two tugs that they can fill with soldiers, and whatever works in their Navy will be heading up to us in first light from Boma. Now, regardless of the soldiers and their actions, if we do hand them over, I will not be responsible for the deaths of them or their families. Nor will I be responsible for the deaths of the pygmies, so no matter what is decided here, I am going to try to take this ship down the river tonight.'

There was a buzz of talking and movement as those in the room turned to converse with each other. Harry again held his hand up.

'Wait, I haven't finished. It will not be easy. The bridge is guarded, probably heavily, with troops, tanks and machine guns. We will not know until we get there. We have a plan to get under the bridge. The tugs will need to be let go and drift under the bridge, and at the same time we will try to sneak past on the other side. It will be raining and it will be dark. I think we have a good chance. After that, I intend to hole up during daylight somewhere along the river and wait for night before passing Boma. That's the best I can tell you. Soon you will go round the ship closing down all the deadlights; tonight all non-essential lighting will be off inside the ship and all lighting on deck will be off. We have weapons and if required we will use them, especially as we have troops on board. Now before the questions come, let me say this.

This is not a warship and you are not paid for this kind of thing. I cannot morally or legally order you to sail. There is a chance that some of you may be injured or possibly killed, so this evening when it gets dark, for those who do not agree to make the Devil's Cauldron, we will arrange a boat to take you to the other side of the river. You can make your way up into the hills to join those from the town who are probably hiding out up there waiting for the thugs to finish looting the town. I cannot land you in Matadi as you know what will be waiting for you there. Now, questions.'

There was an instant uproar of noise as everyone talked at once. Harry waited a moment until he could see a few crew trying to question him.

'Quieten down!' Sandy roared. 'It's like a fucking women's tea party!' The noise dulled.

'Yes, Davy?' It was the 3rd Engineer Davy Wilson.

'What about the government? I mean our government.' The room quietened.

'Davy, the situation is that Zaire now has no government. As a result, there is no law and order in the country. It appears to be ruled by whoever is leading the biggest pack of thugs. Regardless of whether our government is going to be bothered about an old ship with a bunch of merchant seamen on board, these thugs are not going to listen to anyone. If they kill us all, what do you think will happen? I'll tell you. Nothing, except a few feeble protests and maybe a mention on page 20 in some newspaper. Anyway, there is no time. It will be over before the phones even start ringing. Then everyone will deny responsibility and it will blow away on the wind. What's a few more hundred dead in this country?'

Harry saw the Bosun's hand up. 'Yes, Bosun.'

'Captain, I can see a chance of us getting under the bridge, but what about getting through the Cauldron, then down the river past Boma to the sea?'

'Bosun, there are no guarantees, but once under that bridge, I'll get the ship through the Cauldron and down the river. As to Boma, we will have to think about that tomorrow.'

Sandy spoke up. 'Lads, I know the Captain well. I have sailed with him on many ships. Let me tell you, if he says he can do it, then he can. If any Captain can get us out it is him. I'm going, even if none of you are.'

The Bosun stood up and so did the deck officers. They were all calling out that they would go. Others started to stand and the noise grew again. Harry again held his hands up.

'Quiet please.' He saw Peter standing quietly looking down at the deck. He was saying nothing. 'Peter, what do you want to do?'

'Can I answer that?' It was the Colonel who had appeared in the doorway behind Harry. 'Excuse me, Captain, for intruding but I have been listening to what you have all said.' He turned to the crew placing a box on the mess table in front of him. There was now silence in the room. 'First, I know we, how can I put it, insisted that we come on your ship. If you had been in our position you would have done the same. If it had just been my soldiers, then I believe that we could, or at least some of us could, have fought our way through and escaped over the border. But not with our families. I heard what was said would happen to us if the ship goes alongside. The Lieutenant and I can assure you of that. We have no family with us. They were caught in the Palace compound before we could rescue them. We arrived after they had been caught. I will not tell you how, but they were all killed. Our wives and children. I will not let that happen to the families of my men.' There was now complete silence in the room. 'Those that go ashore will be butchered. The Captain can talk about landing you on the other side and of escaping into the hills. That is laughable. You will be as they say, 'babes in the woods'. I promise you will be dead within days.'

The room was silent. The Bosun stood.

'We have already talked about this before the meeting. We had a few questions, and these have been answered.' He looked around the room. 'I think that I can speak for all the crew. We have to get the ship through.' There was a murmuring of agreement. Harry looked at Peter and raised his eyebrow. Peter sighed and nodded.

'Then it's unanimous. We go.'

The Colonel then stepped forward and held both hands up. Slowly the noise died down. 'You mentioned your families. The Captain said that you weren't being paid enough. Let me try to help.' With that he opened the box. He tipped it forward and hundreds of crystal-like stones poured onto the table. The crew stood up and crowded round to look. 'These are gem grade natural crystal diamonds. They are each worth $5,000 on the open market. In this box are several million dollars worth of diamonds. My men have the other half of the box. Now this is your pay.'

'Holy Mary, Mother of God,' breathed Sandy. 'Will you look at that.' There was a brief silence as the crew looked on in disbelief.

Sandy spoke up again. 'Well, lads, you were all wondering what you were going to do once you were thrown off the ship onto the streets. There is your answer.'

The Bosun sat staring at the box. 'That will settle me and the wife for life.'

Others were talking of the possibilities, to pay off the mortgage, buy a shop and never sail again. Words were humming around the room. The excitement grew. Even Harry was mesmerised.

He shook his head. 'Just a moment. Let's keep our feet on the deck. This doesn't get us out. We still have to get out to sea before these are ours.'

Even Peter's face had brightened. 'That certainly makes a difference,' he said looking round at the other engine crew. 'I think I can say the same for the others,' and they nodded in agreement. 'We're off down the engine room, Harry. You'll have the engine fixed as soon as possible.' With that he led his crew past Harry. 'What time do you want the engine tonight?'

'Any time after 0100.'

'You'll have it. And the other one will be on line by tomorrow afternoon, I promise.'

'Thanks, Peter.'

Harry went over to where the officers were standing, still chattering excitedly.

'Now cool it, gentlemen. Let's talk a moment.'

Jake couldn't help himself. 'Sir, do I get a share of the diamonds?'

'Of course you do. Equal with everyone else. Now get your minds off the goodies for a moment. We have to earn them and it won't be easy. Vijay, when we heave anchor you will take one of the daughter craft and make fast on the starboard bow. Graham, take the other boat on the port bow.' Both officers nodded. 'Now the real test will be when we go under the bridge. As soon as we are under, I'll bring the ship hard round to port so that we are parallel with the cliffs at the bottom of the Cauldron and facing the exit channel. I don't know what the current will be like but with this rain it will be strong. You must get my bow round and pull her as hard as you can to help get her to the exit before we are swept onto the cliffs.

Now look at me, both of you. It will be touch and go; it will be dark and you will have no lights. You cannot see the whirlpools but they are there. If you get into one, the only way to get out is to slack down on your line and turn the boat up river and give her all you've got. Once you are clear you can pick up on the line again. And finally you could be under fire from those bastards on the bridge. I hope you won't as they most probably will be concentrating on the ship and we have the rain but you never know. Do you understand?'

'Yes, Captain,' they chorused.

'Keep in constant touch with the bridge. Jake, you will be bridge officer tonight until Sandy gets back. You will have to take the wheel while we are heaving the anchor. There's no one else. Once the Bosun is on the bridge, apart from the radar you will be running the communications.'

'Yes, Sir.'

'Bosun,' he called. 'You will heave anchors tonight, then make the two boats fast. It will be a long job heaving the anchors as we can only do one at a time.'

'Do you want me to grease the cables as they come in to keep the noise down?'

'No. I thought about that but the rain will deaden the noise and anyway, if we are slipping the tugs and going under the bridge just after them, it doesn't matter if they do hear us getting under way. In fact it may help. One more thing, no lights are to be shown. Once that's done, come up onto the bridge and take the wheel. Have one seaman stay on the forecastle in case a line goes and we have to put another out.'

'Aye aye, Captain. I'll make sure that there are another two lines faked out ready.'

'Now, after finishing the preparations, I want you all to get some rest. It's going to be a long night. We'll call everyone at 0115. You will all come up to the bridge for a final briefing. We will start heaving anchors then and the rescue boat will leave the ship at 0200.' They all nodded. 'Sandy, are you happy as to who is doing what, where and to whom?'

'Everyone is briefed, Captain, except the Colonel here,' he said indicating the Colonel who was still standing behind the Captain.

Harry turned. 'You certainly know how to make an entrance.' The Colonel waved his hand.

'Just diamonds, Captain. Money is the best persuader in the world.'

Sandy laughed. 'I'll put the diamonds in your cabin, Captain. Don't want any sticky fingers in them do we. See you all later.'

'Colonel, I will want two of your men in the boat.'

'I will send my Lieutenant and another good man. They won't let you down.'

'If there is any gunfire, Colonel, the game is up. They must understand that they are there solely to protect my crew while they let the tugs go.'

'I know that, Captain. Don't worry, they are very good with their knives. I want to raid your weapons stores and get out what we need to deal with any enemy fire from the bridge.'

'Go ahead, Colonel. Where will you be when we start the passage?'

'I will be by our AML ready to return fire if required. I want to place Delilah up above the ship's bridge with an RPG also. One of my soldiers will be manning the machine gun there.'

'Colonel, you take charge of the ship's defence. Do as you wish, but the rules of engagement are that we do not open fire unless we are directly fired at. Hopefully in the dark with the rain they won't be able to see us and I want to keep it that way.'

'I understand, Captain.'

The room was clearing now as crew went about their various tasks or to their cabins. Harry went over to where Carole and Andy were talking. Jake was with them talking to his girlfriend.

'Were you involved with the baby?' Harry asked Andy.

'They all were,' Carole replied, 'and just as well. It was not easy.'

'How are they?'

'The baby's fine but the mother's not out of the woods yet. She lost a lot of blood.'

'Andy, when you're not busy on deck tonight I want you to stand by in the sickbay just in case. Carole, what have you told our passengers?'

'The soldiers' families understand but the pygmies are a little confused. When I told them that the 'canoe' might be attacked they wanted to get off. Their idea is to fight in the forests where they can hide.'

'Not the only ones, but you will have to keep them calm if we do get into a fight. Also I want everyone away from the port side. That will be the side exposed to the bridge when we get into the Cauldron.'

'I'll organise that,' said Carole. 'The idea is that I will be with the passengers. Andy and Monique will be ready in the sickbay on call.'

'Good,' said Harry. 'Let's hope you aren't needed.'

'I've checked all the first aid kits,' said Andy. 'As well as on the bridge, engine room and galley, I've put two kits on deck, just in case, and one in the rescue boat.' Harry took his arm.

'Well done, Andy. Now remember, most of our people will be in the boats or busy elsewhere. Everyone is excited but most of the lads have never been under fire before. If the shit hits the fan, I will depend on those of you who have.'

'Don't worry, Captain. We'll be all right.' Harry squeezed his arm.

'I know we will, but all the same occasionally go down to the passengers and keep them calm.'

Chapter 13

Harry left the messroom and went up to his cabin. Sandy was sitting in his office waiting.

'Pour us a couple of beers, Sandy,' Harry said. As Sandy went into the cabin Harry sat at the desk. Just one more thing to do, he thought. Picking up the sat phone he dialled the office number. The phone rang and after a few tones David came on the phone.

'Hey, Harry. Now that you have your spares I was hoping you were out of my hair for a while. How are things?'

'Hold on to your hat, David. There's bad news and worse news.'

David groaned, 'Christ, what now?'

'We have the spares and are making repairs. Just before leaving the remnants of Mobutu's army appeared and I now have a Colonel and twenty soldiers on board who want out and this ship is their exit route. Before you say anything they are armed and will not leave. I also have a missionary doctor and a bunch of natives under her protection who are sheltering on the ship and if they go ashore they will be killed and eaten.'

'This isn't a joke is it, Harry?

'I wish it was.'

'Did you say eaten?'

'Wait. The rebels are now in Matadi, burning and looting the place and say we cannot leave and want us to go alongside. There's no way we can do that even if we wanted to with the Colonel and his boys pushing guns down our throats. If we stay here we've had it, well at least those sheltering on the ship have, and I shouldn't think the Mission to Seamen will be waiting on the jetty to greet us either. I've no choice but to try to get out tonight.'

'And do what?'

'Try to get out to the sea. One point is that I have port clearance from the last government and I shouldn't think that this new bunch of murderers have been recognised by anyone except the usual suspects yet.'

'What about Boma? Can you drop all these people off there?'

'The rebels hold Boma as well. The Angolans are also supporting them so on one side I have the rebels and on the other the Angolans.'

Sandy came through and quietly placed Harry's beer on his desk.

'I thought the ship couldn't go without the engine being repaired. Christ, Harry, can you do it?' questioned David.

'No idea but I can try, in fact I have to. Before you say anything there is no alternative. They're coming for us in the morning regardless of who we are. After all what's a hundred more dead when added to a few million.'

There was a pause.

'I don't know what the owner is going to say.'

'David, I really don't give a flying fuck what the owner says. He is the idiot that ordered us here in the first place. Tell him to look in his '*How to Own a Ship for Dummies*' book.'

'Then there's the insurance.'

'Listen, David, don't be stupid. Don't tell the insurance people. Wait until it's over then hopefully we can make up a story between us that everyone is happy with. They can pay out and we can go home. That's what everyone wants. No fuss.'

David sounded very unhappy. 'Harry, as soon as I tell the owner he'll blow his top and order you to remain where you are.'

'He can order Chinese takeaway for all I care. Listen, David, unless you can get your hands on a friendly frigate or two by tomorrow there is nothing else I can do but to try and get through. Now stop covering your arse for a minute and do me a favour. I want to be on my way before you tell the owner.'

'Harry, that's not possible. I must tell him about the situation. I am sure that his office, if not him directly, will tell you to stop.'

'Yes, but then I will have a gun held to my head by a very pissed off Colonel.'

'You know who they will blame for this.'

'That's what Captains are for.'

'Harry I am going to say something very stupid. 'Be careful with the ship.' Harry laughed aloud and looked at Sandy. 'He says be careful with the ship.'

'You know for one minute I thought you were going to say be careful with the crew.'

'Well obviously that too,' David said.

'It's all right, David. We just live on different planets. I guess the shipowner will have insured it for more than it's worth and if there isn't a charter for it, he will probably be grateful if we sink it.'

'Listen, Harry, why don't you delay and let me try to talk to the government.'

'Yes and in a month's time they'll send someone out to arrange for the bodies to go home. David, I told you. I am going. Now all being well I will try to call you tomorrow and update you. I'll not be answering this phone so don't try to ring me.'

'Harry, for the record I have to tell you that I ordered you to wait until the owners decided what they wanted.'

'And, David, for the record, I told you to piss off.'

'I will wait until end of business today, Harry. That's all I can do.'

'That will have to do. You'll understand that I am having problems with communications. They may be working by tomorrow sometime.'

'If you must go, you must. You will contact me tomorrow?'

'If I can, David.'

'Good luck, Harry.'

'Thanks, David.'

Harry put the phone down and looked across at Sandy who was sitting opposite holding his beer. Harry reached for his and slowly drank it. Then he reached out and rang the bridge. 'Switch off the satcomm phone system; it's just broken down.'

'Well, your Honour, looks like you are going to piss off a lot of people.' Harry shrugged. 'Just as well you didn't mention that we are going into the Cauldron with no tugs, no pilot, all the weapons that are on board, and the bridge guarded by tanks and God knows what. Oh, and the small fact of letting two tugs go adrift into the Cauldron. Then there are the diamonds of course. As I have said before and hope to say again, sailing with you is really interesting.' He raised his glass towards Harry.

'Seriously, Sandy, what do you think?'

Sandy looked across at Harry. 'For what it's worth, you have no alternative. If you don't someone's going to kill us or at least a lot of those on board. You can't be responsible for that. You've come up with a plan that gives us the best chance. The ship is ready, you've done all you can and all the officers and crew are with you.' He saw the worried look on Harry's face. 'You're thinking about some of us getting injured or killed aren't you?' Harry nodded. 'Don't. We're seamen. It goes with the job. How many men have you seen killed or injured in your time. A number, right?' Again Harry nodded. 'So have I. Sir, you have one job now, get us down the river and out to sea. Save a lot of people.' He got up draining his glass. 'I'm off to see the ship secured down. Are you aware that we have no shutters for the after bridge windows? They never expected waves to hit the ship there.'

'I'll bear that in mind once we get under the bridge.' Harry looked out of the office window. 'It's started to rain. Let's hope it continues.' He drained his glass.

He suddenly stood up and followed Sandy down onto the deck.

'Sandy, we're going boating. Get the Colonel and Delilah. Just the four of us. We'll take the FRC.'

'Somewhere nice?'

'We're going to take a peek at what's on that bridge. Bring a couple of pairs of binoculars with you.'

When they arrived on the main deck, the Bosun was waiting. A small boat ladder was rigged for the boat which was alongside. Sandy went first and got into the helmsman's seat. He switched on and checked the instruments, then pressed the start button for the water jet engine. It rumbled into life and Sandy immediately cut back the throttle to where it burbled contentedly.

'Ready for boarding, Captain.'

The Colonel and Delilah boarded followed by Harry. As soon as Sandy signalled and took the weight off the headline, Delilah let go the boat rope which the Bosun heaved inboard.

'Take her right over to the far bank, Sandy, then slowly come back down until we can see the bridge. I very much doubt that they will see us there.' Sandy nodded, and the boat lifted as he gave her power to edge over to the bank. The river ran more smoothly as they closed to the bank and Sandy shut the engine down to a low murmur as the boat drifted downriver with the current.

'There's a small spit of land jutting out into the water ahead, Sandy. If you can put the boat in there, we can get out onto the spit and see over it. That should give us a good view of the bridge without being seen.'

Sandy headed for the spit and gently eased the boat into the undergrowth. Delilah got out with the headline and, tying it to the stump of a tree, held the boat in until they had all climbed out.

They pushed their way through the trees until they came to the top where, as they guessed, there was a view of the bridge two miles ahead. Sandy gave one set of binoculars to the Colonel and the other to Harry.

'There are plenty of soldiers on the bridge,' said Harry.

'It's not them I am worried about,' said the Colonel, 'Do you see right in the middle of the bridge? A tank, T62 from the looks of it, and at the Matadi end another one.'

'I can see that but there doesn't appear to be anything at this end of the bridge.'

'Not on the bridge but there could be one off the bridge towards the airport.'

'That doesn't matter, as long as we can get under the bridge before it sees us.'

'Well, from the looks of it, Captain, if your plan works and we can attract that centre tank towards the Matadi end, you might be able to get under.'

They passed their binoculars to Sandy and Delilah who also scanned the bridge.

'There's a machine gun in the centre as well,' said Delilah.

The Colonel took the binoculars off Sandy. 'You're right. Good eyesight. The soldiers may also have weapons we don't know about, including rocket propelled grenades.'

'Has everyone seen what they want? Then let's get back to the ship.' They crawled back down below the crest of the hillock where Delilah pulled the boat in to the shore. He held it there until they had embarked then pushed off, starting the engine.

The rain was getting heavier. Harry looked up at the darkening sky.

'Just what we wanted. Let's hope it continues.'

'It's going to be a wet night for us in the boat,' said Sandy. 'We can't wear our wet weather gear. Its bright yellow with reflective strips built in.'

'You're right,' said Harry. 'I hadn't thought about that.'

They approached the ship and came alongside where the Bosun was waiting. Sandy sniffed. 'At least it's warm rain. See you all at dinner.'

The officers' mess was crowded for dinner. Carole sat with Harry and Sandy. She looked tired but satisfied.

'Our patient is a lot better now.'

'Pleased to hear it,' said Harry. 'Are you ready in the sickbay?'

'Of course. Just try not to give me any business,' she said smiling at him.

Delilah was bustling around in his usual efficient manner. It was hard to see him as the cool soldier they had experienced recently. 'The Colonel told you that you are up on the bridge tonight when you get back?'

'Yes, Captain, makes sense. If they open up from the road bridge I have room to reply from there. At least it will keep their heads down and, as the Colonel says, I know the weapons.'

'We've also mounted a heavy machine gun up there.'

'I know. Let's hope we don't have to use it.'

'When are you going round the ship,' Sandy asked Jake, who was sitting with his girlfriend.

Jake looked at his watch. 'In about 10 minutes, Sir. Just waiting for the crew to finish their dinner.'

'Don't forget to keep the engine throttled back. As quiet as you can. If you see any light then give me a call and stay watching until we fix it.' Jake nodded.

The Cook poked his head into the messroom.

'Shall I prepare some sandwiches for tonight, Captain?'

'That's a good idea, Cook. Would you have them in the messroom for 0100?'

'I'll see to that,' said Delilah.

'I'll do the same for the crew,' said the Cook and ducked back into his kingdom.

The others finished their dinner and one by one they left the messroom leaving Sandy and Harry sitting with their coffee. 'Anything we've missed?' Harry asked.

'Bound to be,' said Sandy, 'but we've covered all the important bases.'

'If there's any problem tonight, get out fast and come back on board. It's not worth getting anyone killed. Not our people anyway. I'll put a stern light on to help you find us when you are coming back. It's low down and doesn't show ahead.'

'As I keep telling you, you've got the beer. I'll find you.'

Harry smiled. 'Just take care of yourself. You're not a youngster anymore.'

'If I don't come back you can have my zimmer frame.'

Just then Jake came to the door. 'All the lighting is out, Sir. There were a few chinks but the Bosun dealt with them. She's totally blacked out.'

'Thank you, Jake.'

'Is there anything else I can do?'

'Yes. Finish your watch on the bridge then get your head down. It's going to be a long night,' replied Harry.

'Goodnight, Sir.'

'I'll take that advice as well,' said Sandy. 'See you in the morning on the bridge, Captain.'

Harry went up to his cabin and, going to the bookcase, picked out a book and sat trying to read. He had kaleidoscope flashes of thoughts and consequences driving like spray in a gale all with no conclusions, just appearing and disappearing in the mist of his mind. He shook his head and went up to the bridge.

Sandy went down to his cabin, looked at his watch and decided not to undress. He was turning towards his bunk when there was a tap at his door. He opened it and was surprised to see Carole with two of the pygmies.

'Come in', he said. 'I presume, Carole, that you are not here after my body unless you have something really interesting in mind.'

Carole smiled. 'I wouldn't put it past you, Sandy, but I think we would shock our friends here. This man is the Kombeti,' she said indicating the older pygmy, 'and this other man is their best hunter.' Sandy looked puzzled.

'They hunt with poisoned arrows, Sandy. Instant paralysis and death very quickly after. The poison paralyses the whole system, no breathing, heart stops and that's it but completely silent and deadly. Sandy, these guys can kill an elephant with one arrow.' Sandy looked at the pygmies with new interest. 'You see what I am getting at. Once the Kombeti got the picture as to what is going on tonight, he brought me this man. I am told he never misses and hunts at night.'

'He knows what we are going to do?'

'Completely and he wants to go. He would regard it as a great honour to get one of those animals who killed his people.'

Sandy looked at him. 'He's only a little guy and I reckon we can squeeze him in. Thank him from me and tell him it will be a privilege to have him along.' Carole turned and gave a thumbs up to the pygmies and spoke a few words. Their faces instantly lit up with broad grins. They took Sandy's hands and shook them rapidly, chattering and clicking with their tongues.

'I don't know what they are saying but they seem to be pleased.'

'They are a very intelligent people. They know what is going on and want to be part of it.'

'What's his name?'

'You can't pronounce it. The nearest I can get to it is Beckle. I'll see he's ready for the boat when you go,' said Carole. 'Goodnight, Sandy.'

It was dark on the bridge except for the faint glow coming from the dimmed radar screens and other instruments. The shutters on the windows gave a strange closed effect to the bridge and Harry felt hemmed in with only three windows to see through. Not that there was anything to see with the rain sleeting down.

'Graham?'

A figure came out of the gloom. 'Good evening, Sir.' Graham had been sitting in one of the bridge chairs. 'She's not moving. Still raining and the barometer is low and steady so this rain looks set in for a while.'

'That's good. It gives us more cover. How are you feeling about tomorrow?'

'A bit scared. I just don't want to screw up.'

'You won't. Being scared is normal. It will keep you on your toes. Have you ever towed before?' Graham shook his head. 'There's nothing to it, at least not for boats our size. Just a few things to remember. No sudden weight on the tow line, bring your speed on slowly and then keep the line tight. The one thing you don't want is to allow the tow rope to come off the stern onto the quarter. That will pull your boat down and then as the rope comes further round onto your beam it could capsize you. That's how most tug accidents happen. If for any reason the rope does come off the stern, take the power off immediately and let the rope come slack, then bring your boat back on course and pick up the slack again. Just watch we don't run over you, got it?'

'Yes, Sir.'

'Don't try to keep power on and fight her back round. Now this could well happen if you get into one of the whirlpools. As it's dark you may not see it, but you will feel it and could lose the heading of the boat. Don't worry. You are bigger than the whirlpools. Just remember to take the weight off, drive her out of the water then take up the tow again. Keep in touch with Vijay. He's been around and knows the score.'

'Thank you, Sir.'

'Good. I am depending on you both to get us through. Now, I'll take the watch. You go down and get some rest. I want you alert tomorrow. We've a busy day ahead.'

'I'm fine, Sir.'

'I'm sure you are. Hand over.'

Andrew began reciting the handover routine. 'I have both radars on, one on 5 mile range the other on 3. VHF is on 16 and 9. Both anchors are out 8 shackles on each. All three boats are down and alongside. Engines are on 15 minutes' notice and presently the engine room is unmanned. Duty watchkeeper is down below. I piped him down already to get some rest.'

'Good thinking. What time did the engine room crowd pack in?'

'Just a few minutes ago. One thing, Sir. We still have the watertight doors open.'

'That's a thought,' said Harry. 'We must close them before starting. At least those in the engine room. When you go down, see one of the engine crew and tell them to close them now, then we won't forget. Thank you 3rd Mate. I have the watch.'

As Graham left, Harry felt his way to the front of the bridge and, settling in the command chair, stared out of the centre window at the rain sleeting down. Although the bridge was set forward on the ship he could hardly see the bow.

He thought back to the bridges on which he had been sitting in command chairs as storms raged; as fog encompassed the ship in silence; pushing through frozen seas, listening to the gunshot crackling of the ice as the ship broke through; approaching the twinkling lights of the shore; awaiting for pilots to arrive or berths to be made ready. Always the smell of coffee, cigarette smoke and the tang of the shore. Every port smelt, some many miles away, especially in the east where the smell of wood smoke drifted offshore. Even the sea smelt. And always the weather. Morning, noon and night the ship lived by the weather. Harry suddenly felt very tired. Like many sailors he wanted what was over the horizon, but never got there to find out what it was he wanted. Again like many sailors, he promised himself that he would leave after this voyage. His reverie was interrupted by the bridge door opening.

'Harry?' It was Carole. 'Over here,' he said. She peered into the semi darkness and, making out the shape of the chair and him slumped in it, felt her way over. As she reached him she nuzzled his cheek.

'You need a shave.' Only a woman could say that to someone at a time like this he thought.

'You know, when my Father was on his cruiser in the war, when they knew they were going into battle, they'd put their best uniforms on.'

'That sounds very romantic and noble.'

'I used to think that too but my old man told me that most of them had paid so much for their best uniform that they still owed the tailor for it and they weren't going to leave it behind if they were sunk.' Carole laughed.

'Was he like you?'

'Hard to say. He didn't want me to go in the Merchant Navy. He was Royal Navy through and through, at least until they threw him on the scrap heap. His ship was sunk at Crete and he got shrapnel in his ear. That was no problem at the time and they kept him on, but as soon as the war ended, that was it. He never quite got over it. He didn't want me to go to sea. He was doing well in business and that was where he wanted me to go. He had thoughts of Oxford and company law. Trouble was that he had brought me up telling me all these stories about the sea so I didn't want anything else. After two schools decided that my presence would not enhance their record, he eventually gave in and sent me to the Conway hoping that they would knock it out of me. I was in heaven, 14 years old and training to be an officer. In boats every day. Seamanship instead of Latin. It was a hard place but by God they made seamen and officers of us.'

'What was the Conway?'

'HMS Conway, a training ship for cadets. It used to be an old wooden ship of the line but by the time I went there it was shore based.

It was hard but then they were getting us ready for a tough job and to lead men. We weren't boys when we left either. It's gone, of course, with the decline of the Merchant Navy.'

'Many ships and seas later.'

'As you say, many ships and seas.'

'Why, Harry? I mean why the sea?'

'Why not? It's a big place and every day is different. It's a challenge, it's honest, no politics here. All I have to do is look ashore and the quiet desperation with which many men live their lives and that gives me the answer. I couldn't do what they do. They are the brave ones. I've run away. Remember I did try the marriage and family route once. Anyway, it's the only thing I'm good at.'

'But she left you.'

'Hell, I was hardly there anyway so I don't really blame her. What got me was that it was a bloody lawyer.' Carole laughed again.

'I can smell coffee. Is there a percolator here?' She fumbled around and found it. 'Good, it's hot. Coffee?'

'Yes please, as it comes.' She poured out two mugs and carried them over.

'What about the children?'

'They hardly knew me. She brought them up and we sent them away to school when they were old enough. Anyway, they have a rich lawyer to look after them now. And you,' he said to Carole, 'are you going to carry on with this missionary thing.'

'I don't know. At times like this I feel like staying in the good old USA but out here we are needed so much. There's nothing much for me back home. Every time I see my parents, they look at me with sympathy and want me to get married again. That's not on my agenda.'

There was silence for a moment as they sipped their coffee.

'Are we going to make it?'

Harry paused before answering. 'I wish I could ask that rather than answering. I don't know, Carole. I really don't know what's on that bridge. I don't know if the boys will manage to let the tugs go. I don't know what is waiting at Boma. But I will say this. The ship is old but she is tough. She's designed for ice. A crew of sailors like this you would be pushed to find on any ship on the oceans today. Even the younger ones are going to give all they've got. If any ship can do this we can. Is that good enough for you?'

He got up from his chair, took her in his arms and crushed her to him, kissing her deeply.

'Now you are going to bed, regrettably alone. I'll make up for it when we get out to sea.' She laughed and held him to her.

'That, my Captain, I will demand. She let him go.

'Goodnight, Captain.'

'Goodnight, Doctor.'

Chapter 14

The bang of the bridge door caused Harry to start in his chair.

'What's this, Captain, sleeping on watch?' It was Sandy. Harry could make out his figure in the gloom.

'I was catnapping. What's the time?'

'That's what they said on the Titanic just before they hit the iceberg. 0120. I've brought you some sandwiches from the messroom.'

He placed them on the chart table and turned on the dimmed down chart light. Harry came over and found that he was surprisingly hungry. He then noticed that Sandy's face was blackened.

'Good idea,' he said pointing to Sandy's face.

'I told all the rest of my party to do the same.'

'Crew getting up?'

'They are already up. I think they are a bit too hyped up to sleep. The other officers will be up in a minute. Still raining though, which will help.'

'I meant it about breaking off if there is any problem.'

'There won't be, Captain, unless it's me getting soaked.'

At that moment the engine rumbled into life and the bridge door opened again as the rest of the deck officers and the Bosun entered.

'Boat crews are all standing by in the boats, Sandy,' he said.

Jake immediately went to the engine controls. 'I'll test gear, Sir.' He put the engine controls ahead and astern checking that all was in order, then went to the wheel putting it to port and starboard watching the rudder indicators. 'Steering and engine all in order, Captain.'

'All in order,' Harry repeated.

Vijay had all the walkie-talkies with him and was passing them out. 'All are set on Channel 6 for tonight, and they are all charged up.' They picked up their sets and tested the comms between them. Jake switched the bridge VHF to Channel 6 and their voices came through the speakers.

'I'll stand by on the forecastle, Sir,' said the Bosun addressing Harry.

'Right, Bosun, port anchor first. Let me know when you're ready to heave.'

The Colonel appeared, joining the others. 'Take one of the walkie-talkies Colonel. It's all ready. You talk to the bridge and to Delilah on top of the bridge with that.'

'I don't want to hear anyone on my set,' said Sandy. 'I'll speak but no one reply.'

'Put your set on Channel 9, Sandy. We'll have the other VHF on that channel then we will have a dedicated one just for you.'

Jake went over to the other bridge set and switched it over to 9. Sandy gave a quick test and nodded. The bridge speaker crackled. It was the Bosun.

'Ready to heave away on the port anchor, Sir.'

Harry turned to them. 'Gentlemen, time to man your boats. Good luck to you all. Vijay, Graham, stand off the ship until we are ready to make you fast. Sandy?' He put his hand out and Sandy grasped it firmly. 'Remember, Sandy, we have a lot more sailing to do before we finish.'

'Bugger the sailing, Captain, just give me the women.' There was nervous laughter. He smiled and squeezed Harry's hand. 'See you soon, Sir. Don't go without me.'

They cleared the bridge quickly leaving Harry, Jake and the Colonel.

'Do you mind if I stay, Captain,' asked the Colonel.

'No problem,' replied Harry. 'Bosun, let the starboard cable run easy as you heave on the port. How is the port cable?'

'About three points port bow, lot of weight.'

'Coming ahead, now heave it in as it slackens. Jake take the wheel. Port 10.

'Port 10, Sir.'

'Wheel port 10.'

With that Harry pushed the engine controls forward. The engine rumble increased and the ship started to swing to port. 'Let me know when the cable is right ahead.' The ship was swinging to port.

'Midships the wheel.'

'Midships, Sir. Wheel midships.'

'Cable right ahead.'

'Steady on that.'

'Steady.'

The orders flowed smoothly. The Colonel was impressed. 'You repeat everything?'

'Yes. It ensures everyone understands the order and provides a check on the order given.'

On the forecastle the Bosun was working in the darkness feeling the shackles as they came in for the marking wire which would tell him how much cable was still out.

'6 on deck cable leading ahead. Moderate weight.' Harry increased the engine speed. The cable was coming in easily now as the weight of the chain came off the bottom. Before long the Bosun reported cable up and down and then anchor aweigh.

'Anchor aweigh?' the Colonel questioned.

'That means the anchor is off the bottom.'

One of the bridge VHF set's loudspeakers crackled. It was Sandy.

'Leaving the ship now.' Harry reached for the mike but instead of speaking just clicked the send button to show Sandy that he had heard.

'Starboard 15. Bosun, I am coming round to pick the other anchor. Heave away when you can.' Harry eased down the engine as the ship came round.

'Cable coming up to right ahead.'

'Midships and steady.'

'Midships and steady,' Jake replied.

They could hear the clank of the cable coming in over the windlass.

Harry went over to the main radar and studied the dimmed screen. 'Shit, the rain is cluttering up the screen. I was hoping I could see Sandy's boat but reducing the clutter has also cut out his echo. Never mind, we can see the banks clearly.'

'Port anchor sighted and clear,' the Bosun reported. 'Starboard anchor aweigh.' The ship was now free in the river. Harry kept just enough speed to hold her in position.

Harry called the Bosun. 'When you get both anchors up and stowed, don't secure them. Take them out of gear and have them ready for letting go, just in case.' Shortly after, the Bosun reported that the starboard anchor was clear, then that both anchors were ready for letting go. On Harry's orders both the daughter craft moved in to take their tow lines. 'Give them a long lead Bosun. I want them able to be manoeuvred if they have problems.'

As soon as the boats were fast, Harry stopped the engine. 'Rescue 1, Rescue 2, I've stopped the engine to let her drift astern. Keep the weight on your lines and keep my head up into the current as she comes astern.' Both the boats were now ahead of the ship allowing themselves to be pulled astern with the ship while holding the bow towards the current.

The FRC had been lowered to the water and gently brought away from the ship. Sandy was already drenched. He sat on the helmsman's seat peering into the rain with the FRC easing towards the bank while drifting down river with the current. The two soldiers were sitting forward while Delilah was standing by Sandy with Beckle crouched down by his feet.

'Can't see bugger all in this rain,' said Delilah.

'We won't see the bank until the last minute,' said Sandy. 'That's why I'm taking it easy.' They both sat staring intently into the rain.

Suddenly Delilah pointed. 'There, look!'

Sandy instantly put the engine in neutral, letting the boat drift forward. 'Can't see a thing. No. Just a minute, yes, there's the bank!' He immediately turned the boat parallel to the bank and nudged the engine ahead. The bank was only several metres away.

'Any idea how far we have to go to the jetty?'

'Not a bloody clue, but looking at the way the bank is going past, the current is pretty strong. Could be anytime.'

'Look at that,' said Delilah. The soldiers were also pointing. On the port side of the boat was a flickering redness in the sky. Then they heard gunfire. Sandy immediately stopped the engine.

'What the hell's going on?'

'It's the town.'

'What do you mean?

'It's the town burning,' said Delilah. 'The so called advance party have started their fun. That's what the gunshots are.' The reddish glow in the sky was strong and filtered through the rain.

'The poor bastards,' said Sandy.

'Poor or not, it means there is enough going on to distract them from us. Every rebel will be up there getting his hands on his share.'

Sandy put the engine ahead again and shortly the bank changed to concrete.

'There's the jetty. We won't get out here. I'll take the boat down the jetty until we come to the tugs.'

The sound of shooting was louder now and there was a faint crackling noise of burning buildings. Sandy tucked the boat in tight to the jetty and let the boat drift down with the current. Soon faint lights appeared ahead in the water.

'There are the tugs. Stand by with the line forward, Delilah. The next ladder we see we'll secure the boat there.'

Delilah moved the soldiers out of the way and stood in the bow. Sandy cut the engine and the boat drifted down the jetty. An iron ladder running down into the water appeared out of the rain. Sandy angled the boat against the concrete and drifted down to the ladder, where Delilah grabbed on and quickly ran the headline around one of the rungs. The boat immediately swung round to the line until it was against the jetty heading back upstream. They waited in silence for a minute.

Sandy spoke into his mike. 'We're at the jetty now.' There was a click in reply. He then went forward. 'Delilah, have a quick look on the jetty. Don't go on it yet. Just look over the top.' Delilah nodded, and climbed up the few rungs of the ladder. When he reached the top he peered over. The jetty surface was slick with rain. The only light was coming from the tugs which were alongside a short distance down the jetty.

Delilah came back down. 'It's all clear. There doesn't seem to be anyone on guard by the tugs but I can't see if there is anyone on guard on board. I think if we keep to the edge of the jetty we can approach the first tug without anyone on the tug seeing us.'

They gathered together. The Lieutenant spoke. 'Mr Mate, we should go first. If anyone is there they will think we are same as them. Good?'

'That makes sense. OK you go first. Take Beckle here with you, then we will follow with the tools.'

The two soldiers climbed the ladder, stopped for a moment at the top then crawled onto the jetty. Beckle, carrying his short bow and quiver of arrows followed. He was far more agile than the soldiers. There was still silence from above.

'I'll go next,' said Sandy. 'You pass the tools up.' As Sandy reached the top he saw that the soldiers and Beckle were crouching at the bow of the first tug. He took the tools from Delilah and together they joined the others. The glow from the burning buildings now showed up their faces and the sound of burning and shooting was an intermittent background of noise.

'Is anyone on guard on the ship?' asked Sandy, not bothering to whisper.

'We cannot see.'

Sandy pulled the Lieutenant's arm. 'The only way to find out is for you two to go to the gangway. If there is anyone, call them down. Beckle here can be waiting. If he misses then you must use your knives.'

The Lieutenant nodded and speaking briefly to the other soldier, stood up. As they approached the gangway, Sandy held Beckle and pointed to his bow and then towards the gangway. Beckle stood up and took an arrow from his quiver ready. The soldiers stood by the gangway for a moment then beckoned Sandy.

'Come on,' Sandy said and they ran towards where the soldiers were standing.

'No one here,' said the Lieutenant. Sandy could see only a few dim lights shining inside the tug. All the portholes were dark. 'I can't hear a generator. I think those lights must be oil lamps.' He turned to the Lieutenant. 'We need to let the next tug go first. You three do the same again there and, if it's clear, we'll come down and slip the stern lines first then we'll cut through the bow lines and do the same with this tug.' They looked puzzled. 'OK, check the next tug,' said Sandy pointing at it.

'Ah,' the Lieutenant realised and spoke to the others. They set off but Sandy grabbed Beckle. He put his finger to his lips and Beckle nodded, then set off at a slower pace. Sandy and Andy watched them as they got closer to the next tug. They were at the tug's gangway looking when Sandy heard them talking.

They were staying at the bottom of the gangway and Sandy could see them pointing at the town.

'Lie down,' said Sandy and they lay down on the jetty. 'Where's Beckle?'

'He's down too,' said Delilah. 'He can't get a shot from where he is.'

'Fuck,' breathed Sandy.

They watched and then saw a figure coming down the gangway and approach the soldiers. The figure joined them, and then Sandy saw the flash of a blade as the Lieutenant stabbed from the front at the same time as the soldier grabbed the figure around the neck. There was a brief struggle then all movement ceased and the soldier let the body fall to the ground. The Lieutenant beckoned and Sandy and Delilah ran to the tug.

'Take the body and lower it into the river,' said Sandy.

They carried on to the stern of the tug and, as Sandy thought, the stern line was slack. They quickly slipped it and went to the bow. Using their saws, they started sawing through the rope lines.

'No wires thank Christ,' commented Delilah.

'The rope's pretty rotten as well,' said Sandy.

The lines started to fray where they were sawing and almost together they parted with the end of the ropes dropping in the water with a faint splash. Immediately the tug started moving astern.

Sandy keyed in his mike. 'One tug let go,' he whispered. A moment later came an answering click. 'Come on, next tug.' They ran to the stern of the next tug and again quickly slipped the rope. The soldiers and Beckle joined them.

'Right,' said Sandy. 'The bow and then we're off home.'

They bent down and started to saw through the headlines when they were startled by a shout. They looked up and saw two soldiers coming towards them. Sandy could see that they had their arms full, obviously going back to the tug to stow their loot before going back to the town.

'Don't shoot,' Sandy hissed seeing the lieutenant and his man starting to bring their weapons up. 'Wave to them.' He stood up and waved. 'For fuck's sake show we're friends,' he said. The Lieutenant got the picture and called out to them. They approached warily shouting out.

The Lieutenant turned to Sandy. 'They ask what we are doing, who are we?' Before Sandy could reply there was a hissing and then a thud. The nearest soldier fell to the ground then again another hiss and the remaining soldier dropped his packages, putting his hands up to his throat from which an arrow was sticking out. He then also dropped to the ground. Sandy turned and saw Beckle standing calmly.

'Bloody hell, Beckle, I'll take you ashore with me any time.'

The soldiers came up to him and patted him on the back. Beckle was now grinning broadly.

'OK, let's save the congratulations till we get back,' said Sandy. 'Put the bodies in the river.'

They carried on cutting the ropes which parted like the others and again the tug immediately started to drift astern. The last body was being let down into the river.

'It's still twitching,' said Delilah.

'Not for long,' said Sandy as it floated off face down. He lifted his mike. 'That's the last tug gone.' Again came the answering click.

'Right, me buckos, into the boat.'

They swiftly went down the ladder into the boat. Sandy pressed the starter and the engine coughed into life. Delilah let the rope go and Sandy took the boat quietly away from the jetty.

'Now all we have to do is find the bloody ship and get dry.'

Chapter 15

Back at the ship, Harry was pacing up and down on the bridge, occasionally peering into the large radar screen. The Bosun had come off the forecastle after making the boats fast and was now on the wheel while Jake stood by the engine controls. The ship was slowly drifting down towards the bridge stern first close in to the bank but the bridge was not visible through the rain. As the ship came abeam of the port, flickers of red broke through the rain from the burning and the faint sound of gunfire could be heard.

'Start the bow thruster,' said Harry. 'We'll use it to help us turn.' Jake reached forward and pressed an illuminated button on the engine control panel. Immediately there was a rumbling noise from forward of the bridge.

'I assume that they push the ship sideways,' said the Colonel.

'Not the whole ship, just the bow.'

'Can we use them to help us through the Cauldron?'

'No, we'll be going too fast. They are only effective up to 6 knots, but we'll keep them on in case we are slowed. At least they will be ready.'

Harry looked up at the bridge clock glowing green.

'0230. We should have heard something by now. I can make out the tugs alongside on the radar through the rain but I can't see the crash boat. The tugs are not moving yet.' They waited in silence.

Harry started as Sandy's voice came through. 'One tug gone,' he bent over the radar peering intently at the screen, while turning down the clutter to remove the effects of the rain.

'I think I can see the tug moving. Yes, there is a gap opening up between the tugs. Come on Sandy,' Harry muttered. 'One more.' Again they waited. Harry heard the sound of footsteps on the ladder going to the deck above.

The Colonel spoke. 'That's one of my men going to man the machine gun, Captain. I'm going down to the deck now. Good luck.'

'Same to you, Colonel.'

Sandy's voice came through again, 'That's the last tug gone.'

'Great,' said Harry. He picked up the mike. 'Rescue 1 and 2, pull to port. We're going to turn the ship round and head down river. Full thruster to port.'

Jake responded, the rumble from the thruster increased as the bridge began to tremble. 'Wheel hard to port. Slow ahead.'

The ship began to swing slowly round. As soon as the ship was pointing at the river bank Harry stopped the engine and let the ship come round with the boats pulling and the thruster working.

'I'm coming astern,' he told the boats. 'I want to hold position here for a few minutes to allow the tugs to get under the bridge. Keep my head steady on 250. Switch on the stern light.'

He went over to the radar to watch the progress of the tugs towards the bridge and look for the rescue boat. 'Jake, tell Andy to stand by to hoist the crash boat when it returns. Stop engine.'

He watched the radar intently. Through the darkness came a series of flashes closely followed by explosions.

'It's worked!' shouted Harry. 'Now let's get going, Full ahead. Rescue 1 and 2, we are going full ahead now for the bridge. Stand by to pull to port as soon as we get under the bridge.'

'FRC coming alongside, Sir,' Jake shouted.

'Switch off the stern light. Tell them to hoist as soon as possible. I can't stop now.'

The ship was picking up speed quickly. The flashes and explosions continued as the ship neared the bridge. Then Jake reported. 'I can see the bridge. We're going under.' Harry went outside to the bridge wing and looked up. He could just make out the underside of the bridge through the rain.

'Hard to port!' The Bosun spun the wheel to port bracing himself against the binnacle while watching the gyro compass.

'What course, Sir?' he called.

'202,' Harry replied. 'Rescue 1 and 2, we're coming round to 202. Come round on that and give us all you've got.' Sandy and Delilah appeared on the bridge. 'Well done, Sandy. We're just going under now.'

Sandy went out onto the wing. 'We're under. Can't see any sign of fire.' At that moment there was an explosion above them. 'Fuck!' Sandy ducked back in the wheelhouse.

'That was a tank firing,' Delilah said. They looked at each other. 'Can't be firing at us,' said Delilah 'They can't lower their barrels enough. They must be firing at the tugs. I'm going up top.' There was another explosion and ahead of them, off the starboard bow came a flash of light followed by a red glow.

'They're hitting one of the tugs!' shouted Jake.

'Let's hope they keep hitting it,' said Sandy.

'Sandy, watch the distance off the cliffs and keep calling it to me.' Harry looked out of the port side door. 'I can't see the bridge anymore through the rain so if we can't see them they can't see us.' There was another explosion from the bridge and another flash from the tug.

'Captain,' said Sandy. 'On this course we are going to cross just astern of the tug. They may see us outlined by the flames.'

'There's nothing I can do about that. Where is the second tug?'

'I can't see it but it could already be on the cliffs.'

'How far off are we?'

'5 cables and closing. On this course we won't make the exit channel.'

'Rescue 1 and 2, pull to port. Bosun, port 20.' Again the Bosun brought the wheel to port. 'Steer 160. Rescue 1 and 2, we are coming round to 160.'

Rescue 2 came in. 'Captain, we are caught in the current. I am slacking off.' It was Vijay. The harbour tug was flaming now and another shell struck home sending debris and flames high in the sky.

'The bearing's opening on the tug,' called Jake, his voice urgent and nervous now.

'At least we'll miss that,' said Harry.

'Be a close thing though,' said Sandy. They could see it quite clearly now. She was heavily down by the bow and sinking fast. Some crew still on board were running aft.

'They won't survive in these waters', said Sandy. 'They'll be sucked down by the current.'

'Rescue 2, how are you doing?' asked Harry.

In the darkness of the night, Vijay was standing staring out of the wheelhouse with increasing anxiety. He had been pulling the ship to port and this change of course had taken him into the heart of a whirlpool which could not be seen in the dark waters. He had let his line go slack and then tried to bring his boat round to port but the current of the pool and the weight of the rope was so strong that it was stopping him coming round.

Pat MacNab gripped the wheel so tightly his knuckles showed white in the dim light of the small wheelhouse.

'She isn't coming, Second,' he called to Vijay.

Vijay hesitated, then ordered, 'Hard to starboard.'

'What?'

'Hard to starboard. Now!' Vijay shouted, as he rammed the throttles full ahead. 'We'll take her right round the other way.'

The boat immediately responded as it turned with the current of the whirlpool. Now it was almost spinning round.

'We're heading for the ship!' shouted Henry the Ordinary Seaman, his voice filled with panic.

On the bridge of the Sea Quest they saw Vijay's boat coming out of the rain heading directly for their bow.

'Christ!' Harry yelled. 'Hard to starboard!

Vijay well knew the danger as he could see the bow of the ship rising above him. He gripped the throttles, still pushing them as if to get more speed. The boat continued to spin round with the bow of the ship now only metres from them.

'Midships!' shouted Vijay.

Pat immediately centred the wheel while Henry watched the approaching ship in wide eyed horror. With the wheel amidships the boat immediately picked up speed and passed ahead of the ship's bow. As it passed there was a scraping sound as the two hulls just touched each other before parting. 'Fuck!' shouted Pat.

'Hard to starboard again. Bring her onto 160.'

As the boat came round to her course, Vijay brought the throttle back to slow ahead with shaking hands. He looked astern and watched the tow line coming gradually taut again. When it was tight Vijay increased to full power.

He called the bridge. 'Back on course and pulling full.'

On the ship all they could do was watch Vijay's boat disappear under the bow, and then moments later Sandy shouted 'Clear from the port side,' as he leant over to watch.

'Hard to port,' shouted Harry. 'Rescue 1 and 2, come round to 110 and pull at full power.' Sandy was back on the radar. 'We're still closing the cliffs.'

But now Harry was watching the sinking tug which was too close on the starboard side. It was blazing with the stern high up in the air, a few crew still clinging to the after end. A fountain of water erupted just astern.

'The tank is firing at us now,' reported Delilah. 'I can't see any target to fire at. They must be able to see us from the fire on the tug.'

'Midships the wheel. We need speed to clear the tug. The boats will keep us up to port.'

The ship's speed increased as the rudder came off and, as they passed the tug, another shell from the tank plunged exploding in the water between them, throwing water over the starboard side of the ship. The tug's stern raised vertical, and after a moment's hesitation it slid below the waters. A swell of air came bursting on the surface amongst a few survivors screaming in the dark waters.

'We're two cables off the cliffs!' shouted Sandy. 'You can see them look! He pointed through the dark and rain on the starboard side and a dark mass could be seen looming above them.

'How far to go to the passage out?'

'4 cables.'

'Port 15.' The Bosun swung the wheel again to port. There was another crack as the tank opened fire again but the shell went far astern.

'At least they can't see us now!' shouted Harry.

'One cable off the rocks and two cables to go to the passage.'

Harry was dripping with sweat as he stood in the centre of the bridge willing the ship to go.

'Port 20. Just a little more, that's all we need.'

The glass windows at the back of the bridge exploded.

'What the hell?' exclaimed Sandy. There was a hammering from above.

'We're being fired on by soldiers on the other tug! It is on the rocks astern of us!' It was Delilah on his walkie-talkie.

Jake went out onto the bridge wing. There was another hammering and he saw the few soldiers on the tug being thrown away like leaves in the wind by the machine gun bullets. The firing stopped.

'One cable to go to the exit!' shouted Sandy. 'We're half a cable off the rocks!'

Harry could see the black rocks almost close enough to touch on the starboard beam. The echo of the ship's engine rebounded off the cliff towering above the ship. 'Please, please, just one little effort. You can do it,' he screamed silently.

'Captain, we're entering the passage. The distance off the cliff is increasing!'

Harry came back into the wheelhouse, soaked in sweat. He went to the radar where Sandy stood aside. His voice was unsteady. 'Ease the wheel to port 10. Tell the boats to stop pulling and approach the bow ready to let go. Jake, take the wheel for a moment. Midships. Have a break, Bosun.'

'Aye aye, Sir.' He let go of the wheel and stopped for a moment looking down. His hands were shaking.

'It's all right, Bosun, so are mine,' said Harry.

Harry went to the radar again and, seeing that the ship was now in mid channel, ordered the course. The bridge was strangely silent.

Harry leant against the bridge front and breathed deeply trying to stop his racing heart. Sandy appeared with a cup of coffee. Harry nodded gratefully, sipped it and spluttered.

'Christ, what's in this?'

'Rum, you need it.'

'I hope you put coffee with it.'

They stood in silence, then Sandy said, 'If we ever tried to talk about that, no one would believe it.'

'I can hardly believe it even though it just happened. I presume we had no casualties?'

'Apart from those who shit themselves we seem to be unscathed.'

'I know one 2nd Mate who did that. That reminds me. 'Vijay?' Vijay came on the radio. 'Vijay, when you've let go I want you to head off down the river to just before Tridente point, you remember from the chart?'

'Yes, Sir.'

'I want you to locate that creek and sound it out. We'll be down there in about 40 minutes. See how far I can go up it, and try to assess how wide it is. In other words see if we can fit. It's still dark, I don't want you to use your search light, it's too powerful. Do you have any other lighting?'

'We've got a battery powered lantern.'

'Good, use that.'

Harry called Rescue 1. 'Graham, when you've let go forward, take the boat down aft. I want you to make fast on the port quarter and be ready to hold the stern up river when I come round to enter the creek. Got all that both of you?' They acknowledged. 'Well done both of you by the way. That was an interesting manoeuvre, Vijay. You must tell me about it later.'

Harry looked at the bridge clock. It was showing 0315. 'Funny, it felt like hours in the Cauldron.' He finished his coffee. 'Better not have another one of those.'

Delilah appeared from on top of the bridge. 'Is that coffee I smell?' He went over to the percolator. The water was dripping off him. 'Now I know why in the past they used to all have black oil skins. At least they could wear them without being seen.'

'Was that you on the machine gun?' Sandy asked. Delilah nodded. 'Building up quite a score.'

'Arseholes didn't expect a heavy machine gun to fire back.' He turned towards Harry. 'Sir, do you want me back up there now?'

'I don't think so, Delilah. Tell you what, you've got a few minutes why don't you go down and change. Sandy, I think where we're going everyone can put their wet weather gear on now. I don't think anyone will be around to spot it and anyway they'll see the ship before someone with reflective tape. I want you in charge of the anchors. What I'll do is close in towards the creek, then let go the port anchor. It should be fairly shallow so be ready to hold on at around a few shackles. I want to use it to spin round on until we're pointing in, then I'll let go the starboard anchor. We'll go in under full power but with the anchors ready to act as a brake. Pay out the chain as we go in, you can judge yourself without me telling you. I want the anchors on the bottom outside the creek as I have a feeling that it will mostly be mud inside and those anchors will help to pull us free when we want to come out.'

'Understood, Captain. I'll put the word around about wet weather gear but I think most are so wet they'll live with it until we are in the creek.'

Harry went to the radar again. 'I'll send the Bosun down when we get near the creek. Bosun, take the wheel again. Steer 180. Jake, take over the con and keep her to the track. We'll stay in the middle until we get near then I'll close the bank again. Hopefully this far up, it will still be quite deep. There's still no river traffic. The locals seem to prefer being on the river in daylight.'

'Not much on the shore either. Can't see any lights on either bank,' said Sandy, 'but that doesn't mean there's no one there. Could be that with all these maniacs roaming around, they don't want to be seen.'

The bridge door opened and Peter appeared. 'Crowded up here tonight,' he said.

Harry slowed the engine. 'Let me know when she stops steering, Bosun.'

'Delilah and I are just going, Peter,' said Sandy. 'Come on, Delilah. Let's at least get dry.'

They departed leaving Harry, Peter and Jake with the Bosun standing rock solid at the wheel.

'That was a bit hairy, Harry.'

'Did you see much of it?'

'I came up on deck when I heard the explosions, saw the tug getting pasted and decided it was better below.'

'Any idea how the passengers are? I can't leave the bridge to have a look.'

'I saw Carole. She was quite calm and seemed to have it all under control.'

The bridge door opened again and the Colonel came in. 'My congratulations, Captain. That was brilliant.' He was smiling broadly.

'Colonel,' Harry said. 'We were very, very lucky.'

'A good commander makes his own luck. I must admit I was wondering how we were going to climb those cliffs.'

'At least we came through untouched and no one is injured,' said Harry, 'and that was the objective.'

'What now?'

'We're hopefully going to hide up in the creek before it gets light and then we can discuss our next move. The main thing is for us all to get some rest.'

'May I suggest, Captain, that when we get there and shut down, all of your crew rest and my men will stand guard.'

'That's sounds good, Colonel. Thank you for that.'

'No, Captain. My men and their families thank you.' He saluted and left the bridge.

Harry turned to Peter. 'Strange bugger isn't he? One minute wanting to kill us and then being polite.'

'They probably said that about some of the Nazis before they hanged them. Anyway, the good news, Harry, is that you'll have your broken engine back on line later this morning.'

'News like that I need.'

'Mind you, you must be careful how you run it in.'

'Can we not start it in the creek and run it up there out of gear?'

'We can, but even then it must be treated gently.'

'Peter, I'll try but God knows what is coming next so no promises. When you go back down please thank the lads in the engine room for what they are doing.'

'Thanks, Harry.'

Peter left the bridge and there was silence for a moment. 'How are you, Jake?'

'I'm fine now, Sir, but I got really scared when we were closing the cliffs.'

'But you carried on, that's what counts. If it helps, so was I.'

'What, Sir? You were scared?'

'Bloody right. I think most of us who knew what was happening were. The worst thing is for those who just have to stand and watch. You did all right. Mind you, it is not over yet. Now, are you tired?'

'No, Sir.'

'We'll be tucked up in the creek soon, then we can all get some rest. I want you alert for the next 30 minutes. Bosun, put the wheel amidships. I'm putting her astern just to slow her up. We're getting near the creek and I want to use the thruster to help get us round and steer us in.' He called up the boats, 'Graham, I'm coming astern now just to slow her up. I want you to keep her heading down river. Vijay, speak to me.'

'Yes, Captain. I'm in the creek right now. Sir, it is difficult getting a sounding owing to the deep mud. I do not know where the water ends and the mud begins. It looks like we can get in but we will be touching the mud. The creek's wide enough though.'

'All right, Vijay. I think I have the creek on the radar. Come to the entrance and shine your torch light.'

Andy MacBride arrived on the bridge together with Delilah.

'Just in case, I'll go back up,' said Delilah and disappeared again.

'All quiet down below, Sir. Thought you could do with a hand up here.'

'Good idea, MacBride. Take the wheel please. Bosun, you can go and join the Mate forward.'

'There's the light, Sir,' Jake exclaimed. There was a dim light showing on the port bow.

'Stop engines. What's our speed?'

'4 knots, Sir.'

'Thruster full to port.'

'Graham, we are coming round to port now. Stand by to hold the stern up when I say so.'

'Sandy,' he called through the radio. 'If you can see that light, that's Vijay at the entrance to the creek. I'm coming round to port now and heading in towards the bank.'

'How far off the bank, Jake?'

'Just under 4 cables and 7 cables to run down to the creek.'

He went over to the engine controls and put the engines slow astern again. 'I'm just taking the heat out of her, I don't want the anchor roaring away when Sandy lets go. Midships the wheel now. It's not doing anything anyway.'

The rain had stopped, but the skies were still sullen as the first streaks of dawn came in the sky. The river was running fast, engorged by the recent rains. The bow was coming into line with the creek.

Harry picked up the mike again, 'Vijay, come round to the starboard bow and hold me up against the current. Sandy, port anchor let go. Hold her at three shackles. Graham, start taking the weight and hold the stern up.' The port anchor ran out with a roar and, with the lightening sky, Harry could see the mud lumps flying off the cable as it ran out.

The ship carried on for a moment and then the anchor and cable caught and the bow sheered around sharply. The ship was still one cable off the creek entrance and was settling off centre to starboard. Harry put the engine to half ahead. 'Port 20.' The thruster was full ahead to port and slowly the ship's bow came to port. 'Starboard anchor let go.' There was another roar from forward and the starboard cable ran out. 'Let out the port cable.' Another roar as Sandy let more cable out. The ship sprang forward heading into the creek. 'Midships. Steer for the centre.' Harry called. The ship was now easing into the creek. 'Pay out the cables together. Jake, take the controls.'

Harry went out onto the wing. 'Full ahead. Stop thruster. Christ, it's tight.'

'Like a snake's arse,' whispered Andy. Jake laughed nervously.

'Stow it!' snapped Harry. 'Wait till we get in.' The ship slid into the creek. As it went further in, the overhanging trees brushed against the ship's upperworks. 'Slow ahead.' Immediately the ship slowed held by the anchors. 'Ease a bit more on the anchors.' Again they rattled and the ship moved ahead. Harry went to the radio. 'Vijay, how much further to go before we're in?'

'About another 30 metres,' he replied.

'Right. Full ahead.' The ship pushed ahead again. Now the trees were overhanging the bridge wings and then the ship came to a stop. Harry let the engine push for a minute then stopped the ship.

'That's it,' he said. 'Vijay, how much are we hanging out?'

'Not much, Captain, about 10 metres.'

'That'll do.' He called the forecastle. 'Sandy, we're in as far as we're going to get. Slack down the cable and then put the brakes on. I think the bow will hold position in the mud but tell the Bosun to get his lads down aft. We must put a couple of breast lines out on the port side to hold the stern in position. I can't let the boats go until they are out. Tell them to double the lines back so we can slip them when we go.

'We'll get on to that now. We'll use Vijay's boat to run the lines. Put them around a tree or something.'

Harry turned around. 'That's it, gentlemen. Jake, stop the thruster and finish with the engine.'

'What notice for the engine room, Sir?'

'Not much point having any here. Tell them where we are and that we'll have two hours' notice. Keep the radars on. Jake, I want you to keep the watch for a few hours. Are you up to that?

'Yes, Sir.'

'What I want you to look out for are any ships going at a good speed up the river. I expect the naval ships to be going up towards the bridge.'

The bridge door opened and the Colonel appeared on the bridge. 'I've told my men to chop down trees and undergrowth. We will have the stern covered soon but my concern are any helicopters flying over. Once the stern is covered, I will carry on trying to cover what I can of the upper part of the ship.

'That's a good idea, Colonel.'

'Also, Captain, I recommend that we tell everyone to stay off the decks. That will stop any movement attracting anyone who is looking for us.'

'Colonel, I have to give the boat crews time for rest.'

'That's all right. We don't need them,' he smiled broadly. 'Look.' They went out onto the wing and looking aft saw that some of the trees which had been overhanging the ship were now bent down towards the deck and were being used as a bridge to the shore.

'Don't worry, Captain, your ship is in good hands. You and your crew can rest.'

Harry picked up his mike. 'Rescue 1 and 2, come alongside. We'll hoist you up then you can go and get some rest. Good job all of you.' Andy looked at Jake and then at Harry.

'Sir, the Cadet is almost dead on his feet. There's nothing up here that I can't do. I'll stay up here and keep a watch. I know how to operate the radar. If there is anything important I'll call you immediately.' Harry looked at Jake. Andy was right.

'All right, Andy. Jake, go below.'

'I don't mind staying, Sir.'

'I know you don't but I need you alert later. Andy will keep the watch.' He looked at the lightening sky. 'I was hoping that the rain would stay, but that was expecting too much. Watch out for helicopters. If the naval vessels don't find us, they will launch them.'

Harry took a last look round the bridge. Ahead all he could see was the narrowing creek of muddy water surrounded by dense mangrove trees crowding in. Astern the overhanging trees were being bent over further by the soldiers who were also bringing branches of trees down aft forming a screen across the stern of the ship. A few more soldiers were scattering undergrowth on the working deck space.

'Andy?' Harry called. 'As soon as it gets light ask the Colonel to give you a couple of soldiers up here on the bridge wings to keep watch for any helicopters. You may be able to see them on the radar if they are low enough but don't depend on it. They don't give off much of an echo. If you do sight any, use the deck loudspeaker system to warn everyone.' He looked at the shattered glass from the stern windows. 'In the meantime you can get this mess cleaned up.'

Harry took a last look around before going down to his cabin.

Chapter 16

Harry opened his eyes. He was looking at Delilah's smiling face. For a moment Harry stared blankly blinking in the light which was streaming in from the porthole. Delilah anticipated his question.

'It's 1100.'

'Shit.' He struggled to sit up. Delilah held up a reassuring hand.

'It's all right, Captain. Everything's fine. I've opened your deadlights. You're not wanted for anything yet and strangely the ship is managing without you for a while. There's tea here,' he said placing a tray on the bunk side table. 'I've run your bath and breakfast will be waiting for you when you're ready.'

Harry struggled to sit up. The ship was quiet, just the usual thump of the diesel generators and the slight hum of the air conditioning still reassuringly cooling the cabin.

'Where is everyone?'

'Just starting to come to. The soldiers have created a jungle outside. Couldn't find the ship if you were 20 yards away. 3rd Mate has just gone and taken over the bridge, and the Mate is in the messroom with the Chief and the 2nd Engineer. No sign of any naval ships or helicopters yet. I'll go and get your breakfast, Sir.' With that Delilah left.

Twenty minutes later Harry, freshly bathed, shaved and dressed, went through to his dayroom and found Carole sitting there, smiling at him.

'Good morning, Harry. I thought I would join you for breakfast if you don't mind.'

'Hell no, who would mind a sight like you in the morning.' Harry bent over her and kissed her. 'God, you look good.'

'That's what I was hoping.'

Delilah appeared at the door with a large tray. 'I hope I'm not intruding but you both have to eat regardless of anything else.' They hastily parted as Delilah laid out breakfast on the low table.

'Delilah, we could have come down to the messroom.'

'I just thought it would be nice to have breakfast together,' Carole said smiling at Harry. 'And Delilah told me to come up so what could I do?'

They sat contentedly. 'I didn't realise how hungry I was,' said Harry tucking in with relish.

'You and me both.'

'How are your tribe?'

'Doing very well. Of course they now have a hero in Beckle. Strange how they are adapting to the ship. The children are having a wonderful time especially as the crew are spoiling them every chance they get.'

'And the soldiers and their families?'

'The same. There is still a problem over the pygmies, but that's mostly from the Colonel and some of the soldiers. The women are mixing in and helping each other. I think Beckle's activities helped.'

There was a knock on the door. Harry looked up. It was Peter.

'Good morning, you two,' Peter said. 'Hope I'm not intruding.'

'Hell no, Peter,' said Harry. 'Want a coffee?'

'No thanks, full up from the messroom. Harry, you are the proud owner of two engines again.'

'That's great,' said Harry getting up. 'Well done, Peter. You and your team have done a great job.'

'Tell you what, it was far better down below last night than where you were. I want to start the engine now and just let it run for a few hours before we start running it up.'

'That's not a problem, Peter. I'll tell Graham.'

'No need, already done that. I'll leave you two to finish your breakfast. See you later.'

'He seems happier now,' said Carole.

'That's because he's fixed his engine. Under the surface he's still upset about this whole business. I don't blame him but then we had no choice.'

Harry sat back down. 'It seems strange after last night to be sitting here in the quiet, having breakfast as if nothing had happened.'

'I expect things will soon liven up again,' replied Carole. As if in agreement with her statement, there was a rumble from the depths of the ship as the starboard engine started. Harry reached for his phone and called the bridge.

'Any smoke from the funnel?'

'Just a small haze, Sir. Nothing that will show,' Graham replied.

'Good. What about river traffic?'

'Small local craft only so far.'

Harry put the phone down. He looked puzzled. 'It's strange. I could have sworn the naval craft would have been here by now.' He thought for a moment. 'Unless they were waiting for us to come down to them. If that's the case, they would not have left until around 0800 which means they are still on their way.'

'Is that good or bad?'

'It's good. It means that if they want to get back to Boma by sunset they don't have too long to look for us. If they're examining their side of the bank on the way, they are not going to get up this way until around 1500 and then by the time they get to the Cauldron, they will be turning back and going full speed back to Boma. It also explains why we haven't seen any helicopters yet.' He finished his tea and stood up. 'I'm going up to the bridge. Want to join me?'

'You'll get a surprise,' said Carole, standing with him.

They left the cabin and walked through the office, up the stairway onto the bridge. Harry certainly was surprised. The bridge was still relatively shaded with only three windows open and he saw that the crew had already fastened ply board over the shattered stern window. But when he stepped out onto the bridge wing a sea of greenery greeted him. The upperworks had branches strapped around all the exposed areas and on the decks a carpet of undergrowth had been scattered to cover up the steel decks. On the stern it looked like a row of trees planted across the ship. Even the Colonel's vehicles were covered.

'Done a good job haven't they?' Harry turned; it was Sandy.

'Good morning, your Honour. What a lovely morning it is now. I am pleased to report that all is well with our little world again, and as you heard we have our engine back.'

'Good morning, Sandy. Where's the Colonel?'

'He's ashore. They've found a road, running down the bank just behind the trees. It's obviously in use because of the vehicle tracks and there's a bridge there over the creek, so he's set up half his men there to guard us from any surprises.'

'The crew?'

'Delilah, Andy and Taffy have got them in the crew messroom going over a few rudiments of weapon handling, hopefully making sure they don't shoot themselves or us if they have to use them.'

Harry looked around. 'It's going to be hot today.' He slapped his neck. 'Bloody mosquitoes. I suppose that's what comes of parking in a swamp. Let's get inside.'

Graham was staring intently into the radar. 'Still nothing, Sir.'

'Should have been here by now,' said Sandy. Harry explained his theory as to why there was no appearance yet of any enemy activity.

'Could well be,' said Sandy. Carole was looking at the chart. 'Harry, why do we have to go past Boma? There's a big island in the middle of the river and we could go the other side of that. We wouldn't even see Boma then.' They joined her at the chart. 'You see these little numbers in the river?' Carole nodded. 'They tell us the depth. We need a minimum of six metres. Look at the depth there.' He ran his finger along the river. 'It's all less than five.'

'But there are lots of places without figures.'

'That means that no one knows what the depth is there. Also you will see that there are no buoys marked, there are also lots of sand and mudbanks. If we tried to go that way and got stuck, we would be sitting ducks for their navy and helicopters. Even if they didn't come, they would put guns on the island and just pound us to bits. We have to go right past Boma to get out. Even then we have problems getting down the marked channel between Boma and the sea. Many of the buoys are out of position, and added to that the sand and mudbanks are always changing. No one has surveyed the area for years and no dredging has been done throughout the years of war. Rivers, especially estuaries, have to be constantly dredged otherwise they silt up. Like this one.'

'But you came in.'

'That we did, because the pilots have local knowledge and know where the banks are. Even then they won't do it in the dark. Each year the size of ship they can take up river is getting smaller.'

'So what are you thinking?' asked Sandy.

'Well, we have to go past Boma, that's certain. The problem is what may be waiting for us. The channel is too wide to block completely. If they have any guns or tanks on the jetty, they will be firing at point blank range as we go past. We saw what a tank can do in the Cauldron. If we do get past we will be out in the estuary with nowhere to hide with their naval craft and helicopters coming after us. One thing is certain, we can't stay here. If not today, they will find us tomorrow. Being stuck here in the creek we can't do very much so whatever happens, we have to go tonight.'

'Could we send one of the boats up ahead of us to see what is waiting?' asked Sandy.

'Only if we are willing to lose the boat and crew. The boat can't hide anywhere. Also if there is any guard at all, they would be seen and then the port would be fully alerted. The only way is for us to arrive at full speed and with as little warning as possible.'

'Can we go very fast with both the engines?' asked Carole.

'On a good day, with the wind up our backside, we can make 14 knots.'

'Which is?'

'Just over 16 miles per hour.'

'That's not very fast.'

'Not when there's a bloody great big tank firing at you it's not,' said Sandy.

Harry was looking thoughtfully at the chart. 'We can't go through without dealing with the naval vessels.'

'The only gun we've got is the one on the Colonel's armoured vehicle and I don't think we can take on all the Zaire Navy with that, no matter how useless they are.'

'No, Sandy. I wasn't thinking of using that, although it could be useful. We are an ice class ship right?' Sandy nodded. 'Then our bow is thick reinforced steel. Those naval boats are just that. Boats, wooden hulls and aluminium, I suspect, or even if steel then very thin. We will go through them like a knife through butter. Graham? Have we got the Colonel on the radio?'

'Yes, Sir.'

'Ask him if he could join us on the bridge would you please? He knows more about Boma than any of us. Let's see what he knows about the layout there.'

Graham spoke up. 'Sir, I think that when we came in, the naval craft were all alongside here,' he said pointing at the jetty on the chart, 'just as the jetty starts as we go in and close to the airport.'

'You're right,' said Harry. 'I think there were two boats berthed one alongside the other.'

'There was another astern of them as well,' said Graham. At that moment Vijay came on the bridge. Harry suddenly noticed the time.

'Change of watch,' said Graham. 'May I hand over, Sir?'

The two officers carried on changing over the watch as Harry turned back to Sandy.

'So the idea is that we ram them?' asked Sandy.

'Basically, yes.'

'We might well take damage on the bow.'

'If we do, we do. The damage won't extend beyond the forepeak bulkhead and if the forepeak is breached so what. It's designed for holding water anyway. I can live with that.'

Graham, who had been watching aft, called out that the Colonel was coming on board. Harry went to look. They had rigged up a gangway of branches and ropes to the shore and the Colonel hauled himself along this and dropped down onto the deck. He was carrying an AK47 in his hand and strode easily towards the accommodation block. A few minutes later he appeared on the bridge. His teeth gleamed as he smiled broadly.

'Good morning, gentlemen, or rather afternoon,' he said as he looked at his watch. He put his weapon down on the chart table.

'All quiet on the road, Colonel? asked Harry.

'Not a whisper so far.'

'We're looking at Boma.' Harry briefly explained their thoughts so far.

'I agree that we have to go through tonight,' said the Colonel. 'And that the naval vessels must be dealt with. If you say your ship is strong enough then that will be the best way of dealing with them. But that still leaves anything on the jetty and, most importantly, the helicopters.'

'We think the naval vessels are here at the start of the Boma jetty. Can you confirm that is where they should be?'

The Colonel nodded. 'We arranged the military area close to the airport as that is where the military aircraft are. Puts all military in one area making it easier to guard.'

'The question is will the naval craft be alongside?' asked Harry. 'If I were them I would have at least one vessel in the middle of the channel at the start of the Boma approach. Although that wouldn't stop us going through the channel, on any approach the vessel will give warning to the port.'

'That's if they see us,' said Sandy.

'With radar on they can hardly miss us can they? There is no rain, it's a clear night and an open river.'

'We don't know that they'll have their radar on.'

'But we can't assume they won't. They can't be that stupid. We could keep as tight to the bank as possible. They certainly can't see us until we round the corner for the final approach. That's still 4 miles to go which at our speed with the current means at least 12 minutes in view of the radar.'

Sandy pointed his finger at the chart. 'We could keep to the Angolan bank. If we do that when we round the bend there will be an island between us and the Boma channel. We can make our approach behind that.'

Harry looked with new interest. 'That could work but we come from behind the island at about two miles from Boma.'

'At least that halves the time in view before we get there.'

Harry mused. 'That gives them 6 minutes to wake up, call the crew to stations and get ready to engage.'

'By which time we will be on top of them and opening up with what we've got,' replied Sandy. 'Their guns will be on the open deck. We have enough fire power with the heavy machine gun and various other weapons to keep them busy.' Harry continued to look at the chart. 'If they have a guard ship stationed in the approach to Boma and if we can get to it, I can hit them with a glancing blow that will open up their hull and should still allow us to turn into the jetty and hit whatever is there.'

'Colonel,' Harry asked, 'do you know what weapons are on these ships?'

'Sorry, Captain, I'm army. But I do know that they have twin cannons mounted forward.'

'That's enough,' said Harry. 'They'll certainly punch through any part of the superstructure.'

'What about the bow area?'

'Probably not as it is ice strengthened.'

'So,' said Sandy slowly.

'So,' said Harry picking up what Sandy was thinking. 'We raise the bow as far as we can. If we pump out everything we've got in the forepeak and forward tanks and fill everything aft, we'll have protection from the bow in the final approach.'

'You'll still need some more protection on the bridge front.'

Harry turned to Graham. 'Ask the Chief to come up for a moment.'

'What are you thinking?' asked Sandy.

'I'm thinking of his engine room plates.'

'What are they?' asked the Colonel.

'They are the floor of the engine room. They are designed as separate steel sections that can be taken up to get at the pipes below.'

'Ah, I understand. You will put these around your bridge front.'

'I hope so, Colonel.'

'May I recommend that you leave a small space between the ship and the plates. I will then get my men to fill that space with earth. That's the best armour of all.'

The Colonel turned to Sandy. 'Do you have any sacks on board?'

'Lots why?'

'I suggest that your crew fill these with earth and put them around the machine gun post above the bridge and anywhere else that we will be firing from.'

'Good idea, Colonel. I'll get them onto it immediately after they have had their meal.'

'That leaves the helicopters,' said Harry looking at the Colonel. The Colonel bent over the chart.

'You can see that the airfield is less than half a mile from the naval jetty,' said Harry. 'If we can hold the ship there, you and your men can get to the airfield, deal with the helicopters and then get back to the ship.'

The Colonel looked at the chart. 'The problem is that with the ship charging into Boma, by the time I get to the airfield they will be fully alert. Even if we can deal with the airport we then have to get back to you.'

'What is the force at Boma?'

'Boma is much smaller than Matadi so I should think that there will be far fewer troops there but I have no idea how strong the force is. Also I don't know if there are any Angolan troops there. We know that they helped take Boma but are they still there?' He shrugged. 'The rebel filth I can deal with but if there are Angolan forces, they are a different story. Not that they fight any better, but they will be well armed.'

At that moment Peter arrived on the bridge. 'Peter, I want your engine room plates.'

'How many?'

'All of them.'

'What the hell do we walk on then?'

'I can supply you with planks,' said Sandy.

Peter rounded on him. 'I'm being serious!'

'Christ, Peter, don't be so prickly, so am I,' said Sandy.

'Let me explain, Peter,' said Harry. 'We are going through Boma, tonight. Things will probably get pretty rough. There are up to three naval vessels there and they have a cannon which is capable of punching through the bridge front. If they manage to do that, apart from taking us out, the ship stops. We cannot carry on without our controls.'

Peter looked around at them all. 'Why can't the Colonel and his men get off at Boma? That was the original intention wasn't it?'

'Because Boma is now occupied by the rebels and probably the Angolans,' said the Colonel. 'So now we are going to take on the Navy and the Air Force and sail through a town in the rebel hands. Let me ask you all this. When do we stop? I mean what happens if we are hit badly and we have people injured or, God forbid, dead. Do we stop then?'

There was silence. Eventually Harry replied. 'There is no alternative. We keep going.'

'Until we sink?'

Harry shrugged.

'You're bloody mad. All of you,' Peter said.

'We need the plates.'

'Is there nothing else you can use?'

'We could cut the main decking up but that would take far too long and we have to be out of here tonight. That would also tend to let the water in.'

'When do you want these?'

'As soon as we can have them. And we'll want them fixed in place.'

'That's all of my lads then as well?'

'I'm sorry, Peter. There's nothing else we can do.'

'I'll get the deck crowd to give a hand in getting the plates up,' said Sandy. 'I'll also show your lads where to fix them. We will also need some steel girder as well. We want to make a space between them and the bulkhead so we can pack earth in between.'

'I hope you've got plenty of planks,' Peter said. Sandy turned to Harry.

'I'll go with Peter and get this started.' He turned to Graham who was hovering. 'Come on, we'll grab a quick bite and get going. We have a busy afternoon.'

Chapter 17

'Sir, there is movement on the river.' Vijay was staring at the radar screen. Harry quickly joined him. Vijay indicated two echoes in the middle of the river.

'I'm tracking them now.' They waited for the computer to produce the target resolution. 'Speed 13 knots and that's against the current. They will be abeam of us in 45 minutes.'

'They're not hanging around then,' said Harry. 'They must be heading up to the bridge.'

Harry went to the ship's tannoy system and switched on all the stations. 'This is the Captain. We have two naval vessels approaching up the river. We expect them near the ship in 30 minutes. All personnel must clear the decks by then. That is all.'

'Do you want any weapons manned,' asked the Colonel.

'You can man your AML. That's about the only weapon we have that can outrange them,' said Harry.

The Colonel picked up his radio and called his Lieutenant. 'They will be ready in 15 minutes.'

'I am hoping that as they are speeding up the river, they are not too bothered about searching, which means that when they come back down, they will hopefully be searching their side of the river,' explained Harry. 'That's the theory anyway. Watch them, Vijay, and let me know of any change.'

'So,' Harry said turning to the Colonel, 'we were discussing the airport. Look here, Colonel. You said the main problem is that surprise would be lost.' Harry was pointing to the turn just before the final approach to Boma. 'See this island here. Opposite there is a village marked on the chart.'

'That doesn't mean it is still there,' said the Colonel. 'Things change fast in this country.'

'Never mind, there must still be some form of road or track leading there from Boma. What about if I dropped your party off there?' He measured the distance to the airport. 'You have four miles to go to the airport. No one will be expecting you from that direction. If I wait until I hear your attack going on, then make my move, you will have surprise. It will take me 20 minutes to get from there to the naval area by which time you should be on your way to join me. You only have half a mile to go to reach me from the airport.'

The Colonel looked thoughtfully at the chart. 'That half a mile may not be easy.'

'The way I see it, when you start an attack, anyone waiting on the waterfront for us to go past will hear that and immediately head towards the airport. Then when we attack, they will turn back towards us. We will catch them from two sides.'

There was silence for a moment. 'How long can you hold in the naval area? Remember, as you have told me, you are civilians. If I attack the airport I have to depend that you can hold where you are for my men to get out.'

Harry looked at him steadily. 'We will be there for you, Colonel.'

They looked at each other for a moment then the Colonel looked back at the chart. 'Did you know our vehicles are amphibious?' Harry shook his head. 'Out here, with all the rivers and swamps, it is essential that we have that ability. That is why we ensured our armoured vehicles had that capability. Now that island you mentioned. Look, there is a small waterway between that and the main bank of the river. It might be possible either at the village or somewhere along that bank for us to get the vehicles out. If not we have not lost anything. I can send them back to the ship. Can you approach as close as possible and put us over the side? If we can get the APCs and AML to the airport, we will have an advantage and a good chance of getting through anything they can put in our way to get back to where you are.'

'That's easy, Colonel. We can use the crane and launch you in the river off the village. We can send in one of the boats with a scout party to assess the village and whether it is suitable to land. The boat can then guide you in.'

'Then that's what we will do. Between us we will get the ship through Boma.' The Colonel looked up at Harry and grinned. 'If not then we will give them something to remember us by, eh?'

'Abeam in 10 minutes, Sir,' said Vijay.

'Thanks,' said Harry and he picked up the microphone. 'All personnel clear the decks.'

Delilah appeared. 'Shall I man the machine gun, Captain?'

'No, Delilah, the range is too great. Just stand by here in case they do see us and close in but at the moment they are heading up river at full speed and I want to keep it that way.'

Harry picked up the binoculars and went out onto the bridge wing. He peered through the branches that were fastened around the bridge and was joined by the Colonel. 'Can't see much at this range but they have a gun forward. I would estimate the patrol boats to be about 30 metres long. At that speed they'll be at the Matadi bridge in roughly an hour. Then they'll come back down. They'll have about 4 hours before it gets dark and will need three of those to get back so they can't spend too long looking for us. If they call out a helicopter they will probably do that in an hour.

The patrol boats were slowing down and then speeding up, turning into the bank where they thought that there was a creek where the ship may be. They slowly came abreast of the ship but stayed on the far side of the river. Harry could see that their deck guns were manned and turned towards the river bank. They gradually passed by and continued up the river towards Matadi. Harry turned away. 'Vijay, broadcast that the decks are open again. By the way, that was an interesting manoeuvre you pulled in the Cauldron. Where did you dream that up?'

'I remembered when you told me about coming out of that bay in Japan into a typhoon with a light ship and how you could not bring the ship around so turned in towards the rocks and took her around the other way.'

'So I did, Vijay, but not with a bloody tow line on the other end. Didn't you think about running over it?'

'Yes, Sir, but I thought that with waterjet engines and no propeller, and with the bow raised up with the speed, I would ride over it.'

'Well you did that but what about nearly colliding with me?'

'It was worth the risk, Captain. If I had let go, I doubt I would have been able to take on the line again before you hit the cliffs.'

'You know, Vijay, there is a saying that nothing succeeds as well as success. You did well. What a shame you want to join the Coastguard Agency.'

'But they need seamen.'

'We'll see, Vijay. Let me know when you see the naval boats coming back down the river and keep a good watch for any helicopters. I expect them soon.'

Harry was sitting at his desk after lunch when the phone rang. It was Vijay.

'Sir, the Colonel says that they have movement ashore.'

Harry shot out of his cabin and ran down the stairways to the main deck. He was just about to climb the branch gangway that had been constructed when there was a flurry of gunfire ashore, followed by further explosions and the crack of a heavy weapon. Harry crouched down on the deck and waited. There were a few short sporadic bursts of fire and then silence again.

Sandy appeared, 'What was that?'

'No idea. I had a call from the bridge saying that they had company ashore, so I came down to check it out. Come on.'

Harry swung out on the tree branch and clawed through the branches to the shore. Landing on the muddy bank he crouched down and worked his way through the mangrove trees until he could see a group of soldiers standing on the rough track. From their black berets he could see they were the Colonel's men. He shouted out and held his hands up. One of them turned and seeing him, grinned and beckoned him forward. Harry stepped out of the trees and saw a wrecked truck on its side off the track and a jeep against a tree. There was a body half out of the front seat. Further up the track was a smoking APC while on the ground were more bodies. The Colonel was standing with a group of his soldiers surrounding a small group of soldiers holding their hands above their heads. They were wearing a mix of blue helmets and berets.

The Colonel turned and waved. 'Captain, we have visitors. I believe you are acquainted.' With that he pushed forward one of the prisoners. It was the UN Major. 'Would you believe the fools came down the track as if they owned it. No scouts, no precautions, straight into our arms.'

The Major had lost his hat and one of his epaulets was torn off. He had blood coming from a graze on his cheek.

'Captain, you are crazy. We are UN troops. This is Angola. You cannot attack UN troops like this. You must stop this madness.'

Harry looked at him. 'I didn't do anything, Major. You had better speak to the Colonel before he shoots you all.'

'He will not do that.'

'Really? Didn't he tell you? Your friends in Matadi killed all his family. I don't think he is too concerned about who you work for. I think you are in real trouble, Major. I'm going back to the ship.'

'Captain,' the Major pleaded. 'You must help. Don't leave us here! If he kills us it will be murder!'

'Just like those young girls who disappeared from Matadi, Major?'

'I had nothing to do with that, Captain. I was obeying orders.'

Just then there was a shot. Harry turned to see the Colonel with a smoking pistol standing over a figure by the jeep. He looked up and saw Harry staring. 'He was badly injured, Captain. It was for the best.'

'You bastard!' said Harry. The Colonel shrugged and calmly holstered his pistol.

Sandy looked at the Major. 'If you're religious, I would think of something to say.'

The Major looked at Harry desperately. 'Captain, what is it you want?'

'Why you're here and what is in Boma. You are going to tell us everything you know.'

'I do not know anything.'

Sandy stepped forward and took the Major by his collar and shook him. 'Listen, arsehole, you have one chance. Tell us everything you know now and you might just live. If you don't, that man there,' he said indicating the Colonel, 'will really enjoy making you talk and then you will be killed. He enjoys it. Anyway, the UN will be better off without filth like you.'

The Major looked around wildly. 'There's no help coming, Major,' said Harry.

The Colonel stepped forward. 'I'll take him now, Captain, you go. You don't want to see this.' He called to his men and two soldiers stepped forward and dragged the Major down to the ground while the Colonel drew his knife and bent down towards him.

The Major started to scream. 'OK! Please! Stop! Wait! I am searching this side of the river for you. The boats from Boma are searching the other side!' He was panicking.

'That's better. Now calm down. Tell us about Boma. Are there any Angolan troops there?'

'There were but I think they have gone back. I don't know. I think so.'

'What about Kabila's soldiers? How many are there in Boma?'

'I don't know. I promise you, 'I am speaking the truth!'

Harry looked at the Colonel. 'What do you think?'

The Colonel shrugged. 'I can cut his hands off to see.'

'No! Please No!' the Major screamed.

'Are there any other UN or Angolan troops near here?' asked the Colonel.

'No, Sir. We are the only ones. Sir, I speak the truth.' His eyes were round and white with fear. He was shaking as the soldiers held him on the ground.

'I'll shoot him now,' said the Colonel. 'He's no use to us.' He took his pistol out and raised it up to the Major.

'No!' shouted Harry. 'Let him up. I don't think he is lying. Who are you reporting to?' He asked the Major.

'What?'

'I said who are you reporting to? You must be going to tell someone if you find us.'

'I am reporting to the General in Matadi.'

'On the radio in the jeep?'

'Yes.'

Harry looked at the Colonel. 'The Major may have some use to us alive after all. What are you going to do with the other prisoners?' asked Harry. There were several UN soldiers huddled together being guarded by the Lieutenant and his men.

'Shoot them,' said the Colonel.

'No, you're not going to,' said Harry. 'That's murder. They were just doing what they were ordered to do. You are unbelievable. You think that is the answer to everything.'

The Colonel sighed. 'So what do you want, Captain? If we let them go they will report what has happened and where we are.'

'We take them with us.'

'Then what?'

'We will let them go in Boma.'

'This is stupid, Captain.'

'I say that is what will happen, Colonel, and what I say goes. Do you understand?' The Colonel shrugged and held his hands out.

'All right, Captain, if that is what you want. No wonder your country lost an empire.'

'Better than wandering the planet killing people. Listen, Colonel, these guys have given us our way into Boma. You can take their uniforms. The sight of UN troops appearing at the airfield will cause whoever is there to hesitate before they open fire. That will give you the edge. Put the UN flags on your vehicles and that will add to the confusion. What about the radio in the jeep? Does it still work?'

Sandy went over to the jeep. He leant forward and turned on the ignition. 'Well, the radio lights up, so I presume it works.'

'Do you think they sent out any report when they were attacked?' Harry asked the Colonel.

'No chance. It was very quick. The jeep was the first to be hit.'

'What about if the Major sent out a report this evening that he had us under surveillance and that we were broken down in the creek and requested a helicopter attack at dawn. Then he confirmed later in the evening just before we attacked. Would the General in Matadi not relay that to Boma? If he did then they would not expect us to attempt a passage during the night.'

The Colonel rubbed his chin. 'Who knows, it might work. You can't tell.'

Harry persisted. 'But it might work. At least it could cause confusion. It's worth a try.'

'All right, Captain. We can do that. But I'll be in charge of these prisoners. If they make one wrong move then they are dead.'

'Not the Major though.'

'Not the Major. Meanwhile we'll get these vehicles off the track into the trees.'

'Colonel, we are expecting a possible visit from a helicopter soon. Can you get your men to man what machine guns we have, just in case, but no firing unless they attack us. Do you have any experience of the Stingers?'

'No, but your steward Delilah might.'

Chapter 18

Harry and Sandy went to the bridge to inspect the plating. Hissing blue flares were coming from the two welding machines as the plating was being welded to the girders. In the finished areas, crew were putting earth from sacks, infilling the gap.

Sandy turned to him. 'Almost finished. It'll take a lot to get through this.'

Jake was covered in dirt from the earth and was working with the crew. He grinned at Harry. 'At least someone's happy,' commented Harry.

'Pure bloody ignorance of youth,' said Sandy. 'He's a good lad though.'

'As good as we were?'

'Better. He doesn't get pissed as often.'

'The warships will be coming back down river soon.'

'Vijay's watching out for them. Strange there haven't been any helicopters yet.'

'They probably haven't been called for. I'm going down to see how Carole is coping with the passengers. Call me when the warships appear and clear the decks. I'll send Delilah up to man the machine gun on the monkey island.'

'Tell him to bring one of the Stingers up, Captain. That's what they are for.'

On his way down below, Harry poked his head into the galley where Delilah was working with the Cook.

'How's it going, Cook?'

'Apart from trying to run a 24 hour a day café and supply the hordes down below while at the same time every son of a bitch wanders in and out of the galley like it's the local park, not a problem, Captain. And another thing, I'm fed up with cooking food no one eats, especially Captains. Not you of, course.' Harry smiled. 'Good to hear that, Cook. Delilah, I want you topside on the machine gun just in case we get a visit from a helicopter. Do you know anything about the Stingers?'

'A little, Captain. I used them in Iraq.'

'Take one of them up with you as well.'

'Already stashed up there beside the gun, Sir.'

'Right. On your way, check in with the bridge and tell them to call me as soon as anything is seen.'

Harry carried on down to the next deck and the workers' quarters. He found Carole in the galley watching the women preparing food for the evening meal. Even with the air conditioning, it was hot and steamy and the smell of cooking food was heavy in the air. In the alleyway outside, clothing was drying on lines that had been rigged to the pipes running along the deckheads.

'There is a laundry you know,' he said to Carole. Carole smiled in greeting and brushed her damp hair from her forehead.

'With all the laundry we have, it would be overwhelmed,' she said. 'They don't mind, except Sandy told us to bring the clothing off the decks and inside for drying in case it attracted any attention.'

'Probably would as well,' he said eying the bright clothing that was hanging outside the galley. 'We have just had an incident.' He briefly told her about the UN soldiers.

'Are any of the prisoners injured?'

'I don't know. Certainly not badly injured. The Colonel has seen to that.'

'Evil bastard,' she said. 'I'll go and see if there is anything I can do. What are you going to do with them?'

'I'll let them go in Boma. Can't do it before in case they talk to anyone.' He waved his hand around the galley. 'You're going to have to talk to them all about Boma,' he said. 'It could get bad there.'

'How bad?' Harry outlined the plan.

'Can you really ram other ships?'

'I've not had much experience. The type of ships we intend ramming are flimsy compared to us. We'll be damaged, but nothing we can't deal with. The main problem will be any weapons they have there. We don't know what or who is waiting for us. The starboard side will take the brunt of any firing so you must have everyone on the port side and keep them there until it is over. The Colonel has briefed the soldiers and they will tell their families, but you must deal with your pygmies.'

'We are definitely going tonight?'

'We have to. If we stay they will find us.'

'Will this be the end of it?'

He looked at her for a moment and lied. 'Yes. Once through we will be heading at full speed for the sea.'

'Thank God for that.'

He gave her a quick kiss. 'Just keep your head down.'

She smiled. 'The same for you.'

On the way back along the alleyway, the ship's tannoy called. 'Captain to the bridge.' Harry broke into a run and dashed up the stairway to the bridge. He threw the door open. Vijay was standing with Sandy, both of them with binoculars looking aft over the river. Vijay turned holding out his binoculars to Harry.

'Helicopter,' he said indicating down the river. Harry steadied the binoculars and focused them, sweeping the river slowly until he found the insect-like helicopter which was slowly working its way up the river. Harry grabbed the microphone, checked it was switched to the general ship's address channel and clicked the transmit button.

'This is the Captain. There is a helicopter approaching the ship. All personnel clear the decks. Stand by the machine guns. There is to be no firing until my direct order. I repeat there is to be no firing until I order.' He turned off the microphone and called the engine room. 'We have a helicopter approaching. Stop the engine.' He turned to Vijay. I don't want any smoke or heat haze coming from the funnel. Does the Colonel know?'

'Yes, Sir,' said Vijay. 'I told him on the walkie-talkie.'

The rumbling of the engine died away as Harry picked up his binoculars again.

'It seems to be more over the other side of the river,' said Sandy, 'but it's definitely searching.'

'Can we see it on radar yet?'

'Not yet,' answered Vijay, 'but I have two targets coming down the river at 20 knots. They must be naval vessels.'

Harry walked over to the radar. 'They are coming down the middle. At that speed they are not searching so they are heading back to their base in Boma, leaving it to the helicopter.'

'What about the radar?' said Sandy. 'Will they pick up any transmissions from that?'

'I think their equipment is pretty basic,' said Harry. 'Anyway it's too late now. If they were going to pick anything up they would have done so by now and be heading for us rather than steaming along the middle of the river.'

'I see the Colonel has his guns ready,' said Sandy pointing down on the deck. All the armoured vehicles had their weapons trained aft towards the river. 'If they do see us they're going to get a nasty shock.'

'The trouble is that even if we shoot them down, we will have lost any surprise and we will have no chance of getting past Boma,' replied Harry.

They stood in silence watching the approaching helicopter flitting around the sky and the naval vessels coming down the river. The naval vessels passed first not deviating from their course. They left a stream of dirty exhaust smoke behind them. As they got near to the helicopter, it hovered over them for a moment before heading back to a search pattern, still concentrating on the Zaire side of the river. 'With luck we may have got away with it,' said Harry looking at his watch.

'Where's the Cadet by the way? He should be on watch by now.' 'He's up on the monkey island with Delilah,' Sandy explained. 'Delilah needs someone to fire the machine gun and he has shown Jake how to do it. Delilah's got the Stinger.'

The helicopter was now level with the ship within its view. It was hovering and swinging around as if studying all the area. Harry held his breath. It swung around again but this time started moving slowly along the far side of the river.

Harry slowly let out his breath. 'At least we know they can't detect heat or radar emissions. If they intend getting back by dusk they only have another hour to go.'

The bridge door banged open and they turned round to see Chalkie, the 2nd Engineer, coming through carrying the radio set from the jeep. 'I was told to bring this up here, Captain,' he said. 'Where do you want it set up?'

'Can you rig it on the side of the chart table?'

'As long as there is a 12 volt power supply,' Chalkie replied. He put the set down. 'I can link it into the power supply for the emergency VHF and also link in the aerial. That should get it working.' He took his tools from his pockets and set to on the wiring.

Harry turned to Sandy. 'As soon as it gets dark and that helicopter has disappeared we'll get the Major to make his first broadcast. Once that is done we'll start up and get out of here. Where's the helicopter?'

'Going further up river, Captain,' Vijay replied.

'Right, ask the Colonel to come up to the bridge. Broadcast for the Bosun to come up as well. Vijay, get Jake down from the monkey island to take the watch.'

Chapter 19

Harry went to the chart table and put the chart light on, dimming it down. The shadows were deepening now as dusk approached. He measured the passage past Boma. Just over 1 mile and then 36 miles to the sea. Even then there was another 30 odd miles before they were in international waters. There was no way they could be clear before dawn. Jake had come into the wheelhouse and was taking over from Vijay.

'Jake, all I want from you is to watch for that helicopter coming back down the river.' Jake immediately went over to the radar. 'You will probably see it with binoculars first but watch with both. Give Delilah a pair up top and he can keep a lookout as well. Vijay, Sandy, come over here.' The Colonel arrived on the bridge. 'Good timing,' said Harry. 'Out of interest, where are the prisoners?'

'On the main deck being guarded except the Major. We have locked him up in one of the APCs. The Doctor has seen them and patched a few up. Otherwise all they want to do is go home.'

'Don't we all,' Sandy murmured.

'All of you, look at the chart. You see we have 12 miles to go to the drop off point for the vehicles.'

'That's if we can find somewhere to land,' interjected the Colonel.

'I'm coming to that,' said Harry. 'When we get out of here, we will launch Rescue 1, which will go ahead to the village near Prince's Island and see if we can land them there. If they can't be landed, they will navigate up the passage between the island and river bank to see if there are any other places, but I am hoping that, if there are boats at the village, there will be a slip or a sloping bank for landing the vehicles.'

'Do you have any matting on board, Captain?' asked the Colonel. 'If you have and we can lay that on the river bank, that would help the vehicles grip when they land.'

Harry looked at Sandy who shook his head. 'No call for those on a ship,' he said.

'We have the safety nets, Captain,' said Vijay.

'What are those?' asked the Colonel.

Sandy replied, 'They are put under the gangways to stop people from falling off into the water when the ship is alongside. We have a couple of those and of course we have the scrambling nets for putting over the side when rescuing people. Two of those as well.'

'Can we have those, Captain?'

'Of course, if you think they'll help.'

'Believe me, when you see these vehicles on mud, anything will help.'

'We will need some soldiers in the boat in case the vehicles are seen from the village.'

'I was thinking that, Captain. It will be better if we have enough to take over the village before we land then we know that there will be no trouble.'

'Do you think there will be any rebel soldiers there?'

'Unlikely. It will only be a few huts and there are more attractions in the town, but just to be sure we want to control the place. I will send 8 men and the Lieutenant. That should be plenty. They can also check out the track towards Boma.'

'We will start out from here at 2100. That should give us ample time to get out, launch the boat and then drift along until we hear from the boat. Then we can speed up to a position off the village and land the vehicles. Sandy, before we start, I want you to lighten her as much as possible forward. That will help her to come off the mud. Once we have done that we can keep her like that ready for Boma. Now can anyone see anything we haven't covered?'

'Just a walk in the park, your Honour,' said Sandy.

'One small point. What about if we cannot find a place for the vehicles to land?'

Harry turned to the Colonel. 'It's your decision, Colonel. Whatever happens we must take out the helicopters, otherwise in the morning they will come for us unless we can hide anywhere else.' Harry pointed to the chart. 'You can see that once we pass Boma we are in the open. It is too shallow to approach either bank.'

'Then that settles it. We have to go in. So we will return the vehicles and then go in on the boat.'

'Do we have to bring the vehicles back?' asked Vijay.

'We don't know what is waiting at Boma,' said Harry. 'We may need all the firepower we can get. At least if they are parked on the deck with their guns facing the shore, we will have something.'

'If we have to bring them back I will leave a few soldiers to man them,' said the Colonel.

Harry turned to Sandy. 'How long will it take to put them in the water?'

Sandy thought for a moment. 'About 20 minutes for each one. Allow a total of one and a half hours in case anything goes wrong.'

'Colonel, if we get them ashore how long to the airport?'

'Allow an hour, for the same reason as Sandy.'

'So, if we start to land them at 2300, we can expect the attack to go on from 0130. That means we have to be at Boma shortly after. We will not make the final 4 mile approach until we hear your attack Colonel. Once that starts we will head into the channel. If there is a guard ship we will ram that and then head into anything alongside. If there is no guard vessel and they are all alongside we will head directly at them. Then we will wait for you and your men.'

'That's the problem,' said the Colonel. They all looked at him. 'With all of us off the ship, what's to stop you sailing away and leaving us once we have destroyed the helicopters?'

'Considering you told us you would happily kill us all, it's certainly tempting, but we need each other and that means we have to trust each other. I have told you we will be waiting for you and that is my word.'

The Colonel looked at him steadily. 'Colonel, don't worry. We will be there, that's a promise.' The Colonel thought for a moment. 'I could always take your Cadet with me,' he said looking around them. Harry replied abruptly. 'Don't go there, Colonel. He would love to go with you but absolutely no.' The Colonel shrugged. 'It was worth a try. I have to remember that there are people like you. I trust you, Captain. I have to.'

'How are you going to hold the base?'

'We will try to get there and be ready for when you arrive, but if we are delayed, then you may have to hold the position.'

'Not just that,' said Harry. 'If there are any other naval craft alongside we must try to deal with them as well.'

Sandy spoke up. 'That's why Delilah and Chalkie have been busy instructing some of the crew, Captain. We have a landing party already arranged.'

Harry looked surprised. 'Who?'

'All the ex-military lads supplemented by some of the younger crew members. We have a party of around 10 ready.'

'You will stay on the ship, Sandy. You're too old for this.'

'Absolutely, Captain. I know my place. Delilah will lead them.'

'There you are, Colonel. Everything is ready.'

'Have you considered what might be waiting further up the jetty?'

'We can't prepare for everything,' protested Harry. 'All we can do is get you back on board and get the hell out as fast as we can.' Harry turned to Vijay. 'It is going to be a tricky passage throughout the night. I will want you on the bridge from when we leave until morning. Go down and get some kip now until we leave. I want you bright and on the ball tonight.' Vijay looked as if he was about to protest but then nodded and left the bridge.

'I'm just going down below to see the Bosun,' Sandy said. 'I want to get the pumping in the tanks started.'

'The helicopter's in sight again, Sir.' Jake was standing at the bridge door looking through a pair of binoculars. 'It's coming down the river in the middle of the channel.'

'What are their night flying capabilities?' Harry asked the Colonel.

'Depends who's flying, us or Chinese. Either way, they don't do much of it.'

Harry took another pair of binoculars and watched. 'It doesn't appear to be searching. Hopefully it's heading home.'

Sandy found the Bosun in the crew messroom clutching a large mug of tea. He called to the Peggy for tea and sat down beside him.

'Have you finished the plating on the bridge front?'

'All that we can. There's no more plating left in the engine room and they're not too happy about walking around on planks.'

'Can't be helped, John. We've made our plans up there and they sound good but there are just too many suppositions. I think we are in for a tough few hours and so does the Old Man but he's not saying. The problem is that all the soldiers will be ashore going for the airfield and that leaves us. If we could ram into the ships and then get away we may still have surprise but having to ram into them and then wait for the soldiers to join us means that we have to hold on till they arrive.'

'So what can we do?'

'I want every spare hand armed. Divide them all up into two parties with equal numbers of experienced men in each party. I'll take charge of one party and I'm thinking of putting Delilah in charge of the other. Any objections?'

'No. Good choice. Why two parties?

'Because one will have to hold on at this so-called naval base while the other will have to deal with any other craft and may have to deal with anything that is at the other end of the jetty. You will be on the wheel and the 2nd Mate will be navigating. The Chief will be in the engine room. I don't want the Cook involved. He can stand by to assist the Doctor.'

'Old bugger would probably shoot himself anyway,' grinned the Bosun. 'What about the 3rd Mate and the Cadet?'

'The 3rd Mate I want standing by for damage control on board. God knows what will happen when we start bumping into ships, apart from that they may be firing at us. I've never rammed ships before, at least not deliberately. I'll take Chalkie the 2nd and Taffy the Fitter. The Cadet's been helping Delilah with the machine gun, so I think he knows it by now, at least as much as any of us. He can man the gun and you can give him the Peggy as his loader. It should also keep the youngest two on board the ship. Lastly, if the Colonel's soldiers are wearing the UN gear then get what you can of their uniform. If the rebels see black berets they might think that we are army units rather than a bunch of sailors on a jolly ashore.'

The Bosun sighed. 'I had a feeling we were going to get those diamonds a bit too easily. It sounds as if we're going to earn them tonight.'

'And tomorrow. We still have to get out to sea and once we're through Boma there's no stopping.'

'Right, I'm off down to the engine room to see the Chief and to sort out the ballasting. As soon as it gets dark, get the boys to clear the jungle off the decks. Are all the boats ready?'

'The Fitter went over the engines today and all the tanks are topped up. Which boat are you sending off tonight?'

'Probably Rescue 1.'

'That'll be the Chief Coxn then. I'll send Stewart as well.'

Sandy hesitated. 'Tell everyone no heroics, John. We just want to get through and on our way.'

'Don't think we've got many heroes on board, Sandy, unless they're impressing some woman ashore.'

Sandy went down to the next deck and opened the engine room door. The heat hit him immediately together with clatter of the generators. Christ, he thought, this is bad enough without the noise and heat of the main engines roaring away. Why anyone would want to be an engineer was beyond him. But they always seemed happy enough. He went down the steep metal ladder to the next level. Looking down, he could see all the planks laid in place of the engine floor plates that were now around the bridge front. Chalkie was wearing the traditional officer's white boilersuit and working on one of the pumps. He waved to Sandy. There was no point in talking as he was wearing his ear protectors so Sandy carried on towards the small insulated control room. Peter was sitting at the desk writing up the engine log. As Sandy entered he looked up.

'Good Lord, a deck officer. What's the matter? Lost your way somewhere or decided to watch people working?'

Sandy smiled. 'Just came down to talk to you about ballasting.'

'And there's me thinking you came down to give me back my engine room plates. Have you seen down below? Just as well we're not at sea; your planks wouldn't last a minute.'

'As soon as we get out of the river, you'll have them back. I promise.'

Peter got up and went over to the percolator. Just then Chalkie and Taffy Williams, the Fitter, walked in.

'What are you doing here? Looking for a job? Sorry, we don't employ unskilled labour,' teased Chalkie.

'Very funny,' said Sandy.

Peter gave Sandy a cup of coffee. 'So what's the latest?'

Sandy sat down and ran through the plans for the night. They sat sombrely for a moment.

'I'll keep the 3rd Engineer with me,' said Peter, 'just in case. The others can join in with the rest of the crew.'

Sandy nodded. 'The 3rd Mate will be on standby for damage control. He can join him if there is a problem.'

'Fair enough. I guess there's no point saying what I think about this again.'

'Peter, you know Harry's position.'

'Yes, but the soldiers are leaving the ship. That gives us the opportunity to contact Boma and give them the soldiers in return for safe passage.'

'I'll go up shortly and talk with Delilah,' said Taffy. 'It might be an idea if those of us with military experience get the crew together and run through a few more things. What about weapons?'

'You've a free hand to take what you want once the Colonel has taken his share,' said Sandy. 'Except for the armoured vehicles. I think the Colonel wants those.'

'How long are we going to wait at Boma for the soldiers?' asked Peter.

'No idea. Until they arrive I suppose.'

Taffy looked worried. 'The longer we wait the harder it's going to be. Every minute will count, especially once we lose the element of surprise and they realise how few we are. I hope the Old Man knows that?'

'He does,' said Sandy.

'We don't even know what's there, right?'

'Right.'

'Then it's going to be an interesting night. I should have stayed running trucks in Nigeria,' said Chalkie.

'Why didn't you?'

Chalkie laughed. 'Too dangerous!'

'Before you all disappear, I want the forepeak emptied and the afterpeak tank filled. That will help us get out and then we'll keep that trim on the ship to keep the bow high for Boma.'

'Watch you don't get the props too low, Sandy. You won't get out at all if you damage them,' said Peter.

'There's plenty of water aft, Peter. We need to break the mud suction forward. If there is still a problem you might have to transfer more water and fuel from any forward tanks to aft.'

The engine phone rang and Chalkie answered. 'The helicopter's gone,' he said. 'We can run the engine again.'

'Good,' said Sandy. 'I'm going before the racket starts.'

Sandy came out of the engine room and walked along the alleyway to the stairway. He was thinking about what Peter had said. This was something to talk over with Harry.

Harry and the Colonel were sitting in Harry's cabin with Carole when Sandy arrived.

'Come and join us,' said Harry.

'Helicopter didn't hang around long then?' said Sandy as he sat down.

'Luckily, it seemed to be more concerned with going home. Is all sorted below?' asked Harry.

'As much as can be expected. The crew are all briefed or being briefed now. The decks are being cleared as soon as it gets dark and then we are ready.'

'You'll be on your own tonight, Carole,' said Sandy. 'Andy will be wanted for the decks.'

'That's all right,' she replied. 'I have Monique and I can use some of the other women if they are needed.'

'Let's hope they are not,' said the Colonel.

Carole looked at him. 'What are you going to do after all this, Colonel?' she asked. 'I mean you have no home, no family, no country. Your only skill is killing.'

The Colonel thought for a moment. 'Doctor, I know you have your own opinions about me but you know, I always worked for this country. Mobutu was no saint but then what rulers in Africa are? Just think, we held together two hundred different ethnic groups for so long. Of course we don't have democracy but that is a luxury for rich countries and rarely is your democracy really free. This is Africa. I know you have been here for a few years but that is, if you excuse the expression, a scratch on the elephant's bottom. Do you really think that this Kabila is going to make anything better? I tell you, the country will descend into barbarism that we have never seen before. I will return and I will be needed. I will take my revenge on those who murdered my family and who knows, maybe I will help establish at least some form of order, but it will take a long time. But this is my country and one day we will govern it the way we want to, not the way the west, east or religions wish to tell us. If it means killing a few more thousand people then so be it. I tell you my particular skills will be needed for a long time. I don't mean to lecture, but you all judge us without knowing us.'

'You're unbelievable,' whispered Carole. The Colonel waved his hand without replying. He turned to Sandy. 'After dinner tonight, I would like to raid your weapons store.'

'That's easy, Colonel. We are getting everything out and distributing what is needed. I want some of your uniform bits that you are not using so I suggest we all meet in the crew messroom after dinner and sort out what we want. Delilah, Taffy and Andy MacBride will be giving some final points to the crew. Perhaps you can also brief the crew on anything you think will help.'

The Colonel looked at Harry questioningly. 'Go ahead. It sounds a good idea,' responded Harry.

'I have something else to raise,' said Carole. 'The pygmies also want to help.' She looked at their faces and raised her hand. 'Before you object, I know that they cannot use your weapons but they do have their bows and, as you know, they are deadly in close range.'

'How many are there?' asked the Colonel.

'Seven including their Kombeti.'

'I cannot use them or want them,' he said contemptuously, 'but maybe they will be useful to you,' he said to Sandy.

'I've seen what they can do,' Sandy said, 'and yes, they could be useful. But their bows are only short range and I hope I don't get close enough to the enemy for them to be used. Carole, please ask them to come to the messroom after dinner and perhaps you can come to help translate.'

Harry looked at his watch. 'Talking of dinner we had better go down before the Cook throws the food over the side. One point before we go. The prisoners.

I intend to let them go in Boma. I thought as soon as the Colonel and his men arrive back, then we let them go. Is everyone happy with that?'

'Does that include the Major?'

'It does.' He looked at them. 'No objections? Good. Let's eat.'

They all left the cabin except Carole who lingered. As soon as the others had gone Harry held her.

'He frightens me,' said Carole.

'Don't worry. At least at the moment he is with us, not the other side.'

'I hope you're right. Kiss me. This is a very strange romance,' she said. 'We seem to meet for a few minutes, grab a quick feel and then back to war.'

'I'll make it up to you when we get to sea. Moonlight strolls on the boat deck, then we can lie on the bed and play with the diamonds.'

'Rather play with you.'

'That can be arranged.' They smiled at each other.

Chapter 20

The crew messroom looked like a village jumble sale, except for the presence of the weapons and the air of excitement that permeated the mess. On one table Andy MacBride had an RPG out with crew gathered around. He was once again going through the firing system. Delilah was distributing ammunition for the AK47s stacked by the door. The soldiers were milling around collecting weapons and equipment and handing over their berets and other uniform bits to crew members. Taffy the Fitter was waiting with a box of hand grenades.

Sandy shouted out, 'Everyone settle down for a minute. I want to run over tonight's little party. Don't get any big ideas. The aim tonight is to land the army boys before Boma. They head to the airfield and take out the helicopters. We then carry on to Boma which is only 4 miles away, ram into as many naval ships as we can, which should be no problem, then take back on board our heroes and head off through the port and into the channel. Then it's full ahead to the sea. Now, if all goes well, these weapons will be for decoration only. We will be divided into two parties. I will lead one and Delilah here will lead the other. We have experience and knowledge; you must listen to us. Joining us tonight we have our new friends,' indicating to the pygmies. 'They're very nasty lads if upset.'

Once we're at Boma for the approach and while alongside and leaving, everyone who is not immediately required must stay clear of the starboard side of the ship. Carole, ensure that all the passengers are kept down in their quarters on the port side. If we take any fire, it'll be initially on the forward part of the ship and then on the starboard side. We'll start the fire pumps before we arrive and have the hoses run out ready to go on all decks. The watertight doors will be closed on sailing tonight. Once again full blackout with all the deadlights down.

Finally, no one fires without orders, no heroics, no one gets hurt and the bar is closed until we get out, so that should give us all an incentive to get out to sea. Then the beer's on me!'

All the crew burst into a cheer to the puzzlement of the pygmies but they grinned seeing the laughter of the crew. Sandy put his hands up. 'Quiet. Any questions you have direct them to your team leaders. Colonel, do you have anything to say?'

The Colonel stood. 'Just remember this, if you see any rebel soldiers, remember they are more scared of you than you are of them. Very few of them have had proper military training although there may be a scattering of regular army soldiers amongst them. If you see any youngsters or even children with weapons and they are pointing them at you, don't hesitate. They are just as dangerous as an adult. When they fire it is mostly just spraying in your general direction so as long as you keep under cover you will be fine. Don't try and tackle any fixed position or vehicles. Leave that to those with military experience. Finally, I promise you I will be back from the airfield as soon as I can. Hopefully I will be waiting for you when you arrive. Good luck.'

The bridge was dark now, the only glow came from the various instruments except for a dimmed lamp over the chart table. Harry was waiting on the bridge when two soldiers arrived escorting the Major followed by the Colonel. He looked at the clock. It was 2000. 'Time for your first broadcast, Major.' The Major looked angrily at Harry; he was nursing his right eye.

'Fell down,' said the Colonel calmly, then drew his automatic.

'So you know what to say?' asked Harry. The Major nodded. 'You have to convince them that you have found us, not here but five miles further down river, that we are doing repairs and that you want an airstrike at dawn, got that?'

'Yes,' the Major replied sullenly.

'Tell them that you are staying here watching us and that you can stop us leaving if we try to go. Again have you got that?' He nodded. The Colonel placed his weapon gently against the side of the Major's throat. 'If you shoot him try not to get any mess on the chart table, Colonel. Right, pick up the mike and start.'

The Major carefully picked up the microphone, dialled in the frequency, then started to call. Harry looked at the Colonel, not able to understand what was being said but the Colonel nodded reassuringly. The voice at the other end became heated as did the Major who was sweating now. He shouted into the microphone and the voice at the other end calmed down.

The Colonel nodded again. He whispered to Harry. 'The General is going to send troops down at dawn.' After a moment the conversation finished and the Colonel shut off the set. 'That was good, Major,' said the Colonel. 'You might live.'

'Do you think it worked?' asked Harry. The Colonel shrugged.

'They seemed to believe it. We'll know when we get to Boma.' He spoke to the soldiers who pushed the Major towards the door. 'They can take him back now. So, Captain, we get on our way soon?'

'In a few minutes, Colonel. Are you and your men ready?'

'Of course. I gather from the Chief Officer that you specialised in amphibious warfare in the Royal Navy.'

'He talks too much.'

'Nevertheless, you have done this kind of thing before.'

'Only in exercises but yes, in Norway.'

'I will tell you a secret. I never have.'

'Colonel, by taking the village you ensure that you have an unopposed landing area. There is no enemy air and the river is calm. That means we can take our time and ensure that everything is done safely. That is half the battle. I worked in amphibious warfare for a long time. We mostly had old ships and obsolete equipment. I told a Minister of Defence once that we were trying to do surgery with kitchen spoons. Plans usually started breaking down five minutes into an exercise. We still got the job done. I did it for a long time and never became 'expert' or met anyone else who was. Common sense, seamanship, good weather and good luck. Hopefully we'll have all those. One thing, don't hurry.'

The Colonel placed his hand on Harry's shoulder. 'You know, I almost believe you.' His teeth gleamed in the dark. Harry turned to Graham. 'Call Stations. Start up the other engine and switch the thrusters on.'

The ship shook as the other engine joined the port engine and then settled down to a steady throbbing. The door banged as Sandy appeared on the bridge. 'Well, your Honour, the adventure continues.' He picked up his walkie-talkie. 'How do you want to do this, Captain?'

'Put both anchors in gear. When I'm ready we'll heave away on both anchors and as she comes out we'll let her swing to the port anchor. Once she has steadied with the bow up river we'll fall back and pick up the starboard anchor, then I'll bring her up to pick up the port.'

'Let's hope she comes off smoothly,' said Sandy as he headed to the forecastle where his anchor party was ready. Vijay arrived on the bridge with the Bosun and after a quick handover took over as OOW as the Bosun took the wheel.

Harry turned and spoke to the 3rd Officer. 'Graham, you know what you have to do. Be careful approaching the village. Any opposition then pull away immediately and head back to me at full speed. For your passage down stay close to their side of the river bank. There is deep water all the way down. When you approach the landing at the village cut your engines down to minimum and try to drift in. There is enough light from the night sky to see the bank so don't use any light unless it is essential.'

'I've photocopied the section of the river from the chart.'

'Nice and easy, Graham. Any doubts pull away and call me.'

Two crew were standing by the port breast lines aft ready to slip. 'Anchors in gear ready to heave away,' Sandy reported.

'Right, Sandy, heave easy on both.' The clanking of the chain over the windlass started and progressed evenly but then slowed.

'That's the cables tight and the windlass won't take any more.'

'OK, Sandy, we'll give her some power. Slow astern both.'

The engine rumble increased as the engines were engaged. Harry went to look over the side.

'Give her half astern.' The engine revs increased and the ship trembled. 'Any joy, Sandy?'

'Nothing yet, Captain.'

'Right, give her full astern.' The ship now shook as the engines increased to full power. 'Hard to port.' Harry waited a few minutes, then tried hard to starboard. Still there was nothing.

'Stop engines. Half ahead both. Hard to port. This will take the mud underneath out.' Again he ordered the wheel hard to starboard. The stern was now moving. 'Stop engines. Midships the wheel. Full astern both.' Again the ship shook.

'She's coming, Captain,' Sandy called.

'Let go the breast lines. Dead slow astern. Don't want to burst out like a cork from a bottle.'

The ship was sliding smoothly from the creek out into the river where the current caught the stern taking it down river.

'Stop engines.' The ship was swinging. 'Slow ahead both. We'll keep the engines on just enough power to take the weight of the cables as they come in,' Harry said to Vijay. Once Sandy reported the port anchor aweigh, the ship dropped back. Once the starboard anchor came off the bottom, Harry brought the ship round and slowly resumed the passage down the river. 'You have the con,' Harry said to Vijay. 'Tell the boat deck to launch Rescue 1 when ready.'

As soon as the order was given the davit motors hummed and the boat was swung out over the water. The engines started and, as the boat lowered to the water, it was released and headed away into the darkness.

'We have plenty of time. I don't want to get to the village until 2300 so adjust speed for that ETA.'

'Very good, Sir.' Vijay went to the chart and made a quick calculation then adjusted the engine throttles. The engines reduced to a low throb and the ship slid quietly through the black waters.

'Any traffic on the river?' asked Harry.

'Not a thing, Captain.' Harry stood in the centre of the wheelhouse peering through the one window that had been left open.

Chapter 21

Rescue 1 was now up to 21 knots, not full speed but sufficient on a dark night in a river where floating objects could not be seen. Olav, the Chief Coxn, gripped the wheel, adjusting course as Graham ordered the changes. The Lieutenant stood behind them and the soldiers were packed in forward of the small bridge control in the survivors' area. A dim red light was the only illumination. On the foredeck the cargo nets were piled up ready to be offloaded onto the river bank. James Stewart, the Ordinary Sailor, was peering at the river ahead with a pair of binoculars looking for any objects in the water. The boat was close enough to the bank for the trees to be dimly seen.

Graham turned to the Lieutenant. 'I'll cut back the engines for the last mile and let the current take us down towards the village. We'll have to look out for any boats on the bank to show us where the landing is.'

'What if there are no boats?'

'Then we have to look to see if we can see any sign of the village huts.' The boat lurched sharply and then steadied again.

'What was that?'

'It was something we hit in the water.' Graham eased the throttles back slowing the boat.

'Sorry,' James called, 'Couldn't see that.'

'It's all right, James. I was going too fast. I don't think there was any damage.'

'What about the propellers?' asked the Lieutenant.

'We don't have any. Water jet propulsion. Best kind for rescue and shallow water work. I'm sorry, Lieutenant. I must concentrate on the river now.' He bent over the radar screen again and passed another course change to Olav. The river bank glided by in the darkness.

The ship was also gliding down the river with the current. There was an air of tension about the ship, even though a silence pervaded the bridge. Harry relaxed in the command chair while Sandy leant against the side. Vijay stood by the radar, frequently checking the constantly changing dimmed display. Pat MacNab, the Second Coxn had the wheel, but presently it was switched to autopilot so he was also silently watching the course and adjusting the autopilot by the few degrees ordered by Vijay who gave the engines a few short touches ahead to assist any alteration. Jake was out on the bridge wing acting as lookout with a pair of binoculars glued to his eyes as he swept the area ahead of the ship. The Colonel stood at the back of the bridge as a silent observer.

He was impressed. Both by the ease with which these men slipped into their coordinated positions but also by their air of confidence at taking the ship down a dark unknown river, especially knowing what was expected in a few hours.

Sandy turned and looked at the Colonel. 'Coffee?'

'Please.'

'Jake,' he called out to the bridge wing, 'fix us all with coffee.' Jake came in and busied himself at the percolator.

'You all seem to be taking it pretty casually,' the Colonel remarked.

'Don't be fooled,' said Sandy. 'This is way out of our depth. We're just seamen, admittedly lucky to have a few ex-service types like Delilah around and a tough old ship like this, but nothing you won't find on many other oceans.'

'You've been around though. Vietnam, Iran, Iraq war. Whose side were you on?'

'Whoever paid the most. If you spend your life at sea in the more interesting parts of the world, you're bound to become mixed up in someone else's problems, but that doesn't make us soldiers.'

'Seamen aren't soldiers.' Harry had turned and joined in the conversation. 'Even in the Royal Navy, the general rule is never give a seaman a weapon unless it's too big for him to carry. That's why we have Royal Marines. Ask Delilah about sailors with guns.'

The Colonel persisted. 'Yet you're still doing this.'

Harry sighed. 'Colonel, I would like to say it's because of the refugees on board and we want to save them. Yes, we all agreed to give this a go but sadly, with a few exceptions, if the push really came to the shove, most would look after themselves. The real incentives now are your diamonds and the money that they'll bring, along with the major factor that you threatened to kill us. Once we get out, these men are finished, deep sea anyway, and they know that. It's not like changing job ashore. This is changing a whole way of life. That money means they can decide what they do instead of taking what they can get. It's more money than any seaman sees in their lifetime. They think it is worth it. Simple as that.'

'It seems strange that they cannot carry on work at sea.'

Sandy interrupted. 'We're not wanted anymore. No one wants to pay for the best, only the cheapest.'

Sandy drained his coffee. 'With that, I'll head down to the deck and see how the Bosun's doing getting the vehicles slung ready for putting over the side.'

'We'll need some work lighting when we put them over,' he said to Harry.

'Understood, but keep it as low as possible.' Sandy nodded and left the bridge.

Rescue 1 was heading in towards the target area. The night was black as were the waters of the river. Graham put the engines in neutral and Rescue 1 was drifting down towards the village. 'About one kilometre to go, Lieutenant. You'd better get your men ready. I'll stop the boat off the village then we'll wait and take a look. If it seems clear I'll put the boat into the bank and your men can disembark over the bow.' The Lieutenant squeezed his arm in acknowledgement and called orders to the soldiers who immediately stood up and gathered their equipment and weapons.

Their voices rose and immediately Graham called for quiet. 'Sound carries across water. No talking.'

The boat silently drew level with the village bank about one hundred metres out in the river. Graham slowly engaged the engines and held the boat against the current. They studied the river bank. There were two boats drawn up on the bank opposite the dark outline of several huts. There were no lights. All was quiet. They waited a few minutes more and still there was silence.

'What do you think?' Graham whispered.

'We go,' said the Lieutenant.

'Right. When you're ashore, I'll pull off again and then, if it is all clear, signal me back in and we can land the nets. First though we must clear those boats off the bank.'

Graham slowly opened the throttles of the engines. 'Put her between the two boats,' he ordered Olav, pointing at the bank. Olav allowed for the current as the boat edged slowly in. The boat crunched to a stop and then lurched as the soldiers jumped off the bow and scrambled up the bank, disappearing into the darkness of the village. Graham immediately put the engines astern and backed off the bank.

There was no sound from the shore and the minutes passed. 'Should we take a look, 3rd?'

It was James Stewart. 'I could nip ashore and see what is happening.'

'No,' said Graham brusquely. 'We stay put until told otherwise.'

The silence was overwhelming though and he was desperate for news. Suddenly there appeared a figure on the bank waving a dimly lit torch. Graham edged the boat in until they could see the Lieutenant, who now was joined by other soldiers. As the boat grounded, the Lieutenant grinned broadly.

'OK!' he said. 'We have put people in one hut. There is a road to Boma!'

'What do you think?' asked Graham. 'Can you land the vehicles here?'

'Yes, I think so,' said the Lieutenant, 'but I've never done it before.'

'Me neither. Let's shift the boats and get the nets down and feel how the ground is.'

He turned to Olav. 'Olav, keep the engines just turning ahead to keep us on the bank.' With that he jumped ashore. His feet sank into the mud but not too deeply. They quickly pushed the boats away from the bank and they drifted off into the night. Next the nets were pulled from the boat and stretched over the mud of the river bank slope.

'What do you think?' asked Graham. The Lieutenant walked over the netting.

'Good, but we should cut down trees and put them on top.'

'So I can tell the ship we are ready?' The Lieutenant nodded, grinning again.

Graham reached up to the foredeck and pulled himself on board. When he reached the wheelhouse he called the ship on the VHF. 'We are at the village. It is all secured and there is a landing beach of mud but not too deep. The nets are laid.'

On the bridge, Harry took the call. 'Well done, Graham. We are about 20 minutes away from you now. Stand by to escort the vehicles in and show them the landing area. When we arrive off the village come out and meet the ship.' Harry turned to those on the bridge. 'So far so good. I think it is time we continued our act with our star guest.'

The Colonel smiled. 'I'll bring him up. I have added a little to it as well.' He disappeared for a few minutes and returned with the Major in his white underwear accompanied by two soldiers.

'Good evening, Major. Time to broadcast again.' Harry handed him the microphone. 'You say as before, that the ship is still there and you can hear the noises of the repairs.'

The Colonel interrupted. 'We have added a little to that. May I introduce two deserters,' he said indicating the soldiers. 'After the Major has finished his little speech he will hand over to these men who will tell them of the trouble on board, the engines not working and the poor conditions which is why they left the ship.' Once again he took out his pistol and placed it on the Major's neck.

'You know what is required, Major. If they don't believe this, you're dead.'

'If you must, then do it outside,' said Harry

The Major nodded. He was no longer sweating but instead had an air of resignation about him. He keyed the microphone and called. After a few calls the reply came and the Major relayed his information then passed the microphone to the deserters who talked excitedly. After replying to questions they handed the mike back to the Major. Harry looked at the Colonel who nodded. After a brief conversation, the Colonel took the microphone from the Major.

'That wasn't too bad was it?' He was smiling as were the soldiers. 'Just as well these boys aren't deserting; that last part was the Major being ordered to shoot them.'

The Major turned to Harry pleading, 'I have done as you wanted, Captain. When will you let us go?'

'As I promised, you will be released in Boma, Major. Take him down.' The Major was taken off the bridge.

'The Chief Officer has arranged for them to be locked in a storeroom when we go,' the Colonel explained. 'It will be interesting to see their reception in town.'

'Colonel, it's up to you now. Take one of these walkie-talkies with you. It's set on our working channel. Let me know how things are going.'

The Colonel put his hand out. 'Just in case, Captain, it has been a pleasure to have met you and your men. If anything does happen, I know regardless of what you said about the diamonds and me, you will look after our families.'

'You have our word, Colonel. I'll see you in Boma.'

'In Boma, Captain.' The Colonel quickly left the bridge.

On the work deck, the AML was already attached to the slings and ready for lifting. Sandy was standing with the Bosun watching the crew holding the guide lines. As the Colonel approached, Sandy turned and waved at the AML.

'Colonel, your limo awaits. Sorry we didn't clean it.'

The Colonel smiled. 'Never mind that; the question is does it float?'

'Are you serious?'

'Completely. This is a first for all of us. We have followed the book and prepared the vehicles but never done it for real except in a few shallow river crossings.'

'What we will do, Colonel, is lower you down into the water but still keep the weight on the crane. Only when you are ready will we continue to lower you down. We have our boat standing off over there,' he said indicating to Rescue 1 which had returned to the ship and was waiting to guide the vehicles. 'They will be alongside you on the way in and direct you to the landing position. When you're ready to slip, all your man has to do is pull the lever on the top of the vehicle and the crane hook will fall way.'

He put his hand out. 'Good luck, Colonel.' In his hand was an ornate hip flask. 'Good Irish whisky, Colonel, not that cheap Scottish rubbish. Something to keep you on your toes tonight.'

'I'll bring it back.'

'You'd better. Saw me through a few problems in the Old Country. Hope it does the same for you. Take care.' He gripped the Colonel's hand firmly.

The Colonel climbed up onto the top of the AML and disappeared into the hatch. A moment later he appeared in the driver's position and gave the thumbs up. Sandy waved and the crane took the weight swinging the vehicle out over the side as the engine roared into life with blue exhaust smoke spewing from its exhausts into the dimmed lights from the crane floods. The crew pulled on the guide lines as the vehicle was lowered to the water and then stopped half way in. A soldier wearing earphones sitting on one of the APCs called and put his thumb up. Sandy called again and the crane completed the lowering until the AML floated. Rescue 1 closed in as the crane hook was slipped and then took up position ahead of the AML as it rumbled into the night.

'That's the first away,' said Harry to those on the bridge. He put the engines ahead. 'Let's move back up into position again before the next one goes.'

It was very tempting to call Rescue 1 to see how it was going but that was the last thing they wanted. If there was a problem they would call soon enough. The bridge door opened and Carole stepped in.

'Can I come and watch?' she asked.

'Nice to see you,' said Harry. 'You can get a better view from the bridge wing. We have sent the large AML away. The two personnel carriers are left.'

Graham led the AML to the landing point and held off while watching the vehicle approach the bank. As it reached the shallows, it increased its power and bit into the bank, sending mud and water spraying up as it drove up onto firm ground.

Graham slapped Olav on the back. 'It's going well. Let's get back for the next.'

Sandy and the deck crew had already lowered an APC into the water and they were waiting for Graham. As he approached, Sandy checked that all was well and then called to the APC to let go. The APC's engines roared as the power was increased and it also followed Rescue 1 towards the village. The next APC was swung out in readiness.

The Colonel had powered up the bank into the village with ease and was now standing on the bank of the river waiting for the first APC to arrive. The Lieutenant had reported that the track to Boma and the airfield was clear and the villagers were all safely confined. The soldiers were all wearing the blue UN helmets and their vehicles all flew the UN flag. Soon, out of the dark came the first APC. It approached the bank at less speed than the AML but managed to reach the safety of the top of the bank and joined the other vehicle. The soldiers got out and waited in a group for the last vehicle. This eventually appeared and, spewing mud and water, with full power reached the top of the bank.

'Mount up,' the Colonel ordered and went to his AML which was going to lead the convoy.

He keyed in his walkie-talkie to the ship. 'All safely ashore, Captain. We're heading out now. Listen for the noise.' The vehicles headed out of the village.

The ship was still holding position off the village when Rescue 1 appeared out of the darkness ready to be hoisted on board once the crane had been stowed. Sandy called Harry on the bridge.

'Captain, do you want Rescue 1 to be hoisted inboard or should we make it fast on the port side. I was just thinking that if there is any fire from the shore in Boma it will be on the starboard side and the boat could get damaged.'

Harry thought for a moment. 'I can't afford to have it in the water. It could get damaged when we ram the ships. Tell you what, use the crane and hang it off that on the port side.' Sandy quickly ordered the Bosun to get the canvas cradles rigged.

Harry called Graham on the radio. 'We're going to put the maintenance cradles in the water on the port side, Graham. When they are in place drive the boat into them and we will hoist you up on those. We're doing that to try to keep the boat away from any damage in the port. How is our blackout?'

'Good, Captain. No lights except from the main deck work area.'

Sandy turned to the Bosun. 'I'll leave you to get on with that. Pipe the lads down when you finish and let them get some hot food before the fun starts. I'm going up to the bridge.'

'I'll get a mug of tea and a smoke then I'll be up to take the wheel,' John said. 'Going to be a busy night.'

'You can say that again,' Sandy smiled. 'Never mind John, soon you'll be sitting on a beach somewhere with a dusky lady and swigging rum.'

'Just as long as the wife doesn't find out.'

Sandy arrived on the bridge. Harry turned towards him. 'The Colonel called. All the vehicles are ashore and they are setting off for the airfield.'

'So now we wait.'

'Until we hear the first bang, then it's our turn.'

'I was talking to Peter,' Sandy said. 'Has he spoken to you about his idea?'

'No, what's that?'

'He feels that as the soldiers are off the ship we could make a deal with the port that we hand them in as a condition for letting us sail through.'

'What do you think?'

'Probably the same as you, desperate and stupid.'

'Not only that, but there is another small problem. We gave our word.'

'That we did, Captain.'

'Come here a minute. Vijay, you too.' Harry led them to the chart table and switched on the light. He picked up the chart pencil. Here we are now, stemming the current off the village. It is one mile to the corner where we turn and head towards the Boma Channel. From that time on we will be exposed to radar. However, following your idea Sandy, we will cross over and make our approach behind Roca Island which will give us radar cover for another mile. After that, we come out into the open, carry on a further mile and then turn for the final run into Boma. It is then one and a half miles to the naval base. If they have any ships in the channel waiting for us, they could be anywhere along that final run.'

'Do you think they will have ships waiting?'

'They will be bloody stupid if they don't. But if they believe what we told the UN Major to tell them they may not. Don't depend on it. If they have a ship there, we will head directly for it and try to ram it on the side.'

'How will you do that?'

'Unless it turns to show us the beam, we approach it to one side and then turn in towards it. I'll broadcast a warning for everyone to get down. Carole has already told all the passengers to sit down on the deck with their backs towards the bow. She has also made sure that everyone is on the port side. Sandy, make sure the crew know that too. As soon as we hit, I'll come full astern and pull out which will open the hole in her side and get us free to then go against any other ship alongside. Once we get in amongst any ship alongside, it's up to you and Delilah.'

'How did you know I was going?'

'I know you too well. If there are any small armed launches try to put them out of action as well. Who's got weapons?'

'A lot of the stuff was taken by the Colonel and his men. We have the usual collection of AK47s, a box of grenades, a couple of grenade launchers, and a mortar. There are six in each party and some of the pygmies with their bows. Everything except the AKs will be with Chalkie, Andy, Delilah and Taffy. Most of the crew are familiar with the AKs from on board practice. Jake will be on top of the wheelhouse with the heavy machine gun. We still have two Stingers left; the Colonel took two, but we thought we would leave the other two up with the machine gun.'

Harry nodded. 'Is there protection up there?' he asked, pointing up.

'It's all bagged with earth around them and provided they don't stick their heads out they should be all right.'

'Once the Colonel starts his party, I reckon it will take us 30 minutes to get alongside. The airfield is only half a mile from where we will be parked so I expect the Colonel very soon after we get there. Regardless of what is happening, we get them on board and head out. Now hold the fort for a few minutes, Sandy. I'm going below for a quick tour round before we start heading to Boma.'

Harry went down the stairway and headed to the galley first. Willie the Cook was inside making sandwiches.

'Make sure everything is well stowed and lashed down, Cook,' advised Harry.

'Aye, doing that now, Captain. I've had the deck boys secure the messes and store rooms. I'm making up the last batch of food for the bridge now.' Harry nodded. 'Most of the lads are in the crew mess getting ready.'

'Takes me back a few years this does, Captain. You're lucky we have a good crowd on board. It's the lads that make the ship and a good skipper to lead them. You're not so bad.'

'From you, that's praise indeed. Mind you a good Cook makes the ship as well.'

'Captain, I'll tell you something I couldn't tell many Captains. I've never spat in your soup.'

Harry laughed. 'You've restored my faith in cooks.'

Harry passed through the galley and found the crew mess crowded with crew dressed in various military garb. Delilah turned round from his inspection.

'We got the uniforms from what was left by the Colonel's mob, Sir. Boot polish courtesy of yourself and Sandy.'

'Good to see it being put to use. Everything ready?'

'As much as possible.'

'I hope it will be a quick in and out, Delilah. Take care of them.'

'I will, Sir.'

'Keep your heads down, lads,' Harry shouted over the noise. 'We'll be as fast as we can. I'll broadcast just before hitting anything, make sure you are sitting or lying down on the deck, with your backs towards the bow. Good luck.'

He carried on to the ship's hospital. It was also busy. Carole and Andy had first aid packs ready on one of the beds and Monique was putting any loose items into the cupboards. Carole looked up and flashed Harry a smile.

'Come to check up on us then?' she asked. Andy also looked up.

'The dispensary's ready, Sir. I'll take these first aid kits to the messroom. There is one for each party and one for the bridge.'

'We already have one.'

'There is more kit in here. Burn gauzes and I've included morphine injection capsules.'

'Thanks, Andy. I'm going down to have a look at our passengers.'

Carole pushed her hair back which had fallen over her eyes, 'I'll come with you, Harry.' She turned to the others. 'Back in a minute.'

They went down to the workers' quarters. Harry could see that many of the passengers were sitting on the decks ready. Some of the children were running around being chased by their mothers and pulled back down again. He went round them reassuring them with a smile and patting some of the children. Concern showed in the eyes of their mothers.

Carole grabbed Harry's hand and led him back up the stairway. There was no one there and she pressed herself against him.

'Hold me, Harry, just for a moment. Christ, I'm sorry. I'm behaving like a stupid schoolgirl. It's just that we have had no time to ourselves.'

'Hey,' Harry said softly, holding her. 'We will when we get out of this mess.'

'Will we really? Is it worth it? We could just give up and see what happens. Look at us, Harry. We are all going round putting a brave show on as if this is normal, but people are scared.'

'I'm getting tired of telling people that there's nothing wrong with being scared. There is with giving up. We're in too deep now. What do you think would happen to all these people? They will be murdered, that's what and that's not going to happen. I'll get this ship through, trust me. Your job is to keep them as calm as you can, regardless of what happens. Remember she is a strong ship, stronger than any she will come against. And we've got a mean bunch of bastards determined to get her through. How can we fail?' He smiled at her and squeezed her to him. 'You take care of these people and I'll take care of the ship. Deal?

She looked at him. 'Deal.'

'Good. I'm heading back to the bridge. Remember, keep them squatting on the deck and away from the sides of the ship.' With that he strode away quickly without looking back.

Harry arrived back on the bridge. John the Bosun arrived at the same time carrying a large plate piled high with egg and bacon butties.

'Cook sent these up for everyone, Captain.'

'Much appreciated,' said Harry taking one. The plate was quickly emptied. The Bosun took the wheel.

'I'll head down now, Sir,' said Sandy. 'I'll make sure that everyone knows what's what. Delilah and I will have walkie-talkies and Carole also has one. Jake has one up top and the Colonel and Graham each have one.' He shook hands with Harry. 'What about finding ourselves a nice peaceful container ship after this? We're getting too old for all this excitement.'

Harry smiled. 'I was thinking of a nice farm. Take care, Sandy.'

'You too. Good luck everyone.'

Jake was next. 'I'll get settled in up topside, Sir. Higgins is up there already.'

'Just remember, keep your head down. Don't fire at the ships if they are not firing at us.'

'Sir, can we put the Red Ensign up? I know we're not a British ship anymore but the lads feel that as we are all Merchant Navy, it's still our flag.'

Harry thought for a moment. 'Well done, Jake. Hoist the Ensign, whatever happens, it's our flag.'

Friday 23 May

Boma

Chapter 22

Harry looked at his watch. 0115. All was quiet. The sky was dark; the clouds were hiding the moon and stars. Towards the east where Boma lay, around the bend in the river, there was a glow of light from the town. The river matched the darkness, just a faint sound of water washing past the ship mingling with the throb of the engines at low speed to counter the river current.

'Let her ease down towards the river bend,' he ordered Vijay. 'Just as long as we stay around this side.' Vijay adjusted the engine controls and the ship started to slowly edge down river.

'How long has it been since the soldiers landed?'

'About an hour, Sir.'

'They should have been there by now,' Harry muttered.

The Colonel had travelled along the track from the village to the road between the airfield and the port without any problems. They had now pulled off the road before reaching the airfield. They were hidden in the trees that bordered the airfield and the Colonel was peering through his binoculars, as was the Lieutenant. There were two helicopters on the field and two aircraft.

One was small but the other was a military transporter. That was strange. He didn't know that they had one in Boma.

'There's a machine gun position on top of the control tower and another by the main gate. Most of the soldiers are in the garrison hut by the control tower. There are also lights on in the hangar.'

'So do we go in from here?'

'No, we are UN soldiers remember?' The Colonel grinned. 'We go up to the main gate. I want that taken without any shooting. We get out and approach the guard post as if we own the place. We deal with the guards then replace them with our own soldiers who will hold it for when we leave. You will take the two APCs to the control tower and the barrack hut and do the same. The blue helmets should get you into the control tower. From then on kill them all. I will take out the aircraft and helicopters but I will wait until you reach the control tower before I start. Once you have the control tower and barracks, head for the hangar. We will meet there. No prisoners. Remember what they did to our families.'

The Lieutenant grinned. 'It will be so, Colonel.'

'Then let us go and meet these bandits.'

The AML joined the waiting APCs on the road and they set off to the airfield entrance with their lights blazing. The entrance to the airfield was blocked by a white and red painted pole where two guards stood, shading their eyes from the glare of the headlights. The Colonel and four soldiers got out of the AML and approached the guards.

'We are here to take over the airfield,' the Colonel said. The two guards looked bewildered but proffered no resistance as they were disarmed. From the next APC eight more soldiers got out and they went past the barrier and stood pointing their weapons at the two soldiers manning the machine gun post just inside the gate. They stood up holding their hands in the air. The four prisoners were made to lie down on the ground. The Colonel drew his hand across his throat and while they were held down four soldiers came behind and, using their knives, cut their throats.

They pulled the bodies to one side and raised the barrier. The Colonel ordered two soldiers to man the machine gun while the rest clambered back into the vehicles. The three vehicles raced across the field, the two APCs heading for the control tower and barracks while the Colonel in the AML headed for the first of the helicopters. A minute later the sound of gunfire erupted from the barracks.

'Fire!' shouted the Colonel and the AML opened fire with the cannon. Immediately the helicopter jumped in the air as the first incendiary rounds hit home and then as the fuel tank was hit it exploded in a ball of flame.

The sound of the explosion reached across the river to the ship.

'That's it!' said Harry. 'We're on our way. I have the con, Vijay. Hard to starboard.' He split the engine controls putting the port engine half ahead and the starboard engine half astern, bringing the ship rapidly round to face down river again. 'Full ahead both.' The ship shook as the engines built up their power. The bridge phone rang.

It was Peter. 'Harry you can only have 75% power on the starboard engine.'

'Understood, Peter. We'll compensate for that on the steering. We're heading in now. I'll broadcast if we are going to collide in the channel. I'll stop engines just before we hit. Just in case, make sure the watertight doors are closed, put the emergency fire pump on and be ready with the bilge pumps.'

'Already done, Harry.'

'I should have known. Take care, Peter.'

'Hey, I'm tucked up in my cosy engine room. You watch your arse on the bridge.'

Harry stood watching the radar display. The river and banks showed clearly. Steer 236. John eased the ship onto course as the ship steadily increased speed, shaking a little as the power of the engines built up.

'Vijay, we hold this course heading direct for the other bank and then bring her round just before she's 1.7 cables off the bank. Keep me advised of the distance off.'

Vijay called out the distances as the ship rapidly came closer. 'Three cables off, Captain. Two point five, two.'

'Hard starboard,' Harry called and John brought her round. 'Steer 315.'

The ship was now heading directly at the small island hiding Boma from the ship and the ship from Boma.

'We now have cover for one and a half miles then we are in the open.'

There was silence on the bridge as the ship closed with the island. Harry went to the second radar and peered intently into it watching the distance closing. He held the course for as long as he could then ordered the wheel to starboard.

As the ship came out from behind the island, Vijay instantly reported, 'Two ships in the channel, Sir.'

'I see them, Vijay. Damn. I didn't think of two ships there. Give me their speed and course.'

Looking through the one open window, Harry could see the lights of Boma clearly now but nothing yet of the ships ahead. On the starboard bow a fireball went up into the air. The Colonel was busy.

'No read out, Captain,' said Vijay. 'I think they are anchored.'

A surge of excitement coursed through Harry. 'The fucking idiots! If they are, we have them! They can't manoeuvre!' He turned to John. 'We'll bring her into the channel now, John. Give me 5 degrees to port.'

The ship slowly came round into the Boma Channel. The lights of the port were bright now, and in the light Harry could see the shapes of the two darkened ships anchored in the middle of the channel. The ship was vibrating now as the speed continued to build.

'They are almost opposite the navy base,' said Harry. 'John, can you see them?'

'Yes, Captain.'

'I want you to steer to the side of the outboard ship. When I say so, you will turn into her and hit her amidships, got it?'

'As you say, Captain.'

He picked up the walkie-talkie. 'Sandy, there are two ships. I am going to hit the outer one first then the inner. I want you to concentrate your fire on the inner ship until I can get to her.

'Understood, Captain,' said Sandy.

'Jake, watch the deck of the outer ship. If they fire hit them all you can.'

'Yes, Sir,' Jake replied.

'One mile to go everyone. Everything looks quiet and still.'

They could hear the sound of gunfire and explosions from the direction of the airfield. In the sky there was the odd flash and flickering of light from the fires. The ship seemed to be surging ahead anxious to take the battle to the enemy. Harry found he was holding the bridge front rail with a grip of iron disregarding the pain. No reaction yet from the anchored ships. There was a flash from the deck of the outer ship and the scream of a shell passing over.

'Take them out, Jake,' yelled Harry. There was no reply from Jake but instantly there was the hammering of the machine gun above. Then came the chattering of fire from the crew as they took on the inner ship. The noise was deafening and Harry found himself shouting, willing the ship towards the anchored warships. There was another flash and then a massive thump and a spew of flame that encompassed the front view from the bridge window. They all staggered on the bridge and were enveloped with a surge of noise and heat. The ship lurched slightly and dust filled the bridge.

'Fuck!' shouted John. 'What was that?'

'Steady everyone! We took a hit on the bridge front. It doesn't matter. We've got the armour in place.'

Another flash and another scream as a shell passed a few feet on the port side. Then the search light blazed out from the monkey island and the foredeck of the outer ship was illuminated, showing the gun and the gun crew around it. The machine gun above immediately hammered out and they were swept away like leaves on the wind. A whoosh sound came from the starboard side and there was an explosion on the inner ship as one of the crew fired an RPG.

'Turn into him now, John!' Harry shouted, John immediately turned the ship heading towards the enemy vessel which was only 50 metres away. Harry picked up the speaker for the ship's broadcast system.

'Hold on, everyone!' he shouted and then held on to the bridge front rail again. He could see crew running from the bridge of the enemy ship and others jumping from the deck before the ship disappeared under the bow. 'Stop engines!' yelled Harry.

At first, it was as if there was nothing in the way as the warship initially absorbed the impact. Then Harry and those on the bridge staggered as the ship lurched, followed by the bow rising up in the air. There was a screeching noise from the bow and it continued to rise. Harry rushed to the bridge wing and looked over the side. He was amazed. The ship was lying on top of the enemy ship, which was now almost completely rolled over. Water was boiling from the ruptured hull and churning around several drowning sailors in the water. Then the weight of the ship pressed down on the enemy vessel and it broke in half. The bow end stood up in the water pointing like a finger at the sky before sinking down.

'Full astern both!'

The ship shook as the engines came astern and there was a groan of grating broken metal. Very slowly the ship reluctantly pulled herself back away from the wreckage. All the time the crew were firing into the other vessel on which a large fire was burning caused by the hits from the various missiles.

'There's another warship alongside the base, Captain!' It was Vijay who was sweeping the shore with his binoculars.

'Let's deal with this other one first!' shouted Harry. 'Stop engines, full ahead again. John, hit her midships. There's no need to hit her hard, just enough to put a large hole in her. She's already in trouble.' The crew were abandoning the ship and there were life rafts in the water.

The ship slowly built up speed ahead. The Bosun turned the ship to point directly amidships on the burning vessel. Harry looked at the speed log, 7 knots; that would be enough. The distance closed rapidly and then as they braced themselves, the ship crunched hard into the warship with a shriek of metal and splintering wood but this time the bow sliced into the hull like a knife. The remaining crew were spilling out of the doors and hatches on the deck to throw themselves over the side. Sandy and his men stopped firing as there was no one left capable of firing on the sinking ship. Immediately Harry put the engines full astern and with an initial hesitation the ship pulled out of the deep 'V' shaped hole in the warship's side. As soon as the ship was clear, the warship started to list heavily to starboard still held by her anchors.

'John, head directly at the warship alongside. Can you see it against the lights?'

'Yes, Captain!'

Again Harry put the engines to full ahead. There was a flash of light from the warship and a spout of water grew in the river about 50 metres away from the ship.

'They're firing on us, Captain!' shouted Vijay. Then there was a hammering noise, not from Jake's gun but from bullets striking the metal of the ship.

'They're firing with machine guns as well!' cried Harry. A louder hammering from above was Jake's reply and this was joined by the crew's weapons.

The lights grew brighter from the town and the jetty as the ship grew near. Explosions and flashes were still illuminating the sky from the direction of the airport. The sky behind was red from the fires on the sinking ship. A shell streaked by on the side of the bridge and hit the water behind the ship. The ship surged on, getting closer to the warship. Another burst of hammering hit the bridge front. There was a crashing from the bulkhead behind them and bullets ricocheted around the wheelhouse causing sparks to fly where they struck.

Harry cried out, 'Just hold on, John. We're nearly there.'

Firing from both ships was constant now. There was a crash and the bow erupted in smoke and flame. The ship staggered slightly but now it was only a few metres away and the crew on the warship deck were being hit by the fire from Jake and Sandy's men. An anti-tank missile streaked out and hit square on the deck gun which was blown to bits together with the gun crew whose bodies were tossed into the air. Then the ship hit and bit in heavily. The warship was crushed between the jetty and the ship. Harry stopped the engines and, looking down, saw Sandy and Delilah leading their men over the side screaming and shouting. What crew remained on the warship cowered on their knees with their hands in the air amongst the blood and the smoke. Harry eased his hands off the bridge rail and found them to be shaking. He looked round at the Bosun and saw he was slumped down by the wheel clutching a shattered hand.

'Shit!' He grabbed the loudspeaker mike. 'Medic to the bridge! Medic to the bridge!' Turning to Vijay, Harry ordered, 'See to the Bosun. Now where's the fucking Colonel?'

Chapter 23

Colonel Saolona was having his own problems. At first it seemed easy. They streaked across the airfield and destroyed the helicopters sitting on the grass. Next the small aircraft crumpled under cannon fire. The transport was next, and as the cannon fire hit the fuselage there was a flash and the entire aircraft blew apart. The hot blast surged across the field to the AML. Ammunition, thought the Colonel. The Lieutenant's party headed for the control tower and the barracks. The control tower was in flames having sustained a direct hit with a Stinger but the troops in the barracks had been alerted and were spilling out and were now pinning the Lieutenant's party down. They were crouched down behind their troop carriers returning fire.

The Lieutenant called the Colonel. 'There are many soldiers, Colonel,' he said desperately. 'They are fighting hard and I cannot get any further.' Shit, thought the Colonel. They seemed to be around the hangar area and he had to get there in case there were any helicopters inside.

'Hold on. We will come at them from the airfield. See if you can shoot the lights out.' The area around the hangar was illuminated by lights on the roof. The Colonel looked around desperately. His small force and one armoured vehicle were not going to turn the battle. The heavy chatter of the personnel carrier's machine guns continued in the night and he could see that the lighting was slowly going out but heavy fire was replying. At the side of the field he saw another vehicle.

'Drive over there!' he ordered. As they approached he could see it was a petrol tanker. He jumped out and ran over with his men. There was no key in the cab.

'Can anyone start this?' he shouted. Three of his men offered. 'Get it going!'

He went round to the back and opened up the valve. Aviation fuel flooded out. The truck started with a roar.

The Lieutenant called the Colonel. 'It is not good. Already I have one APC destroyed and one man killed. I have two others wounded.'

'Arthur, hold on for a few minutes longer. I am coming in directly from the airfield and will make an attack on the hangar. When that starts I want you to withdraw back to the ship. Is that understood?'

'What about you, Colonel?'

'Never mind about me. After I attack, I will follow. Just get your men back to the ship.'

The Colonel ordered the men out of the cab and jumped in.

'I'm going to drive this directly towards the hangar. When I jump out let it get inside and then fire on it. The valve is open so there will be fuel everywhere. That should give them something to think about. Follow me in the MRL and open fire on what you can. Once the truck blows we will head for the ship.'

The two vehicles roared across the grass directly towards the brightly lit hangar which had its doors wide open. As the Colonel got closer he could see a helicopter inside. Flashes of gunfire could now be seen coming from soldiers in front of the hangar doors but immediately the MRL behind him opened up with the cannon and machine gun scattering the soldiers. With the bowser directly heading for the opening, the Colonel jumped out and landed on the grass. He sprang quickly to his feet and ran towards the MRL which was stationary with the door open. Once inside he pushed his way through the soldiers to the driver. The gunner was loading another round in the cannon and fired directly into the hangar. There was a spurt of fire and then a muffled whumph followed by a fireball bursting out of the hangar entrance. The roar of the explosion reached them. He slapped the driver on the back.

'Come back out of the light and then head for the road!' The driver frantically turned around back to the welcome protection of the darkness. 'OK. We're clear now. Swing back slowly and head for the road.' The driver brought the MRL slowly round towards the road. 'Good. Now we head for the ship. Fuck! Stop! What's that?'

They peered forward into the dark. There outlined against the light of the fires were two dark objects.

'Shit! Tanks! Turn round! Quickly!' He picked up his microphone. 'Arthur? Arthur? Where are you?' The wireless crackled into life.

'Colonel? We are just coming to the ship. I think the crew have it all clear.'

'Good. Get on board as soon as you can and tell the Captain to leave immediately. There are two P62s by the gate on the road. I will try to distract them away but he must get out immediately.'

'Understood, Colonel. What about you?'

'Never mind me. Get the ship out. You must do that.'

'I will Colonel. Colonel?'

'Yes, Arthur.'

'I am sorry.'

'Don't worry. Your job is to get the men and their families out. I can look after myself. I've survived so far. Now get going.' The Colonel clicked the radio off then reached into the MRL and took out a Stinger. He switched it on and waited until the batteries lit up and showed that the weapon was ready to fire. He then placed it on the MRL to steady it and pointing it at the barracks, sighted and fired. The missile streaked out and hit the barracks in a flash of flame and smoke.

'Shift out of the way,' he said, taking over from the gunner. 'Now we play a game. We fire and then we run and hide and then we do it again. We have the speed so we use it.'

At the port the ship was now welded into the warship alongside.

Sandy's party had swarmed over the bow and across the warship, rounding up what crew remained into a hut on the jetty. Then they had stood on the side of the jetty and thrown hand grenades into the various launches alongside. They were now a mass of flaming wreckage on the water. Delilah's party had immediately headed for the buildings opposite the ship that were obviously administrative buildings for the base. They had almost reached them when firing had burst out from the upper floors. One of the pygmies immediately spun round and went down on the ground. Two of his comrades dragged him into cover.

Delilah keyed in his walkie-talkie. 'Jake, we're taking fire from the upper windows of the building opposite the ship. Can you cover us while we get to the building?'

'We've only one belt of ammunition left, Delilah, but we have a couple of grenade launchers.'

'Jake, you lovely boy. Do you know how to fire them?'

'No.'

'It's easy. Just pull up the fore and aft sights on the top, move the safety switch on the left side back, point and press the trigger.'

'All right, Delilah.'

'I want you to aim for the windows at the top of the building. Use what's left of your ammunition on the windows, then with the grenade launcher aim for the top of one of them, then lift the launcher about 10 degrees above the window. That should be right.'

There was a pause and then from the ship came the deep chattering of the machine gun which caused a shower of broken glass and masonry chips from the building. There was a pause and a grenade streaked out towards the building only to hit the wall by a window and fall onto the ground in front exploding in a cloud of dust and broken masonry.

'Sorry,' said Jake.

'Try again.'

Another grenade streaked out and this time went through one of the windows. The whole upper part of the building exploded with debris and dust billowing from the windows. Delilah sprinted for the building followed by his party. All fight had gone from those inside and they herded together the surviving enemy from inside the building.

'Captain,' called Delilah, 'we have the road approach to the base secure. It all seems quiet. We had one casualty. It was one of the pygmies and he has been taken back to the ship.'

'Well done, Delilah. Sandy, how about you?' Sandy had moved his party up the jetty after destroying the various launches.

'All quiet this way, Captain. We have no casualties either. How far should I go?'

'I don't want you too far away, Sandy. As soon as the Colonel and his mob appear we hit the road. Just hold on where you are.'

Carole had arrived on the bridge and was kneeling down beside the Bosun.

'There's a lot of blood. How is he?' Harry asked.

'There's always a lot of blood from the hands,' said Carole. 'He's lost a finger. There is a splinter of metal still in his hand. I'm giving him a local to get it out and he also has a broken finger. I'll take him down and deal with it in the hospital.'

'No you won't,' groaned the Bosun. 'Patch it up here. I can still steer the ship.' He got up.

'Don't be stupid,' said Carole.

'Listen, lass. On the fishing boats when we were injured there was no one and we managed for days. This is nothing to what I've seen there.' His voice softened as he patted her on the shoulder. 'Save yourself for what may be coming. I'm all right, really. Just get the splinter out and stop the bleeding. A nice cup of tea will fix me.'

Carole looked at Harry helplessly. 'If he says he's all right then he is. I need him here. Give him a pain killer,' Harry said.

The VHF buzzed. 'Captain, it's Delilah. We have the soldiers in sight. Only one vehicle though and they're belting it down the road.'

'Right. Sandy, get your people back on board. The soldiers are back.'

'On our way, Captain.'

Harry rang the engine room. 'Peter, we're going to get underway very soon. The soldiers are nearly here. I'll need all you've got for the next 20 minutes and then we're clear.'

'Do what I can, Harry.'

'Delilah, as soon as you get on board, let the prisoners go ashore.'

The APC skidded to a halt by Delilah who was holding his hand up. The Lieutenant jumped out of the passenger door and the soldiers bailed out of the back.

'Where are the others?' asked Delilah.

'They're not coming. I lost one man and three were hurt.' Delilah called the bridge. 'Can we have three stretchers down here, Captain?'

'Andrew!'

'Yes, Sir.'

'Get three stretchers down to Delilah.'

Harry called Jake. 'Jake, the two of you go with the 3rd Mate and get the stretchers ashore.'

'Delilah!' the Lieutenant shouted. 'Two P62 tanks came. The Colonel tried to stop it but I think no good.'

Delilah called the bridge. 'Captain, we're coming back on board. No more soldiers are coming and there are two tanks on the way. They can give us serious grief. We have to get out of here pretty soon.'

'Where's the Colonel?'

'Last heard of he was still at the airstrip trying to hold them off for us.' Harry immediately called Sandy. 'Sandy! Get your men back here now! There are tanks coming!'

Harry saw Graham and Jake running across the jetty carrying the stretchers.

Sandy called his men together and they began to run back to the ship but a shot rang out and Sandy went down. 'Fuck,' he groaned as he fell holding his leg. They started to shoot back into the darkness.

'For fuck's sake, never mind that!' Sandy shouted. 'Get me back to the ship!'

They grabbed him and helped him hobble back along the jetty. Delilah's party carrying the stretchers were manhandling them onto the ship from the wrecked warship. Slowly, too slowly, the crew and the soldiers clambered onto the ship, the last being those carrying Sandy.

Harry looked down on the deck. Everyone was back on board now. A few minutes later the Major and his men spilled on to the foredeck, clearly visible in their white skivvies. Behind them was Delilah herding them along. They stumbled over the wreckage of the bow and one by one dropped down onto the deck of the warship. When the last one was ashore Harry turned to Vijay.

'We're getting out right now.'

He put the engines full astern. The ship trembled and then shook as she tried to break herself free but she stayed rigidly held embedded in the guts of the crumpled warship. Hard to port, hard to starboard, he tried to break the ship free. The ship ground and metal groaned but still the ship held. The last of the prisoners jumped from the wrecked warship and ran across the road to shelter in the buildings there. Delilah arrived on the bridge.

'The tanks are coming, Captain.'

'I fucking well know, Delilah, but the ship doesn't seem to care.'

He stopped the engines and immediately rammed the throttles full ahead. 'What's happened to Sandy?'

'He caught it in the leg. Just a flesh wound I think. He's gone to the hospital. There are some wounded soldiers as well and a few cuts and bruises amongst the crew from jumping around in the dark. Nothing serious.'

He put the engines astern again. The ship moved but still held.

'Delilah, are there any hand grenades left?'

'Yes, Captain.'

'Go forward, bung a few over the bow and then get clear. Let's see if that works.' Delilah looked at Harry incredulously.

'You mean it?'

'Course I do. The bow's damaged anyway, can't get much worse. Grenades won't bother an ice bow. Get on with it. Just make sure you duck.'

'What's happening?' Harry turned round. It was Sandy holding onto the door frame.

'What the hell are you doing here?'

'No room in the hospital. Andy looked at me, told me I was lucky, gave me a crutch and told me to find a first aid station. Can you imagine it's lucky to get shot? Mind if I sit down?' He limped over to the command chair. Harry looked at the blood dripping from his leg.

'Vijay, get the first aid kit and bandage him up. We're just about to blow ourselves up.'

Harry watched Delilah climb across the foredeck and, crouching for a moment behind what remained of the bulwarks, he pulled the pins on two grenades and dropped them over the bow then lay flat on the deck. Harry had the engines full astern when there was a series of flashes from the bow and then an explosion that threw debris high in the air with a flash of flame and smoke. The whole ship shuddered and then with a scream of metal the ship dragged out of the wrecked warship. Harry pulled the ship out into the channel then stopped her.

He grabbed his walkie-talkie. 'Colonel? Colonel?' he called.

There was a crackle. 'Captain?'

'What's your situation.'

'All the helicopters are destroyed. Sorry we cannot join you for the rest of the cruise, Captain. We cannot get out and we are pinned back now to the edge of the airstrip. We have managed to keep one of the tanks here but the other we cannot see. There is no chance we can reach the road.' Harry quickly looked at the chart.

'Colonel, never mind the road, get to the river bank directly from where you are. I'll have a boat there for you.'

'Captain, leave us. Just get our families out.'

'I'm not leaving anyone!' Harry shouted. 'Now do as I say. We go together or not at all.' He switched the mike off.

'Sandy, take the ship down the channel and once you get clear of Boma wait there for me. Keep her at full speed until you are well clear of Boma.'

'Where are you going?'

'To get the Colonel. She's all yours.'

'We could leave him, Captain. He's done what we want. He's an evil bastard.'

'Is that what you want?'

Sandy paused. 'No, you're right we can't.'

Harry ran off the bridge, down to the crowded mess deck. 'Delilah!' he shouted. 'Get Andy and Taffy and bring your weapons. We're going boating. We'll use Rescue 2 on the crane of the working deck. Deck crew outside and let us down.'

'Andy's in the hospital.'

'Leave him then. Olav you come in the boat. Come on! Move!'

The Colonel and his men were grouped around the AML which now sat dark and silent at the edge of the airfield with no ammunition. The crackle of gunfire swept the field and bullets whispered in the air above them.

The Colonel called into his walkie-talkie, 'Captain. Captain?' but it was silent.

'All of you, back away into the trees. We are going towards the river.'

'We will be trapped there, Sir,' said the Sergeant.

'No, we won't. There is a boat.'

'What about the wounded?'

'Bring those who we can. Kill anyone who cannot be moved. We leave no one for these bastards.'

The Captain's words were catching he reflected. A week ago he would have left them. They gradually backed to the trees and melted into their protection. At least the tank could not see or reach them here, but the soldiers would follow. As they backed towards the river they continued to lay down a covering fire.

'Get the wounded down to the bank first!' shouted the Colonel. 'Sergeant, you and I will hold until they get the wounded on the boat. Anyone got a torch?' Some of the men shouted. 'When you get to the bank, shine them out into the river. Now get going.'

The Colonel and the Sergeant crouched down while the rest of the men moved back towards the bank. They could hear the shouting of the pursuing troops.

'Fuck,' said the Colonel. 'That's why we had a hard time. They are Chinese. What the hell are Chinese troops doing here?' The Sergeant, instead of replying, fired a burst into the dark. Instantly bullets whipped around in reply.

'Move back, Sergeant. Slowly now, and no more firing until I say so. We don't give our position away. They can't see us until we fire. They are trying to find out where we are.'

Chapter 24

The hospital was crowded. All the beds were occupied with the wounded. The walking wounded were standing around waiting for attention. The deck was streaked with blood where the injured had been dragged in. Some of the soldiers were peering in the door at their friends. Carole and Andy were bending over the couch that they were using as an operating table. Monique was patching up the less seriously wounded. Carole rang the bridge.

'We have to operate. Please try to keep the ship steady.'

'Will do my best Carole,' said Sandy.

'Where's Harry?'

'Gone boating.'

Sandy turned round and saw John the Bosun on the wheel with his heavily bandaged hand. 'What happened to you, John?'

'Got a splinter in my hand and lost a finger.'

'Christ. It's getting like a Belfast accident ward on a Saturday night. Vijay, take your binoculars and watch astern. I want to know as soon as you see the boat coming. John, just keep her in the middle.'

'Aye aye, Sir.'

'Anyone checked for damage forward yet?'

'Not had time,' answered the Bosun 'But she seems to have settled down a little so it looks as if the forepeak has a leak.'

'Not surprising,' said Sandy. 'It's not designed to hit three ships. Just as long as the bulkhead holds. If that goes and the flooding spreads further aft we really have problems.' He reached forward, picked up the phone and called the engine room. Peter answered.

'Peter, we have the forepeak leaking. Can you see if you can get the pumps on?

'On to it now, Sandy.'

'I'll get one of the sailors to get soundings done as soon as I can.'

'How's it going up there?'

'Ask me in an hour.'

'Right, where's Jake?' Sandy picked up the walkie-talkie and called. Jake answered immediately. 'What's your situation, Jake?'

'We came back up top here, Sir, after taking the stretchers ashore. We've no ammunition left. Just a Stinger.'

'Right, come down both of you. I want you to go and sound the forward tanks.'

The ship was picking up speed now.

'Sir,' Vijay shouted, 'there's a vehicle coming along the jetty. I think it's the Colonel.'

'He's missed the boat then.' Sandy grabbed a pair of binoculars and went out to the bridge wing. The vehicle was racing along the jetty trying to catch up with the ship.

'Sod it! That's not the Colonel; that's a bloody tank.' He called the engine room. 'Peter, I need everything you've got. There's a fucking big tank chasing us.' He slammed the phone down.

'John, take her over to the far side of the channel.'

'We might go aground.'

'I'll worry about that. You just steer the ship!'

'Vijay, on the radar!'

He went back out on the wing in time to see a flash from the tank followed by a sharp crack and the howl of a shell passing overhead. The ship had now reached the end of the jetty and ahead was darkness and the widening passage to the sea. Just a couple of minutes thought Sandy desperately. Another flash and above the bridge was a deafening explosion. They all flinched and ducked instinctively, then there was a groan of metal and a screeching noise overwhelmed the bridge. With a final groan the top mast came crashing down over the bridge front onto the foredeck. Smoke and dust billowed up from the wreckage which covered the bridge front and the deck.

'Radars gone, Sir,' shouted Vijay.

That was not surprising. Both radar scanners were now wreckage on the foredeck amongst the ruin of the mast. There was another flash followed by water spouting up on the starboard side showering over the bridge wing. The ship was shaking with the vibration of the engines in the shallow water of the channel. 'Come on! Come on!' Sandy was shouting aloud now.

There was a moment of silence. A vacuum of air sucked out all sound from the bridge, and then there was an explosion behind the bridge that sent up a spiral of debris in a tower of flame. The shock knocked them all to the deck. Sandy knelt there, the pain in his leg forgotten, his ears strangely numb until sound then returned with a strange cracking noise. There was a red glow from the back of the bridge that was expanding into flames along with the smell of smoke and burning. Slowly his senses returned and the noise reached his ears. Jesus! He held onto the command chair and picked himself up. The Bosun was sprawled on the deck beside the wheel. Vijay was sitting on the deck coughing. Sandy dragged himself over to the wheel, pulled himself up and peered out ahead through the wreckage of the foremast. He kicked the Bosun's inert body.

'John! For Christ's sake! John, get up!' The figure stirred and groaned, then got onto hands and knees.

'What the fuck was that?'

'John, what course were you steering?'

'What?'

'I said what was the course, John? I can't see fuck all.'

Vijay spoke hoarsely. 'Put her on 260.'

John staggered to his feet. 'I'm all right. Give me the wheel.' Sandy handed over the wheel without protest. He hobbled to the bridge control panel and hit the emergency alarms sounding the general emergency signal. The flames were visible at the back of the bridge and there was the acrid smell of burning. He then switched on the broadcast system.

'This is the bridge. We have a fire aft of the bridge. Fire aft of the bridge.' He then called the engine room. 'Peter, we have been hit badly behind the bridge. I've no idea of the situation. Can you send up anyone you can spare to help.'

'They're on their way, Sandy. Do you want me to isolate the area?'

'Yes. Can you cut off all power to the shore office area?'

'I'll isolate that deck.'

'Also stop all ventilation and shut down the air conditioning.'

Harry had taken Rescue 1 to the position where he thought the Colonel would be heading for. The boat was stopped and drifting off the river bank. They could hear the sound of gunfire but it was difficult to place where it was coming from.

He keyed the walkie-talkie. 'Colonel? Colonel?' There was no reply.

'There's a light!' Delilah shouted. Harry looked and could see a dim light waving in the dark on the side of the river bank some 50 metres ahead. Harry put the throttles ahead easily.

'Head in towards the light, Olav.'

The boat veered in towards the bank. Delilah and Taffy sat at the bow with their weapons ready. The sound of gunfire drew near.

'Colonel? Colonel?' Harry called again.

'Captain, is that you?'

'We can see your lights and we're within a minute of your position.'

'We have some injured so I am sending them to board you first. The Sergeant and I will be holding the enemy off until all the troops are on board. We have a number of Chinese troops closing in on our position.

Harry took the wheel off Olav. 'I'll drive her in. You go forward and help get them on board.'

The boat softly drove on to the bank of the river then Harry saw Delilah and Taffy slip over the bow and disappear into the trees. The soldiers started boarding, helping the wounded into the boat first. Delilah and Taffy went into the dense trees for a few metres. In the dark shadows, soldiers were passing them heading towards the boat. 'You hold here, Taffy. I'll go ahead, find the Colonel and bring them back.'

Delilah worked his way forward. Bullets were whipping through the air above him, snapping as they hit the leaves and branches. 'Colonel!' Delilah called. Immediately a burst of firing came from close by. He edged his way towards the position and found the Colonel and the Sergeant.

'Thought you might need some company, Colonel.'

'We have nearly run out of ammunition,' said the Colonel. 'Just hold on for a moment,' said Delilah. 'He worked his way forward and started to string up grenades from the low branches of the trees. They were linked with a fishing line. 'That'll give them something to think about. Now let's start backing towards the boat.' The Colonel spoke softly to the Sergeant who wordlessly passed his weapon to the Colonel and moved back towards the river bank. He is wounded, so I told him to go to the boat.

'I don't know how many troops there are,' whispered the Colonel. 'I would think about five or six. They're good. Now I know how the rebels moved so fast to take Boma.'

'I want you to head back to the boat. I'm throwing a grenade,' Delilah said. 'We'll move back when it explodes. I want to attract them towards the grenades I've fixed in the trees.'

The Colonel nodded. Delilah fired a prolonged burst and then pulled a pin from a grenade and threw it towards the trees ahead. They both ducked down as it exploded and then moved back. The returning gunfire shredded the branches above them as they backed towards the river.

'Can you swim?' Delilah asked the Colonel.

'Yes, why?'

'Give me the walkie-talkie.' Delilah called Harry.

'Captain, the Sergeant will be boarding next. After he's on board you'll have to back off the bank. They're too close and if we try to board they'll be able to fire on the boat. Lie off and we'll swim out to you.' Harry could see the sense in this. The boat was a target. The Sergeant stumbled out of the trees and Taffy and Olav helped him board.

'Taffy, we're backing off. They're going to swim out. Stand by to cover them.'

Harry put the engine astern and the boat slid off easily and backed into the darkness of the river.

'Now we wait.' They all listened. There was a series of explosions from the river bank followed by screams.

'Delilah!' Harry called. There was no reply.

'They will be drifting downstream,' said Olav.

'So are we,' replied Harry. 'Take the wheel. Let's get clear of that bank area. Keep shouting.'

They drifted with the current for a few minutes and then Harry stopped the engines. When silence descended on the boat they faintly heard the sound of splashing in the water.

'On the port side,' shouted Olav and there out of the dark they could see Delilah and the Colonel swimming towards them. Bending over the side they hauled them aboard. They arrived in the wheelhouse coughing and spluttering water and slumped down on the deck exhausted.

Harry immediately put the engines astern full and backed away from the bank into the river stream. As they backed away there was a burst of gunfire from the bank and one of the wheelhouse windows shattered. Taffy immediately opened fire at the flashes on the bank and they stopped. As the bank disappeared into the night Harry put the engines ahead and bent over the radar.

'We'll be back on board in a few minutes. Steer 290, Olav.' He turned again to Delilah.

'Too many heroes on this ship. You all right?' Delilah nodded. The Colonel raised his head and looked at Delilah and then Harry.

'I don't know why you did it but thank you both.' Harry was about to reply when there was the sound of explosions from Boma. Harry picked up the binoculars and focused on a brightly burning fire. It was the ship. Sandy's voice called on the VHF. Harry answered.

'Captain, don't come down the Boma Channel. There's a tank on the jetty and it's just hit us aft of the bridge.' Harry pulled back on the throttles.

'What's the situation, Sandy?'

'We've got a fire aft. The emergency party's tackling it now.'

'What about casualties?'

'No reports yet.'

'Right, if there's any danger of the fire spreading get the passengers in their lifejackets on the afterdeck and get your boats in the water ready.'

'What are you going to do?'

'I'll take the boat around the other side of the island and meet you somewhere along the river. Where are you now?'

'We're clear of Boma. I want to keep the fire and smoke away from the bridge so I'm heading down river at about 5 knots. That gives a slight wind from ahead.'

'OK, Sandy, we'll see you soon.' He turned to the others. 'You all heard that. We'll go round the other side of the island and meet up with them along the river.'

'I thought you said we couldn't go that way?' said the Colonel.

'The ship couldn't but this boat probably can.'

'Probably?'

'Hell, I don't know. We have no chart so there's only one way to find out.' He looked at the radar. 'We're going to have to go back up the river and then around the island. Turn her round, Olav, and then head 090. Delilah, get the first aid kit out of the locker and see what you and Taffy can do for the wounded.' Delilah got to his feet. 'Colonel, what was on that tank?' asked Harry.

'It was a P62. They have a 105 mm gun and all kinds of shells. I don't know. A high explosive 105 mm shell can really make a mess of things. Also it was being driven by Chinese.'

'What?'

'Chinese. Don't ask me why the Chinese army are here. All I can think is that they are helping the rebels. They may have some kind of missile. I really don't know. When we see the damage that might tell us.'

Back on the ship the flames were searing into the sky and the smoke was billowing around the afterdeck. From inside the fire came the cracking of equipment and furnishings that were burning.

Sandy called Graham. 'When you can, get Rescue 2 down to the boat deck ready to go if required.'

Graham had set up his base on the main deck. Looking up he could see that all of the added on maintenance offices were ablaze. Already there was one hose party in action from the deck and steam came from the fire as the jet of water poured onto the wreckage. In front of him the fire suit party were almost ready to go. Chalkie the 2nd Engineer and Pat MacNab were adjusting their breathing apparatus and the crew were preparing the hose and nozzle for them.

'Once you get in, find a hydrant as close to the fire as possible and then use that. I want to hit the fire from all sides. Watch out for any secondary fires. As soon as we can we'll start boundary cooling. I want a report, when you can, of the situation inside.'

Chalkie nodded and put his mask on. The two of them entered the accommodation door on the main deck. Another hose was being readied on the deck and would soon be in action.

He reported to the bridge. 'One hose party in action from the main deck and another will be starting any minute. I've got two in BA sets and suits going in now with a hose to start tackling from inside. When they report back we'll know what the situation is.'

'Any news of the passengers?'

'Sorry. Haven't got round to that, Sir. I am using everyone I've got to fight the fire. They should be all right as they are away from the fire but it's the smoke I'm worried about. Can you organise a hose from bridge to hit down on the fire. I've no one left down here. That way the fire will be covered from three directions.'

'I'll get onto it now, Graham.'

Jake came on the line. 'Finished the soundings, Sir. The forepeak is showing two metres but all the others are dry.'

'Where's Huggins?'

'With me.'

'Send him up to the bridge. You go down to the shore workers' accommodation and check on the passengers. Go in through the main deck door. That way you should avoid the smoke.

Next Sandy called the hospital.

'Yes?' It was Andy.

'How are things there?'

'We're busy. What's going on?'

'We've been hit aft but it's under control.'

'There's a strong smell of smoke down here.'

'You're in no danger.'

'Bloody hope not. We've got patients that we can't move at the moment. We've lost one of the soldiers.'

'Sorry, Andy.'

'It happens. Got to go.'

Chapter 25

Rescue 1 was heading back to the ship through the shallows and was hidden from Boma. Harry had reduced the speed of the boat after rounding the island. Even though it was mud, if they went aground at full speed, they might not get her off again. Even so, they were making 12 knots and pushing through the dark river. Harry could see the ship on the radar 8 miles ahead and they were rapidly overhauling her. As they got nearer they could see the flames at the back of the accommodation, then the ship lit up. For a moment Harry thought there had been an explosion but then realised that Sandy had sensibly put all the deck lights on.

He called the ship. 'Sandy, I'm about 6 miles out and will be there in 30 minutes. Where do you want me to come?'

'Come alongside on the port side of the working deck. We can put you on a boat rope there and keep you in the water while things get sorted here.'

'I have three wounded soldiers to get on board.'

'OK, I'll organise a stretcher party and warn the hospital.' Sandy called Jake. 'Get what soldiers you have and any others who can help down there. Go to the hospital and tell them that we have three more injured soldiers coming on board. Then get the stretchers along to the port side of the main deck.'

Jake made his way to the hospital and saw the door was closed. He opened it and went in finding Carole and Andy bending over a patient on the couch which had been pulled into the middle of the room. The beds were all occupied with the wounded. Monique was standing by them with a tray. Her face lit up when she saw Jake. Carole looked up without stopping and then turned back to the patient.

'What do you want?' she asked.

'We've got three more wounded coming. We need the stretchers on the deck.'

'Take them.'

'We're still fighting the fire.'

She looked up again 'Fire? It keeps getting worse. How's Harry?'

'I don't know. He's not back yet.'

'Stop telling me things in bits! Tell me what has been going on.' Jake related the events.

'So where is Harry?'

'I don't know.'

Carole looked at Andy. 'Does Delilah have any battlefield first aid experience?' Andy nodded. 'Tell Sandy that I want Delilah to come here.'

'He's on the boat.'

'Then as soon as he gets off.'

On the afterdeck, Graham called the bridge.

'Sir, we have some bad news. The Cook is dead. Chalkie and Pat worked their way up to the crew deck where the heat and smoke are bad. They went by the galley and it is a disaster area. The explosion caused the after bulkhead to buckle. The cooker came off the base and all the tiles broke away. Willie didn't stand a chance. Apparently there is blood everywhere.' Sandy slumped in the chair.

'What the hell was Willie doing in there? He was supposed to be on the port side until we cleared.'

'Apparently he thought we were and was trying to make something for everyone. It must have been quick.'

'I'd hoped we were going to make it without anyone getting killed. Poor Willie. What about the fire?'

'It's bad, Sir, but we're holding it at the moment.'

'Do what you can, Graham. The Old Man is due any minute. He's coming alongside the port side with three wounded. Jake is bringing a stretcher party down to the main deck.'

'He's beside me now.'

Harry approached the port side of the ship. The fire was still burning with flames flickering from several parts of the after accommodation. He could see where the heat inside was blistering the paintwork and in some areas it was alight. The flames illuminated the thick clouds of smoke and steam billowing into the night sky. Water was streaming from the scuppers and even spilling over through the rails to stream down the hull sides. As they came alongside, the boat rope was thrown and made fast. Harry brought the boat under the crane which, once Delilah had made the hook fast, hoisted the boat level with the main deck. As soon as they had all cleared the boat, Jake and the stretcher party boarded and started to move the casualties to the hospital.

Jake called to Delilah, 'Carole wants you in the hospital, Delilah.' Delilah nodded.

The after work deck was a mess of water streaming from the fire across an entanglement of hoses and fire fighting equipment. Two jets of water were being directed on the fire from the deck.

Immediately, Harry went to Graham. 'What's the situation?'

'I think we're on top of it now, Sir.' He indicated to Chalkie and Pat who were sitting on the deck dirty and exhausted. 'Chalkie and Pat have just come out. They rigged the hose inside and started putting water on the fire. Then we pulled them out when their time was up. We have changed the air bottles and the next team are suited up ready to go. Boundary cooling is going on now but we are short of crew. Captain, I've bad news. Willie's dead.'

Harry looked shocked. 'Oh shit. How?'

'I'm told he thought we were clear and he was preparing a meal for us all. The force of the explosion on the bulkhead shattered the galley.'

Harry nodded. 'How's the bridge.'

'Still functioning, but I haven't been there.'

Harry looked up. 'Where's the topmast?'

'That's down over the foredeck.'

Harry looked at his watch. It was just after 0400. He felt very tired.

'Be dawn soon. Let me get to the bridge and have a look at the situation there.'

'You have to go up the outside ladders, Sir.'

'You've done a fine job, Graham.'

'In another few hours we'll be able to get the vents going and clear the smoke from the accommodation.'

Harry wearily climbed the ladders to the bridge. The smell of burning enveloped him as he entered. Sandy was sitting in the command chair with his now bandaged leg stretched out in front of him. He turned and held his hand out. Harry grasped it.

'Good to see you back, Captain. Have you heard about Willie?'

'Yes, I'm so sorry. I had hoped to carry this off without any deaths.'

The Bosun spoke from the wheel. 'We all knew the odds when we started, Captain.'

'Yes, I know, but it doesn't make it any easier.'

Sandy pointed out of the open bridge window. The top mast was lying down over the bridge front onto the foredeck. Wires and rope halyards decorated the window.

'You probably noticed the ship has been slightly rearranged.'

'I leave the ship for a few minutes and look at what you do.' They smiled faintly.

'How's the navigation going without any radars?'

'Vijay has it in hand. He's using the satnav and living at the chart table. Harry looked over to see Vijay bent over in concentration.

'We'll wait until they have the fire out before increasing speed.'

'What will we do with Willie?'

'Sunset this evening if we are still afloat.' Sandy nodded.

'I'd like to help sew him up, if I can,' said John. 'He was a good shipmate.'

'No more grumbling about you stealing his food.'

'I'll miss that.'

The bridge wing door opened and the Colonel appeared. His uniform was torn, wet and dirty and he looked exhausted. Harry turned to him. 'We're sorry for your losses, Colonel.'

The Colonel shrugged. 'They were good men and loyal. I'm also sorry about your Cook.'

'How are the wounded?'

'The Doctor is dealing with them. I know one man died but the others will pull through.'

'You had a tough fight.'

'More than we thought we would. We didn't expect to see Chinese troops there.'

'What's going on, Colonel?'

'I have been thinking about that. I am sure that they were helping Kabila. Not that it can be proved. I think that now they have been seen they will get them out as soon as they can.'

'How did they get here?'

'That's another strange business. I blew up a small transport that was containing ammunition. It was probably Chinese but it was too small to bring that many troops in. I can only assume they came in from Angola which means Angola was supporting these rebels while pretending to support the government. In a way that helps you, Captain.'

'Why's that?'

'They are not going to want to make any official noises about your escape otherwise all of this could come out.'

'Do you think so?'

'Why not? It will also show their incompetence that they were not able to stop a single merchant ship. No, Captain, you watch. There will be silence. They just want you to go away.'

'We haven't escaped yet. We have to get out to sea.'

'Another very interesting piece of news that my Lieutenant has reported. While on the field they caught one of the soldiers. Not Chinese, but one of the rebels. It seems they have not taken Banana, the port on the coast. Our forces are still holding the port and the area around there. With your permission, I want to contact the port to try and confirm that.'

'Go ahead, as long as you don't mention the ship or that you are on board. Sandy, can you hold on a bit longer here? I want to go back to the main deck.'

When Harry had gone, the Colonel put his hand in his pocket and drew out Sandy's hip flask which was still half full. He passed it to Sandy. Sandy raised it. 'Here's to those who didn't make it.' He took a long drink and passed it back to the Colonel who also raised it in salute and drank.

When Harry arrived back at the fire scene he could see it was now nearly out. Thick black smoke continued to rise from the wreckage of the maintenance office block and was being blown away by the gentle flow of wind from ahead. Four hoses were now playing on the fire; they had been switched to spray to cool it down. Women from the shore workers' accommodation had come out on the deck bringing cold water, tea and sandwiches and some of the crew were standing around eating and drinking. A number of them had blackened faces with white circles from wearing their face masks. Amongst them was Jake.

'The hoses curled around the deck amongst the streaming water. Just about out, Sir,' Graham said as he came up to him. 'I won't complain about fire exercises ever again.'

'Just as well you were a good student,' said Harry.

Peter appeared on the deck. 'How's Sandy?'

'Wishing he was down here crutch and all,' replied Harry. He looked around. He could see they were all exhausted.

'I just want them to hold until this evening. Then it will be over one way or the other. The Colonel thinks that Mobutu's mob are still in control of Banana.' Peter looked puzzled. 'That's the port on the Atlantic where we picked up our pilot coming in. Seems years ago doesn't it?'

'Just a week,' said Harry. 'Can you remember the ballast situation? I know we raised the bow as far up as we could, but maybe you can shift something further aft.'

'Why?'

'It would be good if we could see to the bow damage. We might be able to put a doubler on and cement patch her. Either way it would be good to know what the damage is, just in case we have a long sea passage to make.'

'What are you thinking?' Peter asked.

'Let's see,' replied Harry.

Chapter 26

Harry went through a door on the main deck and up the stairway to the hospital. The door was closed so Harry knocked and went in. All the beds were full and there was a mattress on the floor with a soldier in a stretcher lying on it. The body had gone. Carole and Andy were still working over the patient's couch that they were using as an operating table. Carole looked up and on seeing Harry her eyes warmed.

'So, back from your holidays I see?'

'No more package tours,' Harry replied.

'There's a tea urn in the corner courtesy of the ladies in the shore workers' galley,' Andy said.

'That would be wonderful.' Harry went over and poured a cup. 'How are you doing?'

'We have a production line. This one on the deck will be the last,' she said indicating to a soldier in the stretcher.

'Just dug a bullet out of this chap,' she raised her forceps showing a bloody bullet in them. Delilah and Monique are working in the dispensary dealing with minor wounds. Thank God I brought my instruments with me otherwise we would have had to depend on the ship's antiquated surgical tools. I've used up most of the morphine as well as the gas.' She looked up again. 'We put the body in the cold store. I didn't know what else to do with it.'

'That's all right. Good place for the time being. I'll ask the Colonel what he wants to do.'

'I can finish up,' said Andy.

Carole put the instrument down and took off her mask. She wiped a bloody hand across her brow leaving a streak of blood above her eyes.

'You're tired,' said Harry.

'Everyone's tired. I'm so sorry about Willie.' Harry shrugged in resignation.

'We all are. The only good thing, if that can be said, is that he had no family, only us.'

'What about the rest of the ship?'

'Battered but she'll survive. Everyone has done a magnificent job.'

'Is it over Harry?'

Harry chose his words carefully. 'I hope so. We are still in the estuary, but when we can we will increase speed. We will be out to sea within 4 hours. Let's see.'

He gave her a quick kiss. 'You look a mess but you're still lovely. Just a few more hours.'

When Harry arrived back on the bridge he found the Colonel in jubilant mood. 'We still hold Banana and all the country around it,' he said. 'That Kabila scum have been held. Zaire is too big for them to hold it all.'

'So what does that mean, Colonel?'

'It means we can leave your ship there, Captain. Once ashore we can help organise resistance to Kabila.'

'Are you sure that's what you want, Colonel? I was planning to go straight out into international waters as soon as I could and then up the coast to Nigeria.'

'No, Captain, this is what we want. This is our country and we do not wish to leave it.'

'So you want me to take the ship to Banana?'

'Yes please, Captain.'

'Colonel, I hope you are right.'

'I have spoken to the military there and I know them. There will be no problem.'

'Sandy, what do you think?'

'It'll take one major problem away, Captain. Arriving in Lagos with a bunch of soldiers on board.'

'All right, Colonel, Banana it is.' Harry turned to Vijay. 'Did you hear that, Vijay?'

'Yes, Sir. I will start putting the tracks into the satnav. We already have most of them from when we came in. I just have to reverse them. Sir, Banana is the pilot port and there may be a pilot who could take us down the rest of the channel.'

'Good idea, Vijay. Colonel, can you ask your chums if they can send us a pilot?'

The Colonel picked up the VHF and called the port. He talked for a moment and turned smiling to the Captain.

'They will help, Captain. They will try to get a pilot and bring him to you but they don't know when. Meanwhile they suggested you proceed at a slow speed. One more thing, Captain, the pygmies. We can land them as well.'

Harry shook his head. 'There's no way that the Doctor will allow that even if the pygmies agreed. They regard you as their enemies regardless of who you fight for.'

'It is true that they are treated badly but I tell you it will be no different in Nigeria for them. At least here they know the country and the ways. North of Banana in the forests, there are other pygmies living. They can go there safely.'

'How will they get there?'

'I will take them.' He looked at Harry. 'Strange coming from me isn't it? But I owe you a debt. You came back for me when you could have left. The Doctor is also saving my wounded. I know the Doctor's opinion of me and she may want to oppose this but I give you both my word. I will protect them and get them to the forests. I cannot say more than that.'

Harry thought for a moment. 'Just a minute.' He phoned down to the hospital; Carole answered.

'Carole, not an emergency but can you come to the bridge for a minute.' He put the phone down. You can try to convince her, Colonel.'

After a few minutes Carole arrived on the bridge. 'That's the last of your soldiers patched up Colonel. Three of them will need more time in hospital but it's the best we can do.'

'Doctor, we have been lucky to have had you on board. I know my men are grateful to you.' Carole shrugged.

'Carole, the Colonel is leaving with his people in Banana. It is still in government hands. He wants to suggest something to you. All yours, Colonel.'

The Colonel began explaining his plan and as he continued Carole's face contorted in fury. 'Are you mad? Do you think I will place them in the hands of butchers!' She rounded on Harry.

'Do you go along with this?'

'Hey, leave me out of this. Whatever you decide is all right with me but wait, Carole. You're letting your opinions get in the way. Just listen to the man.'

'Doctor, please just forget who I am or what uniform I wear. We have all been through a lot together and I respect you all. I have always done what I said I would do. Please listen to me. If these pygmies are landed in Nigeria, what then? You will not be allowed to go with them. They may be put into some shanty town in the city. They will die there. They will not be allowed to do what they want and that is to go into the forests. They will be as disliked as much there as here. I promise you this is true and you know it. I am offering them protection from the best soldiers in the country. I will ensure that they get back to their forests. Once there, no one will find them except the other pygmy tribes. There is no war in the north of Banana nor is there likely to be. There's nothing there to fight for. One thing more, you cannot go with them.' He held his hand up again as he saw Carole start to protest.

'In the forest you will die. It is totally different to anything you have experienced. Neither the forest nor my country is for you at present. We are a country at war and no one knows what will happen next.' Carole looked stricken. She turned to Harry.

'What do you think?'

'I think you must ask them. It's their lives not ours. The Colonel is right about you not going. That would place too much of a burden on the pygmies and that would be wrong.'

'So I can't go here and I can't go in Nigeria.'

Her eyes filled with tears. 'So what happens to them?'

'They will live as they did before, Doctor, in the forest which is their home. You must ask them.'

Harry spoke. 'Strange as it may seem, I believe that the Colonel will keep his word. In his own way, it is as important to him as it is to us.'

There was silence on the bridge while they waited. 'We will go now,' she said with resignation. Harry looked at the Colonel and nodded. The Colonel and Carole left the bridge together.

'He's right,' said Sandy.

'I know but she has to decide that for herself. Now go below and get some rest.'

'I'm fine.'

'So I see. Every Chief Officer has a crutch. Bosun that applies to you as well. You're welded to that wheel.' He could see the protest coming.

'And don't tell me about the fishing boats. No one shot you there. You are both ordered to go to the hospital.'

He called the hospital. 'Andy, the Bosun and Mate are coming down. Please can they be seen to?' Then he called down to the main deck. 'Graham, can someone find Olav and Jake and get them up on the bridge please. Go on Sandy. I'll wake you when we get to Banana.'

'There's still a lot to be done.'

'As long as we're not sinking, it can wait. Now bugger off. I mean it. If I see you on the decks, I'll stop your tap till Hull.'

'Shit, that's serious,' said the Bosun.

'The same goes for you,' said Harry. Olav and Jake appeared with smoke-stained faces and after the Bosun handed over the wheel, he and Sandy left the bridge.

'Vijay, are you happy to hand over to Jake?'

'The courses are all on the chart and in the satnav, Captain. All we have to do is follow them and hope the sandbanks haven't shifted.'

'Right, Jake, take over navigation please. Vijay, get a few hours' rest and come back for arrival in Banana.'

Harry sat down in the command chair. He was so tired. Dawn now streaked the sky with grey light and the river was reflecting the colour from the sky, turning it from black to grey. The breeze was freshening as it came through the window and wavelets disturbed the surface of the river. Best of all, he could smell the sea. Freedom.

Not much freedom on the bridge. The next to appear were Graham and Peter. They also smelled of smoke and dirt was encrusted on their faces and hands. 'You've been busy, Peter.'

'He took charge of the hose parties, Captain,' commented Graham. 'Fire's out. We now have access to all decks. It's a bit of a mess down there but only the galley is damaged. The galley and messroom deck has smoke damage but it will be able to function once it's cleaned up. The Bosun has got the crew onto that now.'

'He is supposed to be resting.'

'You know the Bosun, Captain.'

'The power is back on that deck as well as the ventilation. I'll put the air conditioning back on soon,' said Peter.

The whole office block is burnt out. We have taken Willie's body out; it's in the cold room with the soldier,' said Graham.

'We will bury him this evening. The Bosun will arrange for him to be sewn up.'

Peter spoke. 'One of the sailors has cleared his cabin. His papers are on your desk. Do you know what, he only has one suitcase of things? Imagine, just one suitcase.'

'Not much to auction then.'

'I've been and looked at the top mast. Not as bad as it appears. One of the radar scanners is bust, nothing we can do about that, but the other may be all right. Surprisingly the cabling is intact. I think that we can swing the heavy crane around, fix a pulley system and lift the mast back into place. If we can lift it back up into position we can weld a collar round the break which should hold it in place until we get home. Then you'll have one radar, provided the scanner works of course. Otherwise you'll have to switch one of the radars on in one of the boats. Some of the engine plates on the bridge front will have to be dumped. They certainly did their job though. If they hadn't been there you wouldn't have much bridge left.'

'Thanks for that.'

'Anyway we'll get those off and then we'll be able to walk around the engine room again. Regarding the workshop, that's gone but at least it was an add-on containerised block so the damage is mostly confined. We can cut that away and dump it over the side. By the time Sandy's boys have got to what's left and sloshed paint on, it will look as if it was never there. Sandy's been up forward and the windlass is in good order so you have a port anchor.'

'He is supposed to be in his bunk as well.'

'Well anyway, you still have a port anchor. The starboard anchor is crumpled into the hull though. It makes an interesting addition to the forecastle store. The galley will be useable once we can get the cooker back in position and the place cleaned up. So, all in all, not too bad. Give us a week and most of the damage will have been fixed.'

'Thanks for that, Peter.' Harry reached forward and put both engine throttles ahead. 'I'll take her up to 12 knots. We'll see if the forepeak can take that.'

'Oh, one last thing, all the soundings are fine. Everything dry except of course the forepeak which you rearranged. I can't make a new bow unfortunately.'

'You look bloody awful.'

'So do you.'

'We might be calling at Banana in a few hours and getting rid of all the passengers.'

'Then I would like to use a boat and look at the bow. I might be able to put a doubler on and stop some of the holes.'

'No problem, Peter, and thanks again. Now go down both of you and get a few hours' rest.'

'I think I will, Harry. How about you?'

'I will shortly.'

Peter disappeared only to be replaced by Delilah carrying a tray of food. 'Breakfast, Captain. Fry up and coffee.' Harry suddenly realised he was hungry. Delilah placed the tray beside him on the bridge front.

'You do know that without you we would have been in real trouble?' Harry said.

'Sir, without you we would never have made it.'

Harry laughed. 'Without me you may never have got into this in the first place. Can you manage in the galley?'

'If you mean can I replace Willie, no I can't fry everything like he did but I'll do my best.' Delilah smiled. 'We'll miss the old bastard.'

When Delilah left, the bridge was quiet again for a moment.

'I wonder how you're going to tell your parents about this voyage, Jake?'

'I'm not sure I will, Sir.'

'Why not?'

'They wouldn't believe it. Nobody would. I'm not sure I do yet.'

Harry smiled. 'Well no matter what you do with your life, you'll never forget it.'

The ship gave a slight lurch to starboard and sheered to port. Harry got up quickly and looked at the log, she was still under way but slowed down. He immediately pulled back on the throttles. 'Starboard 15!' The head came round. 'Steady.' He looked over the side and saw black mud swirling around at the stern of the ship. 'Put her back on course. It was a mudbank. He looked across at the antiquated echo sounder. Not showing on the machine either.'

Jake looked worried. 'She was right on the line.'

'I know, Jake. Not your fault. These mudbanks come and go. I would slow down but I want to get as far away as I can. Dawn's coming.'

Chapter 27

Daylight pierced the gloom of the bridge. There was no sight of the river banks so it looked as if they were out on the sea but it was an illusion. Like all estuaries, as they become wider they become more shallow with sand and mudbanks hidden beneath the water.

The ship slid to a stop and heeled over to 6 degrees to starboard.

Harry groaned. Aground again. 'Stop engines. Full astern.' The ship shook and black mud boiled up around the stern as the propellers stirred up the mudbank. He put the wheel to port then to starboard with no result. 'Stop engines.'

'Olav, get a leadline and sound around the hull. I just want to see how far we are onto the mud.'

Harry rang the engine room and Chalkie answered. 'Chalkie, we're aground on a mudbank on the port side. You might want to change your cooling water intakes to avoid them clogging up.'

'Already done it, Captain. Peter knew we were going into shallow waters.'

Sandy arrived on the bridge. 'Bloody rivers,' said Sandy. 'If you don't dredge them, they silt up. This place hasn't been dredged for years. At least it's a rising tide.'

'Yes but we don't want to hang around here, especially now it's getting light.'

'I can start changing over tanks to lighten her on the port side.'

'That'll take too long, Sandy. Get the boats down and put them on the bow. Let's see if they can help pull her off. Otherwise we might have to use them to take out the port anchor and use that to pull us off. Tell you what, we've still got that truck on the work deck. Hoist it up on the starboard crane and hang it off out on the starboard side. That will heel her over even more and should help her come off.'

Harry waited. Soon came the sound of the boat davits working to lower the boats. Olav arrived back on the bridge with the soundings. As Harry thought, the ship was aground along the port side with deeper water on the starboard. 'We'll wait till the boats are fast and the truck swung out, then we'll give her another go astern,' Harry said.

It was a peaceful dawn, with the streaks of light beginning to cross the sky above. Across the water, flights of birds were heading seawards in search of food. A light cooling breeze rippled the surface of the water.

Harry went out onto the bridge wing to watch the crane preparing to hoist the truck. The boats were being lowered to the water and the Bosun was standing by on the forecastle to give them the tow lines. He turned aft. He looked at the birds in the sky. They were all wheeling and diving around the stern where the water had been stirred up, except for two in the distance. They were black spots on the sky, not moving but getting larger. He stood for a moment then suddenly rushed into the bridge. 'Sound the general alarm!' he shouted at Jake grabbing the mike. 'Aircraft approaching aft! I repeat aircraft approaching aft!' then grasping the binoculars ran back onto the bridge wing and searched the sky. He located the two approaching aircraft. The bridge door opened with a bang and Delilah rushed through shouting at Jake to get the other Stinger from forward. Jake ran off the bridge together with Olav. On the main deck the Colonel and his soldiers spilled out. Sandy came panting up onto the bridge.

'We have no machine guns!'

'I know!' shouted Harry. There was a roar as the first plane hurtled in at the ship. The soldiers on the deck were firing their weapons as the plane passed over with three black objects dropping from the fuselage. 'Bombs!' Sandy shouted. The bombs dropped and hit the water alongside the ship on the port side. The crash of explosions stunned their senses as three black water spouts erupted from the river and towered over the ship before the mix of water and mud crashed down on the decks. The ship was hurled to starboard as she heeled over with the force of the explosions. On the main deck the truck which was suspended from the crane swung wildly out over the river before swinging back inboard where the crane wire snapped causing the truck to crash onto the deck below just missing two of the soldiers. Those standing on the deck were thrown down and only the side bulwarks prevented them being thrown over the side. Harry and Sandy were also thrown onto the deck where they crawled to the bridge front and pulled themselves up.

'Bloody hell!' exclaimed Sandy as he peered out ahead. The river around the ship was a swirling mass of black water and mud. 'She won't take any more of this!' Harry looked out at the river. 'At least she is off the mud! Look, she's turning!' He rammed the engine throttles full ahead and spun the wheel. 'Where are we going?' asked Sandy. 'I'm turning her round,' replied Harry.

Delilah's voice sounded through the speakers. 'Hold her steady! The next plane is coming in!' Harry turned the wheel, steadying the ship. They were now pointing directly at the rapidly approaching plane. There was a roar of noise, and then from the deck above a streak of flame and smoke headed directly at the plane. The aircraft seemed to try and go higher just as the missile hit on one of the wings. The plane wheeled off to one side crashing into the river a few hundred metres off the ship. The river once again boiled for a moment and then settled around the sinking wreckage which rapidly disappeared beneath the water. They ran out onto the bridge wing. The other aircraft was now far higher and it circled around where the wreckage of the plane had sunk. After a few circles it departed back up the river. Harry stopped the engines. He was panting.

'Get a damage report,' he said to Sandy. 'And get the boats back on board.'

Sandy nodded and limped off the bridge. Harry phoned the engine room. Peter came on the phone, his voice shaky. 'What's going on, Harry?'

'It's all right, Peter. It's over, at least for the time being. We went aground, then a couple of bombers found us. One dropped its bombs, just missing us. Delilah used one of the Stingers and brought the other one down. His friend has left us.'

'Thank God for that. Chalkie was sent flying and he has a bad cut on his arm. I've sent him up to the hospital.'

'I have a feeling that he won't be the only one. Is there any damage down there?'

'Not that I can see, but we will have to wait until we've done all our checks. At least the main engines and steering seem to be working. I'll let you know if there's any problem.'

He put the phone down as the Colonel arrived on the bridge. 'How are your people, Colonel?'

'Apart from bruises, OK. That applies to the other passengers as well. I've just come from the hospital. The usual cuts and bangs but at the moment no serious injuries. Who fired the missile? Delilah?' Harry nodded.

At that moment Delilah came onto the bridge followed by Jake and Olav. 'Well done, Delilah,' said the Colonel. Delilah grinned. 'I think it was lucky we had the Stinger on board. The one left is standing by. I'm sorry I couldn't get one ready sooner but it had to be switched on and then acquire a target before I could fire.' Harry waved his hand. 'At least they've gone. Now all we have to do is get the hell out of here.' Sandy's voice came over the speaker. 'I'm going to put the damaged truck over the side. It's scrap metal now. We need a new crane wire and there's a dent in the deck where the truck landed. I've got Graham and Vijay going round the ship looking for any problems but so far so good. The ship's covered in mud as are those who were on the deck, otherwise she's done us proud.'

Harry ordered, 'Let's get under way. Take the con again, Jake.' The ship steadily came back onto her course and trembled as the revs increased again. 'Keep her at half speed, Jake. Just in case. We don't want to get stuck again.' He turned to the Colonel. 'Where did those bombers come from?'

'They can only have come from Angola, Captain. Zaire hasn't got any. I shouldn't think Angola has many either. They looked like old soviet ground attack planes. Angola was employing Serbian mercenary pilots, so it could have been them. Well there are a few less now. Just in case, I will keep four soldiers up here on look out.'

'I will also stay up above with the Stinger, Captain,' said Delilah.

At last it was quiet. Harry turned to the Colonel. 'I really thought that was it. Having made it so far, it seemed that we were going to lose it.'

'I thought so too.'

They stood together in silence.

Carole appeared on the bridge. She looked tired and for the first time older than her years. 'Apart from various parts of the hospital flying around, and nearly running out of plasters and bandages, all is in order.' She looked at them. 'Is that it now. Is it finished?'

Harry shrugged. 'I hope so, but we are watching just in case.'

They were silent for a moment. 'What did the pygmies decide?' Harry asked.

Carole drew a deep breath. 'They want to go with the Colonel.'

'I should think the bombing made certain of that,' said Harry. He looked at the Colonel.

'I have promised they will be under my protection until I get them up to the forests in the north. I will go now and get my people ready. When will we be at Banana?' Harry looked at the clock. 'Difficult to say. I have had to slow her down because of these mudbanks. Hopefully I'll be there by 1100.'

After he had gone, Carole and Harry looked at each other. 'They're not pets you know,' he said gently.

'What do you mean by that?' Carole asked indignantly.

'Well you obviously feel some ownership of them. I can understand that. They have been totally reliant on you for so long. You have cared for them, worried about them and in the end undoubtedly saved their lives, but they are adult human beings with a mind of their own. They will leave but they will never forget you. It is time to let go.'

Carole stared at him and abruptly left the bridge. If he hadn't been so tired he may not have said what he did, but it had to be said.

The next thing he remembered was being shaken gently. He started. 'What?'

'Sir, Banana in one hour.' It was Vijay. He sat up, his mind whirling for a minute as he adjusted.

'I was asleep.'

'We left you, Sir. Everything is fine.' Vijay handed him a fresh coffee. His mouth felt like sandpaper. He sipped the coffee and came back to earth. The sun was streaming in through the windows. The deadlights had been removed.

'The port anchor's cleared away ready for letting go.'

'Thanks, Vijay. We made good time. When did they take the deadlights down?'

'A couple of hours ago, Sir. They left the engine plates up as they didn't want to wake you.'

'How's the ship?'

'The Chief and Sandy have good news. We have no real damage from the bombing, just things shaken up and some small internal damage in the accommodation. The damage to the forepeak is not as bad as we first thought.

There is water coming in but the pumps have been able to deal with it and they have lowered the water.' Harry looked ahead and saw the bow was now higher.

'Peter says that when we anchor at Banana he will put his people over and see if they can put a doubler on. Sandy thinks there is a split on the starboard side about one metre long. Once the doubler is on he will get the lads to put a cement patch on inside.'

He eased himself out of the chair, feeling the stiffness in his back. 'Let's see where we're going.' They bent over the chart together. 'I don't want to anchor too close just in case. Let's keep her 3 miles off. Here.' He pointed to a position on the chart. 'Depth is 15 metres; that's good enough.' He turned back towards his chair.

'What's that?' He grabbed the binoculars from Vijay's hand and pressed them to his eyes. He focused on a ship on the port bow.

'Is it the pilot vessel?' asked Vijay.

'It's too big for a pilot boat. And it's coming from the wrong direction. Fuck! It's a warship! Sound general emergency stations!'

The strident sound of the bells ringing throughout the ship could be heard.

Instantly there were urgent feet on the stairway and the door burst open. It was Sandy closely followed by the Colonel, Graham and Jake.

'What's going on, Captain?' shouted Sandy.

Harry pointed at the horizon. 'A warship. It's about 5 miles away.'

'Oh shit! And we were so close to getting out!' The bridge was getting crowded.

'What weapons have we got?'

'We've still got a Stinger. Delilah is up above with it.'

Harry turned to the Colonel. 'Can we use them against ships?'

'Don't see why not.'

Harry went to the chart and quickly measured the distances. We have three miles to go and we're out of the river. Then we can head north to Banana.

'It's heading to intercept our track, Captain.' Vijay called.

'It's not going to let us get out,' said Sandy.

'I've not gone through all this to give up now,' said Harry. He went out onto the wing. 'Delilah!' he called. 'Go down to No 1 boat. Tell the Bosun to stand by to launch and bring the Stinger. We're going boating!'

He rang the engine room. 'Peter, I want everything you've got. We've got a warship chasing us!' He slammed the phone down.

'What are you up to?' asked Sandy.

'We just need another 20 minutes,' said Harry. 'Now you get out of the river then head like the clappers for Banana. Delilah and I will keep them busy while you get there. Colonel, get on to your chums in Banana. Tell them we have a warship after us and need help.'

'Are you raving mad?' shouted Sandy. 'You can't fight a fucking warship with a boat.'

'I can give you time to get the ship clear and you're in no state to go. I've no time to argue. Just get the ship out. That's a fucking order.' With that Harry ran off the bridge.

'It's a patrol boat of some kind. It's got a deck gun,' said Sandy looking through the binoculars.

'How far off do you estimate it is?' asked the Colonel.

'About three miles.'

'Boat away,' shouted Vijay from the starboard bridge wing. They watched the boat heading in a wide arc towards the warship, smoke belching from its exhaust as Harry slammed the throttles to full power.

'Delilah, you get up forward with the Stinger. I'll get as close as I can.'

'OK, Captain. The Stinger will give them a nasty shock but it won't stop them. It only has a very small warhead.'

There was a cloud of black smoke from the warship. 'She's moving, Captain.'

The bow of the small warship lifted as she built up speed. A flash came from the bow and shortly after there was a spout of water ahead of them. Harry swung the boat sharply to port and then to starboard.

'I'll have to zigzag,' he shouted to Delilah who was lying down on the foredeck holding on to the rail with one hand.

'I can't bloody shoot like this, Captain.'

'Just hold on,' Harry shouted back. 'I'll get in closer.'

'They're shooting at them!' shouted Vijay. Sandy was watching through the binoculars. Jake and Graham were now also on the bridge. 'And they've got another gun down aft.'

Sandy turned to the Colonel. 'Have you got any weapons?'

'Just some grenade launchers and our own weapons.'

'That'll do.' Sandy pushed the Colonel towards the bridge wing. 'Get some of your soldiers with them down to the port boat. He turned to Vijay. As soon as you get to the alteration point, head for Banana. Don't stop for anything, you understand. Vijay nodded. The Colonel's told Banana we're coming. I don't know what they've got to help but just get there. If you can't anchor and that ship is still after you, then put her into the port or aground. Just so everyone can get off. Got it?'

'Aground?'

'Just get them off. She's all yours!'

'I'll come!' shouted Jake.

'No you fucking won't. You three will get this ship to Banana, you understand.'

Sandy disappeared down the outside ladder and hobbled along the deck towards the port boat. The Colonel and two soldiers were aboard and the Bosun together with Olav and Andy were standing by.

'We're coming,' they said.

'No you're not. Christ, what is this, a bloody debating society? The 2nd Mate's got the ship. Go up to the bridge and see what he wants.' Sandy dragged himself on board with a groan and grabbed the wheel. He hit the starters and the engines roared into life.

'Lower away, Bosun,' he shouted. 'Hold on tight; she'll kick like a mule at this speed.' They hit the water and immediately Sandy rammed the throttles to full and pulled the auto release. The boat slammed against the hull and then curved away.

'Port boat's away,' shouted Jake.

'Four minutes to the alter course,' Graham called to Vijay.

'They're firing!' cried Jake.

'Not at us though,' said Vijay.

Harry was swinging the boat from side to side and the water spouts were getting closer.

'We're still too far away,' shouted Delilah.

'I'm trying to get closer, but the bloody thing's almost as fast as we are and the closer we get, the better their accuracy.'

'Try to get under the gun,' shouted Delilah.

'Fucking hell, Delilah. That's what I'm trying to do. Just a moment! They're turning.'

The warship was turning broadside to them. 'Oh shit, they've got another gun down aft.' Both the guns fired together and the boat was bracketed. The bow slammed into the turbulence from the shells. Harry spun the boat hard to starboard.

'I'm going round their stern,' he shouted. 'That'll keep the forward gun away.' The forward gun fired again but the shell they expected didn't come. Harry turned around and saw the port daughter craft.

'What the hell?' The VHF crackled. It was Sandy. 'You idiot, Sandy!' Harry shouted. 'Get out of here!'

'Too late, Captain. We've only got some RPGs but we'll hold them for you to get in,' replied Sandy.

'What's the range of these, Sandy,' asked the Colonel.

'About 1 kilometre. They self-fuse and explode if they don't hit anything.'

'Fire one anyway. Try to attract their attention.' The Colonel took a launcher and loaded it. Then pointing it up in the air in the warship's direction he fired it. About half way between the boat and the ship the grenade exploded in the air. Immediately, the warship turned its forward gun towards them and fired sending up a spout of water 50 metres away. Sandy now started to weave his boat.

'We're at the alteration point,' called Graham.

'Starboard 5,' Vijay ordered Pat Macnab who was on the wheel. 'Steer 355.' He looked at the log. 'We're making 13 knots.'

Jake shouted, 'The warship has altered course and is heading after us.'

'The warship's altered course!' Delilah called. 'Look. It's going after the Sea Quest and it's increasing speed.'

'This is a chance,' said Harry. We'll head for her starboard side. He picked up the VHF. 'I'm going in, Sandy. Keep her busy.'

He turned the boat directly towards the warship. 'Get forward, Delilah. Fire when you can.'

Sandy swung his boat in between the Sea Quest and the warship. The Colonel fired another RPG which exploded closer this time. At the same time the warship fired but now aiming at the Sea Quest. The shell landed astern of the ship. Vijay called the engine room.

'Chief, we must have more speed.'

'There's nothing left, Vijay. We're at full speed now.'

Harry had the boat at full speed and it was rapidly approaching the warship. Delilah was sighting down the Stinger. Just as he fired and the missile streaked out, the after gun fired and there was a crash as the shell landed just off the bow, throwing the boat up in the air before it landed heavily back in the water. The Stinger shot harmlessly over the warship. 'Oh Christ,' groaned Harry. 'Now we're fucked!'

The VHF crackled on the bridge.

'Sea Quest, Sea Quest, this is the warship Kinshasa. We are heading towards you from Banana. Keep coming on your present course.'

'Kinshasa, Kinshasa, this is Sea Quest. We are being attacked by an Angolan warship.'

'We can see them. Keep coming. We will protect you.'

'I can see the ship ahead,' shouted Jake.

'Delilah came back into the wheelhouse.'

'I'm sorry, Captain.'

'It wasn't your fault,' said Harry.

'Not for that,' Delilah said, 'but for this.'

He grabbed Harry and pushing him towards the rail outside the small wheelhouse, tipped him over into the sea. Delilah then took the wheel and put the boat back on course heading directly for the warship. The after gun fired and the shell went screaming over the boat as it closed in. Harry watched spluttering from the water.

'No, Delilah. No!' He screamed.

The boat hit directly into the beam of the warship and immediately there was a sheet of flame as the fuel tank blew. Black smoke blossomed from a hole in the side of the warship and it turned away and slowed down. Its guns were firing but they were still out of range of the Sea Quest.

Sandy watched in horror as Delilah rammed the boat into the warship. 'Sandy!' It was Vijay. 'Rescue 2,' Sandy answered. 'Sandy, there's a friendly warship heading towards you at full speed. Sandy could see it in the distance.

'Too fucking late,' he said bitterly.

The Angolan vessel had also seen the approaching warship and was heading back to its own waters. It was listing to starboard and smoke was still billowing from its side. Sandy approached where Harry was swimming in the water. He brought the boat alongside and he and the Colonel hauled Harry on board where he lay on the deck panting. 'You saw?'

'We did. He shouldn't have done it.'

'He missed with the Stinger. He wanted to make up for it. It was all we had left.'

They looked at the retreating warship in the distance, still smoking from the side.

'He was quite a man.'

'Let's see if we can find anything.'

Sandy steered the boat towards the floating wreckage in the water, still watching the departing warship. As they got closer, Harry and the Colonel were in the bow. The wreckage was spreading with a light breeze paying over the water. Sandy stopped the boat and switched off the engine. There was silence.

'Delilah!' called Harry. 'Delilah!'

'What's that, over there?' Sandy said pointing a little away from the wreckage. 'There's something floating in the water.' He started the engine and eased the boat over to where he had pointed.

'It's Delilah!' called the Colonel.

Delilah was wearing an orange lifejacket and floating motionless in the water with his face staring up at the sun.

Without waiting Harry jumped into the water and swam to him. Sandy brought the boat alongside them. Harry pushed Delilah into the side of the boat where Sandy and the Colonel lifted him in, followed by Harry.

They crowded round him and pulled off the lifejacket. His eyes were closed. Harry felt for a pulse but could feel nothing. Quickly, they put him on his back. Harry bent over him and opened his mouth feeling around to check it was clear. Then he started pushing rapidly down on his chest.

'For fuck's sake, Delilah!' Harry shouted. 'Wake up!' He hit him across his face, in frustration.

Delilah's eyes opened and blinked.

'He's alive!' shouted Harry.

Delilah turned his head to one side and coughed, then threw up.

'You stupid bastard,' said Sandy. Delilah still couldn't speak. He shook his head weakly.

'Let's get him back to the ship,' said Harry. Sandy opened up the engines to a roar and they sped back across to the Sea Quest. The boat was hoisted on board to find a cheering welcome party of the ship's crew and passengers. They helped Delilah off the boat and Carole pushed through with a stretcher.

'I don't need that,' Delilah said weakly.

'Get in,' said Carole. 'No arguments.' He was carried away to the hospital with Carole following.

'Let's get back to the bridge,' said Harry to Sandy and the Colonel.

When they arrived, the Banana warship was now stopped close by.

Jake handed the mike to Harry.

'They want to speak to you, Sir.'

'Sea Quest, we congratulate you on your voyage. The Zaire government welcomes you and your passengers to Banana.'

'Sounds like a bloody tour guide,' Sandy declared.

'Hold on a moment,' said Harry.

The warship called again. 'Can we speak to Colonel Saolona?' Harry held out the mike to the Colonel. As the Colonel talked his face lit up with a broad grin. He turned to Harry.

'My friend is in command in Banana. He is the Military Governor.'

He resumed talking then put the mike down. He slapped Harry on the back. 'We are heroes! They have been listening to the military communications all the time the ship has been travelling down the river. Apparently there is trouble between the Chinese and rebels over your escape. They are also complaining about why UN troops are in Boma. The troops are still locked up and the UN are negotiating to get them back. The warship has your pilot on board but they suggest they lead the way to where they want you to anchor. Then we will take all the passengers off. If there is anything that you need, they can supply you.'

The warship had now turned round and was ahead of the ship making way again.

'Follow the warship, Vijay. Keep about a mile away.' Then he turned to the Colonel.

'Colonel, you say that this guy in charge is a friend of yours.'

'Yes, he is a good man. I served under him a few years ago.'

'And he is the Military Governor, right?'

'Correct.'

'That makes him the representative of the Zaire government.'

'Yes,' the Colonel was looking puzzled.

'Could he issue me with an indemnity for any damage that we may have caused in escaping from Matadi, bearing in mind that we did this under your orders?'

'Ah,' exclaimed the Colonel. 'Now I understand. Of course he can. I will get it done.'

'Also I would appreciate a requisition letter stating that the ship was requisitioned by your government for transporting government officials and ordered to sail from Matadi.'

'That too is easy.'

'Excuse me, Sir.' It was Jake. 'What about Monique? Is she to go ashore here?'

'She can,' said the Colonel. 'There will be no problem I assure you.'

Harry looked at Jake. 'What does she want to do, Jake?'

'She wants to come with us to England.'

'Has she a passport?'

'No, Sir.'

'I thought you would say that. You know the problems.' Jake was about to speak when Harry held up his hand.

'Wait. She is an illegal immigrant. I know she can claim asylum but it is still very complicated.'

'She understands that, Sir, but she doesn't want to stay here.'

'What about her mother?' asked Harry.

'Her mother would want this.'

Everyone was listening. Harry thought for a moment. Sandy cleared his throat. 'She was very useful caring for the wounded captain.'

Delilah spoke. 'She would be very useful with the cooking, Captain.'

Harry sighed. 'It seems I have no choice or you will sulk all the way back home. All right, she can sign on as a passenger, officially this time.'

Jake's face lit up with joy. 'Thank you, Sir. Can I go and tell her?'

'Yes, go on.'

They followed the warship into the anchorage area and soon the ship was swinging gently to the port anchor. The remaining rescue boat was brought down to the embarkation deck, and before long the soldiers and their families were boarding, shouting their goodbyes to the crew. The warship had come alongside as well; their crew were lifting the body and the wounded on stretchers into the ship. The Colonel and his Lieutenant stood with Carole, Sandy and Peter on the deck by the boats. Delilah had also arrived on the deck, still pale and shaky but smiling. Except for those in the rescue boat all the crew were there as well.

The last to leave were the pygmies, who seemed to be carrying far more than when they boarded.

'The crew wanted to give them a few things to take with them,' said Sandy. Two of the pygmy men then appeared dragging a mattress. 'That's for the Chief,' said Sandy. Harry looked up to the sky and shook his head.

'Dogs, children, sailors and pygmies.'

The pygmies were all round Carole now who was clutching them and weeping. They were touching her and calling softly in their strange clicking language. The Kombeti came over to Harry with Carole and the translator. He stood in front of them and spoke. The translator also spoke. 'I can't understand it all,' said Carole, 'but they think you are a big chief.' The Kombeti then took Harry's hand and turned up the palm to which he put some paste from a pouch. Then he spat in this and closed Harry's palm.

'He has given you part of the tribe's spirit, Harry. It is a great honour.' Harry found he could not speak. He took the Kombeti's hand and shook it. They boarded the boats. The Colonel went to Carole. I won't shake hands, Doctor, you don't like me and that is your choice. Let me tell you something. You people come here and by your actions criticise us. We do need you but not your opinions, Africa needs people like me, the whip, and people like you, the balm. I'll tell you this though. Without you these pygmies would have died. I made you a promise that the pygmies will be looked after and I will keep my promise.'

She blinked through her tears. 'Please do that, Colonel.'

He then went to Peter and Sandy. 'It has been an honour.' They shook hands. The Colonel turned to Harry. 'May I speak to your men, Captain?' Harry nodded and the Colonel turned to the crew.

'I know I forced my way on board and the Captain had no choice but to take me, my men and their families. What you may not know is that I told him that I would shoot you all without his cooperation. He had no choice but to do as I wanted. Maybe you would have done the same. It doesn't matter. I want to thank you from us all for what you have done. I hope that you enjoy your rewards.'

'Delilah,' he called. Delilah came forward. The Colonel put his hand in his pocket and pulled out a case. He opened it and inside was a medal. 'I got this some years ago. Apparently I did something that was considered brave. Anyway, Mobutu gave it me. The Captain said that you people don't get medals. I want you to have this.'

Delilah looked embarrassed.

He turned to Harry. 'We're from different worlds, Captain, but I tell you the only thing that separates us is the accident of birthplace. I see it in your eyes. You could be me.'

'I hope I never have to find out,' responded Harry. They shook hands. 'Thanks for the diamonds. I think you overpaid us.'

'Hah, there are a lot more where they came from. My children used to play with them.' His face darkened momentarily at the mention of his family. 'Now revenge will begin.'

They saluted each other and the Colonel boarded the boat. The Bosun signalled with his arms to lower away and the boat lowered to the calm waters below, then roared away towards the port.

The decks gradually cleared.

'I'm really pleased I'm not on his hit list,' said Sandy as they watched the boat depart into the distance. 'Evil bugger, yet at times quite human if you see what I mean.'

'Do you think he was right about me, being like him?'

Sandy looked at him. 'I think that you would do what was required, your Honour, but you have compassion. He doesn't. That's the difference. Now I have to get on. At least I won't have to look for work to do. When are we sailing, Captain?'

'That depends on Peter. He's got the Fitter and his lads over the bow. 'Peter!' he called. 'When will you be finished with the bow?'

Peter was talking with some of the crew.

'Give me a couple more hours, Harry, and I will have a doubler on the forepeak tank,' said Peter. 'That will do her till Hull. Are we going to make it in one leg?'

'You gentlemen have assured me that we have enough water and fuel so really it depends on food. I have put in a request with the Colonel for fresh salads, potatoes and fish so let's see what comes out. If not then we will stop off at Las Palmas.'

'What about Willie?' Sandy asked.

'At sunset this evening if we have sailed by then. Will the Bosun be ready?'

'They are sewing Willie's body up now.'

Harry looked at his watch.

'Just after noon. We will sail at 1500 if that suits you.' They both nodded. 'Good. Now is the officers' bar usable?' Sandy nodded. 'Then let's go and have a well-deserved beer before lunch, whatever it is. Carole, come and join us.'

Chapter 28

Lunch was over and Harry sat at his desk. The cabin, like the rest of the accommodation, smelt of smoke and there was a film of black oily residue covering every surface. The cabin windows were still shuttered with the engine plating outside. That could wait until they had finished with the bow repairs and sailed, Harry thought. He looked on his desk at the small bundle of papers that were lying there. Poor Willie. He opened the bundle. Discharge book, cook's certificate, fire and first aid courses. Even a boatman's course all obtained back in antiquity. A birth certificate. Harry looked at it, 1923. The man had been seventy four years old. His discharge book said sixty four.

Harry smiled. There were more documents. One was an orphanage discharge paper. So he had been an orphan like many sailors. Straight from the orphanage to sea. Out of this document fell a cutting from a local Scottish newspaper. Harry picked it up and put it under the light. It was faded and folded many times but it could still be read. It stated that Mrs McBraith, her child and her mother with whom she had been staying had been killed in a raid. They had been visiting Liverpool to wait for the convoy with Willie's ship to arrive. So he had been married and lost it all. No wonder he stayed at sea. He looked up. John the Bosun was at the door.

'Come in, John. Sit down.' The smell of rum drifted over.

'Willie is ready now, Captain.' He put a small tobacco tin on Harry's desk and sat down. Harry looked down then opened the box. It contained a number of medals. Harry turned them over. The Atlantic Star, the Pacific Star, the Africa Star, the Italy Star, the 39-45 Star, the War Medal.

'He did his duty,' Harry said. John did not reply. Harry looked up. John's head was bowed. He was quietly weeping. Harry got up and shut the door. He went into his cabin and poured two glasses of whisky and then sat by John. 'He was your friend wasn't he?' John nodded. 'I'm sorry. I didn't know.'

'No reason for you to know,' replied John. He reached for the whisky. 'We sailed together on many ships. I knew him in Aberdeen as well. He used to stay in some cheap hotel. I invited him home many times but he never came. It was losing his family you see. He arrived in Liverpool only a day after the raid. No one thought to tell him. When the Merchant Navy ships came in they were paid off and left to fend for themselves. He went to the house all spruced up and they were still digging them out. Since then, he couldn't face being with a family ashore so he made each ship his family.'

He took another gulp of the whisky. 'I'm sorry, Captain. I've had the usual rum for doing the sewing and…' His voice tailed off.

'John, you don't have to apologise.'

'I'm leaving the sea when we get back, Captain. I don't want to end up like Willie. Just one battered suitcase and a handful of medals no one cares about to show for all those years at sea. You and Sandy should think about it too. There's nothing left for the likes of us here now.' John finished his whisky. 'Thank you, Captain. I must go and see to the ship.' He smiled wanly. 'Can't leave the Mate too long by himself. Don't know what he'll get up to.'

'The medals, John.'

'Yes, Sir.'

'He had no relatives. I think they should go with him. I know you have sewn him up, so we'll put them on top of the Ensign.'

'That would be fine, Captain. I have used the old Ensign we had hoisted to come down the river. It came down with the topmast. It's a bit battered but then so was he.'

'That will be most appropriate, John.'

The Bosun left and Harry sat for a while. Then with a sigh, he went over to the desk and called the bridge.

'Let's see if the satphone still works. At least the aerial wasn't on the mainmast.' He waited a moment, then picked it up and dialled the office. It worked. It rang a few times then David answered. 'Christ, Harry! We've been going frantic here trying to get news. Where the hell are you?'

'We are anchored at Banana.'

'Where the hell's that?'

'Still in Zaire on the Atlantic. We are out of the river, the engines are repaired, all the passengers are landed and we are getting ready to sail for Hull.'

'That's incredible.'

'We have damage.'

'What?'

'We have a dented bow and the top mast is down but we can repair that. We were hit by a tank shell or something that blew up the maintenance workers' office aft of the bridge and damaged the galley and killed the Cook.'

'How the fuck can I tell the owners this? You deliberately disobeyed orders to stay there. This is all down to you.'

'David, I really don't give a damn.'

'You'll lose your certificate for this. You'll never sail again.'

'Shut up, David, and listen to me or I'll put the phone down. We sailed from Matadi with port clearance on the orders of the Zaire government. We were requisitioned and I have the papers to prove that. On the peaceful passage down the river we were attacked by rebel forces.'

'They were government forces!'

'No, they were rebel forces. We were carrying government representatives. I doubt if we have recognised Kabila yet especially as he is still fighting for control of the country, which by the way he will never have. Take my word for that. Now back to where we were. We were attacked by rebel gunfire on the way down the river. That caused the damage aft and killed the Cook. He has no relatives so there will be no claims. Then one of the rebel naval vessels tried to ram us but we got through successfully. That is what caused the damage to the bow. I also have or will have an indemnity from the Zaire government for any claims that may be held against the ship for any damage caused by us.'

'What damage?'

'I don't know but just in case. Now that is what is going in my logbook and I suggest that is what we tell the insurance people.'

'Don't be ridiculous. There will be an inquiry!'

'No there won't. Even if there is one, that bloody flag state you registered the ship with will want it all to go away as well.'

'What about the new government in the Congo when they tell the truth?'

'They won't and I'll tell you why. One, they are too embarrassed that we got out and two, there are Chinese troops here. They don't want that to get out or the fact that it was the Chinese troops who attacked us. Everyone will want this to quietly go away.'

'You really think you can get away with this?'

'Think about it, David. I have. Our ETA in Hull is 15 days from now. We may need a stop at Las Palmas on the way to top off fresh water and fuel.'

'I'll see you swing for this. You will never get another ship again.'

'David, you're sounding boring. We stopped hanging people a long time ago in case you hadn't noticed and another small point, London no longer controls the world's shipping. I'll send you an update of our ETA in a week's time and see you in Hull. Last thing, we will not arrive of course until all the pay which is due to the crew is paid into their accounts and we have confirmation of that. By the way, please accept my resignation effective from arrival. Goodbye, David, and thank you for your support.' He put the phone down and sat back.

The bridge called. 'There's a boat coming out, Captain. It looks like it is the supplies.'

'Thanks. Tell the Bosun.'

Harry went up to the bow. There were ropes and cables around and blue arc lights flashing from over the side. Chalkie was standing by the oxyacetylene bottles, his arm in a sling. 'How's it going, Chalkie?'

'Nearly finished, Captain. There may be a little seepage around the repair but a cement box will fix that. It's amazing. We sink two ships and ram into another, it's hit by a shell and then you bomb it and so little damage.'

'Not really. The ships we rammed were only patrol boats made of wood and aluminium. This ship is built in Russia to go through pack ice so she is much stronger than them. We won't see ships like this again.'

As soon as the stores were on board one of the sailors came to Harry with a package. Inside was the letter of indemnity together with a very official stamped document requisitioning the ship and ordering him to sail from Matadi. That looked impressive. There was also another document. It was a letter of appointment for Monique as a cultural attaché for the Zaire government to the UK. Harry laughed aloud. Let the immigration sort that one out.

'They said there was no bill, Captain.' Harry looked up.

'It was Bailey. Thank you, Bailey. Are you enjoying the voyage?'

'I'll never forget it, Captain.' Harry smiled. 'No, I don't think you will.'

At 1500, they heaved anchor and sailed away, the ship rolling very slightly in a low westerly swell. At 1700 Sandy came to Harry's cabin, smart in clean uniform with his cap in his hand and his Iranian war medals in place. He was still limping, his leg bandaged but with no crutch.

'Everyone is ready, Captain. It's almost sunset. Harry came out in full uniform with his medals pinned in place. He touched them. 'I thought that as Willie had his on, I would wear mine, although his mean far more.'

Sandy smiled. 'He would like that, Sir. Taffy has printed these out. It's the words to *Abide with Me*. He felt it was more appropriate than *Eternal Father*. After all he wasn't saved was he?'

'Was he religious?'

'Who knows, but I don't think he would mind.'

Harry rang the bridge. 'Stop engines. When she's stopped, come down to the main deck. Tell whoever is in the engine room to come up too. We'll wait until she's stopped.' He looked back at Sandy.

'The Bosun said we should leave the sea, Sandy.'

'That's not a bad idea.'

'What do we do then?'

Sandy shrugged. 'I don't know. Run a pub?'

'You'd drink yourself to death in a few years.'

'Well we'd find something.'

'Would we? We don't belong there, Sandy. We're not going home now. We are home.'

'That's sad.'

'That's the truth.'

The ship had stopped when they went down to the main deck. The bier was on the port side facing the sun which was now low on the horizon. The Ensign covering Willie was flapping gently at the edges. It was on a board slightly tilted over the side with the Bosun and Delilah on each side. Facing the body, the crew were drawn up in two lines, and to one side were all the officers in their uniforms, with Carole in a white dress. Monique stood beside her. He looked at them. Bandages, slings, plasters, cuts and bruises, eyes red from tiredness, but they were still standing there. He was proud of them. Harry took his place in front of the Ensign-draped body, the book with the committal service in his hand. He had done it before but not enough that he was familiar with it. He looked out over the sea. The sun was now nearly on the horizon, streaming a path of golden crimson along the sea directly at the ship. There was silence except the lapping of the water on the hull. Sandy called, 'Off caps.' Harry started to speak the words. When he finished, Taffy began the hymn, their voices soft at first but strengthening as the emotion caught them. Sandy called, 'On caps.' No more words were needed. Harry nodded to the Bosun, and together the officers raised their hands in salute. John gently patted the top of the body, and then together with Delilah tipped the plank and the body slid from under the Ensign into the sea with a faint splash. As the plank tilted higher the medals, catching the remains of the setting sun, also slid into the sea.

The deck slowly cleared and Sandy turned to Harry. 'Captain, the crew would like to ask you to join them in their bar.'

'Tell you what. I'll hold the bridge while you all drink to Willie. I think it is better that way. Sandy, remember we are at sea. I am not imposing rules. I know it is a special occasion but I am sure you will watch over things, understand?'

'Yes, Captain.'

'Good. We understand each other as always.'

Harry slowly climbed the ladders to the bridge and after taking over the watch, eased the throttles forward to full ahead and then settled in the command chair. This was one of the best times to be at sea. On the bridge at the end of the day and alone. The steering was in autopilot, just the quiet tick of the gyro occasionally changing its heading. Dusk was now darkening the sky which was beginning to show the early brightest stars. The sea was slowly rolling in at the ship in a slight swell and the ship rose to meet it gently. It had been a strange few days. Even now he was slowly coming back to reality. When he contemplated what could have happened, he shivered. He had got away with it. Only just, but still they had pulled through. The bridge door opened. It was Carole. She slid into the chair next to the command chair.

'That was beautiful.'

'It's a clean way to leave. How is the wake going?'

'They are all so tired. Sad for Willie but exuberant that they have succeeded. The Bosun will have a headache in the morning.'

'Not surprising.'

They sat in silence for a while.

'Sitting here looking at the stars and the sea, I can understand why you love it here.'

'It's not always like this.'

'But then you sail stormy seas, Harry.'

Harry smiled. 'You don't exactly live a quiet life yourself.'

They sat again in silence.

'You were right,' said Carole quietly.

'Right about what?'

'Letting go. There is always a time to let go. The trouble is admitting when.'

'That's what we learn at sea. Each voyage, each ship is a new beginning. We're always letting go.'

'And after this voyage, this ship, do we all let go?'

Harry didn't reply.

'So we have fifteen days to England.'

'So I gathered from Vijay.'

'Harry, if we are to let go, can we pretend to be in love till we arrive?'

He looked at her. Her eyes were large and luminous.

'I would like that.'

He put his hand across and took hers and together they looked out onto the darkening sea.

EPILOGUE

Sailors' lives are generally not tidy; they tend to be like torn tapestries that hold their stories but with whispers of threads untied, for their life at sea and their life ashore are separate. They meet, they sail, they part, only to re-emerge on another ship with other shipmates. One day they leave and are forgotten by the ships they've sailed on, scattering to the corners of the world which they found pleasant and they settle there, usually close to the sea to which they will always belong.

Now to what is known.

Harry was right. There was no mention by any of the parties involved in the events during the ship's passage down the river. There was no inquiry. Just a few statements were required together with the logbook extracts showing the 'true' events that led to the damage and Willie's death. The insurance companies accepted the account of the attack on the ship and paid up. The ship was then sold to Indian interests. The ship's name was changed and later sold to owners in Hong Kong. It was recorded that the ship was converted to an inter-island ferry. The whereabouts of the ship today is unknown.

Harry and Sandy arranged the sale of the diamonds in London. Each crew member received in excess of £255,000. A marine charity received a cheque in the name of Willie McBraith to set up a trust in his memory for needy seamen.

Peter retired from the sea and took up a full time hobby making model steam engines. Chalkie went back to Nigeria and set up a successful engineering company.

Vijay obtained his Master's Certificate and joined the Maritime and Coastguard Agency. He left two years later and became a lecturer at a maritime college.

Graham is now Captain of a search and rescue ship in the North Sea. Andy and Olav are also working in the North Sea. Taffy is on an oil platform.

John the Bosun left the sea and bought a pub in his fishing port where he tells stories of the sea that no one believes. He still sees many of the crew who gather there occasionally and embellish the story of the ship and river.

It was good news for Jake and Monique. As Harry thought, her letter confused immigration and they gave her limited status in the UK. Jake finished his cadetship, obtained his nautical degree then went on to study marine law. Monique joined him at college, where both gained marine law degrees. They are now married, living in Singapore as marine lawyers with a five year old son. They called him Harry.

As to the others, most left the sea. A few stayed on working on ferries or the oil support ships, but none could find deep sea positions again.

Of the Colonel, months later Monique received a postcard given to her mother by the agent in Matadi, who had eventually returned to his business. It was addressed to Carole and passed to her. It showed a forest scene and on the back was simply written, 'As promised.'

In 1998, there was a battle at Banana between the forces of Kabila and those who opposed them. The Kabila forces were defeated.

And of Harry, Sandy, Delilah and Carole, well that is another story...